Keith began to 1

Not more than five minutes had passed, and already he could feel his strength drain every time he said a word. The more powerful or creative the word, the more strength he lost. Shafari, too, began to look weary, though Keith knew he was not about to lose to a slave. The young man glanced at the glowing circles.

"Tired yet?" he heard Shafari's mocking voice.

What word doesn't have an opposite? Think, Keith! What's one thing I know that has ultimate power? Even something as simple as...

Before Keith could finish the thought, Shafari blasted his opponent with a fiery storm, which the young man countered with ice.

"Curse..." Shafari breathed, closing his eyes as a crimson glow lit up the floor beneath him.

Keith saw it coming in wide-eyed horror. Shafari's confident expression told all as he crossed his arms and waited to see what the young man would say. Exhausted, beaten down by each spell, Keith could not think fast enough.

The floor shuddered beneath the young man's feet, and with each twist sheer agony arched its way through his body. The force of the blow threw him to his knees. He dug his nails into bloody sand. Eyesight dimmed. Waves of dizziness numbed his thoughts while faintly aware of laughing.

"Too bad illusion couldn't help you now." The headmaster chuckled wearily.

"Illusion..." Keith whispered.

He had not intended it to be a spell, but as soon as the word escaped his lips the circle of power shifted. Shafari must have sensed it, for he called instantly upon another word he thought would surely bring victory.

Keith waited.

It's not shifting, he realized. The haze in his eyes began to clear, and when he looked up he could see fear on Shafari's face.

Blue Moon Rising Trilogy
Wisdom Novels® Music

Capture part of the adventure and mystery through Spotify, Groove, YouTube, Amazon, CDbaby, iTunes and more!

Original compositions by artst: SupaBon
www.WisdomNovels.com

Bonnie Watson

Wisdom
Book One of Blue Moon Rising Trilogy

WISDOM

BOOK ONE OF BLUE MOON RISING TRILOGY

Published by Foreseer Productions℠

ISBN: 978-1539679943

This novel is a work of fiction. Any resemblance to an actual person, living or dead, is entirely coincidental. The characters, names, plots and incidents are the product of the author's imagination.

Copyright © 2016, Bonnie Watson

All rights reserved; no part of this publication may be reproduced, stored in a retrieval system, or transmitted, in any form or by any means, electronic, mechanical, photocopying, recording, or otherwise, without the prior written consent of Bonnie Watson.

Cover Design by Bonnie Watson.

Printed in the United States of America

Author's Website: www.WisdomNovels.com

A warm thank you to everyone who supported me and helped make the story grow. You are all my greatest fans.

WISDOM

WISDOM

PROLOGUE

The clank of chain echoed within the confines of her dungeon prison. She worked the shackles, with no luck at loosening them beyond the downy feathering covering her cloven hoofs. White hair bristled along her neck in anticipation of someone approaching. A toss of the head loosened several strands of long mane around a single ivory horn perched upon the forehead. She waited. A unicorn must always be patient.

She flared her nostrils at the smell of wood burning beneath a nearby cauldron. The warm glow from the fire illuminated a few bare tables. She could even make out a corner shelf displaying a number of multicolored bottles and vials. One such had overturned. A constant drip suggested a liquid had been inside.

It was not long before the scent of human mingled with burnt logs, and she craned her neck to peer over her shoulder at a winding staircase. It was difficult to see beyond the firelight. Even when the figure finally came into view, his face remained hidden under a black hood. He dipped his head in greeting.

"My humble apologies. One such as you deserves far better, but under the circumstances I hope you will understand the reasoning for your..." he paused as though searching for the right word "...predicament." A moment passed before he continued, "A pity the huntsman never knew your true worth, but in return for sparing your life you offered me a favor. I now come before you to obtain that which was promised."

He reached up and slid the hood back around his shoulders. Long sideburns grew down to a small beard, lightly tinted with grays woven in between brown. It was a replica of his hair, which stuck up in static waves.

The unicorn huffed and shook her mane. She remembered that fateful day. The dark-eyed alchemist had appeared as if expecting a hunter. That was when she had been a mere foal – she *and* her sister.

Blue eyes watched his every move, even when he had finished ladling a bubbling liquid from the cauldron and placed it before her in a bowl. Thoughts reached out to him, her kind words filled with wisdom.

Echoing in and out of his subconscious, the alchemist remained still and allowed his mind to link with hers.

"It is not wise for a non-magic-user to take power and expect to master it in one evening. You are an alchemist and well-known illusionist. Do you not wish to further your studies? If knowledge is what you desire, then mine is more than enough."

"But what good is knowledge without the power to use it? Think how much more I could accomplish if I took the title of *Mage*. Illusion isn't real. It lasts only for a short period, whereas magic stays. Magic *is* real, and far more effective." He gestured to the bowl. "This is the one favor I ask. Likely, it'll be the only one I'll ever see. Grant me this, and I swear to you I will use it in good faith."

The unicorn dipped her head.

"You underestimate your own abilities. Without proper understanding, your desire will only lead to destruction."

The alchemist waited while she paused to sniff the contents of the bowl.

"I will grant this one favor as promised, but be warned. Power bares a great consequence. Do not expect it the way you think it should be."

Slightly red-faced, the alchemist swallowed back his impatience while the unicorn began to drink. His heart beat faster. So many years, so many nights mixing and pouring, and now the moment he had been waiting for had come: the ability to coax magic from another body into his own. No longer would he be a mere illusionist, but a full-fledged magic-user. When the last drop had disappeared, he reached for the horn, its knowledge and power so greatly desired.

The horn flared in a brilliance that caused him to jerk his hand back. Just in time, the horn snapped up as panic sent the animal rearing so quickly that a shackle broke. Her hoofs pawed the air, filling it with shrieks and high-pitched squeals. The to-be mage jumped back as the animal tumbled down, landing hard on one side. Blue eyes polluted to a crimson that drowned out the pupil. Its soft coat spoiled and rotted, charring all the way to its cloven hooves. Darkness fouled the horn's color until all shimmer died completely. Teeth elongated to fangs. Whinnies changed to growls, and it began to find its footing by scraping great welts in the stone floor.

Frightened beyond reason, the alchemist sought the handle of an axe that lay unused in a dusty corner, hoping to strike before it could fully stand. For years the blade had dulled to a rusty brown, but in his haste he failed to notice. When the axe hit, instead of severing the horn, it merely cracked from forehead to tip.

A scream penetrated the air. The unicorn's head thrashed back and forth, catching its horn on the man's clothing and flinging him across the room. The force of the throw against a table snapped its legs, and he collapsed on top of it. Painfully, he fought to relocate the axe.

The snap of chain warned the alchemist that another shackle had broken. He looked up. The creature's horn crackled as though electrified. Fangs flashed in the firelight, tainted crimson from piercing its own lips. Eyes radiated with an unnatural light as it slowly turned its head to focus on the human.

The alchemist made a quick scan of the area and discovered the axe on the opposite side of the room. He glanced between object and creature, and kept an unbroken table between himself and the animal at all times.

A lightning bolt struck the floor, and he dived under the table to avoid a second coming from the horn. Hoofs clapped across the floor before something pierced the wooden tabletop, narrowly missing its intended target. With a toss of its head, the furniture was thrown onto some far shelves. Flasks and bottles crashed to the floor. Potions mixed together and exploded into a whoosh of wind that threw back the man's robe and caught the mane and tail of the unicorn. Fire started along the back wall, and it was spreading quickly.

Flames followed the path of the liquid. Smoke poured into the air, smothering the human as he staggered to where the axe lay. He grasped it firmly in both hands when a hoof slammed into his backside. The alchemist found himself skidding on his stomach toward the flames, saved only by an untouched furnishing. Both in pain and exhausted, he rolled away and swung at the looming shadow from the dark unicorn. A glimpse of underbelly sent shivers down his spine.

Impossible! There's no such thing as a male unicorn!

Teeth sought the taste of his flesh. He raised the axe again, but the lowered horn caught and held it. The smell of decay huffed with each breath. Fangs flashed in the flickering firelight.

The alchemist sent a wild kick to the neck. For a moment it seemed to retreat a step, but then lowered the horn again for the final blow. The man did not hesitate. His next swing landed with a thunderous *crack!* A piece of horn clattered to the floor.

The unicorn screamed. Its body writhed and twisted upon itself. Stumbling, it finally collapsed. A thrashing foot upset the bubbling cauldron, and its contents spilled over the approaching fire, though not soon enough to keep from catching fire itself. In moments it was over, with the remaining liquid smothering the ashes.

With shaking hands, the alchemist sat up and wiped his face. By his side lay the fragment of horn.

"So much for a favor." He coughed from all the smoke still lingering in the air, then lifted the horn. A sharp edge bit into his palm. Blood mingled with still-active magic, and a bolt flared around his hand. Unable to let go, he held it aloft, fighting to contain the power, to understand its sheer essence. Crimson flooded his eyes, then slowly receded, a mere glimmer now and then in the darkness.

"At last!" he rasped, his voice not his own. "Both power and knowledge...is *mine!* Illusionist I shall be no more. From this day hence, I claim the title of *Mage!*"

Laughter resonated within the chamber, each echo hinting the unicorn's warning of his actions...and an awakening of something yearning to be free.

Part One

Jenario

CHAPTER 1

A ladybug captured the boy's attention, its polished red and black shell reflecting the afternoon sun. After a few moments of crawling, it spread its wings and lifted lazily into the flight. The boy shielded his eyes, his mind imagining the bug's journey. Stories of distant places his father often told when he was home from work came to mind; the people he met, the sights and sounds. Surely, an insect had no trouble accessing those places. He imagined how different his life would be as a bug and followed his father's stories through his mind.

Keith....

His mother's voice interrupted the daydream, soothing like the nearby stream running through the woods as it linked to his mind. It was not unusual on lazy days when his father was pressed for work, leaving his wife and son to tend to the house and yard. Those days, the boy would be in his favorite location: the forest. Something about it called to him, and so his free time was spent exploring various areas of Nature.

Without a second thought to how his mother's links were done, he turned for home, white curls bobbing as he ran. It was not far, just through the thicket and down the path he had traveled so many times the grass no longer grew. Even before he had cleared the trees he could see his mother waiting on the threshold of their two-story cottage. She was every bit the opposite compared to her son, he being fair-skinned with deep blue eyes while she retained long dark hair that cascaded over one shoulder. Her smile was as warm as the color of her eyes when she saw him coming, and Keith could smell fresh cut herbs on her clothing when he came close.

"I have a surprise for you," she said.

Keith took a guess. "He's home?"

At a nod, the boy rushed inside, garden scents forgotten at the excitement of his father home early. He found him just hanging up his coat when entering the room. Upon hearing his son, the large man turned to scoop him into his burly arms. Keith did not mind the prickly dark stubble against his cheek that pressed to his father's face.

"My, my!" his father mused. He gently set his son down. "You're growing too fast for me to keep up. I'll have to stop work if I want to enjoy more time with you."

A servant entered the room with a tray and set it on a table by the fireplace.

"Ah, Ullyaemus," Keith's father greeted. "How are things with you, my friend?"

"As always," the servant replied. "Good to have you back, even for a short period."

"Thankfully, I've got some time."

Keith watched Ullyaemus pour a couple of drinks. His mother soon joined them and savored a kiss from her husband.

"Look what I've brought you, Greverlend. I had Ullyaemus fix this for you. Your favorite." Her husband picked up a cup and handed it to her.

"Spiced peppermint?" she asked.

"Finest spice in all the land."

"It's been so long! I can barely remember the first time I had it."

The servant chuckled. "We don't often get many luxuries, but it's a treat when we do."

"Speaking of which," the large man patted his son's head, then pulled out a small object from an inner pocket, "I believe someone's turning ten?"

Keith's eyes grew wide in excitement.

"What is it?" He turned the object over to examine. Several round reeds joined together with opened holes on each end. Down the sides were four more. Bits of colored thread wove delicately around the edges, crossing at an angle to the opposite side.

"It's a pan flute," his father said. "You blow on this end." He pointed to the tip of the instrument. "Hold your fingers over these to create different sounds. Go on. Let's see what it sounds like."

Keith placed his lips lightly upon the opening and blew. A faint whistle coursed through the reeds, and he stopped to look where he had placed his fingers. Lifting one at a time, he piped his mother's lullaby, with a few blundering notes here and there.

"Not bad," Ullyaemus mused. "Bet he'll have it mastered within the hour."

"It's great!" Keith admired the gift. He cradled it against his breast as though it were made of gold. To him, it was priceless, and the fact it came from one of his father's travels made it all the more special.

"It does make a good sound," his mother said. "Where did you find it, Jonathan?"

"From a merchant in Lexington," her husband replied. "First week of the month brings new business. Yesterday, they were selling all kinds." He turned to Keith. "I know you'd probably like to try your gift some more. There's some business I need to discuss, so why don't you go enjoy. I've plenty of stories to tell afterwards."

Keith's slight look of disappointment was soon replaced by a wide grin. Stories were always worth waiting for, and with a nod he slipped from his seat and headed down the hall. He had nearly reached the stairs when he paused. He was just out of sight from the family room where his parents sat talking, but something about the conversation caught his attention. Intrigued, he remained silent to listen.

"...Have to pay a visit to my brother tomorrow," his father was saying. "There's just not enough work going around. With this constant traveling, I'm losing time when I could be here."

Keith cocked his head. He had never met his father's brother, though he had seen his dwelling not far off through the woods. Keith had even ventured that way to get a closer look. His thoughts soon returned to a change in conversation.

"...Won't stay a child forever," his father continued.

"I know." He heard his mother sigh. "He shows great interest in Nature. It's enough to realize one day..."

Keith stepped back when the servant came through the hallway.

At the sight of the boy, Ullyaemus stopped in puzzlement.

"Unless you have something to add," he said in a soft tone, "I suggest you leave them to their discussion. Besides, weren't you going to try your gift?" He pointed to the pan flute in Keith's hand.

"I was just wondering," Keith kept his voice low, "I've heard them discuss work before. Is money that hard to come by? I mean, we don't live in town. There's no tax where we are."

Ullyaemus chuckled. "And how do you think your father gets around these days? It's expensive to travel. You need lodging, food and clothing – not to mention transportation on business meetings. Of course, he'll probably expect you to travel one day."

"You think he'll ask me to come with him?"

"I wouldn't doubt it. Now, that being said, why don't you run upstairs to your room. I want to be able to hear *that* from the kitchen."

Keith did not hesitate. He bounded up the stairs, skipping every other step until he had reached the second level, then out onto the balcony to test another song. He recalled one his father sang after hearing it one day in town. It did not capture the spirit like his mother's lullaby, but it was good enough to bring footsteps to the balcony door. He turned, hoping to find his father. Instead, his mother leaned against the door frame.

"You play beautifully," she whispered, her face ashen.

"Are you all right?" He immediately rushed to her side. "Did something upset you?"

Kneeling beside him, Greverlend whispered, "No. I should have told you long ago..." A cough wracked her body.

"What do you mean?" White eyebrows lowered in confusion. She seemed paler by the minute. "You don't look well at all. Maybe you should lie down."

His mother tried to catch her breath, but every other word seemed to get fainter and fainter.

"I'm sorry, my son." At this point, Keith was straining to comprehend her rasping whispers. "All I can say is this: one day you will find out what you are, and where you came from..."

She fumbled with the clasp on her necklace until it came loose, then slipped it around his neck. A gift from her husband, Keith wondered why she would give it to him. As she turned for the hallway, her body teetered to one side. Her son followed, and she glanced back to form the words, *"I love you,"* from silent lips.

The boy watched his mother stumble into her bedroom. It was not long before no sound was heard at all, not even the rustle of her sewing basket that was kept close to the bed.

His father found him at his mother's bedside, her limp hand dangling from the side almost unbearable to touch; she was so cold. Over and over, her message repeated in his mind, though he never uttered a word of what she had said. He kept recalling the many moments of joy and laughter they had spent together. So short a time. Keith felt he hardly knew himself in those years. What had she tried to tell him? Before her final breath, he had felt her mind tried to link, as she had always done. It was comforting at first, but with her weakness came instability. The abrupt disconnection left her young son at a loss of what to do…except cry. What had happened in a day's time to change everything?

"One day you'll find out what you are, and where you came from…"

His mother was gone.

*****

"How do you know they won't give the boy the same drink?" a voice rasped, and a wispy-haired man stepped to the window. From there, he could just make out the cottage through the woods.

Submerged in shadow where the flow of light could not touch, a second person answered.

"I've watched them." His voice was crisp with assuredness. "They *won't* give it to him."

"Then there's nothing more to do than wait. My brother will likely suspect. After all, the spice *did* come from me."

"Don't forget who gave it to you."

A nod.

"Many thanks." He moved back from the window into surrounding shadow. "Such a shame she would be affected. Would've been better had my brother been one of them, and *she* normal."

CHAPTER 2

Less than two weeks after the incident, Keith learned that his father wanted to include him when he paid a visit to his brother. Having never met his uncle, the boy was elated. At the same time, he understood the reason behind the visit. Their money supply was running low, and his father did not want to sell the servant to make up for the loss. Though Keith was old enough to stay by himself, his father insisted having someone they knew and trusted in the family was best.

A quick stop by his mother's gravesite not far from the house offered some comfort that she was in a better place, and provided the boy a moment to ponder her strange words. Many times he thought about asking his father what she might have meant. Yet he could not push past the feeling that she wanted him to discover the answer on his own, so he kept quiet.

As soon as Keith was ready, they hiked a short ways from the site to his uncle's place. Yet what seemed like an exciting first meeting soon turned into disappointment. Once part of a larger structure, the Keep now only housed one individual. The rest had fallen to ruin. The person who greeted them at the door, however, was far too ugly to be called an uncle, let alone a brother. Keith actually mistook him for a servant.

"Well, what a surprise!" his uncle rasped, then coughed. "Do come in, brother." He stepped aside to allow them in. "I received your letter. Can't tell you how…sorry I was to hear about Greverlend. She was," he inhaled deeply, "quite the beauty."

Keith followed his father into a fairly comfortable sitting area. Three seats had been arranged next to a wide fireplace, which illuminated parts of the room in an orange glow. It did little to warm the mood.

"So you came to collect more money, is that it?" Keith's uncle rolled his eyes. "I don't know what Greverlend ever saw in you. She should have been with me. *I* could have offered much more."

"Not all of us are…*fortunate*…like you, Shavary."

Shavary: even the name rang with an uneasy tone. Keith felt those eyes burn through him and wished he had stayed at home.

"Well, what can I say? My appearance has never truly suited any woman's tastes, animal or human—"

"Don't you dare refer to her that way!" Keith's father stood in a rush with hands clenched at his sides. "You know her real name. Use it! As I recall, she came to you first for help, but you refused. Now I have a son to raise and you're going repay her by helping him."

Shavary shrugged.

"I don't know what you expect from me. I can't teach a dog how to be a cat. Neither can you. As far as I'm concerned, she got what she deserved. And you? You're next."

"Wha—" Keith heard his father give a strangled gasp before he collapsed, a dagger protruding from his back. In those few moments, Keith had committed the gold-striped blade to memory.

"I always did favor the back throw." A figure emerged from the shadows. "Less messy."

Keith cringed in his seat, trying to disappear as the assassin strode over to remove the blade. Frozen in place, he stared in fright as the man flipped the dagger between his fingers.

"Careful," Shavary cautioned with a smile. "He might bite."

The assassin chuckled. "May have use for him." He sheathed the dagger. "Got a sack?"

Shavary smirked. "A punching bag? I like that idea."

"Wishful thinking," was the reply. "I've a cart going to Sapphire. I'm sure my friend will be pleased with *this*."

Keith swallowed with difficulty.

"You're not going there yourself?" Shavary asked.

"Didn't you want the servant dismissed as well?"

Keith could hardly believe his ears.

The uncle waved the comment aside. "Doesn't matter. All I care about is—"

Keith never heard the rest, for at that moment the assassin lashed out and gripped him by the throat. His last conscious thought before darkness took him was of his mother. She was never sick as his father had suspected.

She was poisoned.

CHAPTER 3

He waited patiently for the cart to bounce past his hiding spot. A loose barrel rolled to the back where nothing prevented it from falling into the street. He eyed the next dip where the carriage wheel caught and tilted its burden, then slipped from the alley in a mad dash for the tumbling treasure before it hit the ground.

It was a seamless act of thievery, and he was back in the alley before anyone noticed. His black leather boots dispersed puddles of leftover rainwater as he wound his way through a maze of narrow streets and closely built housing. He could feel the assorted pouches tied at his belt thump into one another as he scrambled over some fallen shingles to a more secure location. When at last he felt safe enough to stop, he sat the barrel upright and cut the cord keeping the lid shut.

The barrel twitched.

He stared in stupefied silence as the barrel shook again, then toppled over so that the lid popped open. A boot to the top of it ceased its movements.

"What's this? Treasure that moves?" He chuckled, then reached inside to pull out a struggling boy. "Ah, a stowaway. Or should I say...*stole away*." A flick of a dagger released the boy from his bonds holding his hands and feet together.

As soon as his hands were free, the boy reached up and pulled the cloth from his mouth. He coughed a couple of times before his breath finally settled.

The thief took a moment to study the boy's pale features.

"Huh. That's a poor way to get rid of someone." He pointed to the barrel, "Mind if I use this?" then swiveled it around so he could sit on top. "That's better. Been out all day grabbing me up some fine goods." He jingled his pouches with pride. "So ye had a bit o' trouble, I see. Got a name?"

The boy looked around with that dazed expression of just waking from dream-filled sleep. When he finally answered, the thief coaxed him over to join him on the barrel.

"A pleasure to meet ye, Keith. Don't worry 'bout a thing. Ol' Blackavar 'ill fix ye up! Trust me." He winked.

Rising, the thief turned and gave a deep bow.

"Blackavar, at yer service." He spread his arms. Long sleeves matched dark pants, patched in several places. "Master of the Thieves' Guild and an escaped slave that no one has caught in years. Impressed?"

"I...suppose." Keith hardly knew what to say. He looked around, unfamiliar with the dim-lit alley and tall buildings closing in around him. "Um...thieves what..?"

Blackavar chuckled. "Not from around here, I take it. Well, I'll tell ye. The Thieves' Guild is...sort of like a clan. Ye come and go, taking or leaving. I guess in many ways it's like a contest to show off who's the best thief around, which...ehem...would be meself."

Blackavar grinned, two of his front teeth made of gold. He had large eyebrows for such a narrow face, and his long sable hair kept falling in his eyes. His vest, as Keith noticed, contained some green mixed with the all-black look, and a rather interesting rectangular pouch rested on one side of his waist. Following his gaze to the pouch, Blackavar beckoned him closer.

"Ah, I see ye have taken interest." He lifted the outside flap and reached inside. When he pulled his hand out, it contained a fistful of pink sand.

Keith's eyebrows lowered in confusion. "You carry...dirt."

"Not just any dirt!" The thief lowered his voice. "*Magic!* What else? Ye don't just find sand like this lying around. Ye have to make this stuff." He poured it back in the pouch "But me, I didn't have to do anything to get it."

"Why's that?"

"Well, I *am* a thief." Blackavar's chest swelled with pride. "Stole it right from one of those magic-users!" He pranced around the boy, demonstrating as though one of his greatest feats. "What are they thinking? With the way they hold their belongings, it's so easy to make a steal. And believe me, they always contain something good." He posed with one boot on top of the barrel. "I've yet to come across one that has *nothing* of value to me."

He grinned. "Alright, enough of me. Let's hear about yeself. I'm certain ye must have a family somewhere. Not every day ye find yeself in a barrel riding the back of a wagon, eh?"

Keith just shook his head..

"No," he said quietly. "They're gone. Everyone."

Blackavar's smile faded. "*Everyone*, everyone? Or just enough to say everyone?"

Keith fought to hold back tears. "I don't know what happened. First my mother, then my father. I think they did something to our servant. I don't remember what happened after...after...." He made the motion of someone grabbing his throat.

"Hmmm. Tough one there. Expecting ye'll want revenge later on, eh?"

"No..." The boy paused. "Just...answers...."

The thief tried to think of something to take the boy's thoughts from his deceased parents. Yet it was those brilliant eyes that kept drawing his attention, and he wagered an idea. "A pair of blue 'uns ye got there! Medallion will think ye're a magic-user for sure."

"Medallion?" Keith wiped his face with the back of his hand, the thief's warm personality soothing the pang of loneliness growing in the pit of his stomach.

"Why, the guild's Master Mage, of course! He'll want to take a look at ye sure enough."

"Where is this guild?" Keith asked. "I hardly even know where I am."

"Well, I can help ye with that!" Blackavar spread his arms in welcome. "This, dear lad, is the Realm of Lexington, a thief's paradise. Ye've got the market in the center of town. New merchants come every month to sell and buy. There's never a short supply of anything! They even sell slaves here."

"Lexington," Keith breathed. "My father used to talk about it." He felt his pocket where he had last put his pan flute, then around his neck for the necklace his mother had given him. He smiled at their familiar touch, being the only belongings he had from home. "He often came to find work and would bring back gifts when he could, though he never mentioned anything about slaves."

Blackavar held a finger to his lips. "Not something ye want to get into. Slavery's a whole different business in itself. Been and seen it. Don't want no more of it."

Keith listened to the thief ramble on about great steals and guild members. Though he could not replace the boy's parents, having someone to talk to was comforting. There was no end to the thief's jokes and enthusiasm, and soon Keith felt right at home as though he had never left.

After a while, Blackavar gestured down the alley. "Would ye like a tour of Lexington? I could talk until sundown, but unless ye see for yeself, ye won't believe how easy it is to get some of these things!"

The boy's thoughts were a whirl of colorful images and impressive steals. Yet the growing concern of his uncle's actions against his parents troubled him. Why had *he* been spared? The only reoccurring thought now was to discover what he was and where he came from, and if a thieves' guild was where he was to find the answer, then that was where his path would lead him.

Looking up at the thief, Keith spoke with determination.

"I'd like that."

CHAPTER 4

Keith followed Blackavar through the alley. As they neared the well-traveled streets, distant sounds of conversation and horse-drawn carts reached their ears. The road narrowed to little more than a pathway the closer they came, until they rounded a corner and stopped in the shadowed opening between two buildings.

Keith had never seen so much hustle and bustle. People hurried by, arms loaded with packages. Horses clopped up and down the streets pulling passenger and luggage carriages. Stationed along the sides of the road were merchant stands with an array of goods to sell. Mesmerized, Keith nearly stepped out when he was pulled back.

"Easy now." Blackavar's grin widened. "Ye never want to reveal yeself too soon! Too many escaped slaves said to be hiding back here. That's why guards are stationed in Lexington. Be a mighty fine reward to turn in one, even if ye aren't a slave."

The two peered around the corner. Right away, Blackavar pointed to a couple of men dressed in black with long swords at their sides.

"I'll bet me boots they're from Castle Mire."

"What's Castle Mire?" Keith studied the men.

"A holding place for slaves until trade season. Then they're brought out in caravans and auctioned off like sheep!" He took another look around before motioning for the boy to follow. "Be quick, before they look this way!"

Through the crowd they darted. Almost instantly, Keith found himself lost, separated when a carriage passed between them. Several passersby eyed the small boy with interest. His pale features were not easy to miss. One person shoved past, knocking him to the ground.

Keith yelped, scrambling to find his footing. Instinctively, his hand felt for his mother's gift to hold for comfort.

"My necklace!" The silver charm was gone! Frantically, Keith searched under and around stomping feet. He had to find it, even if it took all night! A loud whinny made him look up see the underside of a hoof bearing down on top of him.

"Watch it!" Keith was suddenly scooped into the thief's arms as a carriage rattled past. "Ye've got to have yer wits about ye if ye want to get around here."

"My necklace is missing!" Keith struggled as he was carried to the safety of the sidewalk. "I have to go back! It was my mother's!"

Blackavar gently set him down.

"Take it easy!" When he held up a hand, jewelry dangled from his fingers.

Quick as a whip, Keith snatched it from the thief. "You stole from me?"

Blackavar shook his head. "Saw it in the street." He eyed the charm as Keith placed it around his neck. "A fine catch it would make, though. Better keep it under yer shirt. Don't want it tempting others."

Keith checked his pan flute. "But you won't steal from me, will you?"

"Nah!" Blackavar waved the comment aside. "Us thieves are the most respectful gents in the area, despite what some folk may say."

Satisfied, the two continued touring around town. There was no lack for inns and taverns along the street. When they reached the town square, they were met by hordes of people to inspect a variety of items on sale. There were many kinds of people, some more amusing than the items themselves. There were some with big-rounded stomachs, some that were tall, and some that were short. There were people whose heads seemed too large for their bodies, redheads, blackheads, droopy-beards and sagging skin. Then there were some who came stumbling from a nearby tavern, drunk as mules on mead and just as heavy when they fell face down. Both shared a hearty laugh.

Then Keith's merriment faded. Huddled together at the edge of town was a group of raggedy looking men and women. They eyed everything from the corner of the sidewalk, nervously checking to see if they had been noticed. Every once in a while, one person would vanish as someone or something blocked Keith's vision. The third time a cart pulled in front. When it left, the group had moved on.

"Peasants," Blackavar said.

"Can guards get money for them too?"

"Not much, but yes." The peasants were quickly forgotten when a particular merchant stand caught his eye. A mischievous grin spread across his face. "But if ye become a thief, ye needn't worry with being poor." He casually began strolling toward it.

Keith stood aside and watched. Expecting the thief to take something and leave, he was surprised when Blackavar calmly asked to see something. Although dealing with another customer at the moment, the merchant gladly offered his assistance. That was when Keith noticed the thief's hand. Inch by inch, a bracelet was removed right under the merchant's nose! Slipping the charm into his pocket, the thief then gestured at something else. There went another. Finally convinced the merchant had nothing of interest, the thief gave his thanks and left.

"Pretty good catch, I'd say." Blackavar showed his prize to Keith.

"That was amazing! But why didn't he see that? I mean, he was looking right at you!"

"They don't expect ye to take something when they're facing ye to do business. All they can see is how much money is coming their way. Other than that, they're pretty blind."

The two started to a second stand.

"But Blackavar, wouldn't it have been easier to take something while he *wasn't* looking?"

"Aye. I've done that before. But ye know what they say. Merchants have eyes at the back of their heads." That mischievous grin returned. "Now here's a trick that takes skill. See that group of men? They're all guards."

"You're not thinking of stealing in front of *them*, are you?" A look of concern crossed the boy's face.

"That's the beauty of being a thief. It only adds to the pleasure of taking." Whistling to himself, Blackavar nonchalantly strolled to a stand and waited patiently until the last customer left.

"Good evening, sir," Keith heard the thief announce from a distance. "I was just with a friend who happened to have the exact same ring…" The story went on as Blackavar craftily stole several of the man's goods right in front of the guards. Yet Keith's attention was not entirely on the group as it was on a lone guard not far off. At first, Keith thought he had his eye on someone else, but from the look on his face he must have seen Blackavar's thievery. At a gesture, the men began marching toward the stand.

The Master Thief was still deep in conversation when people began moving out of their way. This was all the warning he needed. After thanking the merchant, Blackavar calmly walked away as if nothing was out of the ordinary. He changed directions, taking him back to the center of town. Not bothering to make eye contact, he signaled with his fingers in the direction he was headed.

From the sidewalk, it had not been difficult to see where his friend was going, but once back on the street Keith was easily sucked into the swarms of people going in opposite directions all at once. Unable to keep up, Keith backtracked to the side of the buildings and slipped down the alley, hoping it would take him to where the thief might be waiting.

*****

Guards were closing fast. Yet Blackavar's steps remained unhurried. It was now time to lose them in the shadows of the alley.

Too late, he noticed a band of freshly summoned troops approaching from the side, blocking his intended escape. As the two groups fanned out to trap him between the buildings, Blackavar considered his options. Fighting in the middle of town was the last thing he wanted, especially in broad daylight. However, nothing could keep the lineup of guards from going unnoticed. Spectators gathered around, the excitement of a fight eagerly holding their attention. With a sigh, the thief drew his daggers.

So they want a show? I'll give 'em one.

*****

Keith hurried through the alley, following the sound of clanging steel. When he approached the street, a crowd of onlookers cheered wildly. He was careful not to reveal himself as he peered around the corner. For now, the center of attention went to Blackavar. Keith studied his movements as he parried a blow and turned to avoid another. He was not hurt, but was tiring quickly.

There are too many, the boy realized. *He'll never make it alone!*

A strap snapped from a close swing, sending the largest of Blackavar's pouches flying back where Keith was hiding. So enthralled were the surrounding people that no one noticed its pink contents spill near the unguarded alley, nor the small hand that pulled back into shadow.

Keith pondered over the stuff, wondering what made it so special that a magic-user would need. He raised it to his nose to smell, but quickly lowered it when his head felt groggy.

Could this be powerful enough to slow the guards, even for a few moments? He peered out to check on Blackavar. Now he could hear his labored breaths. The circle of men had tightened. There was no room to dodge and barely enough to block. One guard readied chains to bind the rest of the thief's spirit while another cracked a whip to break it.

"Blackavar!" Keith jumped from the alley and raised his hand. Startled, the guards only stared at the child before them, and laughed when he threw the pink sand. One advanced to grab him when he suddenly slumped to his knees in a slumbering stupor. There was no defending against it, and when all the guards lay resting at his feet, Keith motioned for his friend to join him.

Stupefied, Blackavar stared while the crowd cheered for the boy's success. He sheathed his daggers, tired but proud to have the extra help, then took a bow. The twitching of a nearby guard was enough to get him moving, and followed Keith down the alley. After a certain distance, the two paused to catch their breaths.

"Did you know the sand would do that?" the boy asked, grinning from ear to ear. "Bet they didn't even know what hit them!"

Seating himself on an empty barrel, Blackavar rested while Keith continued in an animate speech. He studied the broken strap, having grabbed the pouch while passing. Only half its contents remained now.

Keith briefly studied the thief before asking, "I thought you said you hadn't been caught in years?"

His response was a chuckle. "That depends. Are ye referring to the act of stealing or being dragged off by guards? Even *I* cannot fully claim a clean record of stealing."

"And you're a *master* thief?" Keith grinned.

Blackavar bowed low. "And my thanks to ye for keeping that title safe. As a reward, I give ye this." He loosened a pouch from his belt and held it out for the boy.

"For me?" Keith allowed him to strap the pouch around his waist before peering inside.

"Nothing in it yet, but as our newest member, I'm sure ye'll find just what ye need."

"You're making me a member? But I'm not even a thief."

Blackavar knelt by his side.

"Being a member don't always mean stealing. It's cunning. What ye did back there took more guts than any of our experienced members, even meself." He laughed. "Let's face it, if it weren't for ye, I'd be stuck back at Castle Mire gnawing on metal bars until the slave auction!"

"Really? Me?"

"Just…uh….one thing. Since I *am* master of the guild," Blackavar held a hand over his heart, "got me pride to carry, is all. So…try not to mention it to anyone."

CHAPTER 5

The leaves on the trees grew thick, concealing one whose dark wings blended well within the shadows of the forest. Patterned markings across his forehead and down the cheeks meshed with his dark covering, and he tapped a taloned finger with impatience on the bark, its rich russet coloring nearly matching his skin. Broad and buff, the wings folded only slightly. He was alone…and hungry.

Sharp eyes of amber caught the faint movement of a squirrel plucking an acorn. Unaware of any danger, the small rodent scurried along the branch, its prize tightly held by its sharp teeth. After finding a suitable place, it took the acorn in its paws, rotating it several times while its teeth nibbled away the shell.

Silent wings opened as the Black Wing dove into flight. Like a hawk descending from above, his coming attack reflected in the squirrel's black eyes for only a moment. Then it was over. After gliding to the ground, he nestled in a small clearing surrounded by a protective covering of underbrush to satisfy his hunger.

"You are an expert ambusher," a rich voice commented.

The startled creature raised his wings to their full height and glanced around the clearing.

"You dare to approach a Black Wing?" he hissed with a rugged accent, and let his meal drop from his claws like the squirrel had the acorn. A sound caused him to whirl around, his wings stretched in sable splendor. "You must have a death wish."

A dark-robed figure stepped from the forest shadows, his face hidden beneath a hood.

"Forgive me, but I am intrigued by a harpy-wizard such as yourself, or so I've been told you're called."

The Black Wing narrowed his eyes. He despised that name. So, then, did every other Wing whom had heard it. He snarled in disgust.

"If you're looking for a slave, I suggest switching to a White Wing! Otherwise, I'll have your head knocked from your puny shoulders before you can even turn around!"

"I've no doubt of that…" The man's voice trailed off. He reached up and removed the hood, letting it fall back around his shoulders. "But isn't that typical of most people? Most do not appreciate the remarkable strength or grace your kind have compared to your White Wing kin. To be able to ambush in flight completely undetected due to the simple fact of wing coloring, I find amazing."

The Black Wing tilted his head curiously to one side.

"Flattering, but it will not earn you a slave that easily, and certainly not *this* kind."

"I never said I wanted one," was the reply. "But perhaps it was rude of me to appear without a proper introduction." He took a bow, his long robe grazing the ground. "I am Jenario Onyx, magic-user from the Realm of Sapphire."

"Magic?" The Black Wing nearly laughed. "Humans know nothing of magic."

After careful observation, the Black Wing let his wings relax. At his feet lay the squirrel, and with an eye on the human, he sat cross-legged on the grass.

"Corrigan," he mumbled, and hungrily began ripping off pieces of flesh. Thin ribbons of blood trickled down his chin as he savored each bite. He was not sure what to make of this person, and contrived an idea to pummel him into the ground for interrupting his feeding.

"Have you ever considered living in the human realms without fear of being hunted?"

The question was not without anger rising in the harpy's gullet, for he had a mind to know where this conversation would soon lead.

He wants me as a slave, just as the others wanted my mother. Well, you're not fooling me!

"I can assure you, my home is large enough to accommodate your size."

Corrigan's brow furrowed in annoyance as he licked patches of blood from his lips.

"And your purpose would be for what—entertaining me?" Corrigan tossed the leftovers aside. "I know what you're after, and I'm not about to let you have it!" He stood and prepped his wings for flight.

"I am a man of study," Jenario replied in a calm tone. "I learn from the real thing, not books! Because of this, I have gone from mere alchemist to magic-user within a single day."

"I cannot *imagine* being interested in either." Corrigan scowled. "By the way, it's *Harma' Keyarx*, not harpy-wizard." Sable wings lifted him into the air, but no sooner had his feet left the ground when he was caught off guard by Jenario's final question.

"What about *Lo-ans'el?*"

That stopped him, and the Black Wing allowed himself to settle back down.

"Where did you hear that?" He frowned. "Not from a Healer. I'd stay well away from their clearing, if I were you."

"I told you." Jenario cracked a smile. "My information does not come from books."

"Pah!" Corrigan sat on a nearby log and drew a wing around to preen. "And I suppose you invited one to your place like me?" His gaze flicked to the mage to find him staring in somewhat surprise. "What? You never seen a bird clean its wings before?"

"I didn't think your kind had magic," Jenario said. "But now I see. Your wings can fade when you close them."

Corrigan cracked a smile. "If you had wings as large as mine, climbing through dense treetops could be an issue. They fade to keep from tangling."

Upon lifting the other wing, it immediately appeared so he could show the underside. Up close, Jenario could see tiny bits of color on each feather: dark browns, reds and a hint of green. His eyes scanned the entire length, trailing from the tip of the primary feathers to the smaller ones. Near the base of the wing Jenario noticed several that were longer. The long feathers adjusted separately from the rest, and the mage realized they were used to help guide the harpy in flight.

"You are unique," the mage commented, then added. "But I'm sure that must come from your father's side, not your mother's."

Corrigan shot the man a dirty look. His facial feathering puffed out in an effort to look larger. This only brought a smile to the other.

"What do you want with me! Out with it, mage!"

"Having two different kin as parents must be hard," Jenario continued. "You want things to be different. You want things to work, and yet you're denied that because your mother is missing and your father denies any relations with you to his clan, is that it?"

Corrigan stood and raised his wings in a huff.

"You read my mind, didn't you?" A talon pointed at the mage. "Don't lie!"

"Would you like to find out where she is, possibly?" Jenario turned away as if to leave. "I can help you. You could leave behind the stares and comments. You're not like them."

Corrigan remained silent. He wanted to rake his talons through the man's throat for even mentioning his family.

What if he could help? I can't find out where she is without some form of human contact.

"I hunt alone," Corrigan whispered. "I like shadow. I like silence. I'm not coming so you can take my wings and enslave me because I *will* tear you to shreds if you do!"

Slightly turning his head, Jenario grinned.

"You won't be disappointed, Corrigan. I promise you that. Meet me in the Realm of Sapphire. You'll get the answer you seek, and I'll get to study one of Nature's finest predators of the sky...."

CHAPTER 6

Sunlight warmed the tops of the tree homes, built lovingly to survive harsh weather and constant swaying. Here, Redwood trees were thick with sturdy limbs to support the added weight, while larger leaves sheltered against rain and summer heat. Connected to each home was a bridge. Cleverly concealed by intertwining branches and leaves, the bridges provided safe crossing from one home to the next, and served as a perfect location for a clan of *Harma' Keyarx*.

The door to the central home opened, and a White Wing stepped out. A soft tuft of down sprouted from his chin to resemble a beard. Dark markings around the face gave his kind more of a bird look rather than human, while their bodies were much smaller for the sake of flight. He paused to stretch each snowy wing before crossing the bridge to a balcony. A few of his kind already lay basking in the sun, their wings spread to soak in its warmth. They observed their leader as he stood quietly in an elegant, gold robe. Clothing was not a necessity, and most of his kind preferred not to look so much like humans. After all, humans were responsible for enslaving them. The clothing was just a reminder. Now and then the leader's wings ruffled in silent anger.

"Thinking about humans again, Rusha?" A soft voice startled the White Wing, and he peered up through the dense canopy. Amber eyes returned his gaze.

"You're back early, Corrigan. Was your hunt successful?" He watched the Black Wing slip from the branches and land beside him. He could hear the other Wings shift in discomfort. Corrigan, on the other hand, seemed quite pleased.

"Something you wish to tell me, *my son?*" Rusha lowered his voice for the last two words, and he watched the Black Wing's expression turn sour.

"Yeah, you *would* have to remind me of that, wouldn't you?" Corrigan casually strolled across a bridge with Rusha at his side.

"I can't help what happened to your mother, Corrigan," Rusha replied. "There's not a day that goes by that I don't think of her. Perhaps if she were here, things would be different." He grasped his son by the shoulders and faced him. "But just because she's not doesn't mean I don't care about you, or Chanté."

Corrigan pulled away.

"You only had Chanté to make up for your mistake! Even if he knew I was his brother, he'd never accept the truth."

Rusha smiled faintly. "He would be more accepting than the rest of our kind. For your sake, Corrigan, it's time you start realizing you're half White Wing. This constant behavior of sulking behind bushes, late night hunts, being alone! You've made no attempts to better yourself, or make friends."

"That's a Black Wing for you." Corrigan curled his lip into a sneer. "I'll always have those traits because it's what I am." He turned away. "Perhaps it is *you* who need to realize that I will never fit in."

Rusha sighed. "I had high hopes you would...at least some day."

"Well, some day will never come, because *today* I've decided to leave."

"What!" Rusha stared at him in disbelief. "When did this come about?"

"I met a human this morning." Corrigan balanced himself along the edge of the walkway, tracing a finger down the long vines holding the bridge. "He offered me a place to stay and hunt whenever I like in return for study."

"Are you mad!" Rusha fluffed his wings unconsciously. "Do you have any idea what humans will do to you? Do you know what they did to your mother?"

Corrigan spun on his heels to face his father.

"No more different than here!"

Rusha opened his mouth, but no words would come. His mind sought a reply, something to make him see, to make him stay. Yet in his heart, he knew Corrigan spoke true. He was a Black Wing, a loner, a hunter, feared above any other Wing. Because of that, he was an outcast, no matter what Rusha said. Corrigan would always remain alone.

At last, the White Wing bowed his head in acceptance.

"Whatever you think is best, my son. I won't hold you back." He turned away, but stopped at the touch of a clawed hand on his shoulder.

"Do I think this is a crazy idea?" Corrigan asked. "Yes! But maybe this human will know where she is, where slaves go."

Rusha raised an eyebrow in suspicion.

"And you trust this human will not do the same to you?"

Corrigan shrugged with a faint smile. "He's a magic-user. If he had wanted to take me, he would have already done so."

CHAPTER 7

The coming of night blanketed the sky with fading purples and blues. Many merchants had cleared for the evening. A few people hurried down Lexington's sidewalks, occasionally startled by the growling of some mutt let loose from its master. Horses in their stables snorted and stomped their feet, trying to settle down after pulling carriages all day. A lone guard patrolled the streets, lighting lampposts as he went.

Though travelers and merchants actively walked the town square by day, nighttime brought its own array of hosts. A variety of animals marched the streets in search of leftover food. Peasants, who had had no luck during the daylight hours, now came from hiding. They were soon joined by Keith and Blackavar. After nearly losing to the town guards once, the two were in no hurry to try their luck again. Instead, they waited until the cover of darkness. After checking for the night patrol, they darted across the street to the next alley, continuing until they reached a dead end.

Blackavar cupped his hands over his mouth to produce a convincing night owl's cry. His fingers rapped atop the knuckles of his opposite hand, varying the steadiness of the cry. In all, there were two long hoots, which were promptly answered by two more.

Keith heard a faint click, and a section of wall opened to reveal a figure holding a lantern.

"I was beginning to wonder when you'd return," a soft voice greeted. Once inside, the wall slid in place so that not even a crack hinted its presence.

"He's here," a voice said from above.

Several shadowed figures slid down ropes from the rafters to join their comrade. The middle figure spoke to Blackavar while directing the others with hand gestures. It was a perfect way of communicating. Keith noticed the Master Thief's fingers signal too. Whatever it meant, the thieves understood with no questions asked.

"I've brought a new member," Keith heard Blackavar say, and the boy's attention drifted from the hand signals to the tall figures.

A slender woman laughed, her face hidden under the shadow of a cowl. "Another from the gutter, eh, Blackavar?"

There were several chuckles before the Master Thief cleared his throat.

"Well, what are we waiting for?" He grinned. "Ye know the routine. Snap to it! And mind ye, young ones are far more easier to teach than the grown."

Before Keith could blink, the men scurried back up the ropes. More rustling from above alerted him that others had joined, darting from one rafter to the next. Blackavar gestured for Keith to follow across the room. When they neared the end wall, it slid open, and the two departed back outside. Surrounding buildings boxed in the area, with only a pile of tossed belongings in the center. There were no other exits except the way they had come.

"Another hidden door?" Keith inquired.

Blackavar nodded, and pulled back a rag to reveal a square stone jutting from the smooth pavement. When he pressed it, a trap door opened beneath them. Keith yelped as he felt air whipping past until something soft broke his fall. An array of feathers flew up around him. He sat up.

"Blackavar?"

More feathers went flying as the thief pulled himself out and dusted off.

"The only problem with feathers," he shook his head to loosen any strays, "ye have to keep piling 'em up for the next person." He tapped a finger to his chin, staring at still-falling stragglers. He shrugged. "Oh, well! Come on. It's this way."

Side by side, the two walked through a narrow passageway to a set of semi-circle doors.

"Ready?" Excitement welled in Blackavar's voice, and Keith grinned. Using both hands, he pushed the two doors open until golden light from within flooded the entrance. "Welcome to the Thieves' Guild!"

The room was like a miniature town square, with buildings lining the sidewalls and pathways in between to resemble alleyways. Many long tables arranged in the room's center contained piles of stolen goods, the majority being gold. Around the tables were benches, which allowed members to sit and admire their daily steals.

Already, the room was filled with hustle and bustle as thieves, young and old, came and went. There were women washing clothes and hanging them to dry, men roasting hogs over fires and brewing stew in kettles. Keith even saw animals being led from passages into the back rooms where meat, clothing, and more were produced. The sight of it all was very much like above ground, but with no guards to bother with.

From the moment Blackavar entered, acknowledgements came from every direction. No matter what people were doing, all paused to greet the Master Thief. This provided the perfect opportunity to introduce his newest member who, after a while, received more attention than expected. Keith's unusual appearance drew quite a crowd, curious to see an albino in their midst. Conversations of excitement, even skepticism, broke out, for how was a thief with white hair able to steal and remain anonymous?

"Don't ye fret, lad." Blackavar held the crowd at bay by answering questions using hand signals. "We'll get Medallion to take a look at ye. Now, ye hungry? Been a long day, has it not?"

Keith's grumbling stomach answered, and he smiled sheepishly.

"I can't remember my last meal," he admitted. "That stew sure smells good."

A woman stirring it offered him a bowl.

"We're all family here," she replied. "You don't go hungry like *up there*." She pointed with a thumb.

Blackavar made sure the boy was comfortably seated at a table before venturing elsewhere with a promise to return. Keith did not mind, content to talk to those still surrounding him. There must have been hundreds living underground, for there was no place he looked that lacked movement. Yet the chamber was a comfortable size that accommodated each and every person with any need.

"Ain't hard to miss, are ya? I'm Toby." A boy, no older than himself, plopped down next to Keith. Short red hair stuck up over his brow, accompanied by a few matching freckles around the nose. Pudgy cheeks contained dimples when he smiled, and his soft brown eyes shined with mischief.

Keith returned the greeting and introduced himself.

"Funny sort, ain't ya? What ya call it – albino?"

Keith shrugged. "I looked fine this morning."

Toby laughed. "You and me! I can see the steals already coming our way. We'll make a great team!"

Keith was just finishing his stew when Blackavar returned, parting the remaining crowd of still curious onlookers.

"Feel better?" the thief asked.

The boy yawned with a nod. "Did you find Medallion?"

Blackavar chuckled. "Oh, he'll turn up when he wants. There's no rushing a magic-user." He winked at Toby. "Got a room prepared for ye, and judging from that yawn ye'll soon be using it."

"Already? But I'm not—" Keith broke off into a yawn. "Well, maybe a little."

The Master Thief gestured down one of the tunnels. "Let's get ye settled for the night. Some new clothing could do as well."

"See ya tomorrow, Keith!" Toby called. "Big steals coming! You'll see!"

Shortly after departing, the two entered a smaller room. Here, barrels contained fresh water, several with steam rising off the surface. Carefully, Keith dipped a finger to test its warmth.

"If ye need to bathe, we've plenty of hot water. It runs through channels between the walls."

"You have water in the walls?" Keith asked in surprise.

Blackavar motioned for the boy to look behind the barrels. There, a thin trough ran from the back to a hole in the wall. As Keith watched, water dripped down the channel and was swept away with other connecting troughs.

"They go all over the guild," Blackavar said, "and it's all thanks to a spring we found running beneath a Blacksmith's shop. They always keep their fires burning, so the water's plenty hot. To cool it, we keep it in these barrels. Just have to wait it out."

"How much water is there?" Keith asked.

Blackavar chuckled. "Probably enough to flood the entire main chamber, and still have some left over afterwards." He led the boy into the next room. "So…ye ready to see yer new wardrobe?"

"Wardrobe?" Keith followed the thief and watched him slide back a panel in the wall. Inside, rows of clothing hung in all different shapes, colors, and sizes. Keith stood in awe at all the expensive looking robes. There were leggings and tunics, skirts and gowns.

"We have enough clothing to rival even a prince's wardrobe!" Blackavar exclaimed. "Choose yer pick. Just don't pick yer choose, or ye lose!" He laughed.

"I've never seen so many!" Keith climbed inside and rummaged through them, trying to find one that fit.

"There you are! I missed you earlier."

Blackavar turned to see a young man coolly striding toward him, confident as a falcon. His style of dress was similar to Blackavar's, with the exception of maple-brown leggings. Short, dark brown hair curled around his ears. Over one shoulder he carried a bow and set of arrows in an olive-green case.

"Aldaris, ye proud bird!" Blackavar held out welcoming arms as the young man warmly embraced his friend in a bear hug. "Careful now! Ye're stronger than myself."

Aldaris laughed. "They say I don't know my own strength. How true that is." After setting the case of arrows down, he pulled back his shirtsleeve to flex his muscles.

"Impressive." Blackavar nodded. "Now ye just need to work on appearance."

Aldaris rolled his eyes. "You couldn't match my strength even if you wanted to."

"True."

"So where's this new member I keep hearing about?" Aldaris scratched at a scruffy-looking beard beginning to grow. "I'll take him out with one arm."

Blackavar chuckled. "I'm sure a finger would do." He nodded toward the wardrobe just as Keith stepped out holding a dark tunic.

Aldaris was lost in that sapphire gaze. His head cocked at an angle while he studied the small boy's peculiar appearance. After a moment of silent concentration, he forced himself to look away.

"He ain't a chance up there, not with hair that color. Might get a couple of things, but even with a hood he'd be recognized after a while."

Blackavar placed a reassuring hand on the boy's shoulder.

"I'm sure a little…adjustment…is possible, but I do believe in the long run he'll make an exceptional addition to the guild."

Aldaris was still doubtful when another member walked into the room. A gold pendant gently swayed over his breast. Gold rings adorned each of his ring and forefingers, and in one hand he carried a staff inlaid with swirls of gold and diamonds. Even his long hair took on a golden appearance.

"Good evening to you, gentlemen," the man greeted. A velvety robe of scarlet swished the ground with each long stride.

"Ah, our Master Mage." Blackavar returned the greeting with a bow.

"Medallion," Keith whispered, and sky blue eyes met his sapphire ones.

The mage's smile broadened, his lean facial features complimenting his slender form.

"Uncommon, but intriguing. Do you suppose there's any magic in him?"

"Could be." Aldaris adjusted his bow. "I thought albinos had pink eyes, not blue. Certainly, not *that* blue."

"So...how 'bout those clothes?" Blackavar quickly changed the subject, seeing the confusion on Keith's face. He glanced over what the boy had pulled out. "I think these will do. Why don't ye try 'em on? Look, there's a panel over there. Ye'll have full privacy." Blackavar then turned to Aldaris. "Why don't we have a few steals, hmmm?"

"Now? But there're no..."

Blackavar clunked him on the ear and began dragging him toward the door. "Back in a few," he said to Medallion. "I've got a goon to clobber."

Medallion smiled. "Make that double for me as well."

The Master Mage seated himself on a bench next to one of the barrels and rested both hands on his staff. Behind the folding panels he could hear Keith rustling with his new garments.

"I'm sorry if you were offended, my lad. Aldaris' tongue can be as sharp as his arrows sometimes."

Keith appeared wearing dark pants and belt that fastened over a long shirt. Lastly, he included the pouch around his waist Blackavar had given him. He checked the inside once before folding the flap and securing it, for within he had placed his pan flute for safekeeping. *Better than my pocket,* he thought. *There's more room.*

"Nice touch." Medallion nodded in approval. He rose to study the boy. "But I'm afraid you won't get far with hair that color, at least not directly on the streets. Most people aren't accustomed to oddities, lad. You'd soon be recognized."

"I could find something with a hood," Keith said, but Medallion only smiled.

"No need. I think I have just the thing." He rested a hand over Keith's head and murmured a few words. When he took his hand away, a wave of dark color swirled through the boy's hair, changing it from white to coal black. He then guided Keith to a mirror hanging on the wall. "There! That should do it."

Keith stared in disbelief.

"You like?" Medallion stepped to the side. "I inverted the color, which isn't hard since black is opposite white. A simple illusion that doesn't affect the natural color."

Keith glanced up at the magic-user. "So is this what you do for the guild? Help hide things?"

Medallion grinned with pride. "You're a bright one. Ah, but there's more to it than just illusion. Magic is a wondrous gift. It protects the entrances from curious seekers, like street guards, and only allows members to 'see' the actual doorways."

Medallion turned his head at the sound of footsteps to see Blackavar enter the room.

"You're just in time," he said, and the thief halted in mid-step.

"Where's Keith?"

"I'm right here." The boy stepped forward. "Look! I'm like you now!"

"Above me word!" Blackavar studied him. A mischievous grin spread across his face. "A spitting image of meself. Do you think we could pass as twins?" He lowered himself to Keith's level, receiving a hearty laugh from the magic-user.

"More so if he steals like you," he chuckled.

Keith just cracked a secretive smile at Blackavar.

The thief shrugged. "We'll see 'bout that!"

CHAPTER 8

An eerie stillness hung in the air, disturbed only by the rustle of feathers as the Black Wing hovered a few moments before landing. Silence pleased him. No more suspicious glances from the White Wings. No more whispers behind his back.

Corrigan glanced around his surroundings. The ground sank under his weight from excess moisture coming from the nearby swamp. Various ferns and underbrush peaked his interest toward strange foliage coloration. Here, trees shrewdly slunk upwards to a gray-clouded sky with black-veined leaves. Even the sun retained its early morning warmth, cold and gray-white through the swirl of clouds. It was the same as he approached the charred black gates, marking the entrance to Jenario's home. A morning fog obscured the top portion, and they faded in and out of view as a cold wind picked up.

Corrigan allowed his wings to fade as he passed through the gates, following a well-trodden path. A stone overpass pointed upward in a curving V-shape. Beneath the pass, Corrigan paused to examine a few symbols etched into the stone. Over time erosion had masked the surface. If there had been any meaning to them, it was gone now.

Passing through, Corrigan found himself in a courtyard. Toward the center, a patch of flowers grew, but how unusual! He glanced at what used to be roses, now withered and dry like ashes lined in a row. The feeling of comfort faded to doubt.

I take it visitors must be seldom here.

A thin mist settled around the vacant yard, and he peered up to take in the sight of looming castle. An ornate archway framed the front door as he approached. Designs carved into stone arched high over the threshold in an unpleasant frown. Two matching triangles slanted above the entrance like two narrowing eyes. Corrigan felt a shiver run down his spine at the thought that the very castle may be watching.

He reached for the knocker, and the door opened inward on rusty hinges. Dust stirred from the movement, and a masterful but soft voice echoed from within.

"Come in, my friend," it beckoned.

Not a feather flinched nor reappeared as he calmly entered. The door locked behind him.

"This way," the voice coaxed.

Corrigan turned down a long corridor, following drifts of dust that lifted from the floor as if an invisible force moved them along. It rolled down the corridor until it came to a standstill in the center of a room. Here, four hallways arched away from the main corridor. Overhead, the same type of architecture that he had seen on the exterior of the building decorated the interior. The rafters in the ceiling were long beams of curved iron. The intersection was a cross of several arches, each one layered on top of another like mini highways. No doubt, they made the perfect connections for mice to get from place to place.

Candlelight provided the only light source within the dark hallways, for there were no windows. Even if there had been, thick clouds prevented any sunlight from shining through.

Corrigan noticed the dust swirl in a ring. When he approached, it rose higher, changing from ordinary grains of dirt to onyx flames. It circled until a form took shape from its wrath.

Jenario stepped from the circle. The dust disassembled into fragments once more, and when he walked a breeze from his folding robes swept them off into darkness.

"A pleasure to meet you again. You will not regret this decision."

The Black Wing smirked. "I'm already enjoying the silence here."

Pleased, the mage motioned for his guest to follow.

"You won't find many in Sapphire. Most people prefer the crowded streets of Lexington."

As the two walked together, Corrigan thought of his mother. *This place would have suited her well.*

Jenario's smile broadened. "Feel free to ask me about the human realms."

A frown. "I'll ask when I'm ready."

The mage nodded. "Suit yourself. You can ask about Castle Mire later."

"What?" Corrigan raised a feathered eyebrow.

"A holding pen for slaves," a gruff voice met their ears, and Corrigan ruffled his wings into view as a figure appeared at the end of the hallway.

"Corrigan, I would like to introduce you to a friend of mine," Jenario said. "This is Nathaniel Woodston, my assistant huntsman."

A room off to the right provided a warm fire that lit Nathaniel's backside. Corrigan eyed his belts equipped with daggers and vials of oddly colored liquids. The collar of his boots ascended all the way to the knee. A leather band around one leg held a patch of arrows. Already, there were mud stains on his shirt, and a faint scent of blood floated around his figure. Huntsman or not, he was dressed to kill.

"So this is your Black Wing?" Nathaniel scowled, looking the harpy up and down. "Looks a bit scrawny to me."

Jenario eyed those talons flexing in silent anger.

"Nevertheless," he said quickly, "he's still quite capable of inflicting the same amount of damage, *if* you get my drift."

Nathaniel backed into the shadows of the room, mumbling to himself.

Jenario motioned for his guest to continue into the next room.

"Don't mind him," he said, holding a door open for the harpy. "He normally stays to himself."

"That was no huntsman," Corrigan replied stiffly. "That was an assassin. I don't see how you could possibly trust someone like that."

"I don't." Jenario chuckled. "I keep my chamber doors magically locked. And since Nathaniel has no concept of how to break spells, I needn't worry with it."

Corrigan grumbled. "Remind me to sleep from the rafters then."

Jenario smiled in amusement.

"You needn't fear for your safety, my friend. Nathaniel has a tendency to preoccupy himself with liquor. He'll probably forget he even saw you."

Corrigan shrugged, his only concern being that he did not get locked in his room at night, for nighttime was when *he* hunted.

For the remainder of the evening, Corrigan was shown around the castle. At mealtime he ate in one of many spacious dining rooms, delighted to have a recent kill from the so-called *huntsman*. A glass of wine afterwards in the mage's private study was a treat. Having never tasted wine before, the Black Wing was cautioned by his host not to gulp it down like his meal. Corrigan took the advice seriously, and instead studied his surroundings while listening to Jenario talk more about his work. Off to one side was a bookcase filled with the mage's life-long studies.

Jenario shifted his gaze to the shelves. "I have conducted many a research on various creatures, but my greatest discovery has yet to be seen—or perhaps you haven't noticed." He reached beneath the collar of his robe and pulled out a gold chain. At the end dangled a ruby stone.

Corrigan leaned closer for a better look.

"Looks ordinary at first glance," Jenario continued. "But it's what's *inside* that matters."

Corrigan squinted, trying to peer beyond the surface reflections.

"I see *something*," he admitted. "It's too dark to tell. What am I looking at?"

Jenario gently removed the stone from between the Black Wing's fingers. Leaning close, he whispered, "Inside is the most precious thing in all of *No'va* – the tip of a unicorn's horn!"

Corrigan stared. "Explain yourself."

"Oh, it was quite easy, actually." Jenario leaned back in his chair. "A unicorn will only give favors if you give *her* one. What I asked wasn't much."

"A horn? I thought you would have asked to study the unicorn itself?"

Jenario's lips spread into a thin smile.

"Remember when you asked me how I knew the *Lo-ans'rel* name?"

Corrigan raised a feathered eyebrow. "You asked for that?" His wings ruffled into view, causing him to stand. "You can't possibly imagine the danger you've put yourself in!"

"I only asked to become a magic-user," Jenario replied. "Now my potions are ten times more powerful, and will keep the Healer quiet until I've finished my studies."

"And then?"

Jenario shrugged. "He gets released. Why? Are you worried, Corrigan? Did you want to release him from my dungeon for me? I'd rather not face an angry Healer anyway." He chuckled and rose from his seat to stretch. "It's late. Do what you like: hunt, fly. Don't bother meddling with my things, though. Just a fair warning."

With a slight bow, Jenario slipped from the room. Shadows from the outside hallway enveloped him in darkness until there was nothing left but the faint echoes of his footsteps fading down one of the corridors.

Corrigan stretched his wings. He decided to keep them in view while exploring the many shelves stacked with books. Each one had been titled according to Jenario's research. One such book was labeled *Eúgliactmaent*. Another was *Harpy-demons*.

Harpy-demons? He'd have to crawl through a swamp to reach one! Or did his current magical abilities persuade one out?

He continued scanning the shelves until one title in particular caught his attention: *Lo-ans'rel*. Curious to see what was written about them, he reached up and carefully pulled it out using the tips of his claws. Dust stirred through the air when he opened the cover and flipped through its pages. Detailed drawings marked how shifting was done, accompanied with notes that pointed out specific areas of the body—the use of ears, eye color, even sounds they made. Corrigan skimmed over the notes, then turned the page.

Something clinked on the floor near his foot, and Corrigan peered down to spy a metallic object in the glow of candlelight.

What's this? He bent to retrieve it. A double-sided key, new from the looks of it, had been tucked between the pages of the book. He kept turning it, each end a different size to fit two separate locks. *But what?*

The page he was on suddenly flipped to the next, revealing a crude layout from the lounge to a door not far down the hall.

With a shrug, he ripped the page from the book and carried it with him as he strode unhurriedly to the specified location. *Don't meddle in his stuff, huh? Don't leave keys in books and maps to find things!*

The key fit the lock perfectly, and the whole bar snapped up with a loud click. Corrigan waited, listening for sounds of footsteps. When none came, he gave the door a good shove and watched it open on silent hinges. Darkness greeted. Although he was a night hunter, complete blackness would be a challenge. Grabbing one of the nearby torches lighting the hallway, the Black Wing held it just inside the door. A long stairway wound down in the dark with no railings to hold should he fall.

Good thing I have wings, Corrigan chuckled to himself and began descending, one step at a time. It took a while before he finally reached the bottom, being too dark to see how far he had to go. The torch did little to light the massive chamber, allowing only a faint glimpse of objects too far back against the wall. The sound of dripping water echoed throughout the room as he turned slowly around, straining to see in the dark.

If only I had been part owl.

Close enough, a soft voice entered Corrigan's mind. Wings rose in warning, though he had no idea where the voice came from, nor how to block it.

"No games, Jenario!"

Far from it, the thought continued. *To your right.*

Cautiously, Corrigan took a few steps until the light fell across a small cot. He drew the torch slowly down the length of the bed and over a still form lying on top. He recognized the lightweight clothing of *Lo-ans'rel*, and his heart beat faster. When he came to the middle, he paused. The slender hands were chained together. The ankles might have been too, but for the robe covering them there was no way to tell.

Light passed over the face, and Corrigan took a quick intake of breath. There was no mistaking those wolf-like ears.

So Jenario told true. He does have one.

Like he has you, the voice returned, but now Corrigan understood its location. It was coming from the Healer himself.

"Can you hear me?" he asked.

Just think your answers, was the reply. Golden eyes wearily peered up at the broad-winged harpy. *Jenario must not know you're here.*

Corrigan smirked. *I think he wanted me to.*

He held the key up in the light. The opposite side matched the locks on the shackles, and he wasted no time removing them, then helped the Healer up. He was weak from the potions Jenario had given him, forcing Corrigan to support his frail body. Stairs proved too much, and in the end the Black Wing had to carry him. Once free of the dungeon, Corrigan returned the torch. He would need the cover of darkness to find his way out among the maze of hallways and rooms.

He turned down a hall and stopped. Footsteps scraped the floor, stumbling every other step. Corrigan had a mind who it was, and backed into shadow with his wings blending perfectly as he wrapped them around his body. He waited, the *Lo-ans'rel* gently pressed against his chest feathers.

A figure stumbled into view, and as Corrigan peered between his wings he recognized Nathaniel and nearly laughed at his drunken state. He would prove no trouble to deal with, but the risk of alarming Jenario was too great. Nathaniel passed, mumbling as he went, and Corrigan slipped down the hallway without further incident.

An open window in one of the rooms offered a quiet getaway, though once in flight he cared little if he was quiet or not. Jenario expected him to hunt, and Corrigan would make sure to leave the bones of his nightly meal in clear view.

He made sure to clear the castle grounds before setting the *Loans'rel* down, wondering how the Healer would survive in his weakened state. Yet no sooner had he released him than vines began gathering from the ground. Those that touched the Healer turned brown and withered away while more took their place. It was not long before the Healer could stand without assistance. He took a deep breath, coughing a few times. When he spoke, his voice sounded stronger.

"Thank you, my friend." He held out his hands, and the vines stopped circling. "I am indebted to you."

Corrigan shrugged. "Your kind owes nothing to the likes of me."

"My kind are like yours, whispering behind our backs because we are different, an outcast living among outcasts. They call me Windchester."

Corrigan ruffled his wings.

"You know me, Healer? I don't recall ever seeing you in the shade of our trees."

Windchester nodded.

"It was a while back, but yes. I was there. I left because of humans." He brushed a few strands of chestnut hair from his face. "Seems you left for the same reason."

"I came for answers," Corrigan replied. "And I'll get them, one at a time." He spread his wings and took to the sky, seeing the vines had begun moving again. They rose around the figure in a twist of leaves and soil, engulfing the Healer's body.

"Suit yourself." Windchester bowed his head, but his thoughts carried to the Black Wing. *You've seen his power. You've seen what he's obtained. Be on guard, my friend, and farewell.*

Corrigan did not stay to watch the vines cover him completely, though he did glance down to see them retreating back into the earth, the Healer nowhere to be seen.

CHAPTER 9

"Ain't ya ready yet?" Toby peered into the bedroom just as Keith tucked his pan flute into the pouch Blackavar had given him and fastened it around his waist.

Nearly two years had passed since the boy had joined the guild, and already his room was filled with collectibles that challenged even the Master Thief. Proudly, he admired several diamond necklaces, pottery, even bundles of clothing stored in one corner. Across from those lay various colored glass bottles, which were lined all in a row across a single shelf. There were plates and cups, saucers and teacups, not the plain white ones that normally passed between merchant to commoners. These were rare, one-of-a-kind designs that only the wealthy could claim, and where the wealthy roamed was where Keith found gold; gold shillings, gold fabrics, gold everything. Sometimes he would come across silver.

Slightly larger but lighter than gold, silver coins were easier to take, being far quieter when they clinked together in purses. Occasionally, he would come across copper coins that peasants used to bargain for food. Since copper was not worth much, few merchants accepted it.

There's no telling where I'd be if Blackavar hadn't found me, he thought while following Toby out to the main chamber. *And yet I wonder if my mother meant this way of life for me. I may be good at stealing, but that can't be the reason why my uncle let me live!*

"Can't ya just smell the riches we'll be gettin' today?" Toby beamed as the two boys stepped into the golden lit room.

"Who'll be with us this time?" Keith asked, trying to refocus his thoughts on the day's steals.

"Well, we had Aldaris last week. I think maybe Jasper."

Keith nodded. "Good. I like Jasper. He keeps the merchants busy."

Jasper, whose dark curls reminded Keith of his father, stood waiting for them in a group of ten others. Good at storytelling, Jasper often entertained merchants with wild tales, which made it easier for Keith or Toby to take things from the stands. Being the weakest at steals, Toby often relied on others to steal for him, Keith being one himself.

"So you going to try for a bracelet today?" Keith teased, and Toby's face grew red.

"Ain't promising nothin'," he admitted. "One day, though."

"Yeah. Three in a row. Got it." Keith shook his head.

"I will! Just..."

"Hurry up, you two!" Jasper spotted them approaching. "Where've ya been? Blackavar's 'bout ready to pounce a cat if he doesn't go soon." He laughed. "Ready for another big one, Toby? Got the perfect story."

The boy grinned. "Me n' Keith gettin' that bracelet today."

"Actually, I was thinking of having Keith today." Medallion stepped from the group, staff tapping the stone floor as he walked. "If that's all right with you, Jasper."

Nearby, Blackavar eyed the Master Mage with a smirk.

"Yeself? Taking a partner? That's new."

"Me?" Keith stared in surprise.

Medallion sighed, the glow of magic captured in those light blue eyes holding the boy's attention. Something about him always drew Keith's focus. Something...about the magic...

"Well, if we're all ready," Blackavar broke the moment, and Keith snapped to attention. "To market, here we come!"

Medallion led the way with Keith at his side. As he passed Toby, he saw his lips form the words, *"Lucky!"*

"But you always work alone," Keith whispered, glancing up at the mage's tall frame. "How come today's different?"

A chuckle. "New merchants bring new people. New people mean possible magic-users. I work alone because I have magic. It's not fair to have a partner when I can act as two people. But today I'm in need of something. If I should find it, I'll need you to help me."

"I'll try," Keith replied.

"You'll do fine."

A ladder led to a trap door, which opened to a narrow alley. Medallion went first to check for bystanders. Only when he was certain the alley was clear did he gesture for the rest to follow. Once everyone was out, they made their way with caution to the edge of the buildings.

Blackavar was quick to spy the first guard, and he rubbed his hands in anticipation for the coming steals.

"Relentless!" he whispered. "But fun!"

"Until you're caught," Medallion warned. "Let me go first. I'll cover the passage so everyone can come out at once."

"Aw, where's the fun in that?" Aldaris grinned. "So much better to dodge and duck!"

Jasper nudged him with an elbow. "That only works in twos or threes. We've got ten."

Blackavar waved the mage onward. "Ye do the honors."

"With pleasure." Medallion checked the guard's position before stepping from the alley. A wave of his staff cast a thin aura of illusion around the opening between the buildings to veil their presence. Once in place, the group stepped out in one mass to examine which merchant stand to try first. A few customers walking along the sidewalks carried large purses at their sides. No doubt, by keeping away from the heavy crowds did they think to avoid possible theft.

How wrong they are. Keith smiled to himself, and would have followed when he remembered today he was partner to Medallion.

He turned to find the mage in the midst of weaving illusion around his garments. Crimson robe quick-changed to pants and shirt, not something Keith associated with his friend, or any other magic-user he had seen roaming the streets of Lexington.

"Only those of status think they need to stand out," Medallion said after completing his outfit with a brown belt.

"Have fun, Keith!" Toby darted into the crowded streets with Jasper at his heels.

Keith shook his head and glanced to Medallion.

"You think he'll get those bracelets today?"

After a moment's thought, the mage simply said, "Nope."

Blackavar and Aldaris started off to the right. The Master Thief turned and signaled to Medallion before mingling with the crowd.

"By noon?" Keith questioned the signal to meet back later on. "Is that enough time to get what you need?"

"Should be." Medallion started down the sidewalk, keeping an eye on a few passing guards.

Keith knew the guards were not a bother, especially with illusion disguising his white curls. That, at least, would keep some attention to a minimum. Still, he kept checking the tips to see if any white showed, receiving a chuckle from his companion.

"Don't worry, lad. I'll be certain the illusion doesn't wear off too quickly like last time."

Keith made a face.

"That nearly cost us a member!" he accused, remembering his encounter with a guard when his hair suddenly changed from black to white. "Aldaris nearly got caught trying to get me back to the guild!"

"I'll make it up to you both." Yet a mischievous grin told Keith the mage's thoughts were elsewhere. "There!" He gestured to a stand where a few people gathered. "Recognize that one?"

Keith noted the unfamiliar garment on a tall individual chatting with a merchant.

"Is he a magic-user too?"

Medallion nodded. "See that pouch on his belt? What's inside is what I want. Do you think you can get it for me?"

"Sure, but why me?" Keith asked. "Is it something about the magic?"

Another nod.

"It's highly dishonorable to steal from another magic-user. Should our magics clash, the illusion disguising your hair would fade in an instant. That's why it's better if you do the honors."

"And if he should catch me?" Keith asked.

"I'll be right here," was the reply as Medallion gently gave the boy a push toward the stand.

Keith approached with curiosity to see what wares the merchant sold. He clenched his palms, nervous sweat already building so that he had to wipe his hands for the moment of the steal. The crowd was not too thick in the area, so the merchant seemed lax about keeping an eye on his goods. As the boy positioned himself, pretending to admire items from the stand, he saw the magic-user slip a hand into his pocket, then back to the items for sale. Curious, Keith watched the movement again before he realized the man was stealing. Having seen Medallion do the same, the boy recognized the illusion replacing each piece of jewelry taken.

He's busy concentrating on keeping the merchant's attention. Now's my chance!

The pouch was within reach. His hand inched toward it. A quick glance to the merchant confirmed the magic-user had him locked in full conversation. His fingers worked to unlatch the flap. He reached inside, touched something, then pulled it out. About to turn and slide it into his own pouch, Keith stole a glance to see what he had taken.

He gasped – a little too loud. When the giddy conversations died behind him, Keith knew he had been discovered.

A hand grabbed the boy's shoulder in a firm hold and spun him around.

"Thought ye'd take something of mine, did ye now?"

Keith stared into a pair of angry eyes - magic-user eyes that flared with power ready to release.

"Y…You keep sk…skulls in there?" the boy stammered a reply.

"And I keep adding new ones…every time someone steals from me!" He raised a hand, a spell forming on his lips.

"Medallion!" Keith cried, flinging his hands up in defense. He shut his eyes tightly.

A scream, then someone grabbed his hand, and Keith felt himself being pulled away. When he finally opened his eyes, people were running. The merchant stand was gone, tossed onto the sidewalk as though a great wind had toppled it. The magic-user, flung on his back, was wildly waving his hands in the air trying to get off crates of food.

"Quickly!"

Keith exhaled in relief when he realized Medallion had pulled him away from all the chaos.

"Your hair turned back!" the mage huffed. "We need to get you out of here before guards see you!" The two started toward the nearest alley. "Stay here while I gather the rest," he said once they were safely between the buildings.

"Thanks for stopping that guy," Keith managed.

Medallion glanced over his shoulder with inquisitive expression.

"You think that was me?" With a chuckle, Medallion darted from the alley, leaving Keith with his fingers still clamped tightly around the skull.

*****

"So here I am! Thinking I could go about my business when all of a sudden…" Jasper took a breath to finish the story, another thrill for a merchant while Toby took his time taking a few items from the stand. It was his best one yet, for it drew several other bystanders. They stood together in hushed silence, the grand ending but a breath away when a disturbance from another stand stole the moment.

Toby dropped his treasure and looked around. Curious onlookers started down the street. So did guards.

"Oh. Great." Jasper shook his head. "Just when I get to the good part!"

Blackavar darted through the crowd. A hand signal later, Jasper and Toby were hurrying alongside to get to the alley.

"Is everyone all right?" Jasper kept asking. "That sounded big!"

"So far." Blackavar held back to wait for others. "Get to the guild! I'll be in shortly!"

Disappointment crossed his features. He had lost the opportunity to steal something worthwhile. About to turn in with the rest, Toby's eye caught a vacant stand.

"Ain't that jewelry?" but Jasper was already caught in conversation with other members approaching the alley. "Be right back!"

Toby let himself fall behind. The merchant stand was not far. Most people were too curious in the happenings down the street. Even guards had cleared the area.

"Perfect!" The boy approached and reached for one of the bracelets. "Been wantin' one of you."

A shadow fell over the table.

Toby's hand froze just over a bracelet. He had barely even touched it when he felt someone grip his shoulder.

*****

Keith was glad to be back at the guild and more than happy to give the miniature skull to Medallion.

"A head?" The boy made a face. "Was that truly what you were after? Or did I take the wrong thing?"

Medallion smiled. "I won't tell you what you were supposed to take, but this is fine. I'll just add it with the rest of my collection."

Nearby, Aldaris snickered.

"Better watch that one," he said. "To us, stuff like that are mere trinkets. To him, they're trophies." He shrugged. "So, did you happen to pick up anything else on your way in?"

"Too confusing at the moment. What'd you get?" Keith went to a table where the thieves had piled their latest steals.

"Anyone seen Toby?" Jasper entered the main chamber with puzzled expression. "Wasn't he right behind us?"

"Did he not enter the guild?" Blackavar's expression turned serious. "Ye were his partner. Why didn't ye keep an eye on him?"

"He's probably upset that he didn't get that bracelet," Keith teased. "I'll bet he's in his room."

"Sorry, Blackavar. I'll go back out and look," Jasper said.

"There's no need to if he's already here," the Master Thief said. He pointed to Keith. "Check his room. If he's not there, Jasper will go back out."

"And tell Daumier he's needed for inventory," Medallion added. "Blackavar, you and I need to have a chat."

The thief raised his eyebrows in question. "About?"

Keith heard several mentions of 'magic-user' as he left the main chamber. *What a joke! He's probably telling him how I got caught.* The boy grit his teeth. *The one and only time he picks me, and I fail miserably!*

Keith decided to take the long way in order to vent.

Let me get Daumier first. I'm sure Toby's fine, but I can't go into his room angry when he's probably upset himself for missing a steal.

He stepped lightly over the floor, for rainwater had dripped from the streets to create a slippery surface. As he walked, he watched his shadow roll over the walls. It grew larger, then shrunk, depending on the wall's contours. At an intersection of tunnels, a ray of light shone from a hole in the ceiling. Keith stopped beneath it, watching his shadow slide along the floor. He turned so it stood upright against the wall, toying with shadow puppets using his hands to create animals. He laughed at them dancing across the wall. He created a second puppet, and then a third joined.

The boy turned to catch someone ducking inside another tunnel.

"Daumier!" Keith exclaimed.

"Had you fooled, didn't I?" Shadows rolled over the thief's body as he came into view. He was slightly shorter than Blackavar with years of skill shining in those hazel eyes. He brushed a hand through his sandy brown hair. "I take it you were looking for me?"

"We just got in. Need an inventory count." Keith smoothed a hand over the corroded surface. Several layers of mold flaked off. "I don't remember this tunnel being so…shabby."

Daumier grinned.

"Did Blackavar ever tell you we used to live in the tunnels above?" The thief ducked under a low ceiling as he headed down a tunnel. "Only reason we moved was because the townspeople could hear us. That's why guards constantly keep a lookout. Let me just get something. Tell the others I'll be right there."

Keith could hear him scuffling along the interior of the narrow tunnel. He thought of his missing friend and asked, "You didn't happen to see Toby come this way, did you? Jasper didn't see him come in." When no one answered, Keith tried again. "Daumier?"

Suddenly, the thief came skidding on his back to a stop at Keith's feet.

"Daumier!" Keith bent to help him up, but the thief thrust away his hand.

"Run! Warn the others!" he choked. "You're faster than me!"

"Wha—" And then Keith saw them. Street guards tromped through the tunnel, their dark outfits blending into the shadows.

"Don't let him spread the word!" one shouted. It was as if someone had opened a valve. Guards flooded everywhere.

Keith gasped. "How did they get in?"

"Just go!" Daumier begged. "Find Blackavar!"

There was no other choice, and Keith knew it. The floor was slick, but still he ran, only to discover the way blocked by a guard at the other end. He tried to stop and skidded sideways. Not far behind, the rest of the guards closed their distance. Burly arms reached out to grab him, but because of Keith's size, he went sliding straight between the guard's legs. Without a moment's breath, the boy latched onto a ladder and began climbing to the unused tunnels above.

I'll never get to them like this! Still climbing, Keith dug into his pouch and pulled out his pan flute. *I hope this works.* He took a deep breath, then blew as loudly as he could. Panic short-winded the sound, yet the screeching echo it left behind was sure to be heard, and it was not long before he recognized the warning cries of guild members, much like the rapping of night owls from when he had first met the Master Thief. *I need to get to Blackavar! He'll know what to do!*

From below, guards latched onto the ladder and tried to rip it from the wall. Keith barely reached the top when it collapsed. Making sure his flute was secured in the pouch, the boy raced to find an opening to the main tunnels. He could hear shouts and clanging metal. He followed them, not certain where the upper tunnels would lead, and had just rounded a corner into a room when he suddenly halted.

"There's one!" Two guards came marching toward him. One lurched forward, but Keith sidestepped and made haste down the corridor. He looked back to see how far they were.

A loose board tripped his foot, and Keith went sprawling on his stomach. The boy grit his teeth as stinging pain surged up his arms. It was not long before the guards were upon him, their heavy boots shaking the floor.

The two men, loaded down with weapons and heavy armor, did not hear the snapping floorboards until it caved in. Both fell through, crashing into the main chamber below. Keith recognized the long tables where the thieves displayed newly stolen goods, now a resting place for two broken bodies.

Snap! Keith had only enough time to get to his feet before another section collapsed. Fingers clawed the air for something to hold. He could feel the floor angling, and his feet began to slide.

"Blackavar!" he cried, feeling himself fall. He grasped a piece of wood barely attached, dangling him like string over the main chamber several hundred feet below.

"Keith!" Blackavar jumped on a table to avoid some of the mayhem in the room. "Keith, let go! I'll catch ye!"

"What!" The boy could feel his fingers slipping.

"Trust me!" Blackavar shouted. Guards were pouring into the chamber. "Trust me, Keith."

There was no other option. Unable to hold himself any longer, Keith closed his eyes and let go. Wind whipped past, not fast like he would have thought. It was a gentle breeze, reminding him of lazy days spent outdoors collecting herbs and bouquets of flowers with his mother. He could almost see her, arms outstretched to bring her son close. Her loving embrace soothed away his fears.

Keith opened his eyes, hoping to wake from a dream back at home. He looked up at Blackavar.

"Ye're all right, lad," he said, letting the boy get over the dizzying fall before setting him down.

Blackavar hopped off the table first, then scooped Keith down with him. The room was a mass of confusion, but somehow Medallion and Aldaris had managed to join their Master Thief. Keith looked around at all the guards blocking the tunnels. There was nowhere to run, and no way out.

"How'd they find us?" Keith asked.

"Not sure," Blackavar replied, "but I think we're about to find out." As he said this, the captain of the guards entered the chamber, pulling a boy behind him.

Toby! Keith thought.

"Listen up, scum!" the captain announced. "Here's how it's gonna' work. We march from here to the streets. From there, you'll be taken by wagon, and I think you already know where you'll be headed."

Keith heard Blackavar take a quick breath when Toby was pulled in front of the guard for everyone to see.

"Thanks to one of your own," the captain continued, "I now get to see justice done!"

Keith narrowed his eyes as fury boiled through his veins. Questions spun through his head, each one stirring his anger.

"You make me sick!" Keith said in a hushed whisper. His eyes captured the light of each tiny candle burning from the wall, and they seemed to glow along with his anger. *This can't be Toby's doing!*

The captain smiled triumphantly. Above his head, a chandelier began a lazy swing from side to side. As Keith's anger built, the swings increased.

"Gather this muck together!" commanded the leader, tossing Toby to the side. "And you can tell the headmaster we've got a special addition coming his way!" He nodded toward Medallion.

The motion prompted Keith's temper.

"You can't do this to us!" he shouted.

A crack from the ceiling alarmed Blackavar, and he pulled Keith back as the chandelier broke from its chain. The captain snapped his head up in time to glimpse the underside of a falling object right before it crushed him.

Toby stared at the body, watching trickles of blood collect around the fingers. For several minutes no one moved. Then he turned and ran toward the thieves, nearly jumping into Blackavar's outstretched arms.

"I never wanted to bring them here!" Toby cried. "I'm so sorry!"

"I know," Blackavar soothed. "I know."

"The betrayal is on us!" a guard shouted. "Just kill them all!" The guards rushed forward.

Blackavar met the first in a blur of steal. "Aldaris, get to the pipes!"

"On it!" The thief notched one arrow after the other, severing his way toward the water room.

Suddenly, Medallion was beside Keith and Toby, herding them away from Blackavar toward the back of the room. Like a snake, he lashed out at any guards in his way, his staff arching over their heads to create a magical barrier around the three. Attacks harmlessly bounced off.

"What about Blackavar?" Keith kept glancing over his shoulder. The crowd had thickened, and he could no longer see the thief.

"He'll come!" Medallion pointed the staff at a bare wall, and a secret door opened. "Right now our main concern is getting you two to safety. Quick! Down this tunnel before the guards see it."

"No wait! I can help!" Keith protested, but Medallion's firm grip kept him and Toby from leaving.

"See you at the other end." The Master Mage waved his staff again, and the wall shut.

"Hey!" Keith was angry. He wanted to be where his friends were fighting. He could have helped. He could hear shouts and clanging steel, and thought he recognized Blackavar's slender blades doubling up against a sword. "I have to get back!"

"Only Medallion can open the door." Toby tugged on his friend's sleeve. "We need to hurry. Aldaris will release the water soon. The whole room will go under!"

"I don't care!" Keith jerked his arm free. "Seemingly you don't, since you gave away our hideout."

Tears sprang to Toby's eyes, and he backed away from Keith's accusing gaze.

"I...I didn't mean to." He held his hands in front of him. "It was stupid, I know! I ain't ever been the best at steals. Thought I'd slip away. But then – the captain – he my father...."

Keith's anger cracked light under the wall, and they both looked as it grew brighter.

"Medallion's back!" Forgetting his anger, Keith tried to lift it. "It's stuck! Help, Toby!"

"Ain't we gonna' drown?" Toby shivered. "Th-the water...."

Keith spun around.

"Fine! You flee down the tunnel and let everyone else drown when they would've accepted you back!" The boy's spurt of fury pushed the door open wide enough for him to crawl under, leaving Toby alone.

No one had seen him yet as Keith dodged between fighting thieves and guards. A flash of light drew his attention to the room's center.

Medallion held his staff out to one side, the tip glowing brightly to thrust the guards away from the tunnel openings. Once the tunnel was cleared, he raised it high and caused a sliding section to seal it.

He's closing off the tunnels!

One guard spat at the mage and pulled out a crossbow. Medallion swung his staff over the man's head, stepping to one side as one of the deadly bolts shot past his waist. Another guard took aim and prepared to launch one into the mage's heart. Medallion turned, but jolted to a halt when he saw the weapon. Both stood facing each other, waiting for the moment. Instead, the guard's eyes rolled to the back of his head. When his body slumped to the ground, Keith stood behind with a broken bottle in hand. A piece of glass stuck out from neck where it had punctured the flesh.

Medallion raised an eyebrow, then cracked a grin.

"I knew you were one," he breathed.

Keith wanted to ask what he meant, but at that moment Blackavar's voice rang over the shouts and stabbing metal. Turning, Keith saw the Master Thief wildly beckoning for him and Medallion to a side tunnel. It was the only one left open.

Medallion had to fight harder to keep them back as Keith made his way down a small flight of steps, jumping the last four to dash across the room when a guard crashed through a table and blocked his way. His enormous sword slashed sideways, and Keith barely ducked under it in time. The guard grit his teeth at the miss and turned to slash down.

Dagger met sword as Blackavar intervened, bringing his two daggers up to catch the blade before it could fall on Keith.

"Run!" Blackavar shouted as the guard lifted his sword off the daggers. For the next couple of swings Blackavar's weapons constantly blocked. When at last he saw a chance to retaliate, it harmlessly nicked the guard's thick armor. An unexpected punch to the stomach sent the thief careening backward to the floor. Both his daggers were lost in the midst of feet and noise. As he scrambled to find his footing the guard brought his sword down hard. Blackavar rolled to the right, keeping his body facing the guard as he crawled backward on his hands and feet. Another swing cut into the stone floor. This time the blade was momentarily stuck, allowing Blackavar enough time to get up.

A chain wrapped around the thief's throat, and he found himself thrashed back and forth in an attempt to break his neck. He was held securely in front of the other guard, who at last pulled the blade free and aimed for the thief's chest, only to meet Medallion's staff halfway down.

Metal sparked against jeweled wood. A bolt of electricity spiraled around the mage's hands and up the staff. Upon contact, the sword split in two and threw the guard far across the room. Meanwhile, Blackavar was still struggling with the guard clinging to his back. His head felt light as the chain cut into his throat.

An arrow struck the guard's neck. He dropped instantly, allowing Blackavar to pull the chain off and breathe in fresh air. He spotted Aldaris, then nodded his thanks.

"Come on!" Medallion supported him down the tunnel where Keith waited alongside Aldaris.

A rumble shook the walls, and a large crack appeared. Guards paused in confusion, but began fleeing when steaming water from the underground spring began spewing out.

"Time to go!" Aldaris helped Blackavar to the tunnel. "Hurry up, Medallion!"

The Master Mage nodded and raised his staff to close the entrance to the tunnel.

Keith paused when he heard a faint gasp and turned around. Medallion's eyes seemed closed in concentration. Yet when no wall came down, the boy knew something was wrong.

"Medallion?" he called. Ahead of him, the others paused.

The Master Mage made no response. Instead, his head slowly bowed as he slumped his knees.

"Medallion!" Keith began racing toward him.

"Keith!" Blackavar shouted as a loud crack echoed down the tunnel. A section of wall had collapsed, pummeling guards with steaming water.

Keith reached Medallion and tried to pull him up, then saw why he could not. Faintly, he was aware of guards screaming. A golden aura surrounded the entrance. Medallion had placed it there to protect them, and it had cost him with an arrow in his backside.

"Go..." the mage whispered. "The barrier," he coughed, "won't last long."

"Medallion!" Aldaris came running with Blackavar right behind.

"Look out!" Keith shouted as the first wave of water hit the shield. It glowed brightly, keeping the foaming liquid at bay. Yet the light was fading fast, as it was in Medallion's pain-filled eyes. Another wave crashed against it. The light flickered.

"Go!" Medallion choked. "If I can't close it, you'll be boiled alive!" He struggled to rise. Aldaris and Blackavar helped him to where he could lean against the wall. When they attempted to pull out the arrow, Medallion stopped them.

"Don't do this," Blackavar said. "Don't do this to us."

Medallion smiled faintly, his gaze finally falling to Keith. Their eyes met, and the remaining illusion disguising the boy's hair faded back to its original color.

"I'm glad to have met you, Keith," he whispered, leaning heavily on his staff. Reaching up, he removed the gold pendant from around his neck and held it out to him. "Remember me."

Keith held the necklace tight and watched the mage struggle outside the tunnel where the water had risen well over the fading aura. Several bodies of guards washed against it, illuminating their bloated faces. With little strength left, he balanced himself and raised his staff to finish what he started.

At the same time the sliding wall came down, the barrier broke.

Time froze.

Keith was lost in a maze of sounds and images. Though he ran with the rest to higher ground, the image played over and over in his mind. His fingers clamped the necklace tighter, imprinting the inscription from its cool surface into his palm. He could see the guild's Master Mage standing outside the tunnel, knowing that he was dying. With the tunnel safely closed off, he opened his arms to embrace the warmth of death.

CHAPTER 10

"What do you sense, Eumaeus?" Chronicles sat back with eyes closed, his fingers on either side of his temple. Wolf-like ears twitched at every sound, soft with a light covering of fuzz that darkened at the ear's tips. It was their trait, the symbol that marked the *Lo-ans'rel* kind.

"A stirring," Eumaeus replied. "Nature's energy pulls sharp."

Chronicles let his hands slide down his face and fold together across his breast.

Eumaeus, whose dark salt and pepper hair displayed the ripe old age of centuries past, stood close to his clan leader. Once a brilliant sapphire, Eumaeus' eyes had dulled over time.

The leader relaxed in a chair created from vines. With a gesture the vines grew thicker and curved their stalks around the bottom of the seat to form a more stable base.

"Much better." Chronicles opened silver eyes to glance at his creation. "I'm rather pleased we came here. Not a human for miles."

Eumaeus nodded.

"Humans, no. Yet there's this...*presence*. You can feel it shifting through the earth every so often."

"Humans." Chronicles frowned and leaned back in his seat. "They think they have the means to control Nature." He shook his head. "They are no guardian over anything but greed."

"Greed offered an opportunity, though. With no humans around, it's much safer for our children. Your son will thrive in his training, and make an exceptional leader one day."

A thin smile crossed the leader's lips.

"I plan more than just presenting him as *leader*, Eumaeus. He's nearly seven winters, but already he's capable of things *humans* could not dream of."

Eumaeus nodded. "It's been ages since we've seen an albino. He will be very powerful. He'll do things *we* cannot do."

"Which is why he must be trained now."

As he rose, Chronicles tapped the vine. Without hesitation, it unraveled and sank into the ground. In two strides he had crossed the room of their underground home and slipped out into the candle-lit hall.

Eumaeus stretched, enjoying the pleasant caress of shape-shifting. A faint glow surrounded his body, and when it had faded only the form of a ferret remained. The small animal scurried down a burrow off to the room's side, rethinking the clan leader's words as he went. He let his thoughts explore past the confines of those words, finding new meaning. In the mind's eye he saw woodlands pass, realms and clans until it focused on the entire land in unison...*the world of No'va.*

Yes, he sensed Chronicles' mind link with his. *You understand now why Shy is needed. His abilities must be perfected for the day we reclaim our homeland, and purge the land of humans...forever!*

*****

Silent was the whisper in his dreams, dry and hollow like the sound of one whose presence had long since passed from the living to the dead. Its soul was present, and in the gloom of the night it called out to its servant.

Jenario...

Drapery around the bed frame ruffled from a breeze through the opened balcony doors. Wax dribbled down the side of a well-worn candle upon the nightstand, its light extinguished as another breeze turned its raw flame into withering smoke.

Jenario...

Something tingled in his dreams, and he whimpered softly.

Smoke collected in the air. As Jenario turned to one side, the stone slid from under his nightgown, attracting the wispy puffs. Shadows from the drapes passed over him, and when it had settled a moonbeam glazed over the stone's surface. The crimson crystal glowed in the light, and the smoke that hovered just overhead assembled into the shape of a skull before dissipating.

Jenario...

He bolted into a sitting position. Beads of sweat lined his forehead. After a few moments, he pulled the covers back and slid his bare feet to the floor. He watched the bed curtains waver in the breeze. Unconsciously, he fumbled with the stone around his neck, shivering in the cool night air.

A gentle breeze beckoned, material wavering around his slender form. Entranced, Jenario watched as a swirl of smoke from the extinguished candle rose in the air, riding the air currents out onto the balcony. At first he thought it illusion, but he swore he saw it curl into a skeletal hand and summon with one bony finger.

Is this a dream?

A dying whisper on the wind called, caressed his soul from deep within, and he responded. Gradually, he made his way out onto the balcony. The air was much colder here, and he folded his arms tight against his chest for warmth. He tried to ignore the cold floor against his bare feet.

Jenario...

He snapped to attention. The moon shining down upon the crystal caused it to flare blood red.

"*Jenario...*"

"That voice." Jenario shuttered. Had his own lips formed words? "Am I mad, or just dreaming?"

"*Easier if it had been,*" the mage's voice hissed. "*I have called many a night.*"

"Who are you?" Jenario's breath quickened as a gust of wind sent his nightgown dancing behind him.

"*I am as you are. I am always carried with you.*"

Jenario reached for his necklace and gingerly lifted the crimson stone between his fingers.

"*Yes, my friend. I am here, waiting – waiting at your command.*"

Jenario clasped his hand around it, feeling how warm it suddenly became. He closed his eyes, allowing the sensations from it to burn into the palm of his hand. He winced as pain traveled up his arm and into his chest. Then it was gone, relaxed into his being, his soul, and when he opened his eyes a fire burned within. Lips parted to speak, but the voice was not his own.

"*You wish to study and know things. Allow me to show you how to further study them.*"

Jenario hesitated, but the stone reassured him.

"*You will have no regrets by the end of tonight.*"

The mage relinquished control to the horn, then clenched the stone tighter. A smile only came to his lips as he leapt to the balcony wall. His voice raised to the dying wind as a howl of joy escaped into the night before jumping. His nightgown blew around him, catching hold to branches outlined in silver. As his clothing ripped down one side, his body began to change. His face elongated. Limbs stretched. Fingers and toes grew together as one and hardened, forming cloven hoofs. His hair and beard lengthened to a mane, and a tail sprouted from the end of his spinal cord. Skin darkened and gleamed as tiny hair follicles grew from his flesh. At last the ears stretched upward, and Jenario found he could turn them to better catch distant sounds.

He landed with his front legs extended and his back legs following. Muscles tensed and rippled throughout his body. A horn protruded from his forehead, which he could barely make out by crossing his eyes. When he opened his mouth, long fangs scraped his lips, and he tasted blood on his tongue…*his blood.*

"Now allow me to demonstrate the full power of what you are."

Jenario tossed his powerful neck to one side, dipping the horn, and caught a glimpse of his muscular chest and strong legs. His tail rose behind as he reared and let out a shrill cry. The call of darkness beckoned, and he bolted into the black forest, faster with each stride. His soul felt free as his sable coat blended in with the night, and he was lost to the power of the horn.

CHAPTER 11

Water swirled around Keith as he raced toward the main chamber. He got to the opening in time to see Medallion, a large wave behind him. In an outstretched hand the Master Mage held the gold pendent always worn around his neck.

"Remember me," he whispered. The necklace slipped from his fingers, turning slowly in the air until it tinged against the stone floor. Then he turned and opened his arms to welcome the oncoming wave...

Keith woke in a cold sweat, panting heavily as he reached to pull the covers off, ready to follow the others through the tunnels. He stopped and looked down, and for the first time he realized he was in his room. Movement drew his attention to the side of the cot to find Toby watching him.

"Feeling better?" Toby got to his feet

Keith shook his head, trying to clear away the dream. A weight against his chest drew his attention to the gold pendent dangling from a chain around his neck. Holding it to the candlelight, he stared at its reflective surface.

"What happened? Where is everyone?" he finally asked, letting the necklace settle against his breast.

"You were sick," Toby replied, keeping his gaze lowered. "Blackavar brought you here until you got better."

"How long did I asleep?"

"You're on day two." Toby looked away, and Keith noticed several small scars running across his left cheek.

"That guard, the one who held you, did he do that?" Keith pointed to the scars.

Cautiously, Toby reached up to feel alongside his face. With a shake of his head he left the room, tears welling in his eyes.

"Toby?"

Keith could hear his voice outside the door. There was a shuffle of feet, then Blackavar poked his head inside.

"Ye're awake!" His smile was not the brightest, but it brought comfort to Keith knowing he had survived the flood.

"What's wrong with Toby?" Keith asked. "It looked like he was hurt."

Blackavar came to the bedside and sat next to the boy. His eyes trailed to the gold pendent.

"We were all angry, but none more than yeself."

"I did *that*?" Keith stared in disbelief. "But I didn't think it was his fault."

The thief chortled. "It wasn't. His father used him to rise in rank, then again to find the guild."

"And Medallion?"

There was a momentary pause as Blackavar wiped a tear from his eye.

"A sacrifice to keep the place safe, though we're still checking the tunnels to make sure no stragglers were left."

Keith sat for a moment in silence. "If some of the guards got out, could they come back in?"

"Not if they used the same entrance, but we've completely blocked it so no one can use it now."

"And the illusion needed to cover entrances," Keith inquired. "What about those now that…Medallion is no longer here?"

"Still in good shape," Blackavar replied. "We've a few illusionists around to help keep 'em up."

A fellow thief poked his head inside the room, and Keith's eyes lit up.

"Daumier!" The boy was across the room in moments. "I thought they had you!"

The thief chuckled and rubbed his eye where the skin had swelled from a guard's punch. "Well, that's the good thing about being underground. A little dirt on yer face and people think you're dead."

"How's the arm?" Blackavar motioned to his friend's bandaged elbow.

"Not as bad as I thought it'd be. Few days' rest and I'll be ready for the next steal."

While the two talked, Keith stepped outside the room to look for Toby.

"Where'd Toby go?" he asked the two thieves.

"Down that way, I believe." Daumier nodded toward a tunnel leading away from the main chamber.

"Alone?" Keith asked.

"Should be safe." The thief scratched under his chin using his good hand, but Blackavar shook his head.

"Best be certain. Find him and tell him to stay close to the main tunnels."

Keith agreed before wandering off, calling his friend's name as he went.

He's probably afraid I'll hit him again.

A shadow moved to the side of the next tunnel, and Keith hurried over to it.

"Toby, wait! I just want to apologize."

"Do ye now?" a gruff voice replied.

Keith froze, fear forming a lump in his throat as the shadowed figure stepped from the tunnel to block his path.

"I should hope ye would after what ye did to our captain, ye little traitor!"

Traitor? Keith wondered, but when he stared up into the guard's eyes he saw the look of delirium burning through red-streaked irises. Parts of his face looked swollen as though he had been burned. *Does he think I'm Toby?*

Backtracking, Keith stumbled over his feet and fell. He never took his eyes from the large figure filling the tunnel as he pushed away.

"That gold!" The guard paused. It was not until Keith glanced down at his shirt that he realized the medallion had caught his attention. "Magic-scum! Ye'll pay with yer life!"

In one swoop the guard grabbed him by the shirt and lifted him to his face. With his other hand he grabbed the medallion and ripped it from the boy's neck. There was a clink of pendant thrown to the ground.

"You gonna' scream now?" The guard breathed heavily, his foul breath causing Keith to gag. He tried to struggle, but the guard just tossed him over one shoulder and started down the tunnel.

Keith did scream. They were nearing the end of the tunnel when voices echoed from behind. In the midst of desperate cries and heavy breathing, one voice stood out. The guard started up a ladder to the next level.

It was Blackavar.

The guard had almost reached the top when the thief jumped onto the ladder. Others soon joined. He could hear Jasper and Aldaris ordering others to the top level.

Reaching the top, the guard pushed a heavy lid aside and would have gone through had Blackavar not caught the end of his boot.

"Filthy bastards!" the large man hollered. With one well-placed kick, Blackavar was thrown off. The thief tried to regain his footing and climb back up. A few others had already started, but by that time the guard was through and slammed the lid back over the opening. Still holding Keith in one arm, he dragged a barrel overtop to hold it shut.

Keith ceased his struggling. He stared longingly at the locked lid, hoping, waiting. He could hear them banging against it.

They're locked in. I'm...locked out.

*****

Frustrated, the Master Thief slid back down the ladder.

"I've already sent men up." Aldaris met him at the bottom. "We've still got a chance!"

"We need to head them off!" Blackavar commanded in fury as he rushed through the tunnel and up another ladder. By the time the others reached the alley, Blackavar was already at the street corner searching the multitude of faces for Keith.

"Do you see them?" Daumier joined him.

"Blackavar!" Jasper cantered toward the two on horseback, leading a saddled black. He threw the reins to the thief. "They've already left town!"

Blackavar swung onto the saddle and kicked his horse into a gallop, dodging people left and right down the heavily packed street. Behind, he could hear the pounding hooves of his fellow guild members following. Once outside town, the road divided. Without hesitation, Blackavar charged down the right fork, his fears confirmed by the dust still lingering in the air. It was not long before he spotted them in the distance.

An open cart bounced along behind a single bay-colored horse with the guard repeatedly cracking his whip. Keith lay crumpled in the back, unconscious by the way his body shifted with the swaying cart. At the cry of his name the guard turned, a scowl on his face. A hard yank on the reins turned the cart wildly to the right, and they started through a tangle of trees, following an uneven path.

Blackavar reined his horse alongside the cart. One foot swung over, careful not to tilt the saddle. Then he was in. Good timing, for a low branch caught his horse off guard and sent it stumbling to its knees by the side of the road.

"Keith?" He was at the boy's side in a moment, ducking to avoid another branch. The bay nickered while unseen vines and branches scratched and battered its legs and neck, but fear of the whip kept it going.

After securing the reins, the guard climbed into the back and slashed at the thief with his sword. Just as quick, Blackavar blocked with his daggers.

"Keith, wake up!" he kept trying, to no avail. The wagon rocked dangerously from side to side while a series of branches whipped by, quickly turning into a game of duck and slash every few yards. The guard had a more difficult time due to his size and heavy gear, but each blow was superior to the slender thief's. It was not long before Blackavar was out of breath.

A branch whapped the guard in the back of the head. He teetered to the side, allowing the thief another try at waking the boy. Then it was back to countering blows. A fist smashed into his jaw. Another to the stomach brought him to his knees.

"Keith!" he gasped just as the guard kicked a dagger from his grasp. He felt a hand wrap around his throat and hold him aloft.

"End of the road for you, scum!"

An arrow struck the guard in the arm, and he immediately let go. Blackavar glanced over the back of the wagon to see Aldaris notching another on horseback. Yet he was still too far behind. With the guard temporarily distracted, the thief turned to grab the boy.

The horse screeched and pulled a sharp left. All three were tossed against the cart's side.

Keith moaned as the impact jarred him awake, and he rubbed his burning cheek where the guard had struck him unconscious.

"Ye all right?" Blackavar started to help him up when a swift punch sent him careening over the cart's side and into the underbrush. For several feet he rolled in uncontrollable ways, arms and legs sprawled in all directions. When at last he came to a stop, the cart was too far ahead, even on horseback.

"Blackavar!" Aldaris reined his chestnut stallion to a halt and jumped from the saddle. Not far behind, Daumier and Jasper pulled to a stop and jumped down to rush to the thief's side.

"I'll live." Blackavar grit his teeth in pain as he tried to sit up.

"Careful." Daumier attempted to help, but the thief jerked his arm back.

Jasper felt around the bone, then shook his head.

"It's not broken," he concluded. "Just badly bruised."

"What about Keith?" Aldaris asked grimly.

Blackavar hung his head. "Damn guard still has him!"

"Could use another flood," Jasper said between clenched teeth and helped Blackavar onto one of the horses. "We were so close."

"Not close enough," Blackavar mumbled. "Even so, this marks the borders of Lexington." There was a lingering silence. "Even if we had taken Keith back, we'd still have to avoid the night troops dispatched from the slave compound."

Jasper caught his breath, and Daumier dared to whisper the name of the place they were all too familiar with.

"Castle Mire...."

CHAPTER 12

Sounds of barking drew Keith from his huddled position in the cart. Too weak to fight the guard himself, he simply sat where he was told, and remained still until the ride stopped. When he glanced at the sky, only gray clouds swirled overhead, threatening to storm. Somewhere he heard laughter, followed by a gruff voice.

"So you finally came back! Where are the others?" someone announced, and Keith shrank back into the cart as footsteps approached.

"What is this? A kid, or a white rat?"

"Le'me see."

A masked face peered down at the boy. The longer Keith stared, the more he realized it was not a mask but fine patterned feathers growing from the skin. The markings even continued into the pale hair.

"Ain't no others coming!" The guard spat next to the cart. "He's a filthy magic-user! I say skin him!"

"Hold on a second." A dark-haired man pointed at Keith. "Ye're telling me a kid...eliminated...single-handedly...fifty of our men?"

More laughter.

"Yeah, tell it to Shafari!" someone shouted. "Tell him ya got a sure money-maker!"

Keith was yanked from the cart and tossed to the ground. Bewildered, the boy jerked his head around at all the guards surrounding him. Most of them frowned at the sight of him while others grinned and poked fun at his helplessness.

"That's enough!" The one with face markings stepped through the crowd. "Shafari told you *no children!* What good is he? A doorstop?"

A few chuckled.

"Yer one to talk, harpy!" the guard grumbled. "Shafari had to buy ya when ya didn't sell. Look at him. Look at his appearance. He's a magic-user, I tell ya!"

"Even if he was, do you know what they're worth nowadays? Nothing! Too much trouble."

The big man glared at the smaller figure. One fist swing could have taken off his head, which barely attained chest level.

"If you still had wings, I'd rip 'em off!" the guard exclaimed.

"Someone get the headmaster!"

Others chimed in. "He'll settle this!"

Keith remained close to the creature known as 'harpy.' Though he had no idea what a harpy was, it had saved him from the taunts and rough handling. Now he waited for this headmaster, hoping it would be someone who understood the true place of a frightened boy.

"Silence!" a powerful voice rang out. "What's this I hear about an albino?"

"Magic-user," the guard muttered.

Keith peered up at the headmaster. A crimson robe trimmed in gold reminded him of Medallion, but with a set of keys at his side in place of pouches. Light brown hair curled over a gold headband holding it in place. A small beard curled under his chin. Now and then the headmaster tugged on it as his patience thinned.

"You realize that albinos have red eyes, do you not?" Shafari lowered his voice. His olive green gaze flicked around the area. "And where are the others? Why have they not returned?"

"*He* killed them!" the guard protested. "The captain is dead! Now I demand payback! I demand either *his* death or—"

The guard never finished, for at that moment Keith saw the headmaster's hand weave a pattern at his side. The guard clutched at his chest, then his throat.

"Or *yours*?" the headmaster finished for him as an eruption of blood burst from the guard's mouth, spilling down the front of his chest. He flung his arms wildly and collapsed in a puddle of blood, swimming through it until his movements ended in a violent convulsion.

Keith stared, nearly forgetting to breathe. The sight of it churned his stomach. Vision blurred. He could feel hands shaking his shoulders, but he could not tear his gaze away. The last thing he remembered before darkness took him was the headmaster stepping toward him, a hand outstretched the same way just before the guard had died.

Keith jerked awake, his breath heaving in his chest. A dull ringing echoed with dog howls and loud voices, one of which came from someone standing over him.

"Ain't it always a pleasure when they drag another in?" The young man stepped back as Keith sat up on the cot and drew the ragged covers aside. He rubbed the sleep from his eyes.

He groaned. "What happened? I feel like someone hit me with some of that pink sand."

"Ye're one of the lucky ones. Shafari probably charmed ye, thinking ye'd bring in some money one day."

Keith peered up at the figure, his eyesight still a bit blurry.

"Blackavar?" he asked before noticing the dark bars around him.

"Ye know him too? Ain't that something!" The young man smoothed his charcoal hair from his face and grinned. He had the same build as the thief, but much younger in years. "Did ye hear that, Lavern? I bet he's seen the guild too! Ain't no one known Blackavar and not seen the guild."

Keith followed the young man's gaze up to the top bunk where an older boy sat cross-legged on the edge.

He nodded to Keith. "Kind of hard to miss, aren't ya? What are ya, some type of albino? No wonder Blackavar found him!"

The young man nudged the newcomer. "Look at him! So confused, and we ain't properly introduced." He took a bow. "I'm Lancheshire. That's Lavern. And yeself?"

"Um...Keith."

"Well, Um-Keith," the young man's smile never wavered, "welcome to Castle Mire, the largest slave compound in all of *No'va!*" He spread his arms toward the other cells behind their own, each full of slaves both young and old. Each cell comprised of two to four individuals contained within a square. There were no tops to these cells, allowing one to gaze all the way to the grand columned ceiling.

"Ugly, ain't it?" Lavern grinned. "Heard it used to be nice once, before Shafari took over."

"Shafari..." Keith remembered the dying guard. "He's a magic-user."

"More like *curse*-user." Lancheshire chuckled. "Magic's a rare jewel for him. Ain't nothing but death spells when it comes to his abilities. That's why he's the greatest slave trader around."

Keith stepped to the bars. It was an immense chamber. Cells lined side by side as far as he could see. The floors were made of straw mixed with oil-stained dirt. Across the room two large vats towered in the corner. Steam rose from a bubbling substance he could hear even from far away. He nervously swallowed, but Lancheshire reassured him.

"Don't worry. Ye're with us," he said. "We'll take good care of ye, least 'til ye can fend on yer own."

"My own?"

In answer, Lancheshire pulled up his sleeve and pointed to the scars across his left arm.

"See those? Those are the marks of freedom to come."

Up top, Lavern laughed.

"Yeah! Shafari will boil ya first, *then* think about it." He pointed to the vats. "Those who misbehave get a nice little bath, so be sure to mind yer manners!"

"I'm serious!" Lancheshire winked at Keith. He pulled his sleeve back down. "Don't get too comfortable here. They'll soon make use of ye."

Lavern dangled his legs over the cot's side.

"Ha! At his size, that ought'a be a trick!"

Lancheshire patted Keith's back.

"Stick with us. Ye'll be fine."

"I guess I'll be fine, as long as I have my…" Keith felt for the necklace. He groped, for nothing was there. In panic, he started searching the ground when he realized the pouch containing his pan flute was also missing.

"My things are gone!" he exclaimed.

"Headmaster's probably got 'em," Lancheshire replied without concern. "Don't worry yeself. Wait about five years. Then ask for 'em."

Keith was still in a state of panic when Lavern stood on the top bunker to peer over the cells.

"Hell they ain't!" he exclaimed.

Quick as a jackrabbit, Lancheshire climbed to the top bunker.

"What ye seeing?" He squinted and looked across the compound. After a moment, he reached down to help Keith up beside him.

"What's going on?" he asked, temporarily putting the flute and necklace aside. His pupils enlarged to better take in the direction they were looking.

"Harpy, by that corner cell," Lavern said.

"Harpy?" Keith whispered. "You mean that feathery-faced guy? What exactly is a harpy, anyway?"

"Ain't ye know nothin'?" Lancheshire inquired. "Harpy-wizard? Don't tell me ye ain't never seen one!"

Keith shook his head.

"Course not—if they come from *here*." Lavern cracked a half-hearted chuckle.

Keith peered out over the cells to see two guards wrestling with what looked like a giant bird. Such wonder! The wings alone might have stretched twice the size of a grown man had they been allowed to fully open. Yet, slowly the strength was beaten from it until it took all the creature's might just to stand under the weight of chains tightening around its body.

A cry erupted from its lips, one Keith had to cover his ears from as the sound reverberated throughout the chamber. No human could have created it, for it was a combination of both bird and beast, and only ended when a gag was roughly stuffed into its mouth. Keith welcomed the steady howl of hounds instead, at last uncovering his ears when it was quiet.

Even when his cell mates lost interest, the young boy continued to watch. For the longest time he pressed his face against the bars, his eyes following the procession of guards half dragging the harpy between aisles. As they passed by his cell, the creature's frightened gaze fell to Keith, and paused. In that moment, a rush of images flooded the young boy's mind. It caught him off guard so that he nearly toppled from the bunk. It was gone before he had a chance to focus, and only left a sick feeling rising in the pit of his stomach. He had felt the harpy's pain when taken in flight and realized a wing was broken, though the creature hid it well as it continued to struggle.

For the first time, Keith understood how he had been able to hear his mother's thoughts. She had linked her mind with his, so often that he never thought twice about it.

Now I know...

The group rounded a corner to a private room, though their shadows still lingered against the far wall. A jumble of forms surrounded the winged one. There came a snap of shackles as it was bound between two poles. When its wings spread to either side, Keith thought for sure he had managed to free them. Yet from its sagging shadow, that hope soon dimmed.

Shadows merged, and the harpy was temporarily engulfed. Then screams, worse than the shrill animal cry, echoed within the compound. He saw a shadow step back, and when he did one of the wings dropped to the ground.

Keith jerked away from the bars, gagging.

"Awful, ain't it?" Lancheshire barely whispered.

Keith crawled under the covers. The next scream was worse.

"Best get used to it." Lancheshire stretched out on the bottom bunk. "They usually bring in one a day. It's the whole point of Castle Mire – *to make us slaves!*"

CHAPTER 13

It was not long before Keith grew accustomed to the day's events. New slaves, such as himself, were allowed to leave their cells during certain times to complete various tasks. Yet because of Keith's size he usually accompanied his two cell mates, which gave plenty of time to know them better.

Lancheshire was not the healthiest of slaves. Constant beatings from guards brought down any person's spirit. Yet Lancheshire was one of few who flourished as if it was an endeavor to make himself stronger. Scars marked his arms and back, which he proudly showed as though it symbolized triumph over each master. His soft brown eyes were warm and friendly. At such a young age those eyes had seen many days of hardship, and Keith learned quickly that if there were any questions he had, he knew he could count on Lancheshire to provide the answers.

Unlike his companion, Lavern did not take well to beatings. He was short and stocky, often drawing taunts from some of the guards. Yet if Lavern had an oddity to show, it was his eyes. The left one was a deep brown, so dark that at night the pupil was completely lost. His right eye, however, was blue. The two found it humorous to glance at each other now and then, each one just as curious of the other's appearance.

"Do you think they'll sell me to a master?" Keith asked Lancheshire one afternoon.

"Eventually," he replied. "Shafari probably thought ye'd sell 'cause of yer good looks."

Keith grinned. "How come slaves come back? If you're sold, how do *you* come back?"

"It's all a game, Keith," Lancheshire said. "Ye play along 'til ye win, then the headmaster pairs ye up with another."

Keith thought about his friend's words all day while he worked. Come evening, he trudged along the rows back to his cell. It had been a long day lifting and polishing armor. His whole body ached, but slowly he was growing accustomed to the long hours of labor.

Nearby a whip cracked, followed by the cry of a slave. Rounding a bend, he saw a guard lifting his whip over a dark-haired young man.

"*Lancheshire...*" Keith breathed as the whip came down, splitting the air as its tip cracked again.

"You'll do as you're told, slave!" The guard kicked him in the stomach.

"Stop!" Keith grabbed the man's arm before the whip fell. "You're killing him!"

"Gutter filth!" The guard flung the boy aside.

Now Keith was furious. He could feel his blood boiling with hatred. He raised a hand. His eyes narrowed, and a strange glow engulfed them.

"Stop..." The guard's hand froze in mid-air, and a look of bewilderment came over his face. "Hurting..." The guard's arm began to tremble. "My..." The body jerked from side to side. "Friend..." Keith hissed the last words as the guard rose into the air. Then Keith rapidly moved his hand aside and watched the large man skid halfway down the aisle.

Those close enough to witness the action instantly froze. A few fled the scene while rumors quickly spread that a magic-user was loose.

From across the compound a bell rang, an emergency signal that called not only guards, but the headmaster. Slaves scattered as a mass of armed men tromped down the aisles. They surrounded Keith, who held his friend protectively in his arms. Rage still burned deep, and when several guards came close Keith threw them with a single glance.

"What's the trouble here?" Keith heard the headmaster's voice.

"We've a magic-user!" a guard blurted. "Get rid of him!"

Surrounding guards moved aside to let Shafari through, his hands already weaving a curse. When he reached the center, he paused. Before him sat the smallest of slaves cradling his cell companion. Blood-soaked straw lay strewn about, and he turned an accusing eye to the surrounding men.

"Who's responsible for this?" His gaze swept over the many faces, searching for guilt. "How many times must I repeat myself? *Don't* beat them! How do you expect me to sell a half-dead slave? *No one* would buy! Leventés!"

Keith recognized the feathery face of the harpy he had met upon arrival. Without a word, the servant stopped at his master's side. His eyes locked with Keith's.

"He's hardly big enough to pass for a magic-user," he said. "Think he'll let you touch him?" A smile crept over his face.

Shafari raised an eyebrow.

"I'll deal with that. You take the other up. I want him cleaned up and well within the next week!"

Keith's anger had thinned since the headmaster's arrival. He no longer felt the power coursing through him, and he knew he was no match against a curse. Yet the thought of the guards taking control frightened him, so he kept a serious face. Pretending was his only defense now.

Shafari raised a hand.

Keith cringed, expecting his heart to burst any moment. Instead, sleep overwhelmed him, and the next thing he knew he was waking in bed. The first thing he noticed was the small cot Lancheshire lay on a short distance from his on, and he tossed the covers aside and hurried over. He looked better. At least his breath was not rasping anymore, and his wounds had been dressed.

"He'll be fine." The voice of Shafari startled the boy, and he turned to find the headmaster smoking a long pipe as he sat with one leg crossed over the other. He tapped the pipe over a glass dish alongside stacks of yellowed papers on his desk. A drawer left open revealed a fresh supply of tobacco for his pipe. Yet something else caught his eye.

"My bag!" Keith exclaimed. "You stole it from me!"

"Stole?" Shafari pulled the item out to peer inside the leather flap. He eyed the charm tucked next to the reed instrument with interest. "If anything, you probably stole them yourself."

"But I..."

Shafari silenced him with a look and slipped the pouch back in his drawer, "Be thankful my guards didn't get *their* hands on it. In here, it's safe. And after a period of five years, *if* you survive slavery at Castle Mire, you may have it back."

"Five years?" Keith's shoulders drooped. "I have to be here five years?" He glanced over his shoulder at Lancheshire. "How long has he been here?"

Shafari shrugged. "Three, I believe. Could be longer. But the minimum is five. Gets thieves off the streets for a while. And I," he stroked a pouch of money on his belt, "get to enjoy the spoils."

"But I'm not a thief!" Keith crossed his arms in a huff. "And I didn't steal those. They belonged to my parents."

"Then your parents were thieves. Why else were you caught in a place where thieves gather?" Shafari puffed a ring of smoke from the tip of his pipe. "Hiding from the world because of your appearance, I take it."

He chuckled, puffing a larger ring this time. Moving a finger, he caused it to change to a silhouette of Keith running from the guards. "Or perhaps you knew people wouldn't take to a strange magic-user in their midst, hmmm?"

Keith lowered his eyebrows in confusion.

"Magic-user?" He shook his head. "I can't do magic."

Shafari paused, raising an eyebrow.

"On the contrary, my friend. Those guards you threw will have bruises for quite some time, and will not likely forget you. How, then, do you explain that?"

"That..." Keith froze, his mother's words invading his thoughts so strong he feared Shafari could hear. "Could that be what she meant?"

Shafari was silent a moment, puffing away on his pipe.

"*She* being?" he finally prompted.

The boy licked his dry lips. "My mother." He paused, but Shafari remained still. "Before...before she died, she told me that I would one day discover what I was...and where I came from. I didn't understand at first. I was hoping...maybe in the guild...."

Shafari suddenly broke into laughter.

"That you were a thief? Come now! Surely she meant the magic." He puffed a large ring. "Try using it. Change its shape, as I did."

"But..."

"Concentrate! Your mother obviously knew the secret, and now it's coming out. Besides, why would I throw my own guards? Not that they didn't deserve to be thrown after what they did. What triggered it? Was it love? Was it anger?"

Anger... Keith remembered his anger. It had raged through him like a violent storm. He thought back to the time Medallion had asked him to steal from another magic-user. When he was caught, Keith thought the Master Mage had intervened by tossing the person as Keith had just done. *He knew! Medallion wasn't telling Blackavar how I had failed. He was telling him how I had used magic!*

Keith watched another smoke ring drift overhead. He closed his eyes and concentrated, trying to make it change the way Shafari had. Yet when he looked, the smoke had already dissipated.

"Try again," Shafari coaxed.

Keith relaxed. Anger had already been spent on Lancheshire, but what about his family? Rage built inside at the thought of his uncle. How could he have done such a thing, to his brother, to his own nephew?

Shafari watched the smoke ring begin to shake. The more Keith thought about his uncle, the more angry he became until it was not only the smoke ring shaking, but the room.

"Enough!" Shafari slapped a hand across Keith's face, breaking his concentration.

"Ack!" Keith rubbed his sore cheek. "What was that for?"

"You must learn to control that power of yours, or you'll likely kill anyone nearby. Now try again, but this time concentrate on *one area*!"

The headmaster restocked his pipe and soon had a large smoke ring drifting over Keith's head. The boy was angry from the slap, and after reddening his face thinking of it, managed to stop it from dissipating and hold it in place.

"Good," Shafari cooed. "Keep that concentration. The more you practice, the easier it will come. Now move it backwards. No, not like—"

The ring came bouncing back into his pipe, billowing smoke and ash into Shafari's mouth. Coughing and spitting, the headmaster reached for a drink on his desk to wash the taste down.

"That's enough!" he gasped, holding a hand up to stop the leather pouch from floating to the boy.

"You've no right to keep them!" Keith's magic tugged again, but Shafari was stronger, and he brushed them back into the drawer and locked it.

"Trust me." Shafari gulped down his drink. "It'll still be here *ten* years from now, if you manage to last my own temper." With a wave of his hand, he forced the boy to sit cross-legged on the floor. "Now hear me out, and *maybe* you'll learn to survive this game."

At the mention of 'the game', Keith stared quizzically from headmaster to his friend.

There was a twinkle in Shafari's eye as he continued. "Ah yes, I know what he's told you, and it's true. Learn from your friends, and when it comes time for *you* to play," he grinned, "you will be ready."

*****

Dark drapes wavered as a breeze from the rising storm swept under the balcony doors. A crack of thunder shook the room. It was always storming, in Corrigan's opinion, and yet it did not bother him. Conveniently nestled in one of the towers, it slightly reminded him of home. Although he missed the swaying of the trees, the tower itself was high enough to be one. As he settled in for the evening, he could not help but think about his family.

A shadow passed on the outside of the curtain. Or perhaps the wavering fabric had merely caused the illusion of such. Nevertheless, and not wanting to be caught off guard, the Black Wing whipped the curtains back with the swipe of his taloned fingers and peered through the darkness. A streak of lightning lit the interior, but in its momentary illumination he saw nothing.

"My imagination," he muttered, and turned over to readjust himself in this new type of bedding.

"The mind can also be deceptive," a voice breathed on the back of his neck.

Corrigan turned. Where the curtains once hung, a figure loomed. Another flash lit the room, casting deep shadows along the bony structure of the figure's face - nothing more than a skull with a glowing red-stoned necklace dangling between outstretched fingers. The stone vibrated with power. Corrigan could feel it pulsating with the beat of his own heart. A skeletal hand reached for him.

"Now you are mine!"

Corrigan woke in a fury of flying feathers and bolted upright in bed, his chest heaving. Without thinking, he threw back the curtains surrounding either side to glance around the room. A clap of thunder startled him, and a flash of lightning momentarily cast the furnishings in white light. Amber eyes scanned every nook and cranny. No spider web went unnoticed. No corner left unchecked. He inspected every shadow until, relieved, he lay back to allow his heart time to settle once again.

"Was it really a dream?" a familiar voice whispered.

Corrigan twisted to his left to see a dark-robed figure leaning against a maple wardrobe.

"Jenario!" Corrigan jumped from bed so quickly his wings got tangled in the curtains. "If I were you, I'd be out that door!"

"Quite the storm we're having tonight." Jenario smiled, watching the Black Wing slow his movements in order to release his wings.

Corrigan grit his teeth. One wing was free.

"I hope you can run faster than I fly!" he hissed.

"Oh, come now." Jenario's smile never faded, and only increased when Corrigan became so infuriated with the curtains that he swiped his nails through them. Wings spread wide in an elegant display of battle stance. "'Twas only illusion, same as what you can do with your wings."

Corrigan tossed the ripped curtains at Jenario's feet.

"What are you babbling about, *human?* What illusion? Our kind have never held any power whatsoever!"

"Illusion is not power. *Strength* is power. In that respect, your wings are very powerful. Yet they can fade when you close them, giving you the freedom to climb through the treetops without disturbing your nicely preened feathers."

Corrigan resisted the urge to gut him.

"I can't believe you woke me for this!" He turned away in disgust.

"Because I don't think you realize what illusion can do for you, my friend."

"Exactly as you said." Corrigan puffed up his feathers in irritation. "For climbing trees."

"Ah, but what if you could hide completely, not just fade your wings?" Jenario's eyes lit with another flash. "Think about it. Magic's just another form of illusion, nothing more. Master it, and you may just find out *what you came here for.*"

"And what of *that* thing?" Corrigan pointed to the crimson necklace. "I don't suppose unicorns thrive on illusion, do they?"

Jenario chuckled as he made his way to the door. With a single gesture the torn curtains repaired themselves, leaving no trace of the harpy's struggle.

"You'd be surprised."

CHAPTER 14

"Do that again!" Lavern's eyes danced with excitement. No matter how small the magic, Keith always left his companion wanting more. "Lanc would love this!"

As Keith made his bed with a thought, he answered, "I'm sure Shafari will probably tell him. He's keeping him until those cuts heal." His smile faded when he noticed some of the other slaves watching. Since the day he had protected Lancheshire, none would dare speak to him. Somehow, he could sense their fear, just like the time he had sensed the harpy's thoughts. "I don't think they like me here."

"Shafari's never kept a magic-user before," Lavern said, then thought better of it. "Then again, I don't think he's ever dealt with one."

With a sigh, Keith turned away from the bars. It was hard to ignore the feelings coming from different slaves. Now that he had magic, how was he to control it? Thus far, anger seemed the only way to make the magic happen. Even amusing Lavern took some form of stirring emotion, and eventually he stopped to rest.

"I never realized how much it saps your strength," Keith said.

Lavern climbed down from the bunk and sat on the lower one next to his friend.

"But how ya plannin' to do the bigger stuff if ya always get tired?"

Keith shook his head.

"I don't know. The headmaster helped me, at least, to this point. But there's so much I still don't understand."

A howl echoed across the compound. It was soon accompanied by others.

Keith and Lavern turned toward the southern entrance where a large pen housed a group of black hounds. Over the few months Keith had been at Castle Mire, he had grown accustomed to the different barks and cries, for they served as a warning to the slaves. Lately, the hounds had been silent and either whined for food or to be let out. Now, however, they growled and scuffled, snapped and pulled on their chains, causing such a ruckus that even the guards were irritated. Keith noticed other slaves looking too. A few shrunk back in their cells. One started to cry.

"What's happening?" he asked at Lavern's changing expression.

"Ain't we just had one?" The boy brushed a hand over his face.

"One what?"

"What we all dread most – *slave auction*."

Slave auction. The words hissed from Lavern's lips like a snake. It was hard to fathom how two little words could bring so much fear. Yet fear was all around, more so of the auction than of a magic-user. As they watched and waited, the southern gates to the compound slowly creaked open. They were huge doors compared to the others leading into the main castle, with enough room to haul in six horse-driven caravans at the same time. The wagons pulled to a halt beside several rows, one of which was Keith's. It was not long before the headmaster appeared, his expression as serious as the guards who followed at his command.

Keith nervously swallowed at the spiked whips carried by each guard, and he wondered why Shafari allowed them when he opposed slave beatings.

"Don't worry," Lavern reassured him. "Ya ain't big enough to go no ways. They'd laugh ya off the auction block."

Keith managed a small smile. From the corner of his eye he saw Shafari making his rounds, pointing to cages he wanted slaves taken from. When he pointed to Keith's cell, the guards hesitated.

Shafari rolled his eyes and pushed through them.

"Must I do everything myself?" he muttered, unlocking the cell door.

Lavern bravely walked out, and a guard snapped a metal collar around his neck. He glanced back at the cage to see Shafari tugging on his beard in thought.

"He ain't big enough!" Lavern's blurt received a slap to the head.

"Shut it!" A guard shoved the boy toward the waiting caravans.

Shafari raised an eyebrow toward the motion but said nothing.

Keith could feel the headmaster's concern. His pale features were an oddity, but was it enough to peak bidders' interest, even if they knew he was a magic-user?

Shafari turned to the waiting men.

"Take him." His deep voice rang with authority. "But be mindful of his temper."

*****

"You're even crazier than a drunk!" Aldaris teased as his friend put the finishing touches on his master disguise.

Dressed in a forest green robe, Blackavar posed in front of an oval mirror. Black velvet adorned from shoulder to waist. A gold-trimmed sash matched a cloak fastened with a broach. Around his neck he had placed the gold medallion found lying in a tunnel. He wore it always, for not only did it remind him of his deceased friend, but of Keith.

Aldaris had chosen a less fancy garment, a dark red-brown with black trim and cape.

"Sufficient enough to travel with ease," Aldaris scratched his arms, "but this material is itching me to death! Why can't we just hide in the alley until they announce the auction?"

"Because then we wouldn't have a chance to bid if Keith is present," Blackavar replied. "It's our only chance to free him. No telling' what he ain't been through already!" He shuddered from memories of the slave compound. In his heart, he feared the worst. Keith had been small, too small at the time the guard took him. Normally, the auction only produced strong, healthy looking slaves – never children.

The two made their way to the alley where a few others had already gathered. They laughed at the rich clothing, especially Aldaris' inching problem.

"You try wearing this!" Aldaris kept scratching.

"Right." Blackavar rolled his eyes, then raised a hand to silence everyone. "So here's the plan. Aldaris and I will go to the auction. The rest of ye wait here. Should someone recognize us…ye know what to do." He winked.

"I hope they make this quick," Aldaris whispered. "This stuff's killing me."

"I'll kill ye if ye don't get yer fancy pants out there!"

With a sigh, the thief followed, scratching his arms as he went.

"Been easier if Medallion was still around…"

*****

Keith was relieved when the caravans finally rolled into Lexington, and he gulped in several large breaths as soon as the guards pulled him out. The wagons were packed, with only a small barred opening at the back to let in air. The stench of urine wafted on the breeze before something warm oozed around his bare feet. In disgust, Keith wiped them on a patch of fallen straw. He glanced at Lavern and grimaced.

"*Welcome to auction,*" the older boy mouthed before being shoved toward a wooden platform.

Already, a multitude of people had gathered at the front. In the center of the platform hung a large tapestry, which hid all the bustling of rounding slaves into cages at the back. Now and then it would gently waver, allowing a glimpse of growing crowd.

Each slave was placed in a separate cage. Being the smallest, Keith had plenty of room, unlike others. A few had not survived the journey, and Keith turned away as the bodies were piled into an empty wagon and carted beyond public sight.

"Slavery ain't for the faint of heart," Lavern whispered in the cage next to Keith's. "Be lucky ya even made it this far."

When all of them were accounted for, an announcer called the first slave to the front.

A girl with short strawberry hair was escorted behind the tapestry. Keith listened to the announcer start the bidding, naming the girl's attributes in between when no one offered.

Keith glanced at Lavern when he heard the boy chuckle.

"They've grown soft!" he whispered. "Ya wait. These masters come from all around, but it ain't just buying they came for. They like a show! If they ain't gotten one by the fifth slave, the guards will make sure they will."

Lavern's words held true, for as soon as the fifth slave was off the stage the guards cracked their whips around a hefty male. Keith held his breath at his bulging muscles, and he feared the chains holding him would break.

As soon as the crowd saw him, they went wild. Bids soared into the hundreds while the slave fought in wild fist swings.

Lavern shook his head.

"They make everything seem more than it really is. I know this guy. Ain't bothered no one."

A crack of splintering bone echoed from the front.

Until now. Keith grit his teeth amidst loud shouts and announcing bids.

The noise dulled for a while until a lanky looking slave was hauled to the front. Keith had seen him many times at the compound. With an awkward limp and thin, dark complexion, it instantly drew several taunts.

Keith dipped his head, trying to peer beneath the tapestry. He gasped when something splattered against the platform. An onion rolled to the back and stopped at Keith's cage.

They're throwing food? He glanced quizzically at his friend.

Lavern shrugged. "Could be worse. I've seen torches thrown...lit!"

Keith leaned against the bars. By now, the sun was high enough to shine full force. Yet even under cover the heat was sweltering. What little water was offered did not quench Keith's thirst for long. Soon, the urge to drink returned.

"What're ya doing?" Lavern demanded when a bucket of water inched toward the cages. "Pause it!" he whispered harshly. "Someone's coming!"

Too late, a guard saw Keith's outstretched hand and tromped toward him.

"Ya want water, magic-scum?" He stopped next to the pail. "Ya'll have to *earn* it!" His leather boot sent it flying across the platform, clanking over the edge and spilling water everywhere. "Better save up for the real show, cause it's coming, and this ain't a crowd ya want disappointed."

Keith narrowed his eyes as the guard walked away.

"Save yer strength," Lavern interrupted his thoughts. "He ain't kiddin' ya."

The announcer made a comment, then Lavern was next.

"Remember, it's just a—" Lavern was yanked from the cage before he could finish.

"Just a game," Keith finished softly, watching him disappear behind the tapestry. He waited, pressing his face against the bars. To his relief, only the usual bid took place, and Lavern was passed on to a new master. For him, the game had been played many times. For Keith, it was only just beginning.

A whip cracked against the top of the cage, its spiked tip sparking across the metal.

"Ye're up, scum!"

Keith gulped as his door was unlocked, allowing him to crawl out.

Save my strength? Those things could pull the skin right off my back! There's no way I'd be able to stop it!

"Don't be trying nothin', hear? Ain't the only one holding this." He shoved the spiked tip beneath Keith's throat. "Now move!"

Both slaves and guards kept a steady eye on the boy. Even having the dreaded *cat-o' nine tails* did nothing to ease the doubt of having a magic-user loose.

The tapestry was pulled back, and a man to the side of the platform announced the slave's name. It was just as crowded as the days when Blackavar had taken him to steal in the market. All types of people were present, some he was sure to have seen on various occasions. Yet that was back then, back when his appearance had been disguised. Now, as he mounted a flat box in the center of the platform, he was paler than ever. Fear, instead of anger, had drained all color from his face. The crowd did not look pleased.

"What is this?" someone demanded. "Some kind of joke? I'm not paying for some kid!"

"Look at him!" Another pointed. "He's whiter than my mother's hair!"

Laughter rose all around.

"Maybe he could dance for her as well! Doesn't look like he can do much else."

"Hey, slave! Dance!"

A potato knocked Keith flat on his back. He gasped in surprise and felt around the sore skin. A red welt began to swell on his forehead.

"That put some color on him!"

More laughter.

"Get up, scum!" A guard yanked the boy to his feet. "Now's ya chance to show 'em yer great power. Looks ain't much. Maybe some enticement ought'a help."

Keith glanced over his shoulder at the rest of the guards. Impatiently, some tapped their whips, waiting for more action. If nothing else, they could make it happen.

*I have to get angry. I have to get angry. I have to...*Keith chanted over and over, trying desperately to think of something, anything, to rouse his temper. To make matters worse, the announcer then told everyone that he used magic.

"If that's a magic-user, then I'm a six-foot little girl who shaves whiskers all day! Tell me another!"

Laughter roared through Keith's ears. Not a single bid had been offered. Behind, he could sense the guards enjoying the show. Yet taunts never lasted for long. Soon they would be bored, and there were still more slaves to sell before the end of the day.

"Better hurry, scum!" The guard sneered. "Unsold slaves don't go back. Where's ya magic? Thought ya had a little temper ya wanted everyone to see?"

Another potato slammed into his knee, and Keith buckled over in pain. He raised a hand to stop the pelting vegetables. Anger coursed through him, and for a moment he was overjoyed. The magic had come!

The next instant, Keith found himself staggering back, holding a hand to his shoulder. When he pulled his fingers away, a rock fell to the floorboards, trailing blood with it.

A cheer rose from the crowd. A second rock narrowly missed his head, but a third caught his upper arm. The crowd went wild.

A tiny voice amidst all the possible hundreds gathered caught Keith's sensitive ears. Eventually, it was accompanied by a second. The voices moved through the crowd, calling the boy's name. Far away, yet familiar, they alone kept Keith's mind from fading.

Blackavar?

"Time's up, worm!" The guard raised his whip to finish Keith off. "No one wants yer kind no ways!"

The whip came down but never hit its target. With a single gesture, the guard was tossed into the crowd like a rag doll. People scattered in confusion. How had a mere child managed to pick up a full-grown man?

Keith stared at his hands in disbelief. The magic was there, but anger had not triggered it.

"Keith!"

The boy searched the sea of faces, finding Blackavar waving a pouch of money in the air.

"I place first bid!" he shouted over the commotion.

"We have a bidder! Are there any more?" asked the announcer.

Guards rushed to the front. One guard paused a few feet away, slowing the others with an outstretched arm. A strange smile spread across his face.

Go ahead, it taunted. *Try that trick on me.*

Keith raised a hand...and froze.

The guard merely chuckled.

"You may have power over some of us, but not all. Master Shafari will see to it he gets his money. Now turn around and start selling, or they'll be sampling you in pieces!" The whip cracked to emphasize his words.

Shafari knew this would happen. That's why they're protected.

Another bid came from the back of the crowd, then another from the side. Soon, hands went up from all around.

"I like a challenge!"

"I'll break him in a second!"

"He's mine!"

"Hey, where's my money?"

Aldaris snickered as he hid a large purse under his jacket to keep Blackavar bidding. How long he could keep stealing, he did not know, for soon hundreds turned into thousands. Most people were still unaware of their missing valuables; however, the moment was short-lived as a stork-like gentleman pushed through the crowd.

"I call next bid," he said in a calm voice. "The rest of you might want to check your pockets."

Blackavar signaled to Aldaris, and the two began to back away from the crowd.

Keith gasped when Aldaris dropped a bundle of coins. The noise drew both crowd and guards' attention.

"Run for it!" Keith shouted. "Don't worry about me!" He longed to return to the guild, the one place he had come to call home after being taken from his family. Yet that dream was fading quickly, for a guard grabbed him by the shirt collar and lifted him to his eye level.

"What're ya playing, runt! Thinking of striking it rich? I'll strike ya with this, ya little—"

"That's enough." The tall gentleman strode across the stage. "I've already paid my money. No one else wants him. He's a thief and a magic-user. More importantly, he's *off* your hands!"

Keith followed the bony man off stage to an awaiting carriage.

"Hold out your wrists." A pair of silver wristbands were snapped in place. "These will keep you from using your magic, so don't think you'll get your way when we leave. You're mine now. Soon, you'll be trained like the rest of my slaves, *silent*, and obey without question. Now, in you go. We'll get you cleaned up when we reach the clan."

Keith climbed into a side compartment, not cramped like the caravan. It soon started down the cobblestone street. A barred window allowed him to watch the auction go by. Somewhere, he thought he saw

Lavern with his new master. With a sigh, Keith sat back and watched the town go by. Out on the open road, he perked up when several figures stepped from the alley.

Blackavar... Keith held his hand out through the bars to signal with his fingers.

The thief responded, a last message before he returned with the others to the shadows of the alley.

Be safe, it had said.

The sun was just setting when Lexington faded in the distance. The game had started, and Keith was ready to play.

Part Two

Glory

CHAPTER 1

Keith huddled in a corner at the rear of the carriage. Drifting in and out of sleep, he was faintly aware of the first rays of dawn slowly approaching. It had taken them the entire night to reach the clan of Silver Trails located on the southeastern borders of Sapphire. As the carriage pulled off the main road, fields of grass condensed to forest.

Several times, Keith had attempted to use his magic along the journey, to no avail. Not a single spark coursed through him as long as he wore the bands. Instead, hunger took its place, and he was thankful when the carriage stopped and the rear door finally opened.

Keith crawled out and peered up at his master. His neck seemed too long, with a head too large to fit atop those bony shoulders. Keith could almost picture a walking skeleton with wisps of stringy bleached hair stained with potato mash.

"You will address me as Master Reuphas," he said. "From now on, everything you've ever known will be forgotten. This is your home now, magic-user or no."

Reuphas gestured for the boy to follow him down a well-worn path cut between the most unusual trees. As a breeze rustled their limbs, the leaves shimmered silver in the sunlight reflecting off their waxy surfaces.

"Silver Maples." Reuphas followed the boy's curious gaze. "Lends its name to this place."

At the end of the path, overhanging leaves opened to reveal his master's home. Though not massive like Castle Mire, it instead offered a more stylish appeal. Several balconies protruded from the upper floors, curving around the side in a semi-circle. Vines of ivy stretched to the tops of these, flecking the dull gray stonework with its sap green leaves.

Keith followed his master to the back of the castle where a variety of underbrush created a thick wall of foliage. A small gate opened into a courtyard where several servants busied themselves in a corner garden. They never acknowledged the two arrivals until Reuphas whistled.

Immediately, the servants dropped what they held and turned toward their master. In perfect unison, they lined up along the garden path to await instructions.

Keith stared at the expressionless servants. Not a wink, stance, or appearance seemed out of place. *They stand like statues, like they're not even real.* When he reached out to touch one, Reuphas slapped his hand away.

"You'll learn your place," he said. He puckered his lips again. A low whistle this time brought a single servant from the line. "I want you to take this slave up to his room and get him some new clothes. No slave of mine goes around wearing market muck. And clean those cuts while you're at it. People don't realize slaves make an impression upon a home, and scarring them makes them less desirable to look at."

The servant bowed and began walking toward the castle's back entrance.

"Well, don't just stand there. Get a move on!" Reuphas commanded.

The boy hurried after the servant. Inside, he observed the behavior of others. Their movements were stiff. Joints hardly seemed to bend, and speech was no better. When asked a simple question, the answer was spoken in a flat tone. When they arrived upstairs, the servant opened the door to a bedroom and stiffly set about fixing something for the boy to wear.

Keith glanced around, impressed with the crimson and gold furnishings. Long drapery from the canopied bed grazed over a ginger slab floor, matching the tapestries that hung on the walls. A dark maple desk and chair next to the bed had been carefully arranged with pens and paper for letter writing purposes. Yet the best feature was a crescent-shaped balcony. With no door, the room continued out into the open. Sunrays slanting over the floor created a cheerful glow, and a constant breeze kept the room freshly scented with the smell of pine from the nearby woods.

"Your clothes are on the bed," the servant concluded.

Keith turned from the balcony view. Up close, the servant's face was a mask.

"There are fresh linens in the wardrobe. You must change the sheets yourself and wash the dirty. Washing's at sunrise." The servant then set a dish of water upon the bed with scraps of cloth next to it. "Let me see your shoulder."

"Thanks." Keith held still until the servant had finished cleaning the place where a rock had hit. It was barely a scratch now. Even the redness had gone down on his forehead, according to the reflection in the dish. After addressing several other places, Keith watched the servant move to the doorway, that same stiff walk never altering pace. It was a relief when he was finally alone.

Right away, Keith began tinkering with the locks on his wristbands. Silver designs seemed to overlap the keyholes, making it difficult to pick. Lancheshire had taught him several methods to picking a lock, but he had never seen one where the design intricately hid the keyhole. After several tries, he found a place where the design lifted up using his fingernail.

Now all I need is a lockpick.

Keith searched the room, looking for something small enough to use. Unsuccessful, he decided it best to change and get some rest. The bed looked warm and inviting, and sleep invaded his eyes as soon as he lay down.

He was uncertain how long he slept, but the sound of bedroom door opening awakened him. He cracked an eye to watch a servant place a tray of food upon the desk. Never once did she acknowledge his presence, but went straight to the pile of old clothing. As she bent to retrieve them, a ting of hairpin on the floor caught Keith's attention. The servant, in her usual trance, never noticed a lock of hair fall to one side of her face. With the clothing under one arm, she soon left, and Keith slid from bed to locate the pin.

I know it's here. His sharp eyes caught a glint of thin metal by the door, and he quickly pocketed the find. By now, the smell of warm food soon turned his attention to his rumbling stomach. The bands would have to wait.

Like a wolf, he gulped down large bites of fruit and vegetables without chewing and slurped up his water. The generous portion of meat was left untouched.

"Meat is for the weak-minded," his mother had told him.

"You always knew best." Keith bowed his head in remembrance. "I do for you."

A knock interrupted his thoughts, and when the door opened, Reuphas entered. The master's eyes flicked to the boy's plate.

"Not your liking?" He frowned. "I don't cater for comfort, you know. You'd have to be a master for that."

Keith shrugged. "Maybe someday I will."

Unhurried, Reuphas stepped closer. A smile crept over his face.

"You think you'll ever be worth anything?" He chortled. "Once a slave, there's no going back, not even if you escape. Anyone would be able to look at your wrist guards to know, and they won't come off, not even magically. You see, lad," he held up a finger, "those bands were crafted from a material that keeps its wearer from using magic, such as throwing food like you did so very nicely."

He patted the boy's shoulder in sarcastic amusement.

"I enjoyed your little performance. Unfortunately, until you're completely under my control you won't be using any for the time being."

Like being cursed! Keith grit his teeth in irritation.

Reuphas scooped the plate up to take with him.

"No meat," he said on his way out the door. "I'll keep that in mind."

*****

"So move." Lancheshire crossed his arms and stared at the checkered playing board. He was still recovering from his wounds and had to be careful when moving. Because of this, Shafari allowed the slave access to his private lounge. There, the slave could recover by playing against the headmaster, though at the moment the only movement was the flicker of Shafari's eyes deciding between pieces. Lancheshire sighed. "Don't ye have a slave compound to run, sooner or later?"

"Don't rush me," the headmaster said. "I must decide."

"Ye've been deciding all day! Just pick one! Ye're gonna' lose anyway."

Rubbing his beard in thought, Shafari delicately lifted a pawn and hovered it two squares ahead of his king, then placed it back. He moved the knight at his left, counting out the spaces that were available—placed it back.

"Honestly, Shafari!" Lancheshire laughed. "We've only just begun, and ye're worried over yer first move, which, might I add, ye've yet to make."

"Just a moment! I have it, but I have to think first."

"How much thought does it take to make a move?" The slave rolled his eyes.

"I've let you win a few times, that's all."

"More or less all week." The slave snickered.

"Then let's change it up a bit," Shafari continued. "How 'bout we play *my* way." He closed his eyes. "I was never really good at singles, but I was always known for my doubles." When he opened his eyes, a fire lit their core.

"So does this mean I'm gettin' more of a challenge this time?" Lancheshire teased.

Shafari glared at him from across the table.

"As a matter of fact, you are."

Weaving a hand through the air he conjured another checkered board to replace the current one. Instead of two sets of pieces on one board, there were three sets on two adjoining boards. Wood was replaced with cobalt blue and white marble.

The slave lifted a pawn to examine.

"Nice. Though this ain't exactly familiar lookin'. How's it work?"

"The rules are simple. The board, as you can see, is relatively larger to accommodate twenty-four pieces instead of sixteen. One row of pawns is replaced with two. The third row is the same. The king, however, can move two blocks instead of one, and can destroy his own men - but only on the second move. Pawns still attack diagonally, but can move backwards once during a match to do so. Lastly, knights can move double the number of squares as long as it's backwards from the first move."

"Uh huh." Lancheshire was unimpressed. "And this will increase yer chances of winning how?"

"By the fact that I've never lost this type of game," Shafari said with confidence.

"Ye mean ye've never lost a game after ye've changed the rules," Lancheshire corrected.

"Enough! Just pick one and move!"

"With pleasure, but no cheatin'." The slave selected a pawn and moved it forward two spaces.

"Course not." Shafari smiled innocently. Beside his seat, two fingers secretly crossed.

*****

Keith continually picked the lock on his bands while staring at his supper; only vegetables this time. Reuphas had been kind enough to bring him a second helping after his first meal. Yet something told him not to eat, hungry though he was.

In frustration, he threw the hairpin across the room.

None of the other servants wear bands like these. What if....

A breeze from the balcony gave him an idea, and he grabbed the plate and hurried over. Keith could not stop smiling as he brushed the food off and watched it fall into the bushes below. Returning inside, he set the plate back on the desk, and had just seated himself when the bedroom door opened.

Keith kept his eyes on his plate, listening to his master's footsteps stop a few feet behind.

"And now, slave," Reuphas began, "you will obey my every order. Serve me with your magic!"

A low whistle signaled Keith to turn around. The boy mimicked the slow, rigid movements like the other servants, making sure to keep his face void of any emotion. He nearly lost concentration when Reuphas took hold of each wrist to remove the bands.

"To the banquet hall! There is someone I want you to meet."

In silence, Keith followed behind his master, the game getting more interesting by the minute.

Check.

*****

"Con!" Lancheshire argued. "Ye ain't specified pawns could jump over em'selves!"

Shafari stared at the slave in innocent shock.

"I'm sorry. Did I forget to mention that?" He replaced the pawn. "It was your move anyway."

"Cheater." Lancheshire gripped a knight and slapped it down on the board, causing some of the other pieces to tumble over.

"Easy now," the headmaster soothed. He reached over to pick up a fallen bishop. "Methinks someone's a little angry because he's, shall we say, *losing*?"

Lancheshire cast him a threatening glance.

"Maybe ye would like to know how it feels to get a beatin'!" The slave raised a clenched fist.

Shafari chuckled. "Careful. You'd only end up getting yourself in a mess." He lifted a finger, and a chess piece floated into his grasp. "Or had you forgotten what I am."

Lancheshire took a deep breath, keeping his eyes on the headmaster at all times.

"So move! But no more cheatin'."

*****

It was a standstill between master and slave, although Lancheshire slightly held the advantage at the moment. It was the same between Keith and Reuphas. The two stood, like the pieces in the game, then slowly moved down the middle of the board. Shafari's ebony bishop had tried taking one of the slave's pawns by surprise, just as Reuphas had Keith. Bishop and pawn, two magic-users, passed in between enchanted pawns of slaves. Keith looked at each of them, their faces blank and lifeless like the chess pieces. To win was to be a pawn himself and move accordingly to his master's game plan, and he smiled while following orders. Now the rules had changed, like the rules on the board between Shafari and Lancheshire. To win, he had only to pretend.

CHAPTER 2

"Check."

Shafari could hardly believe he had let a mere slave slip by his ever-watchful eye. Perhaps he had dozed somewhere in between making his next move and watching the rest of the game unfold. After all, they had been playing nonstop all day. Now, as evening settled over Castle Mire and long shadows cast themselves far into the sunset, the two paused to reflect back throughout the day's play and refresh their parched tongues with drinks.

"This time I *know* you cheated," Shafari accused with a sigh. "There's no possible way you could've gotten past me. All directions were blocked."

"Ye're the one who made up the rules in the first place," Lancheshire dangled a pawn in front of his face. "Remember that pawns can jump, or did ye forget that rule?"

"I never specified they could jump over *other* men, only themselves."

"Humph! Should've specified that before the game started." His hand reached for a fresh glass of wine and raised it to his lips. He inhaled deeply as the intoxicating smell rose to his nostrils. Then, in one sip, he took in all its richness. He exhaled in a long sigh as the burning sensation of liquor tingled down his throat. "Now I know the taste of wealth."

"Only the finest allowed." Shafari watched him a moment before sipping his own. He closed his eyes and relaxed in his chair to enjoy the same sensations.

"Gettin' late," the slave commented.

Without opening his eyes, Shafari replied, "Are you implying we quit the game, or are you just speculating the meaning of defeat?"

"Well, for one I'm still waitin' for ye to start playin'," Lancheshire teased. "We've sat here all day, and I ain't seen nothin' yet. Ye've changed the rules so ye could cheat, and ye still ain't won. Not even come close to winnin'. So what now, oh defeated one; change rules again perhaps?" The slave reached for another glass.

"Perhaps." Shafari's gaze fell upon Lancheshire's confident grin. "Unless I spice it up with magic."

Lancheshire slapped his hand on the tabletop and raised his voice in a chortle.

"What would ye do, old man? Curse those whom entered yer side of the board?"

"Shall we find out?" Shafari winked and slid a knight toward Lancheshire's pawn.

"Are ye implying we continue?"

"Indeed."

As each made countering moves, the slave noticed Shafari's men begin to glow, especially those whom were considered higher in status when his pieces came close.

"Can you defeat something you cannot see?" The headmaster tugged on his beard.

"Magic can't hide everything." Lancheshire grinned while he slipped several chess pieces behind his back.

*****

"So what do you think?"

Reuphas instructed Keith to stand before the stranger, a tall, dark-cloaked figure with an impressive looking stone worn around his neck. More impressive still was the harpy that had accompanied him. Unlike those seen at Castle Mire, this one still had its wings intact. Long, sable feathers folded neatly, and had only opened once to display its magnificence upon introduction.

"His appearance alone is enough for a sell. Albinos are rare finds."

"He's a magic-user, isn't he?" The stranger chuckled. "Appearances or not, you'll have to do much better than that, which is why I've come today. The boy's from Castle Mire, isn't he?"

"What slave isn't, Master Onyx? Besides, I don't trust outside dealers. They don't keep contracts, which makes it harder to track escaped slaves." Reuphas followed the man's gaze to Keith. "However, I don't think I follow. Are you implying that I should have? Come now! A magic-user such as yourself cannot be afraid of a mere boy. He may have magic, but I assure you, he's completely under my control."

"Is he now?" Master and harpy exchanged looks. "Then, I suppose if I told him to do something, he wouldn't because only you can tell him. Correct?"

"Precisely."

Keith stared at the one called 'Onyx.' *What a name*, he thought. *It certainly fits his appearance. The harpy too.*

"Young man."

Keith snapped to attention.

"I want you to reach into your master's pocket and pull out the vial he uses to poison his slave's food. Hand it here to me."

Keith lowered his eyebrows. "You're not going to poison your harpy, are you?"

The next instant Reuphas yelped and sprang away from the boy.

"You're playing games with me, Jenario!" he accused. "He can't speak! I didn't tell him to speak!"

The mage laughed.

"Only fools believe they can control those with magic. You've a smart one on your hands, and if I were you I'd give him to someone who knows better. No? Well then, I'll make this brief." He gestured to the harpy. "You've met Corrigan before. He needs to ask your little slave a favor while *we* catch up on old times. What say you? A glass of brandy perhaps? You'll probably need it by the end of the night."

At first, Reuphas was too dumbfounded to speak. Even when Jenario assured him the two would be fine and went off into another room, Keith could still sense his master's anxiety.

"I can already tell you'll be of no help." The harpy's sarcastic tone caught the boy off guard. A wing stretched open, each feather spreading until it had achieved full height, then slowly pulled back into a fade.

Keith stared in awe.

"And no," Corrigan rolled his eyes, "my kind does *not* have..." His words trailed off when a flicker of candlelight hit the boy's eyes. He stared at their wild illumination, much like an animal's when light touched it at the right angle. While Corrigan's mind was lost for explanation, the last word whispered from his dark lips, a whole different meaning in itself. "...*Magic.*"

"What are you doing?" The touch of a clawed hand to his ear sent Keith back a few steps. "Your master said you needed a favor, but for your sake I hope it's not flesh you're after."

Amber eyes narrowed, black pupils no more than slits in the dim lighting.

"I'm no *slave*, unlike you." Corrigan ruffled his wings into view. "And quit staring at me like that! Do I crave flesh? Yes! Do I eat humans? No! You're no better than the White Wings. Always questioning my looks and behavior. And it's not a *favor* I came to ask."

Corrigan took a breath. His feathers had fluffed themselves in agitation. Now, as he paused to relax, the sable wings drooped slightly to graze the floor. After a moment, he continued.

"If it's any concern, I'm actually looking for another of my kind. But I was hoping for someone a bit older."

"I'm sorry I couldn't help," Keith replied in a soft tone. "No one like you has ever come to Castle Mire - at least while I was there. But slaves don't always stay with one master. Eventually, some of them even return."

Corrigan perked an eyebrow. "Doubt it. We Black Wings are famous for our strength and size." He lifted his wings in a proud arc above his head. "Unfortunately, I happen to fall between two different *'Ken*.*"

The Black Wing's gaze shifted over the boy's appearance. When their eyes locked, Keith once again felt the wave of emotions enter his thoughts. He understood Corrigan's sarcastic nature, knew the reason behind his hatred for humans, and toward his parents for creating a child capable of more than he had been offered in life. Now, he had no one—like Keith.

"I know who you're looking for," Keith finally said. "I lost mine too. That's why I'm here, trying to find answers as well."

They could hear the two masters returning. Reuphas seemed to have calmed down enough to enjoy his drink while Jenario motioned to Corrigan that it was time to depart.

Keith waited until the harpy had left before reaching down to pick up a black plume, which had fallen from one of the wings. He recalled several slaves whom had fastened necklaces for themselves using their own feathers. Though Keith was no harpy, the unusual coloring was certainly intriguing. He pocketed the find in hopes to do the same.

CHAPTER 3

It was not long before Keith was back at auction. This continued for several months, some masters even passing the boy between friends to see how they fared. Yet none could tame the magic-user's fiery temper, nor control the outcome of his power.

Friends came easy to Keith in times of need. Some he had known through Castle Mire. Others, he made in a continuous cycle of game pieces. Each master represented a piece. He had played many pawns, even knights. Yet the greatest challenge, and final piece, was yet to come. That was the king.

Four years, he thought while tolerating another auction. He barely flinched when someone tried to throw food anymore. Learning to master his anger came easy now, and much of the times people knew what to expect when they crossed his temper. *Just four more years. That's the minimum.*

Keith's new master, Nunnelly, had a thick skull with little mind to fill the gaps. Day and night, he sat like a shriveled prune and drank until the smell of liquor actually stained, discoloring everything with a bitter perfume. His hair matched the dirty brown bottles, with his fat fingers having to hold the bottoms because they were too short to wrap around the sides.

Nunnelly had little concern for a magic-user living under his roof, especially with the new wrist bands he provided. Five keys were needed to turn the locks all at the same time, and since Nunnelly vaguely recalled anything he last handled other than liquor, Keith was stuck without magic.

Nunnelly had very few servants. Those who actually came to his summons wore toe bands, which Keith despised. A thin strip of metal ran under his foot and tightened under the ankle when he walked. Running was impossible, for the faster he walked, the tighter the strip became.

"Fffeather!" Cranky, Nunnelly sat up in his chair, trying to locate Keith over his mountain of a stomach.

The boy responded to the nickname of "feather" given from the harpy's plume fastened around his neck.

"Fetsssch me sssome drrinssk!"

With a heavy sigh, Keith turned and trudged down the hallway to a flight of stairs. After descending to the wine cellar, he grabbed a lantern hanging from the wall. A large, wooden door remained closed at all times. Over the years, the wood had cracked, filling with mold and fungi around the frame. One side of the door had come loose from its hinges, so it dragged over the floor when Keith heaved it open. Inside, the room was cold. Cobwebs hung across the bottles as Keith reached up to select one.

His ears perked at the slightest movement, and he jerked his hand back. Sticklike, hairy legs jutted out at his withdrawing hand, and a plump body of a Widow crawled from hiding. In the light of the lantern he could clearly see two fangs dripping with venom.

A mouse scampered across a row of bottles directly below, and the Widow pounced so quickly the rodent barely had time to squeal.

That could've been my hand! Keith swallowed, watching the spider slowly back into its hiding place. He made sure it was well out of reach before allowing his hand near the rows again. After grabbing the bottle and blowing the dust off, he slipped back outside and replaced the lantern.

Keith was three steps from the top when the board collapsed under his weight. Flailing his arms, he fought to keep himself from toppling backward. The glass bottle slammed against the steps. Pieces shattered everywhere with the putrid smell of liquor drugging his thoughts.

Keith could not recall how he reached the top, or if he even responded to his master's calls. All he knew was waking in his cot and wondering where the next auction would land him.

*****

Jenario flipped through the many pages of his notes. Since Corrigan had arrived, he had filled two books of information, and now sat working on a third.

I'll soon rival Lord Gracie's collection. He glanced over at bookshelves lined with his work. *It's so much easier to get information when the subject is within my grasp.*

"You could put that subject to use for you and get many more." Jenario felt his lips move, but the voice that spoke was not his own; it was the horn. *"Do you recall the time you met the albino?"*

"How could I forget?" Jenario's voice returned to normal. "He would have made a good study - for a magic-user."

"Did something not stand out when you looked at him? I'm surprised you didn't notice when you studied the last Lo-ans'rel."

Jenario stiffened. "What?"

"The eyes, mage. That's something not even illusion could hide."

"But surely his kind would not have allowed it."

"Unless he's never been with his kind and doesn't know what he is," the horn hissed. "Recall the time your assassin was summoned to a location involving two men, a woman, and a child. Three were killed while the child escaped. This is that child."

"Are you certain?" Jenario rose to examine the book entitled *Lo-ans'rel* resting on a shelf. "But it doesn't make sense to study a creature that doesn't know what it's supposed to be. I wouldn't get any results."

"It's only a matter of time. You don't go through life and not discover what you truly are." Here, the horn paused as though allowing its words to sink into the mage's mind. "Now here's a way to put that Black Wing to good use. He trusts you. Just make it convincing that what he's doing does not go unrewarded."

*****

The wind summoned him, and he obeyed without question. Spreading sable wings he leapt from the balcony high above the treetops, soaring over and through clouds to reappear like a ghost on the other side. Folding his wings he dove down, feeling air whip by him. Just before the forest swallowed him, his wings spread into a glide.

The dark 'Keyarx arched into a sideways turn, the extra-long feathers flexing to turn him back to the castle. Barrel-rolling right-side-up he saw the balcony swiftly come into view. Talons glistened in the moonlight. Hair blew around his face as he came in for a landing. He was the sky at night, a shadow cast by the setting sun. He could come and go as he pleased, free to express his true feelings in flight. He belonged to no one but himself. He was free, and that was just the way he liked it.

Corrigan hovered over the balcony before landing on all fours. He let his wings stretch, feeling the exuberant sensation of tensing muscles as each extended to their limitations. Everything had a limit, he realized, and he was no exception. It would seem that everyone else around him got past those limits while he was forced to be no more than the usual breed, and even that was cheated from him. Disgusted, he did not see a shadow move next to the bed until the person spoke.

"Ah, the majesty of flight," came a soft voice, and Corrigan halted in mid step to find Jenario sitting on its edge. "Always the yearn to fly. Always the call of the wild."

"Why am I not surprised to find you here?" Corrigan replied with a smirk.

"Do you remember the last time we visited Silver Trails Clan?" Jenario began. A smile tinted his lips in the moonlight. "And the albino you received information from?"

Corrigan narrowed his eyes. "What about him?"

The alchemist clasped his hands together, long bell sleeves from his robe falling in velvety folds around the wrists.

"I was wondering – what with your overall appearance – if you'd do a tiny favor for me. Nothing fancy, of course, though it does involve a little investigation."

"Out with it, mage!" Corrigan tapped a claw on the bedpost. "Quit your jabbering and let's hear it!"

Jenario nodded. "Find the boy, and bring him to me."

There was a moment of silence before Corrigan spoke again.

"He's a magic-user."

"Correct."

"You don't just snatch magic-users and expect them to come quietly!"

Jenario strode to the balcony doors. Lifting a hand he let the rising moon's rays display over his palm.

"What if I offered you a taste of power? Enough to subdue the boy until he arrives."

Corrigan hesitated.

"Think of the possibilities," Jenario coaxed. "Unlimited access to a world where only the experienced of our kind may seek. With only a thought, you'd be able to read minds and obtain any information you wanted." He held up a finger. "Think about it. You'd be the only one of your kind with the ability to *use* magic instead of just being a part of it. It may even help you on your own little quest."

"You'd grant me that, just to find this boy?" Corrigan considered the offer.

With a wink, Jenario turned and strode to the hallway door. Already opened, he slipped through without another word and disappeared into darkness.

CHAPTER 4

Keith cherished the few moments of freedom once the ankle bracelet was removed, and as soon as he returned to auction the game picked up where it left off. However, the bands on his wrists stayed, making him a prime target for ridicule by both masters and Castle Mire guards. Without magic, he was no more special than the usual lot. Still, his fiery spirit proved far greater to control than expected. For this reason, he passed quickly to the next match.

Each master used different rules. Keith found it extremely complicated to move between game pieces, for always his path was blocked. The longer he played with one person the more game pieces he lost, and it was not just patience that went with it, but his health.

Keith played with the last bit of strength before two years had ended, and by then he had nearly enough to amount to anything, much less slavery. Word quickly traveled to Castle Mire, and the boy was bargained back.

It was the eve of his fourteenth winter when Keith arrived at the compound. Snow lay dense and pallid as the curls of his hair, though by now those curls were discolored from the grime of his labor. As Shafari laid him on a cot, he wondered if starvation had stunted the boy's growth, for he was still quite small. He noted the feather threaded around the boy's neck.

Chain imprints caught his attention on an ankle, and he brushed two fingers lightly over the area. As the headmaster examined for other marks, his eye was drawn to the rusted bands worn on the boy's wrists. Five interweaving locks wound the dull gray bracelet. Each design intertwined with the other as it curved in a never-ending weave.

Leventés entered the room with a dish of warm water and cloth.

"What is it?" the harpy asked. After setting the items next to the cot, he peered over the headmaster's shoulder. "Some type of band to mark him?"

"Indeed," Shafari commented. "But not ordinary." He went to his desk and rummage inside one of the lower drawers. "I've seen this kind before, and if I'm correct I should have just the thing to open it."

Leventés heard a faint ting of metal.

"Ah, here we are." The headmaster held up a small object. "The key to the locks are contained within a larger one, kind of like dividing puzzle pieces." He lifted one out using the tips of his nails. With nothing to hold the remaining pieces together, they separated into four segments, each resembling the shape of a key.

Shafari slipped each segment into one of the five locks. When turned together, a hidden latch revealed a sixth. After reassembling the key, he opened the final lock, and the band clattered to the floor. The process was repeated to release the second wrist.

Leventés bent to examine the opened bands.

"So what would you use something like this for, if not to mark him as a slave?"

"Oh, it's a mark alright," Shafari replied. He dipped the cloth into the water and wiped around the boy's face and hair. Some of grime flaked off enough to hint its original color. "It's something worn to prevent someone from using magic. The idea came from an old friend in Sapphire. Heard there was one made to fit harpies as well. It prevents the wings from opening so you don't have to cut them."

A glimpse of white feathers ruffled into view for a quick preen before fading.

"You'd best keep those out of sight, if I were you," Shafari said without looking. "Now, that's a bit better." He rinsed the cloth in the dish and slid it aside. "Let's see if we can get some food in him."

Keith faded in and out of consciousness. At times he was aware that another was beside him, but then his mind would blank and he would be lost in the unknown of his own thoughts - those that concerned masters, sometimes harpies, even visions of his family. It was not until the fit of unnatural sleep lifted that Keith began to stir.

The first thing he saw when his eyes opened was a blurred face. Gradually, the haze cleared enough to recognize the headmaster standing over him.

"Still alive, young one." Shafari smiled.

Keith rubbed his head. "Yeah," he breathed. "I suppose I still am. I don't even remember the name of the last master."

Shafari leaned close. "Does it really matter? You can't expect to keep up with every fool you come across." A chuckle. "Hungry? You must be. You're hardly here as it is."

Keith slightly raised his head. With one hand he touched his side, feeling protruding ribs. In disgust, he looked away while Shafari summoned Leventés to fetch a bowl of warm mash and water.

"And see if you can find some decent clothing. Not that baggy stuff!" Shafari commanded. "And bring some brandy." He glanced at Keith. "We are going to celebrate your return."

After receiving the items, Shafari pulled his chair close and spooned some of the mash to Keith. When water was offered, Keith gulped it down in one swallow, choking and sputtering in his haste. When he felt strong enough to sit up, Shafari helped him with the new clothing.

"Better now?" Shafari asked.

Keith shrugged. "I'm still here."

"True, but at least you're alive." The headmaster pointed to boy's wrists. "By the way, I removed those bands. Should make things a little easier, I think."

Keith glanced at his arms.

"I didn't even think about it," he admitted. "Everything seems like a blur. I feel drained just trying to think."

"Drained, eh? Well, maybe this will help." Shafari stepped to his desk and unlocked a drawer to pull out an object that Keith had not seen in three years, yet remembered as though he had carried them every day of his life.

"My necklace and pan flute!" he joyfully cried, and slipped a hand inside the bag to pull them out as the headmaster sat back to enjoy a brandy.

Raising the reed flute to his lips, Keith blew gently to test the instrument. He managed to pipe a short melody before exhausting his breath.

"Easy now," Shafari cautioned when the boy's body began to sway. "Don't be blowing out air when you don't have enough to breathe." He smiled. "I've kept them just as promised. Good thing too. I think some color just came to your face."

"Two more years," Keith said quietly as he stared at his mother's necklace. Not wanting to let go of the past, he hesitated before handing them back.

"I'll bet you're wanting to see your friend again, aren't you?" Shafari locked the trinkets in his drawer.

"Lancheshire? Lavern?"

With a nod, Shafari gestured for him to follow.

The compound was crowded as usual. Guards shoved slaves back and forth from their cells. Hounds wailed. Vats boiled near the side walls. It was all there, waiting for Keith's return as he hobbled behind the headmaster. New faces peered at him from behind bars. Fresh slaves meant new money.

"Well, well. Look what the hounds dragged back in," a familiar, sarcastic voice said from a cubicle, and Keith peered around the headmaster to find the widest grin on his cellmate's face.

"Lancheshire..." Keith grinned. He waited until Shafari had unlocked the door for the boy to enter before exclaiming, "The game's not over yet!"

Lancheshire studied the headmaster.

"See ye've been bustin' yer rear over him like ye did me."

Shafari chuckled.

"You weren't as worse off. Keith here was at death's door. If I hadn't taken him back, that door would have welcomed him in."

Lancheshire nodded. "Ye were lucky then."

"It's good to see you're okay," Keith said. He noticed the empty bunk. "Where's Lavern? Did he not come back?" He glanced at Shafari.

"Still playing, I suppose." Lancheshire shrugged. "Sometimes masters don't bargain back, or else..."

"Well." Shafari coughed. "As much as I love reunions, I must be getting back. There's a lot of preparation to do for next auction."

"Oh, sure!" Lancheshire smirked. "Ain't sticking 'round to watch us fatten for roastin', eh?" He chuckled, watching Shafari lock the cage door and hurry down an aisle. "How the rich can run is beyond me."

Keith laughed. "At least he got you back on your feet. Have you been sold to anyone else?"

"Ye kiddin' me?" Lancheshire seated himself on the edge of the bottom bunk. "Me an' Shafari been goin' at it in a game of our own."

"A real game?"

The slave nodded. "Chess."

"Did you win?"

"Win? Ain't no winning against a magic-user, not unless ye know magic yeself." He winked.

"You cheated." Keith grinned.

"Ain't no other way. Besides, it's Shafari who's cheatin'." Lancheshire's cheeks swelled with pride. "But I got 'im good. Ain't call me a thief for nothin'!" He pulled a pawn from his pocket and held it up.

Keith shook his head. "I suppose he thought it was right since he's headmaster."

"Pish posh!" Lancheshire tossed the chess piece on the bed.

"What?" The boy cocked his head.

Lancheshire shrugged. "Pish posh, nonsense. Don't like something? Call it pish posh." Lancheshire sang the words in a dance around Keith until he fell back in bed. "Ain't no point to a word unless ye make one, the same in which ye make yer point. And if there ain't a word to make yer point with then there ain't no point in making a remark involving it."

Keith laughed, and joined his cell mate on the bottom bunk. As night slowly approached, guards tromped back and forth lighting candles around the compound.

"From what I've heard, ye almost didn't make it," Lancheshire said softly.

Keith trailed a bare toe in the dirt as he stared at the ground.

"I honestly didn't think I'd see you again."

"Ye know, I thought the same 'about ye. My only concern now is for Lavern to return to us. 'Bout time for another slave auction."

Keith nodded in the direction of the headmaster. "So he mentioned." He grinned. "Bet you'll be glad to see the last of them. 'Bout how many years have you been here? I'd have thought you'd been long gone by now."

Lancheshire counted his fingers before holding them up for Keith to see.

"It's over five years, I'm sure. But that's only because some masters keep slaves longer. Ain't counting against minimum requirements."

"Shafari *does* free slaves, doesn't he?" Keith asked hopefully. "That's what he promised."

"Shafari ain't the type for bargainin' when it comes to money. What he assumes often times turns somewhere else. He may do it. He may not."

"He *will* free you," Keith said, stunning his friend to silence when he held up a key. "Three years ago I was taken from the Thieves' Guild. But that didn't mean to forget everything I'd been taught. Shafari turned his back on me just once. That's all I needed."

Lancheshire's look of bewilderment softened to a bitter smile.

"Even Shafari has his limits," he warned, taking the key and stuffing it up his sleeve. "If he ever found out, especially from the likes of ye..."

"He won't." Keith grinned. "You *are* going to be free."

Lancheshire chuckled. "Ye act as though ye intend to stay longer. What with yer magic an' all, I'd be thinking about gettin' out too."

Keith looked doubtful. "But I've barely just begun to use magic. If I stay in the game, I'll continue to learn how to control it."

"Don't be daft! Shafari ain't keepin' ye for looks, ye know! 'Twill do me no good leavin' without ye. If ye're staying, then so will I."

Keith lowered his voice as a guard tromped by the cell. "Shafari won't keep you long either if you don't start selling. Besides, when I leave, I plan to release everyone, not just you."

"Ye'd have to tear the place down for that," Lancheshire replied. "In case ye haven't noticed, it's not just the compound to worry with. There's still a whole castle attached. How ye plannin' to stop 'em both? Set it on fire?"

A cold chill ran down Keith's back.

"First, the game. Then..." He let his voice trail off, the agonizing screeches of a harpy echoing throughout the compound.

*****

The smell of cinnamon drifted through an open vine window where moss-covered walls intertwined with Morning Glories, its white blossoms awaiting the advent of dawn. Though the room lay dormant, the presence of Nature breathed in every corner. Energy pulsed like the life-blood of a child that lay in bed. Moonlight sifted across his long curls in a silver glow. Dark eyelashes drew attention to a round face, his baby cheeks beginning to narrow in a lean appearance.

The silence was disturbed when the child tensed. Muscles tightened from a day of hard training. It settled for only a moment before plaguing his sleep once again.

No doorway existed into the room, but at a gesture the vines pulled aside to allow two Healers within. With a goblet in hand, Chronicles crossed the room to his son. At a gesture from his companion, vines rose from the ground to form a small table. Crumbs of limestone gathered at the base, then climbed upward to produce a stable surface for the goblet to rest. Stepping to the bedside, Chronicles tenderly removed stray curls from around his son's eyes.

"It takes time," he heard from behind. "Once he recovers he'll be able to shift more quickly without delays."

"I know, Eumaeus." A hint of impatience rose in Chronicles' voice. "Though by now I thought he'd be doing that."

Eumaeus came beside his leader. "If we rush the shifts, his body may reject it."

"I understand the risk of *phi'o-'eptén*," Chronicles snapped, switching tongues in mid-sentence. Reaching for the goblet, he ordered the Eumaeus to lift his son's head. The advisor obeyed without hesitation, though not without a disgruntled look.

Force-shifting should not be taken lightly, he thought to the leader. *I've seen one too many taken back to Nature because of it.*

Do not think I don't know my own son's strengths and weaknesses, Chronicles returned. *You assume too much, brethusus.*

Eumaeus glanced at him. 'Brother.' How long had it been since Chronicles had used that word? In no way did he feel close to his leader, yet they were bound together by more than their bloodlines.

Shy is more than ready, Chronicles finished.

Eyes of emerald attempted to open as Chronicles placed the rim of the cup against his son's lips. Pressure was gently applied on either side of the boy's throat, causing the muscles to instinctively swallow. As the liquid took effect, Shy's body relaxed.

"Let him rest into the next day as well," Eumaeus suggested.

Chronicles nodded.

"In two days," he said sternly, "his training will resume."

Eumaeus bowed his head before turning to leave, though their thoughts continued to flow freely.

He will become very powerful.

That's why it is essential that he be trained quickly, Chronicles returned. *He is the key to our people's survival. Nothing must stand in his way.* His ears lay back, listening to the footsteps of his companion fade down the hall. At a glance to the doorway the vines sealed the room. He rested a hand over his son's head, letting his fingers trace along the threads of hair.

"So much depends on this." Chronicles knelt beside the bed. "But I know you will not fail me."

And love? What of that? A familiar, yet strange mind linked with his, and Chronicles snarled when he recognized the thought from years ago. He closed his eyes, seeking the comfort of silence in the unknown void of the mind's eye. The presence of another followed, probing his being until discovering it. *How can there be love without mercy?*

T'jaeto! Chronicles thrust a mental barrier against the intrusion. *I shall not be condemned by one of the same!* He waited before lowering the barrier, but the other mind refused to leave.

Traitor? I was never interested in using my daughter as a tool to sever human lines. By your misjudgments will you destroy our people!

Phv'in! Chronicles commanded, his powerful thoughts reverberating through the minds of the other clan members. *It would be wise for you to leave, Windchester. You no longer deserve a place with us. You chose the life of a half-breed. Go back to them!*

Chronicles probed the area, trying to locate his once formal leader, and nearly laughed when he realized how close Windchester was.

A mind is a fragile thing, my friend, Chronicles said as he made his presence known. At once, Windchester tried to pull away, but Chronicles held him.

You cannot kill me! I am One! Windchester's pleading thoughts struck Chronicles, who slowly backed his probe through the haze of confusion into his own mind. His mental energy, he realized, was quickly slipping from him, so the leader made his point brief before withdrawing.

Know this, he threatened. *If you are caught in our territory again, you will be stripped of Nature's connection! One or no, you know the only element capable of harming us. If you so much as think about coming near my son, I will personally see to it that element be put to good use!*

Rather I take my own life than have you degrade it! Windchester rapidly thought.

His presence winked out.

CHAPTER 5

Keith woke sometime that night, his forehead damp with sweat. Dreams were still fresh in his mind as he tried to settle back down. The large vats against the far wall bubbled in a soft lull, and he was nearly asleep when he suddenly sat up.

An uneasy tension stirred the air. Without a sound, he slipped from bed to the bars and peered down the aisle. Pupils enlarged, enabling him to view the compound in the dim candlelight. No guards, which he figured by now were probably asleep. Still, the air shifted like dust being disturbed after a passing.

Keith took in a deep breath, inhaling the distinct smell of sweat and manure.

Nothing new. He glanced at Lancheshire lightly snoring on the top bunk. *But maybe it couldn't hurt to check.*

Keith slipped back to the bunks and climbed up the side. Cautiously, he pulled back his friend's sleeve where he had seen him hide the key. His triumph was short-lived when Lancheshire rolled over on his side, losing the key in the process. The clink of metal against bars resonated from his cell. Keith waited, planted in place against the side of the bunk, anticipating heavy footsteps to tromp down the aisle any minute.

Silence.

The boy let out a slow breath. He closed his eyes and tried to focus. After climbing back down, he stooped to look under the bunks. The floor was littered with dust so thick it was completely white, and Keith muffled a sneeze while trying to reach the key. He slid himself further under the bed and held his breath. When he could wedge himself no further, he gave up. Every time his fingers touched, it would slip the other way until the key was no longer inside the cell. A thin wall stood between the bunks and the bars, giving some privacy when sleeping, but did not come all the way down. Now Keith wished it did.

Wearily, he heaved himself from under the cot and waited for his temper to cool before dusting himself off. He knew the feeling all too well. It was a time when most of his magic came…and quickly went.

It's not the temper that controls it. At least I don't think it is. He studied the bunks for a moment. The bottom one was bolted into the floor, preventing it from being moved. *Even if I could move it, I'd risk* waking Lancheshire. His mind reeled for answers. *I can throw things with my magic. But can I bring things to me?*

Caressing warmth pulsed down his arm to his outstretched fingers as he lay on his stomach again and pointed at the key. The feeling came and went, and still the key was beyond his reach.

Am I doing something wrong? Maybe I'm supposed to be angry. But if that was true, then it would have worked the last time I saw Blackavar. He sat back on his knees. *I'm completely worthless! How am I supposed to last my remaining years in slavery if I can't use the magic when I need it?*

"You are more than you believe," a soothing whisper answered. The words gathered as a breath of wind carried it through the compound from open windows, rising and receding in volume. There was a hint of feminine dignity to the words, though it sounded many. Keith could not count how many voices he heard. Not all spoke Common, yet he understood as though they did. Mystified, his thoughts carried with it.

What are you?

"Haven't you known the answer?" the voices replied in harmony.

Keith blinked. *It* was the presence he had felt roaming the compound, had driven him to seek the key. *It* was the reason the key was lost. Swift anger built up again, then quickly subsided.

"Anger only plays a small part. It brings temporary energy. To unlock your true power, you must become One."

One with what? Keith thought. *Is Shafari One too? I've never heard him mention it.*

"He does not carry the Gift, as you do. Embrace in the Light of what you are. Become One with us. Only through us will you connect with each living creature, both plant and animal. Become the earth and the sky. Your tears become our own, as it falls when all is dry. Give in to your heart, for your heart is what guides you. In the end, there can be nothing but the purest of emotions. Love—it is the fate of all. So now shall it be yours."

"Love..." Keith breathed. Images of times he had used his magic came to mind. "So when I threw back that guard..." he kept his voice low.

"*Your love was protecting your friend.*"

"And at the auction?"

"*Your friend's love provided the connection.*"

Blackavar? Keith thought. *So is it just Love that controls my magic?*

"The more intimate your feelings, the stronger your magic. However, being One takes more than 'feeling' connected. It takes dedication. Your kind will show you the way."

My kind? You mean magic-users?

A breeze ruffled his curls as it shifted course to the cell door. With a click, it unlocked.

Uncertainty edged its way through his thoughts. Why now? Why not sooner so he could have saved Medallion, or his family? He stared at the cell door silently open before him. The temptation to leave this place pulled hard. Yet, with a glance to his sleeping companion, the boy knew he could not abandon his promise to help the slaves. He slipped out, but only for the purpose of obtaining the key.

She said 'my kind.' There must be someplace I need to go in order to find them. Wonder if that was what my mother meant?

Keith felt the wind retreat and watched a few swirls of dust sift along the ground until it dispersed. Glancing around, he kept his back to the bars as he slipped around the side of the cell. Turning a corner, the faint glint of metal drew his attention to the ground, and he reached down to retrieve it.

As he grasped the key, a small puddle of slush held his reflection in the flickering candlelight. He brushed a hand through his long curls, pulling them back behind his ears. As he stared, the pool rippled, distorting his reflection into light and shadow. When it settled, his ears were no longer human, but long with tiny hairs darkening at the tips. Another ripple, and when it had cleared he was staring into a pair of yellow eyes.

Keith slowly raised his head to the sound of a low growl. A loose hound, probably from a gate left unlatched, stared back. The upper lip curled into a snarl, revealing long fangs stained with blood from its previous meal. It inched closer.

Meat!

Keith jumped when a gruff voice entered his thoughts, words faltering as though trying to speak Common for the first time.

Blood!

Is that what the guards—Keith hesitated—*feed you?*

Saliva dripped around its unclipped toenails.

I hate meat! The hound lunged, knocking the boy to the ground.

Terrified, Keith remained still, the use of his magic already forgotten.

How you get out?

The question caught the boy off guard. Wiping spittle from his shirt, he replied, *I didn't exactly. How did you?*

Guards forget. The large animal sniffed the boy around the face. *You smell different.*

Keith was grateful when the hound carefully stepped off his chest. He noted the indentations in his shirt where its nails had been.

So you're not going to...eat me?

The animal snorted.

Why do that? I once like you.

"What?"

A slave rolled over in sleep, bristling the fur on the back of the dog's neck. It remained still, its stiff posture making Keith uneasy, until remaining silence prompted it to continue.

No sell? He do this!

Who? Shafari?

My memories all dog. He make this!

You were once a slave? Keith swallowed. *Like me?*

He saw its ears perk in alertness. This time a low growl escaped its throat.

Keith did not need to read its mind to know who was coming.

"Shafari," Keith breathed.

A shadow passed down the aisles just as the hound took up a hiding spot behind another cell. The shadow continued to creep over the bars, briefly pausing at certain cubicles before moving again.

Keith kept hidden behind the two bunk beds, the footsteps coming closer, and he cursed quietly for not securing the cell door.

Shafari's no fool! He knows I'm out! A quick intake of breath, louder than intended, drew the headmaster's attention. The shadow moved around to the back of the cell, and Keith braced himself for what was sure to come.

*****

Shafari's mind had been on the magic-user all day as he entered the compound. Rumors had spread that the boy could escape at any time.

Shafari never doubted that possibility. Still, the last thing he needed was an uprising.

Candles cast an eerie glow through the many bars, crisscrossing shadows over his robe. He glanced around the area as he came to Keith's cell. At first, everything seemed in order. Yet what he perceived to be a closed door in a column's shadow was now opened. A quick examination to the lock baffled him. There were no marks to determine how it had been opened.

Foolish. He almost laughed. *To think a simple magic trick could outsmart me.* A few whispered words and a wave of hand revealed a pair of small prints in the sand. With hands folded behind his back, Shafari calmly followed the tracks around the side.

A short intake of breath around the corner made him smile. He readied a sleeping spell, but before he could say a word a low growl drew his attention.

*****

While temporarily distracted, Keith made for the opposite side. Whatever the others did was their choice as Keith entered the cell and dived under the covers, hoping the headmaster's attention held....

*****

Shafari's ears had not failed to hear the faint click of metal door shut. Now the bottom bunk held a sleeping form that was once bare.

With a sigh, he retreated to the far corner of the compound where large vats bubbled with boiling water. A set of wooden steps brought him to a platform overlooking a huddled form whimpering in a mechanical dipping device.

The headmaster just shook his head.

"You should know better," he addressed the hound. "Trying to warn our little magic-user?" His voice grew cold. "I think not."

A flick of the wrist sprung the device into action. In one swift motion, it dropped from beneath the animal's feet, cutting its howls short when it plunged into the water. It did not resurface.

CHAPTER 6

By the time Keith turned fifteen, he had lost all hope of Lavern's return. It was not until later he received news of his friend's passing. For him, the game was over. As Keith prepared for auction, he thought back to the first time he went with Lavern. It had been crowded just as it was now, and even more so because of Keith's magic.

"I'll miss you." He bowed his head in remembrance, though grief for his companion was short-lived. Once again, Lancheshire had missed auction, but it was Shafari's announcement to keep the slave permanently at Castle Mire that brought relief. No more did Lancheshire have to worry about being sold. From this, Keith enjoyed the morning sales until his name was called. He did not even mind the food tossing, if any, from challenging masters who wanted some action. A better understanding of his magic showed in his stance. Bids quickly rose, and soon he was sold and escorted to an awaiting carriage.

Keith's new master, Nicolas, sat across from the boy once inside the carriage. There was a gentle way about him, his voice soft and understanding. Wrinkles of care lined the corners of his eyes when he smiled, a welcoming change from other masters. Once in open country Keith relaxed, away from cracking whips, yelling guards, and being shoved into cramped spaces. To take his mind from Castle Mire, he gave full attention to his master, especially to the emerald ring that complimented an outfit of forest green and gold.

"You like it then?" Nicolas held out his hand. "It was a gift from Lord Gracie."

"Who's Lord Gracie?"

"You've not heard of him?" Nicolas questioned. "How about Luxor Castle? I'm sure you've at least heard of *that*."

Keith shook his head.

"No? I thought everyone knew of the only castle that floats."

"Floats? You mean it's up there?" Keith pointed toward the sky. "But how do you get there? Do harpies carry you?"

Nicolas chuckled. "Well, there are a few of those, but for guests we have special transportation."

"Luxor...That's much more inviting than *Castle Mire*." The boy grinned. "Shafari would be jealous."

"Ah, yes. Always cradling his money, that one."

"You know him?"

"Friend of my father's, *once*. Too many tantrums. Started cursing people up and down. Got quite a hang of turning them into dogs, for some reason."

Keith remembered the night one of the hounds got loose. "Would he still do that now?"

"Oh yes!" Nicolas's brow lowered in concern. "Be glad I bought you when I did. What with the talent you have, and quite remarkable appearance, it'd be such a waste to end up like that! He only keeps slaves for a certain amount of time—five years, I believe. If you don't bring in the profit he's looking for...well, you know the rest. I'm sure you've seen those vicious looking things."

Keith nodded slowly, his face paling even more when he thought of Lancheshire. "I have a friend who just became Shafari's personal servant. He's actually missed several auctions."

Nicolas shook his head. "Let's just hope your friend doesn't suffer too long in the transformation."

"What! But—"

"Have you any knowledge of dream-channeling?" Nicolas changed the subject, then lowered his voice. "It may just help your friend." He winked. "I'll tell you about it later."

The carriage suddenly jerked to a halt.

"Well, we're here."

"Where's here?" Keith stepped from the carriage into a small forest clearing. There was no path, and no sign of other people. Even more startling was the empty carriage pulling away with no other transportation in sight.

"So...are we just waiting?"

"You might say that," Nicolas finished as a faint rhythmic beating caught their attention. "Watch closely."

A white spectacle of prancing hooves and turning wheels cut through a break in the trees. The flapping ceased after a thud on earthen soil, leaving only the pounding of hooves as two horses pranced into the clearing.

Keith gaped in awe. Gold harnesses hitched each horse to a pearl-white carriage, and as they came to a stop their wings folded at their sides. Transfixed, Keith nearly missed his master's guiding hand to another spectacle weaving in and out between the trees.

A harpy glided into the clearing, his white wings outstretched with ease as he descended. He smoothed down his gold-trimmed vest after landing with a slight skid, then tried to comb through his wind-tossed hair and feathers, to no avail. Bits of brown fuzz stuck up on his head as he came close, jade eyes studying each person. When he recognized Nicolas, his wings faded, and a warm smile greeted the travelers.

"Megas," Nicolas embraced the White Wing, "it's good to be going home again." He motioned to the boy. "May I introduce you to Keith, the one we talked about."

"Ah, yes." Megas folded his arms "The magic-user." He cocked his head while studying the boy. "Funny, I thought he'd be older."

"Well, I just turned fifteen, sir," Keith replied, laughing when Megas just stared in disbelief.

Nicolas chuckled. "He just needs room to grow, and I daresay a cage won't allow much of that."

"Well," Megas plucked a feather from his vest, "there's more than enough room where's he's going now."

Nicolas stretched. "It's getting late. Lord Gracie will probably be wondering where his carriage has gone off to."

"Quite right." Megas unfurled his wings, the last rays of sun shimmering upon them. "Sky's clear tonight. You should be able to see everything."

"Then let's not miss it." Nicolas held the carriage door open for Keith before climbing in himself.

When the two were inside, Megas turned to the horses and whistled. It was an unusual melody, one humans could never hope to make. Nevertheless, it was the moment the horses had been waiting for, and they both sprang forward.

Keith gripped the sides of the seat as the carriage picked up speed. He felt it tilting backward, feeling weightless a moment as it lifted. The distinct sound of wings beat the air, and a third pair soon joined as Megas flew to the front of the carriage to lead the way.

"Hang on to this." Nicolas calmly offered a strap suspended from the ceiling.

Keith grabbed it as the carriage jolted to one side.

"How can Lord Gracie expect to have visitors in something like this?" he asked, hanging on for dear life.

"Newcomers like you are always startled. Once it settles down, you'll actually find the ride quite pleasant."

Nicolas was right. At a certain height, the carriage leveled so Keith could hardly tell they were moving at all, save for a gentle swaying.

"Look outside. You can see everything from up here."

The boy released the strap and looked out into the fading sunset. Blue, purple and orange blanketed the sky with a touch of pink in the trailing clouds as far as the eye could see. Below, tiny lights flicked on from town lanterns at the approach of night.

"This is amazing!" he exclaimed.

His master nodded. "Some people take the ride just to get away. You can *think*, and for me there's no better place."

Keith watched even the tallest tree fade from view. "No crowds. No pushing or shoving. No guards..."

"Well, there're always guards," Nicolas said. "Just a different type. You probably mean those that carry whips and pop your ears when they yell at you." He chortled. "Luxor only has guards to protect it from...say thieves, maybe? Not that they could run anywhere once they're exposed, that is."

"Thieves?" Keith curiously asked. "Does Lord Gracie not know who comes and goes?"

"Oh, always! It's because most people think they can slip in."

"Is he a magic-user?"

"No, but he started as an alchemist, one of the first four to come to *No'va*."

"You mean *the first* four humans?"

His master nodded. "We really haven't been around that long. Megas and his kind were here long before we came."

"So who were the other three?" Keith asked.

"Let's see. There was a mage with him—two in fact! One of them you've already met: Shafari."

Keith laughed. "Would've fooled me."

"The second - I can't remember the first name, but the last name was Onyx."

"Jenario Onyx?"

"Yes, that's it." Nicolas eyed Keith. "You've met him too, I take it?"

"We met when I was sold to my first master. That makes three. So who's the fourth? Maybe I've met that person too."

Nicolas smiled. "Well, I can honestly say you've met his son."

Keith's brow crinkled in thought.

"The fourth was my father, Nickademis O'loyté. He lives in the Realm of Trully as local practitioner, or either tends to his garden. He loves gardening."

Keith absorbed the information like blotter paper soaking ink. It was hard to fathom those he had come to know were the first to enter *No'va*. Yet each of them had chosen a different path and gone his separate way.

"You look disappointed," Nicolas said after a while. "Was there someone else you were expecting?"

"It's not that," Keith replied with a sigh. "But I do have one question."

"And I have one answer," his master teased, cracking a smile from the boy.

"Why did they separate?"

"Interesting." Nicolas took a deep breath and let it out slowly. "I'm not sure how actuate my information is because my father told me some time ago." He leaned back and rested his hands across his lap. "From what I remember, there used to be only alchemists. Magic-users didn't exist for a long time. But little by little, the two mages you've seen slowly changed as they began to dabble in the ways of magic. With their knowledge of formulas and whatnot, they made it possible for others to understand the language of magic so they too could use it."

"And now?" Keith inquired.

"Well, *now* is the question. Jenario went his way with an interest in power. Shafari went another way with her curses, and my father? Well, he kept his knowledge of herbal concoctions and gardening to himself."

"What about Lord Gracie?"

Nicolas smiled. "Mostly, he's an observer. Some have even said his library could expand the length of *No'va* for all his writings. He's also the Law Keeper, and therefore has been given the title of Grand Master. Now maybe law wasn't what he had in mind, but it suits him."

He held on to the overhead strap as the carriage dipped. A whinny from one of the horses drew Keith's attention. The carriage dipped again, harder.

"Best hold on," Nicolas said.

A frantic neigh followed by a jolt alarmed Keith.

"What's going on?" he asked.

"Must be getting close."

Megas appeared by the window, hovering alongside.

"I would've thought we'd been there by now," Nicolas said. "What's wrong with the horses?"

"Sorry 'bout that," the White Wing replied in an apologetic tone. "They've caught wind of something. It'll pass. We should be there momentarily."

Suddenly, the carriage's backside dropped, sending Keith flying with it. He could hear Nicolas shouting when it tipped over, throwing Keith against the door. There came a crack, and it flew open. Another lurch tossed him out.

"Megas, the boy!" Nicolas shouted.

Keith was holding to the carriage's side when a pair of hands gripped him around the waist. At Megas' command he let go, and the harpy's wings beat the air furiously to hold the extra weight.

"What's happening?" Keith shouted to him in the sudden wind. Around him, clouds began to darken in large clumps.

Megas fought to keep control. Beneath him, the carriage rolled to the other side, slamming the door as its right side now turned upward. A clap of thunder sent the horses into a frenzy, rearing and bucking in fright.

"Nicolas!" Keith tried to call down to his master, but the high wind took his breath away.

"He'll be all right," Megas answered. "We've been through many storms together."

Gray turned to black, rolling and changing into a vortex of flickering light. Ahead of them, the clouds parted, and for an instant Keith caught a glimpse of silhouetted castle. Light spilled from each window, warm and inviting. Then it was gone, devoured in the building mass of clouds.

A deafening crash blocked out all sound as a white bolt ignited the top of the carriage. Fire flew through the air, eating through the harnesses until, free at last, they pulled away, leaving the carriage to its fate.

"Nicolas!" Keith screamed, but there was nothing he could do. Megas was having enough trouble battling against the winds. Another glimpse of the castle came and went, much closer this time.

Keith could feel the White Wing tiring, and they still had a ways to go. The boy grieved over Nicolas. He had only begun to have a decent master, and now he was gone.

Can my magic save Megas? Can I possibly hold us up long enough to reach the castle?

Keith shut his eyes tight, hoping and praying it would come to him.

"Become One with us!" A gust of wind blew around the two.

Keith could not believe what he was hearing. It was same voice he had heard at the compound, the same multitude of females speaking as one in a language he understood.

Then suddenly it all made sense—the voices, the language, the magic. Like a door being opened to another world, he welcomed the surge of power and understanding of what the voices were asking.

It's Nature's energy I must become One with. You are Nature!

"Give to us what we give to you!" The voices continued. *Fruits of life, flesh and bone, the spirit that's within you. Be ours and we will be yours...forever!*

Keith felt Megas' grip loosen, then gasped when they started to drop. He glanced at the wings. Although they flapped, one was bent back, broken at the joint. Some of the feathers seemed darker, as though they had been burned from the carriage fire.

I wish to be One now! Keith demanded, holding to Megas as they broke through the clouds. Keith saw the tops of trees fast approaching. *I'm yours.*

"Now we are One."

A sudden gust caught the two from underneath, slowing their descent until they were traveling in the opposite direction. Keith relaxed, his eyes aglow with new power. The same glow enwrapped the two, and before Keith could take another breath they were whisked away through the clouds. With closed eyes, he let Nature guide the way to the castle and settle on the entrance landing.

Several people crowded the front when they saw the flaming ball of blue light. Guards took precaution and held their weapons ready.

When the light faded, Keith lay beneath the weight of the White Wing, both mental and physical strength spent. Darkness overtook him as a familiar voice called his name, and the fading image of black wings loomed above.

CHAPTER 7

Amber eyes skimmed along the clouds forming off to his right. The sky was darkening quickly as Corrigan put Jenario's promised power to use.

No 'Keyarx would ever believe one of their own having power.

A dry laugh escaped his lips. With closed eyes, he relished the feel of wind caressing his russet flesh. He let his wings close around him, freefalling to catch the next current. He lifted back into the invading purple and velvety blue hues.

Almost there.

The smell of another *'Keyarx* caught him off guard, and his lip curled into a sneer.

White Wing.

With his sharp eyes, he quickly caught sight of a carriage pulled by two winged horses. The temptation of fresh meat made his mouth water. When was the last time he had truly enjoyed a larger hunt? He slowed his flight to carefully observe the path of the carriage and the position of nearby clouds.

You want it, don't you? A gentle voice spoke in his mind, and Corrigan paused. He knew it was Jenario, and then it was not. The voice was dryer, a harsh rasp he had never heard before. Yet the link clearly came from the alchemist.

Quit toying with me, mage! Corrigan returned the thought. *We may be linked, but what I think stays in my head. I'll get fed when I'm good and ready.*

To stop the carriage, you must first stop what's pulling it. Why not satisfy your hunger in the process?

Corrigan felt a surge of power course through his body. His mind went blank, replaced by a set of different thoughts.

Raising a hand toward the carriage, amber eyes narrowed as a bolt of lightning extended into the sky and dissolved into a swirling vortex of gray smoke rings. The rings grew in size, expanding in height until its mass exploded over the horizon in a brilliant display of light and shadow. It regrouped, in which the harpy concealed himself. He could smell two people inside the carriage, one being the boy. While streaks of lightning danced around the carriage, the horses reared in fright, tipping the vehicle over. When the boy fell out, a smile crossed his lips.

An ear-splintering explosion echoed like rolling thunder as a streak of lightning struck the edge of the carriage, severing the connection between the two horses. The sound was enough to drown out the commands of the other mind and re-awaken Corrigan.

Damn you, Jenario! Corrigan sucked in a quick breath when he saw Keith held by the White Wing. *I said I would...*

The orange glow of the burning carriage plummeting below drew his attention.

The other human...

Corrigan closed his wings into a dive. Feathers on either side of his face prevented the wind from burning his skin as he descended through the clouds and short bursts of rain. The flaming carriage tumbled over, whipping flames back through the sky. Corrigan swerved around spitting décor spewing from its top. He dived below the carriage, careful to avoid its continuous rolls. By now the fire had spread across the top and down one side. An opening into the carriage rolled toward him, and he grabbed hold and pulled himself just inside the doorway. A quick glance out confirmed the sighting of approaching treetops.

Inside, an older man huddled in the corner, his hope of escape fading before his eyes at the sight of the Black Wing. Without a word, Corrigan reached over and yanked the man from his seat just as flames broke through the ceiling.

He could not wait for the vehicle to right itself. With the human in his arms, Corrigan pushed off into the depths of the forest, his sharp eyes helping him through the maze of twisted branches and thick foliage. He continued straight down as the carriage slammed into the first set of trees from above. Wood and fire exploded in a roar of leaves and severed trunks crashing overhead.

A clearing opened before him, and Corrigan spread his wings in attempts to bring them back up. He could feel the heat across his back. In his arms, the man gave a holler.

"You've truly never flown before, have you?" Corrigan grinned as he pulled up through the trees. Below, burning rubble of blackened carriage and smoke was all that remained.

The Black Wing paid no heed to the stares he received when they landed at Luxor Castle, though the moment was short-lived as a blue light hit the ground between him and the surviving human. He averted his gaze until the glow faded.

Keith? He blinked, staring wide-eyed like everyone else. *Was that his power?*

*****

Lancheshire carelessly tossed a white marble bishop through an empty space between two ebony pawns. With a tired sigh, he rested his chin in his hand when his turn was complete and waited for the headmaster to make his next move.

"I'm half-spent, Shafari!" the slave blurt in the midst of the mage's thoughts. "Ain't we quitting yet? We've played so long the squares are just a blur."

Shafari raised an eyebrow in slight irritation.

"Patience, my friend," he calmly glanced at the bedraggled slave. He noticed the bags hanging under each eye, threatening to steal years from the otherwise hyper-mannered young man.

The two sets of game pieces had increasingly dwindled since the game first started, leaving wide open space for the slave to plunge through without delay, yet left little to hide. Even if he could get close to the king, Shafari's enchantments alerted the slave's whereabouts.

The headmaster's content gaze fell upon him now and then with a slight nod of victory shining in his eyes. Soon all talk ceased until only silence threatened to engulf them into each other's thoughts of madness.

Death hid in the headmaster's eyes as Lancheshire watched an ebony knight trample the last of his pawns.

"We're almost through here, my friend." Shafari stretched and yawned. It was well past midnight as he stood and looked down upon the already dozing slave.

"Really?" came a faint reply as Lancheshire rested his head on his arms. "Call it a night then."

Shafari eyed the slave for a moment before heading to his sleeping quarters.

"Call it a night," Shafari yawned again. "Until next time..."

*****

"Keith?"

"He's fine. Look, he's coming 'round."

"Keith? Can you hear me?"

Voices echoed in and out of Keith's head as his eyes opened to a group of faces staring down at him. A buzzing throbbed in his ears, and it took a few moments for the sound to fade before he could focus.

Three men stood around him, one he recognized.

"Nicolas?" Keith slowly sat up in bed and glanced around. The room was filled with an eccentric yellow glow as light seemed to flow from one wall to the other. Tapestries hanging on each side of the room helped keep the glow to a comfortable level. His gaze eventually settled back on his master. "I thought you were dead."

Laying a hand on the boy's head, Nicolas smoothed back a few strands from his eyes.

"So did I," he replied.

"And Megas?"

"Doing fine," Nicolas said. "Though it may be some time before he flies again." He glanced uncertainly at the other two. "We'll just have to see."

A fourth person entered the room, black wings slipping into a fade as he calmly strode toward the bed. A few others that stood nearest the door stepped aside to allow him passage. Nicolas started to introduce the Black Wing when Keith interrupted.

"Corrigan!"

A cool smile expressed the Black Wing's gratitude to see his young friend.

Nicolas glanced between the two, astonished at the immediate recognition.

"'Twould seem no introduction is needed." A new presence entered behind the Black Wing. "Small wonder in the world we live in now. Much is possible."

"Lord Gracie." Nicolas and others bowed as the headmaster approached while Corrigan stood quietly by Keith's bedside.

Thomas Gracie was not one to call handsome, nor had he seen days of good looks in the past. His round face and body fit well with his deep voice, and though he kept his appearance well-trimmed, his garments were another matter. Keith lowered his eyebrows, quizzically studying the headmaster with his vest of multicolored patches and dull brown pants. To him, he looked more like a gardener.

"Not what you were expecting, was it?" Lord Gracie gestured to his lackluster clothing. "I only dress when entertaining, not to tend a castle."

He ran a hand through his thick black hair, parting two white streaks that ran down its length.

"To be honest, sir, I didn't know what to expect," Keith replied. "In fact, I didn't even know I was coming at all. It wasn't before the storm—"

"Ah, yes—*that*." Lord Gracie raised an eyebrow toward Corrigan, who feigned non-interest in the conversation. "Let's not discuss the matter. It's over and done with, and I'm sure our guests would much prefer to be refreshed after all that has occurred."

At a command, a servant girl entered. Petite in size with strawberry hair, she reminded Keith of a slave he had seen back at the auction.

"You're from Castle Mire, aren't you?" he inquired.

"Aye, I thought ye looked familiar," the girl said. "From the auction, right? Ye were that little runt in the back." She sized him up. "Still are, from the looks of it."

Corrigan grunted, suppressing a smile while Keith's cheeks turned pink. The boy looked down at himself after slipping from bed.

"How do you feel? Well enough to walk?" Lord Gracie asked. When Keith nodded, the headmaster turned to Nicolas. "Why don't you take Keith and head down to the bathing room." His gaze returned to Keith. "Ginger will assist you with fresh garments once you've washed. Afterwards, a feast will be prepared." His eyes flicked to Corrigan. "I *do* have raw meat, if you care to join us."

Corrigan tapped his claws against the bedposts in thought. He preened a couple of feathers before nodding his thanks, then slipped out into the hallway.

"Corrigan?" Nicolas called from the door, and the Black Wing paused just long enough to glance over his shoulder. "I never did thank you for saving my life. I…just wanted you to know. Thank you."

There was a brief silence. If Corrigan had not a mask of feathered markings, his flushed appearance would have shown.

"Just don't brag about it," he said softly before continuing down the hall.

*****

Did you enjoy my little…magic trick?

The sudden intrusion of another mind received a fiery comeback, one that ended in apologetic waves of energy to sooth the harpy's temper.

You nearly killed him! I even had to save—

But you've seen his power, Jenario interrupted. *That in itself is far too dangerous for a mere child to handle.*

There came a change in voice, and when the thought came again, it was the same deep tone he had heard earlier before the storm.

You know what he is, don't you, Corrigan?

The Black Wing hesitated. Was this the same person?

His lack of experience puts him at a disadvantage to you. With my guidance, he won't know how to react when he's taken.

With your guidance? Corrigan ducked down an unused hallway. *I've told you before. What I think stays in my mind! After what happened earlier, I'd prefer handling it without your help. And you can take back your power, unless you'd like a surprise visit in your mind!*

Corrigan waited until Jenario's presence faded. A breeze coming from an open window drew his attention. With no one around, the Black Wing climbed out and let the air currents lift him into flight.

CHAPTER 8

Long strands of silver-white hair blew around his face in the breeze. His mental energies extended over the vast forest, connecting with each individual clan member. When his thoughts reached them, he was greeted warmly.

Shy had drifted further this time, the need to explore calling him. He looked up and shielded his eyes from the sun's rays filtering through the leaves. Now and then a few stray beams hit the eye that caused them to glow in emerald splendor.

Where have you gone this time, Shy? A mental link established with his own, trying to locate his physical presence.

Come find me, if you can! Shy laughed.

No shifting this time!

Twilight, you're such a baby! a gruff thought interrupted.

You find him then, Jangus, if you're so smart! Twilight returned.

Shy shook his head and made his way down the bank. He stopped at the river's edge. Here marked the border of Crystal Valley, and the end of the *Lo-ans'rel* territory. He stared across, trying to picture the landscape outside the forest. Out there, he knew humans had reshaped the land to their liking. Though he had never seen it, there were others who had. Tales of plant-less structures scorched his thoughts. How could someone live without Nature close by?

Shy's pointed ears twitched to pick up his stalker's quick breaths. With a faint smile, he ducked and moved across the forest floor without a sound. At certain points, he could look up and see the bridges connecting between the different *Harma'Keyzarx* homes. A flash of wings overhead drew his attention, and he called to the fledgling with a thought.

Come join our game, Chanté!

A winged boy settled on a nearby branch.

"You're going to get me in trouble again!" Chanté called down with a broad grin.

"Afraid of being caught near the ground?" Shy teased.

"Not if you're afraid to be in the skies." The fledgling flipped over the branch and hovered overhead. "Learn any new shifts lately?"

"I'll be taking larger forms soon, like...the one behind me." Shy sidestepped to avoid an older boy's attempts to lunge at him. "At least here's one who never learns."

"Quit ragging on me 'bout that! I realize skunks stink." Jangus picked himself up, his face drawn into a frown. Raven black hair fell in wispy strands to his shoulders. He was much thinner than Shy, and in no way was his appearance pleasing to the eye. Compared to Shy, Jangus grew like a weed. With his tawny flesh and unusual set of opal eyes, he was the least liked of the Healer kind. His sour attitude quickly dulled a game, which in this case was no exception.

From above, Chanté scowled.

Thanks, but I'll play another time, he thought and made haste into the canopy.

Shy sighed. *Another game spoiled.*

"Hey, don't look at me!" Jangus replied. "I didn't ask him to leave."

"So...I guess Twilight's not coming." Shy ignored the comment.

"You know he doesn't come to the border. Neither should you."

"And you're here, why?" Shy grinned when Jangus did not answer.

"Well...somebody's got to make sure the clan's *heir* is safe." Jangus smirked.

Shy glared at him. "Quit calling me that."

"Well, you are," a new voice made the two boys turn toward a young female approaching.

"Come for your lover, Kat?" Jangus inquired in a sarcastic tone.

The girl's lips puckered in a childish pout. "I prefer Katherine," she stated firmly. "Don't make me smack you again." A few fingers combed through her long, strawberry hair. "You really deserve two after taking that form."

Jangus narrowed his eyes.

"Fine! I get the idea!" He stormed off through the trees. "None of us should be this far anyway!"

Katherine just rolled her eyes. "He's just mad 'cause he can't accept the truth."

"You think?" Shy chuckled. He motioned for her to follow. "Come on." His form began to waver as he walked. A faint flow engulfed his body, and when it had cleared a bird fluttered onto a nearby limb. *Let's see if we can find Chanté,* he thought to her. *His company will be much more pleasant.*

*****

A silent observer calmly watched one of the boys angrily pass beneath his location in the trees. In the form of an owl, Chronicles mentally noted their progress, especially his son.

And Jangus? It was no secret that his ambitions to win the leader's approval were desirably great. Thus, the *Lo-ans'rel* leader had accepted him with welcome arms should anything befall Shy.

Chronicles could still hear their playful outbursts now and then as he stepped into the sunlight. For a moment he stood basking in its warmth before silently taking to the sky.

*****

Keith closed his eyes when soapy water was poured over him. It felt good to get a warm bath and wipe the dirt and grime from his hair. With every scrub his curls became a shade lighter until it was back to its original snow white.

"I never knew just how filthy Castle Mire was." Nicolas noted the discolored bath water.

"I'm not surprised." Lord Gracie entered the room with a towel and put it with the boy's new clothing. "The young maid I bought was even worse."

"Did you know we would look that way coming from Castle Mire, or is that any slave in general?" Keith asked as he grasped for the towel.

"Slaves in general from anywhere are going to look like rotten potatoes!" Nicolas scowled. "But anything from Castle Mire is top breed, or so I'd thought."

Lord Gracie nodded.

"Top breed, as in magic-users, you mean. But you, lad, would be the first I've seen or heard of. It was your magic that saved Megas, and for that I thank you. He's doing much better now."

"Will he be able to fly soon?" Keith wrapped the towel around his waist as stepped from the tub.

Lord Gracie looked skeptical.

"Wings are very tricky to set back into place. They're not like a small bird's, which can easily mend in a matter of weeks. But...we'll just have to see."

Spilled water next to the tub made Nicolas and Keith slip, so Lord Gracie called for Ginger to bring two extra towels for the floor. Before leaving, she peered over her shoulder at Keith.

"Ah, ah." Lord Gracie held up a finger, gently sending her on her way. He met Nicolas's gaze. *"Females,"* he mouthed the word.

Keith checked his appearance in a nearby mirror after changing into his new clothing.

"A little big, but it'll work for you," Lord Gracie approved. "I'm assuming the feast should be ready as well. You must be hungry."

Keith and Nicolas followed the headmaster. As they passed rooms filled with different wonders and oddities unlike Keith had ever seen, the headmaster explained what they were and where they had come from. Each room was like a grand ballroom in itself, a chamber with high domed ceilings and colorful tapestries draping along each wall. As they neared the dining area, many wondrous smells of food wafted down the hallway.

There was always movement wherever he went, whether admiring guests or servants hustling to keep things tidy, and no matter where Lord Gracie went, he was always informed. Already, a servant had approached him in mid-conversation.

"I never tire of this place," he said after sending the servant away. "It keeps me occupied." He glanced at Keith. "On those long nights when storms approach and lightning dances across the sky, you're never lonely. And I don't mind sharing rooms with the young ones that come here, scared to death from recent masters who never paid them much mind. I've seen some with little more strength than a child 'cause their backs have given out from heavy lifting all their lives." He shook his head. "Such a shame I can't release you."

"Release?" Keith paused in the middle of the hallway. "Oh, I get sent back all the time."

Lord Gracie chuckled.

"I meant from slavery altogether, not just me."

Keith's brow furrowed in thought.

"But I thought Nicolas was my master."

"No, my lad," Lord Gracie said. "He is a servant here. Or rather, more like an advisor to me." He sighed. "I had high hopes my old friend would change his mind about those documents. Alas, he's more selfish than I realized."

"Shafari never mentioned documents," Keith said. "He just told me five years."

"Then he hasn't told you everything. But come!" The Grand Master gestured down the hallway. "Let's discuss everything over supper, shall we?"

CHAPTER 9

Keith had never eaten so much food. Now he leaned against the high-backed seat staring at all that was still before him: potatoes, corn, stew, and roasted hog with fruits and vegetables around the platter. There were chowders, fish, beef, pies, and cakes. It was enough to feed an entire realm. He even took a sip of Lord Gracie's special Falconberry Wine.

"A rarity, indeed," the headmaster pointed out, offering another sip before passing it to Nicolas.

Keith watched the pitcher pass down the table to both servants and guests, then back up. When it reached the boy, he took another sip. So small a taste, yet still it was enough to make his tongue dance. It was not long before he raised the question about the slave matter.

With a heavy sigh, the headmaster reluctantly swallowed his halfway chewed food and gulped down the rest of his wine.

"Keith," he began. "For all the money I paid for you, I don't exactly *own* you. You see, Shafari has papers listing every single slave that comes through Castle Mire. In that way, a slave can be tracked back to the last paying master, and as long as Shafari holds that paper, *he* has the final say-so."

He sighed.

"Now I'm sorry I couldn't get the documents. I tried to bribe him, but he wouldn't have it, even when I offered more money than you would *ever* be worth." He chortled. "Should have seen the disappointment on his face, but still he refused. I can keep trying though, or I'll just keep you here. He may have the documents, but I have rightfully paid in full for you as a slave owner."

Keith looked down at his plate. "A friend once told me to view slavery as a game. That way it makes things easier, I guess."

Lord Gracie glanced at Nicolas.

"I've heard people compare their lives to all sorts of things, but never a game. Tell me, what type are you playing with each master you come across?"

"Chess," Keith said.

"So when you leave each master," Nicolas inquired, "is that like an entire game won, or an individual piece defeated?"

"A piece—mostly pawns," Keith added. "I figured slavery in general would be a game in itself, and each master would make a piece on the board."

"May I inquire who's winning as of late?" the servant teased, but Keith remained quiet.

"If you ask me," Lord Gracie frowned, "'twould seem a stalemate, at least for the time being. No one can win until the final piece is brought down, and that can only be the king." He glanced at Keith. "Tell me, lad. Have you ever played *real* chess before?"

Keith shook his head. "Only watched."

A sly smile spread across the headmaster's face.

"High time you're taught then," he said. "Who knows? Might come in handy against these 'pieces' you're playing against."

*****

Megas opened his eyes, his vision hazed with a slight throb at the temple. He could not feel his right wing, bound to his side and elevated by a pillow. Servants had come and gone. They had done their best to keep him comfortable. Now alone, the harpy lay staring at the ceiling, a pang of dread that he would never fly again kept at a minimal somewhere in the back of his mind. Gradually, his gaze shifted around the room.

There were no windows. Yet the glow cast from each wall created a mutual peace around a still figure standing nearby. A ruffle of feathers drew the White Wing's attention, and his eyes grew wide at the sight of the Black Wing. He tried to lift his wings in defense, to no avail. There was not even enough strength to lift his head off the pillow.

"Oh, please!" Corrigan scoffed, his sable feathers twitching in annoyance. "You couldn't do anything to me even if I *was* after you."

"How did you get in here?" Megas croaked.

Corrigan shrugged. "I'm only here because of one person in particular, and who apparently saved your life—what good that's done! You've no chance of flying anytime soon."

Megas snorted and looked away. "I could have told myself that."

One glance, and Corrigan knew Megas' wing was beyond repair. His amber eyes trailed to the cast wrapped tightly around the pallid feathers. It was the only thing that held the fragile bones together now.

"Look," he began. "I'm not one for helping or giving advice, but there might be someone here who can."

"And...why would a Black Wing care to associate with a White Wing's business?" Megas squinted at him. "You're not very big. What happened? Growth defect? Fledgling? Doesn't appear to be. Parents rendezvous with a different Wing?"

Corrigan suppressed a chuckle.

"Least we have something in common, though mockery, nonetheless."

Keeping an eye on him, Megas asked, "And who, or should I say, *what* do you think is going to help me? One of your kind, I suppose?" There was a hint of sarcasm, which Corrigan ignored.

"That *what*, you so pleasantly mentioned, I cannot speak aloud. But I do believe he's strong enough to get you back up and flying, if you care to know."

When he received a puzzled expression, Corrigan held up a hand and signaled a word with his fingers. Though his larger talons seemed bulky in comparison to the White Wing's slender nails, the message was still clear enough to receive a look of surprise.

Megas breathed the word, unsure whether to believe it or not.

"*Healer...*"

*****

Keith placed a knight on the small, checkered board, blocking one of Lord Gracie's pieces. The headmaster swiped a pawn. Just as easily, Keith took out a bishop.

"You're a quick learner," Lord Gracie said, counting how many pieces remained. "And a good player too." He leaned back in his seat and crossed one leg over the other. "Nicolas tells me you're going to learn dream-channeling."

"It's to warn my friend at Castle Mire," Keith said. "Even though I may already be too late."

"Have you tried just connecting to his mind?"

"Well...I don't really know how," the boy admitted. "I mean, I've heard people's thoughts before, but they just come to me."

Lord Gracie chuckled.

"So that would explain why you're winning. You can *hear* my thoughts."

Keith's cheeks swelled as an impish grin spread across his face.

"Nicolas mentioned one time about people who can do that," Lord Gracie said. "There's a name for it. It's…" He braced his hand against his forehead, trying to remember. "Give me a moment. I know he told me." He slapped the table, causing a few pieces to tumble. "Sight-reader! On sight is revealed. Beyond that is concealed. That would make you a mind-reader."

Keith began placing fallen pieces back in position. "Do you think I'll ever become one of those?"

The headmaster shrugged. "It's possible. Then again, you're still very young. There are years ahead of you to practice – so long as you survive slavery," he added in a grim tone.

"Hmmm…" Keith stared at the board. After a moment, he moved his queen in between two pawns, cornering Lord Gracie's king. "Checkmate."

The headmaster grinned.

"So much for that." He rose and stretched. "I do have a few things to attend to before the day ends. Why don't you have a look around? Take your mind off 'games' for a while."

It was not long before Keith found himself wandering from one corridor to the next, peering into opened rooms. High vaulted ceilings arched overhead, some so vast that columns supported a good majority. There was no telling how many rooms he passed, nor how many still lined the hallways and upper floors. Each was like a grand ballroom, equipped with a comfortable sitting lounge. Several contained guests, and though Keith was more than welcome to join, he politely refused to check the next wondrous room. Many lavish furnishings captivated him. Priceless objects compelled him to touch, though with caution.

Upon filling his curiosity, Keith was making his way back when a small, dimly lit alley cut between the corridors caught his eye. The amount of light that did show came not from glowing walls, but sunlight from an opened doorway at the rear.

Curious, Keith followed the hallway to an outside garden. A fresh breeze carried many fragrances, and he stopped to admire the many flowers planted along a stone path. The call of Nature tingled his magical senses as he let his finger trail a rose bud. At his touch, their petals unfurled in the splendor of sunlight, beaming their rosy-cheeked faces. So amazed at this spectacle that he tried it again, running along the path opening every flower, until he nearly ran into another person.

"Hey!" a young girl cried.

Keith jumped back, too startled to even say a word. He stared. The girl's hair was pulled back so tight her eyebrows arched in a constant expression of surprise. Makeup adorned her every feature, hiding any embarrassment she might have shown. What that did not cover, her lacy gown got the rest.

Keith suppressed a chuckle as he attempted to apologize.

"You think this is funny?" The young girl scoffed. She ripped a bow from her sleeve and waved it in his face. "Try wearing *your* hair back as tight as it will go, and lace, and ribbons! See how *you* like it!" She took a step back. "What are you anyway? Some sort of albino? Leave me alone!"

She yanked a ribbon from her hair. Dark brown locks collapsed to her shoulders.

"Why would you wear something you don't like?" Keith tried to conceal his smile.

"Fine time to be asking me now. I hate this!" She tossed her shoes over the balcony wall. Something tinged on the ground by her foot, and she reached down to pick up a gold ring. "Stupid thing won't stay on my finger!"

"Maybe I can help."

The girl's eyes darted up and down his figure, studying him. "What part of *leave me alone* don't you understand? I don't dress this way 'cause I *like* it. My stepmother makes me wear this horrid mess!"

"Your stepmother?" Keith raised an eyebrow.

Sighing, the girl took a deep breath.

"You're not one of Lord Gracie's servants, are you? Don't tell him I'm out here. No one must know I'm here."

"Well...okay then. But first you have to tell me who you are. I'm Keith." He extended a hand, which received a tight squeeze.

"That's for nearly running into me." She grinned. "If my stepmother was here, she'd demand you call me *Princess* Alexia, because she says it sounds more," she lowered her voice to imitate an older woman, "*sophisticated.*" She gazed into his eyes, the sunlight catching a glimmer of sapphire. "If you're going to call me anything, call me Glory."

Keith nodded. "I'm sure it's true…on good days."

"Yeah, well, today's not one of them." The blooming flora from Keith's early magic spurt wavering in the breeze drew her attention. "I don't recall those from before."

"I did it." The boy stepped to an unopened bud beside the path.

Glory eyed him in suspicion. "You? So what are you, some type of skilled gardener?"

Keith laughed cheerfully. "No, but I have magic. See?" A touch to the bud quickly turned its petals up.

Glory was instantly awestruck. "Can you make it go back?"

Keith shrugged. "I guess."

"Can you make people disappear? Mainly…my stepmother?"

"So that's why you're out here. You're hiding!"

Glory did not immediately answer and instead took a sidelong glance at him.

"You sound older, but you're smaller than me."

"I'm fifteen," he admitted. "I think slavery's done me in."

Glory raised her eyebrows. "I didn't know they allowed magic-users in slavery."

"Not normally," Keith replied as he toyed with the flower. "Guess I got lucky."

"That's more luck than me. I'm stuck with a witch!"

Keith chuckled. "Oh, really?"

The girl narrowed her eyes. "She calls me a spoiled little brat!"

"And you're sure you're not one now?"

"You cod!" Glory jumped at him, forgetting she had on delicate lace. They instantly tangled in the rose vines and tore, leaving bits of white everywhere as the two tumbled back across the path. She fought viciously, pulling at Keith's hair and clothing, even managing to tear his shirt collar.

Keith kicked her off, but she came flying back.

"Not bad, for a white rat!" Glory breathed heavily when they finally stopped. She looked down at her soiled clothing. "Feels great to be rolling in the dirt again!" When she looked down at Keith sprawled in the flowerbed, she began to giggle. "We both look so silly now. Here, let me help you up."

Graciously, Keith allowed himself to be pulled to his feet before dusting himself off. He fingered the torn collar, testing his magic to see if the stitches would reweave themselves. It was not the best work, but it looked far better than before. A sly smile snaked its way across his face.

"Not too shabby, see? How 'bout I replace some of that lost lace?"

"Oh, no you don't!" Glory jumped away from him. "I feel much better without it, thank you very much." She inhaled deeply. "Maybe all I needed was someone to take my frustration out on."

"Thanks." Keith rolled his eyes. "Course, you *do* realize you could only hide for so long here. After all, we are on a floating building."

Glory's cheeks turned a rosy pink. "Actually, I came with my father on business. Guess he thought the outing would be good for me."

"And was it?" Keith teased, eyeing the dirty spots on her once white dress.

Before she could reply, Nicolas poked his head outside.

"There you are!" he exclaimed, startling the two. His gaze flicked to Glory's ruined dress. "Gracious! What happened to you?"

"Did you find...?" Another followed after the servant, but stopped short upon seeing his daughter. "Oh, Glory! You mother is going to throw a fit!"

"Stepmother," the girl insisted. "And I'm sorry for leaving you, father. But look!" She gestured to Keith. "He's a *real* magic-user. See the flowers? He makes a great gardener."

Keith lowered his gaze from the tall man's concerned expression. He could feel his cheeks flush with color just as the blooming flora.

"Interesting." Glory's father glanced over the boy's unusual appearance. "And you trust him, Nicolas?"

Keith felt the servant's hand pat his shoulder.

"With my life," he replied. "Already, he's proven quite valuable in service, more so than a harpy – and they're pretty loyal."

"Well," Glory's father glanced down at his daughter, "Best we be on our way. Maybe pick up some new clothes for you before we get home."

Keith smiled upon hearing Glory's groan.

Nicolas took the man's hand in a firm handshake. "A pleasure, Master Roland, as always." He escorted them to the garden door before turning to Keith. "Don't wander off. I'll be right back."

While Keith waited. He shot a tiny amount of magic toward the flowerbeds to help clean them up, mending broken stems and raising crushed leaves. While lifting one of the roses, something gold glinted in the dirt. He picked it up between two fingers and brushed it off.

"Glory's ring!" Forgetting the plants, he raced to the door, hoping to catch them before they left the hall. He could hear their footsteps fading down the corridor and decided against the idea of running after them.

It wouldn't look proper with me running down the hall when Nicolas told me to stay. Besides, I'm sure they'll come looking for it...maybe.

CHAPTER 10

Keith had just pocketed the ring when Lord Gracie stepped outside. His casual attire had changed to an elegant green robe. Gold patterns adorned the cuffs of his long sleeves, and an emerald necklace matched the rings on his fingers. His freshly combed hair made it easy to detect the two white stripes running down the sides.

"Lady said I'd find you here," he said pleasantly. "You might want to put that on a chain rather than in your pocket."

"Who's Lady?" Keith glanced down where the ring had just been placed. "I don't suppose this *Lady* said that too, did she?"

There was a chuckle. "Soon, you will meet her." The Grand Master gave the boy a gentle pat on his shoulder. "Then you will know."

Perplexed, Keith allowed himself to be lead back inside. They had just cleared the dim alley when Nicolas, having departed from his earlier guests, greeted the two in the main corridor.

"Sorry," he apologized. "Had to escort one of our guests out."

"Quite all right, my friend. Now that you're here, though, Keith needs to be ready for tonight." He eyed Keith's stained clothing. "Do make sure he's fitted, will you, Nicolas?" Then he started down the hall at a brisk pace.

"Who's coming tonight?" Keith asked the servant as he was led the opposite way.

"Lord Gracie has invited all clan masters to attend, along with their servants," Nicolas answered. "It's a way to not only get to know who's rising to power nowadays, but what new slaves they've harvested." He gestured for the boy to turn down a side passage. At the end, a set of steps wound their way to the second floor. Keith led, flanked by Nicolas. "That's how he gets so many harpies here. He buys them from his guests."

"I feel sorry for them. The way they're treated at Castle Mire..."

"Not another word! I too have seen what they do."

A tug on Keith's shirt kept him from going further, and he turned to watch the servant pull a key from his pocket.

"Not the correct way?" Keith questioned.

Nicolas grinned. "Trust me. It's correct." He felt along the wall, trailing the key over the smooth surface until it clicked against something.

"But we're not even near the top. Certainly, there's no doorway here."

"Oddities lie in just about every corner of Luxor," the servant replied, slipping the key into a lock that materialized from the wall. "One of many illusions that keep pesky guests from entering where they don't belong." He looked up. "Rely on what you see and you'd never reach the top. But for me, we *are* at the top."

Keith looked around. No sooner had the key touched its destination than the never ending staircase faded. Instead, a wall marked the end of their climb. With a push, the door opened.

Nicolas beamed when he noticed the astonished expression on the boy's face.

"When you've been around as long as I, you learn to count your steps." He lit a candle sitting on a small table, then raised it so he could better see inside a nearby wardrobe. "Now I'm sure there's something here that will fit you."

While Nicolas searched, Keith skimmed the room with his sharp eyes. He needed no light to probe the corners where treasures lay shrouded in darkness. Already, a partially opened doorway drew his attention. The servant was still busy when the boy slipped over to peer into the next room. He eyed some of the covered furniture shoved against the back wall. Upon entering, he lifted a sheet to peer at a rustic looking couch, shabby compared to the furnishings seen in the grand hallways.

Maybe they're planning to fix this up for later use. Shame to waste all this. A few other objects scattered in between the covered furniture. Otherwise, there was little else to hold his attention for long. With a sigh, Keith returned to check on Nicolas.

"Find anything?" Keith stepped through the doorway, only to discover the room vacant. "Nicolas?" Keith's brow crinkled in puzzlement. *Maybe he went downstairs.* Then he smiled. "All right, Nicolas. You're inside the wardrobe, aren't you? Very funny." He started to open the doors. "You got me, so you can come," he peered inside, "out."

It was empty.

"But a moment ago there was clothing!" Perplexed, Keith waved a hand through the empty space just to be sure. If stairs could be hidden by illusion, maybe this was too; however, the only thing his hand touched was cobweb, which he brushed on the side of his pants before backing away. "He wouldn't have taken everything and left. That was too much to carry!"

The door in which they had entered was still present, so the boy rushed over and opened it. Bright light made him shield his eyes until they adjusted. Slowly, he lowered his hand and peered around the strange room.

Is this illusion too?

Ahead, sunlight poured in through paladin windows. Bookcases lined nearly every wall, each shelf filled with different sized books. In the room's center was a large desk crowded with papers, inks and quills.

"Hello?"

Keith approached a high-backed chair and sank into its plush seat. *This must be Lord Gracie's chamber.* His gaze continuously swept over the vast room. The quiet location made it a prime place for study, and he began to wonder what was written in the many books.

Something brushed against his leg, and when he looked, a marmalade cat stared up at him with large green eyes. It purred loudly as he reached down to scratch behind one ear.

"Thought I was Lord Gracie, huh?"

In response, the cat jumped upon the desktop. To Keith's surprise, a pair of wings opened to assist in a graceful landing. Fur lightly covered an array of multicolored feathers, fading back to orange near the shoulder. The cat's purr never ceased, and it perched in front of him like an owl, large orbs for eyes watching his every move.

Keith sat back to admire the winged feline. *What other treasures might this place hold?* he wondered. He did not wait long, for the cat spread its multicolored wings to create a semi-circle around its body. Tiny sparks of electricity began gathering in a circle within the limits of the wings' arch. Like the warm light that filtered through the windows, so too did a light begin to glow from the sphere contained within the wings. Various images materialized within this light, and Keith soon recognized his cell companion. The vision panned out to show a small table with a large checkered board. Across from the slave sat Shafari himself.

As Keith continued to watch, a female's voice came not from his thoughts, but within the sphere of light, strong enough that anyone could have heard had they been in the same room.

"You seek a way to help your friend at Castle Mire. He plays an enchanted game with the headmaster with whom he has only to complete within the year to win his freedom."

"And if he doesn't win?" Keith asked, hoping to receive an answer.

"Your friend gambles with his life. The pieces are cursed. One ill turn could be fatal."

"Then Nicolas was right." Keith sighed. "Shafari means to change him into a hound, just like all the rest."

"The headmaster's greed traps him within Castle Mire, and as long as it functions he will remain. His only escape is for the castle to cease routine."

"But how do you stop something that large?"

"There is still time. When you have learned dream-channeling, return to me, and I will show you how to survive the game." The light began to fade, and soon the vision winked out as the cat readjusted its wings so that they rested along the back.

Still mesmerized, Keith thought about what the vision had showed as he watched the cat glide to the floor. Its belly nearly dragged the ground as it rubbed up against his leg. The purring grew ever louder.

"Thank you," he said softly. "I'll get Nicolas to teach me, but if you don't mind, could you show me now?" He glanced around the room. "There's no telling if I'll make it back the same way." He laughed. "I couldn't even see the door to get in."

The cat turned briskly and made for a bowl of water by the window. After lapping a few sips, and with water still dripping from the whiskers, it turned and perched like before on the floor.

A smile touched his lips as he watched those wings open to create the semi-circle around its body.

Don't worry, Lanc. We'll win this game, no matter what it takes!

CHAPTER 11

The cat's words were still fresh in Keith's mind as he scanned the many titles lining the shelves. Behind the first bookcase was another, and so on, until they reached the far wall. It was a wonder at the amount of writing one could put in a book. Curious, he reached to pull one from the shelf, so tightly packed together that they were pushing one another out. While he pressed with a hand to keep them from all coming down on one side, he pulled with his other. Too late, he failed to notice a protruding end book until it slapped the floor with a startling *clap!* It would have gone ignored while struggling with the rest; however, its unusual title drew his attention.

"*Lo-ans'rel*," Keith read. He abandoned his current search, making sure the top shelf was stable enough before picking up the large book. He stared at its cover a long while, as if some meaning stirred in the back of his mind.

He had just flipped to the first page when the main door to the study opened and Lord Gracie entered, a black and white winged cat perched upon his right shoulder. The boy instantly closed the book.

"Ah, here you are." The headmaster rubbed a forefinger under the cat's chin. "Thank you, my friend."

The cat's amber gaze captivated the boy's attention. The same multicolored wings opened, and it leapt from the Grand Master's shoulder in a graceful glide to join the much larger marmalade lazily curled on the window seat.

"I'm...sorry," the boy apologized. "I didn't realize the rooms changed."

"Quite all right, I assure you." The cheery smile across his master's face put any doubts aside. "I see you've met my Lady." He gestured toward the marmalade.

Keith nodded. "She was really helpful."

"They're called Foreseers. It's how I *know* the many happenings here, and with a place this large, the extra sight is useful." He glanced at the book in the boy's arms. "Bit of light reading?" He chuckled, reaching out to take it from him. He ran a finger down the spine, noting no disturbance in the pages. Grinning from ear to ear, he slipped it back on a shelf. "Come, lad. Nicolas eagerly awaits your return."

"I hope he's not disappointed that I left."

"Nonsense!" Lord Gracie led the boy from the room. "He's got everything ready for you, and a bit more."

*****

"He ain't coming back."

Nathaniel's grumbling unnerved the mage, who sat absorbed in one of his notebooks.

"He will return. Of that I can assure you," Jenario replied.

Nathaniel narrowed his eyes and crossed his arms. "You have every confidence in that bird, don't you? That wretched creature was useless. Now you've let him off. Just as well. Feathers everywhere you go."

"They *are* called harpies for a reason."

Casting his gaze beyond the book's contents, the mage stared across the room, eyes unfocused as he planned his next course of action. *The mind of a mage is never at ease. Neither are those who associate with them.* His eyes flicked to Nathaniel, and a malign smile slithered across his face.

An inner voice answered in the void of darkness that flooded his thoughts. *The harpy may come to better use,* it hissed. *Send the assassin in his stead. Bring the boy to us!*

Nathaniel raised a bottle of liquor to his lips, and nearly spewed it out in disgust. With tongue thrashing against his mouth in protest, he examined the various letters written on the side. When he could not decipher the label, he tossed it on a nearby table.

"It's *Eúgliactmaent*," Jenario said with a sigh. "And you'd fair better to place the bottle upright instead of throwing items everywhere." He licked a forefinger before thumbing through a couple of pages, stopping only when something of interest caught his eye.

"Ugly what?" Nathaniel sat up in his chair. When no answer came, he leaned back again. "One of your concoctions, I suppose? Tastes of sour tea." He made a face. Then, thinking better of it, he asked, "Wasn't poison, was it?"

"To you, no. Though it might have taught you a lesson if it had been." Jenario glanced up from reading. "Then perhaps you would at least take note of the words I scribble on the side, and not mix them with your liquor!"

"Oh, so that was *your* chicken scratch." Nathaniel sneered.

"As a matter of fact, it was."

The assassin chuckled. "If you're so concerned, then why not cast a spell so I can decipher the words, or make the words read themselves?"

"Oh!" Jenario balked. "In that case, maybe I could just snap my fingers and make the boy appear before me!"

Nathaniel grinned. "Well, I don't see why you couldn't with all this power you say you have. So much, I thought, that you gave some to that bird of yours. Why *couldn't* you just snap your fingers—"

Jenario suddenly burst into laughter, then held a hand to his forehead to massage his temple.

"You don't think, do you? Corrigan only *believes* he has power," Jenario continued. "And yes, you are correct. I *should* be able to do certain things. But what you don't understand is that there is always a price when dealing with magic. That's why I must be careful with what I have." He slammed the book shut.

Slowly, the reality of Jenario's words sank in Nathaniel's mind.

"Okay," he began slowly. "So...you're telling me he *doesn't* have magic."

The alchemist shook his head. "Corrigan's already attempted several spells. One of which was a storm, complete with thunder and lightning—very easy to create. I know when he wants things because our minds are linked. That, too, was a simple travel-spell placed upon him before his departure. I've followed his movements ever since."

"So you can read his mind?"

Jenario shrugged. "To some degree."

"And these spells – do they go according to what he wants?"

The corners of Jenario's mouth twitched upward.

"Not...always. I wanted to test the boy's abilities. Seems he's stronger than expected, which makes me wonder if he knows what he is." He tapped the side of his temple. "I'll need to learn more, though, before proceeding, which is why that *bird* comes in quite handy."

Nathaniel chuckled. "And if he doesn't do what you want? What then?"

"Oh, not to worry. I believe he'll find me quite...*persuasive*."

*****

"Dream-channeling's not hard to do," Nicolas explained as he sat across from Keith in the private lounge. "A lesser magic-user, such as myself, can accomplish short distances. The stronger you are, however, the greater the distance of communication."

"So how does it work?" Keith hurriedly asked, but the servant held up a finger for patience.

"Now remember, Keith. You can't rush these things. I know you're trying to help your friend, but you'll need plenty of practice before you're ready for long distances."

Keith slowly nodded.

"Yes, sir," he replied in a dull tone.

Nicolas smiled in understanding, then held out his hand, palm up.

"Place your fingertips overtop mine."

Keith did as requested.

"Now relax. Close your eyes and take a deep breath. That's it. Just focus on keeping a steady breath."

It felt strange to Keith as his fingers lightly touched the servant's. He tried not to move, keeping to a placid rhythm that was comfortable enough to pay attention.

Nicolas closed his eyes, sending his thoughts into the mind of the boy. Startled by the sudden intrusion, Keith's breath quickened.

Calm down! Nicolas commanded through his thoughts. It took a moment before the boy's mind settled. *That's better. Now, the most important thing about dream-channeling is that the other person must be asleep, so...*

But wouldn't that mean that one of us has to be sleeping then?

A chuckle.

Quite. We'll start out simple. I will cast a small spell upon myself to sleep for a short period. While I sleep, I should be able to still communicate with you.

That's all there is to it?

That, and the fact that you can send images, or dreams, into the other person's mind. You can also create nightmares.

Really?

Um...well, we'll get to that later. Start simple.

Okay. Keith laughed. *Do I really need to be touching you?* Nicolas squeezed the boy's hand.

No. But since dream-channeling is supposed to work over distances, you wouldn't be touching anything except with your mind. Having said that, are you ready to begin?

Yes.

With a slight nod, Nicolas spoke softly to himself. The words rolled off his tongue in a graceful dance, and Keith listened intently to each word. Again, he repeated the chant. It was halfway completed when his words fell silent. Keith opened his eyes to check on him, only to hear a soft snore escape his lips. Closing his eyes again, Keith sent a mental probe into his friend's mind.

Nicolas?

A long tunnel of thought stretched into darkness. Bizarre lights flashed by his presence. The mind of a sleeper was not a friendly place. Every shadow held a potential dream ready to surface into reality, and every reality became intertwined with fiction. Facts questioned themselves. Myths found truth and were believed. Keith passed all this, searching for his friend's true identity.

"I've never read a mind like this before. What makes it so different?"

"Dreams, lad," the voice of Nicolas echoed in and out of his subconscious.

Keith shuddered. Ahead of him he spotted the slender form of the servant, slightly warped as visions faded in and out around him.

"Is that you, Nicolas? What's happening?"

"In the mind, things aren't as they seem."

"But I'm not asleep. Should I be seeing any of this?"

"It depends on where you are in a person's mind, and what type of mind that person has. I cannot decipher what I see."

"Can you see me?" Keith asked.

"Not yet. You must think of something for me to see in order for my mind to find you. Your thoughts are difficult to follow."

Thinking quickly, Keith conjured an image of himself the best he could, and suddenly he was there.

Or at least I feel here, Keith thought. *I can see inside his mind like I'm seeing a normal person. Am I sure I'm not also sleeping?*

"Much better," Nicolas answered, stepping toward the boy. *"How are you liking inside a dream world?"*

"It's...different," Keith replied. "Am I not dreaming as well? I can actually 'see' you, but my eyes aren't open. How is that possible? Before when I connected to minds, I saw nothing."

"Dream-channeling shows you things what sight-reading cannot offer. You can see things because you're allowing a part of your subconscious to awaken. So...in a way, you *are* dreaming."

"So this is what happens when I connect to other minds? I'll see what they're dreaming?"

"And you'll be able to send your own dreams as well."

Outside his mind, Keith could hear the snores lessen, and the dream-filled world of thought began to flicker, then slowly dim.

Nicolas?

Keith opened his eyes after retrieving his mental probe. His own mind was still filled with the fresh thoughts of his friend still lingering in rainbow fields of shrouded darkness. It was both wonderful and terrifying, but something he knew he would have to do over and over in order to save his friend.

And possibly Shafari, Keith realized. *Lady had said he was trapped in his own greed. But how do you stop a multi-level castle from functioning, complete with guards and hounds and so much more? And the documents Lord Gracie mentioned? They'll all have to be destroyed.*

A droopy-eyed Nicolas gradually awoke, and he raised his head to focus on the boy once more.

"Wh–where were we?" he stuttered a moment, trying to recollect his train of thoughts. "Ah, dream-channeling! Do you understand how it works now?"

"It's all that dream stuff that gets to me," Keith said nervously. "Things moving around in shadow, and when you try to focus, it disappears!"

"Just remember, Keith. It's all in the mind. There's nothing a person can do to you while they're sleeping."

"But if I can conjure things for them to see, can't they do the same to me?"

"Possibly." Nicolas nodded. "It's something you have to get used to. I don't use it very often, so I'm not that accustomed to seeing much in people's minds." He chortled. "Don't want to see it either. Daily events affect how people dream when they sleep, and you have to watch out that you're not still lingering in a person's mind when they wake, especially if they're not expecting you. But we'll leave that for mind-reading purposes. What you're trying to do is sight-read."

"I thought sight-reading was hearing what other people thought?" Keith asked. "What I'm doing is delivering a message."

"But you're still not probing a person's mind too far to get trapped between their mental barriers if they should wake. See the difference?"

Keith sighed. "I suppose."

Rising from his chair, Nicolas stretched and yawned.

"Now I'm feeling sleepy." He smiled wearily. "That's the thing with these silly charms. They can make you want to sleep after you've just finished waking!"

CHAPTER 12

The feathered mattress sank under Lancheshire's weight, forming a mold that held his body in complete comfort. The cramped bunks were too small to stretch out and relax, and there was always someone snoring in the next cell over, not to mention the constant yapping of hounds near each entrance.

The wonders yer own room can do, the slave thought pleasantly. Yet his thoughts were not entirely pacified by the riches of the room, nor the downy mattress and pillows. There was always something bothering him, something that kept him from total rest each night. *It's getting worse. I feel like every part of me is being manipulated.* Wearily, he rolled over to stare at the ceiling.

It's the game...

The game controlled everyone who came to Castle Mire. Everyone knew of it, even down to the youngest member. There was no escaping the way the game was set up, for every person who came was automatically included. It was never-ending, with no beginning to go back to, no redoes, no mistakes. Once lost, there was no one to take the place of the fallen. It only began where it left off, but with a different set of rules and a different way of playing. Even the guards played. They too could lose, though it never counted as a win to slaves.

Lancheshire played his hardest, harder than ever now that too few pieces remained on the board. As much as the slave hated to believe, he knew that in the long run he would probably wind up losing to the headmaster. *And remain a slave forever...or worse.*

Overwhelming dread slowly etched into a checkered board of dream-filled sleep. Turning over, he pulled the sheets over his frail form. He had lost weight, his intellect taxing not only rest but also his stomach. For many nights he had refused both food and drink, determining to come up with a solution to avoid the game at all costs.

Empty...the barrier...no one there...

Lancheshire slept with the knowledge that one of his kings had been taken. He had only one other while Shafari still had two, and both were pointed toward his final stand.

*****

Keith sat cross-legged in bed, his eyes closed in concentration as his mind reached tranquility. For many nights he practiced dream-channeling. Each time he let his mental probe advance farther from Luxor until he was confident he could master the distance without becoming too tired.

Like he had practiced, he heard only what his mental probe sought. He reached into individual minds, passing in and out of conscious thoughts and images. He had to be quick, for time was against him at such a distance. Already, he could feel his strength ebbing away every moment that passed.

I've got time.

He passed through the mind of a guard as his probe trailed along a tunnel of light and visions. The way to Castle Mire was not precisely clear. Here and there a dim white glow trailed off, like an overgrown pathway just discovered after years of solitude. Each turn on the path met a separate mind, a guide to which he could use to determine his location.

The guard's mind he had felt at the entrance led him through a maze of ghoulish illusions in the sleep-filled cells. The hounds were the worst. Keith sensed his body cringe through each one. In their minds, they were not hideous beasts with long fangs and dripping saliva, but humans, most of which recently selected. In horror, Keith watched as the headmaster extended his hand in slow motion, his accursed chanting binding each slave before repulsively mutating them. He saw the flesh and muscle melt away, leaving the bone to grind into its new shape.

Keith moved on, relieved Lancheshire was not among them, and worked his way to the upper levels.

Where is he?

He paused, his probe hovering on the outskirts of sanity. It was the mind of a middle-aged male. Upon entering, Keith was stunned at all the voices floating in every direction. Some faded in and out, echoing softly in the background. Others screamed to be recognized, ones that had been freshly created and were remembering what to do when used. And yet, though all the voices spoke differently, they were all the same person, and could only mean one individual.

*Shafari...*Keith grit his teeth. *No other person dreams of incantations in their sleep.* He nearly laughed. *Lady told me his next moves were for the king. I can't believe Lancheshire has survived as long as he has!*

Keith retreated to the next room and entered the thoughts of Leventés. Dreams of flight through sunlit skies quickly faded into the gloom of thrashing bodies and cracking whips.

Keith's ebbing strength tugged at the back of his mind, and he quickly pulled away into the next room. *Even if I don't get a chance to talk to him, just so I know he's all right.*

A black figure with no face slipped past him in a world of troubled shadows. The boy pressed on, searching deeper for an identity. Gold and silver lay over soft earth. The black figure returned, slightly hovering over the ground. In a way, it slightly resembled Blackavar.

Suddenly, the soil shifted and all went black. White sprouted forth into a patterned haze mixed with ebony and white marble. Stone statues moved accordingly, thrust aside by a gigantic hand. Keith dodged a pawn that scraped along the checkered board. Laughter eluded him, and when Keith glanced up he saw the grinning face of the headmaster.

"Lancheshire!" Keith cried out. *"Lancheshire, it's me, Keith! Can you hear me?"*

"There's no one here, little boy!" the still-grinning headmaster answered. *"There's only the game. You must know of the game!"*

"Lancheshire, I know how you can defeat Shafari, but you have to listen to me!" Keith tried again.

Colors swirled around him. The grinning face vanished, replaced by a solitary figure. A green slime oozed from the ground, slowing Keith's approach. Again, he called his friend's name.

"Keith?" a frail, haggard voice spoke in the darkness. The figure came toward him. *"Is that you?"*

"Lancheshire!" Keith rushed toward him, but seemed to get farther away with each step. The harder he ran, the slower everything became. *"It's your dreams! You're slowing me!"*

"I dreamed of ye last night," Lancheshire whispered, slightly swaying from side to side.

"What's happened to you?" Keith asked. *"Is Shafari starving you?"*

"I've given up," Lancheshire answered without emotion.

Keith sought his eyes, but found only two hollow sockets. His face was deathly pale.

"I can help you! I know Shafari's next moves!"

"Ain't no use, Keith. He's already won, so close now that I might as well let him."

"*But if you lose, he'll change you into a hound. I've read their minds. They're slaves!*"

Keith winced as a sharp pain shot through his head.

"*This ain't real, is it? Ain't ye a dream?*"

"*No, my friend,*" Keith replied. "*It's real. I'm using my magic, but I don't have much time. Now listen! When Shafari makes his next move, stay all the way to the left. Use the leftover pawn. Take out his last bishop. He won't suspect it because he'll get too cocky and have to call it a day. He'll be angry with you, but you mustn't give in!*"

"*Stay to the left.*" Hope reentered his voice. "*Then what?*"

"*You have to intersect him. Don't try running.*"

"*Ain't much to use for that kind of tactic. What'll happen if I sacrifice all I've got for nothing?*"

"*You've still got your king,*" Keith responded. "*Your king can kill too, you know. Trust me on this.*" His head began to throb. "*I have to leave now, but don't worry. I'll return tomorrow night.*"

He never received a response. Memory and time faded. A haze of visions flashed before him. Even after he had retrieved his mental probe, they lingered until the room spun in a swirl of light and shadow and faded into his own dream world of darkness.

CHAPTER 13

The world is full of those who don't know anything, and those few that do are left out... Ah, well.

Corrigan slipped down the hallway under the cover of shadow. Rays of moonlight streamed in through windows along the upper walls, though it mattered little to one whose wings matched the night. Even a passing servant on his nightly rounds failed to notice him.

The boy's bedroom was only a few feet ahead. A stray moonbeam from a slit in the wall flecked the door handle, which turned without a sound. He found Keith lightly snoring in bed where he had passed out earlier.

It was the perfect moment, he reasoned. In a matter of moments, Jenario could have his specimen, and none would be the wiser. *No!* Corrigan shook his head. *I must know for certain if he's truly one of them.*

Corrigan gently shook the boy's shoulder. When there was no response, he shook harder.

"Is it morning yet?" Keith answered in a weak whisper, still exhausted from dream-channeling.

The Black Wing stepped back to examine him.

"What's the matter with you?" he snarled. "Too much for a slave to do nothing all day except explore?" He waved the comment aside when Keith stared at him in question. "Never mind! I need you do something for me."

"What?" Droopy-eyed, Keith sat up.

"Remember the White Wing, the one with the broken wing?"

"How could I forget?" Keith rubbed his eyes. "I was right there when it happened!"

"Calm down." Corrigan cracked a smile and raised his hands in defense. "I didn't mean nothing by it. I just need a little favor."

"At this hour? How much longer before sunrise?" Keith glanced out the bedroom window.

"There's plenty of time to catch your precious beauty sleep!" Corrigan sneered. "Listen! I've been watching you. Ever since the day we first met, I've seen how your powers have grown."

"I'm still learning," Keith admitted.

"But you should have the ability to do it; I'm sure by now."

"Do what?" Keith spoke in between yawns. "What are you talking about?"

Corrigan studied the boy more carefully, then took a deep breath.

"You're a Healer, Keith."

Silence, then, "Come again?"

Corrigan rolled his eyes. "What's there to explain about healing? You *heal!* I know this! My family lives right above your kind."

"I don't understand. What 'kind' are you referring? I'm just a simple magic-user. Are you saying there's a race of different magic-users? I wouldn't be one of them."

"You think?" Corrigan frowned. "Come with me."

Keith watched as the Black Wing extended a clawed hand.

"Wh...where are we going?" Keith hesitated

"To the White Wing. I sort of promised him he could be healed."

"You told someone I could heal when I've never done it?" He lowered his voice. "How do you know this is what I am?"

Corrigan snickered. "Hey, I'm half animal too, ya know." He offered his hand again. "Call it instinct."

After some consideration, Keith carefully took his hand and allowed himself to be pulled close under the large feathers.

"My wings will conceal us from anyone who happens to be lingering at this hour. As it was, I *did* happen to pass a few late-nighters on the way here."

"What if I can't heal?" Keith murmured. "What if I'm not what you think?"

Corrigan glanced down at Keith's small frame and pale features. Yet it was his eyes that drew his attention, as bright as precious stones when the light hit them just right.

No human has eyes like that.

"Trust me, Keith." He smiled, but this time there was no hint of sarcasm.

The two moved stealthily across the floor with Keith nestled comfortably between his wings. The boy clung to his waist while his host moved with incredible speed through the corridors, pausing every once in a while to scan for guards. He took the right-hand passage, keeping to the shadows as he pressed his back to the wall. Beams of moonlight streamed from above, though they were safe from its penetrating rays as it only touched the upper parts.

Corrigan paused at the sound of footsteps and crouched low, pressing himself further into the shadows until he had become one himself.

Keith held his breath as the steps drew closer, and he felt the harpy tense. The footsteps paused, and for a second Keith thought they had been spotted. Whatever caught the servant's fancy, however, did not hold long, for he soon passed. Only after his footsteps had faded down the corridor did the harpy start moving again, with only one other encounter. At a flight of stairs Corrigan paused, then released the boy. He beckoned to the stairwell.

"This way," he said, allowing Keith to go first.

When they reached the top, the Black Wing pointed at a bare wall across the hall.

"Through there," he said.

"Is he *that* bad to be kept secret?" Keith grimaced.

"Could be." Corrigan felt along the wall. A smile indicated when he had found what he sought. Extending a talon, he inserted it as though a keyhole were present. There came a faint click. "If I were pure-blooded, this trick wouldn't have worked. Pure-blooded Black Wings are much larger than any '*Ken*' you've encountered." Corrigan snickered. He braced his body against the door and slid it to one side.

"How did you know where to find it?" Keith inquired.

"Saw some of the servants enter one day and thought I'd investigate." He motioned for Keith to enter. "After you."

The room was dim with only two candles by the bedside. Keith noted a tending servant asleep in one corner before advancing to the bed. The sound of labored breathing greeted him, and he turned to Corrigan with worried expression.

"He doesn't look good."

The Black Wing shook his head. "He knows he'll never fly again. Not with his wing like that."

"Should I wake him?"

Corrigan looked skeptical.

"I suppose it might be best, but keep him quiet. We don't want the other to wake."

"That's easy enough." Keith walked around the side of the bed where the broken wing lay. "Megas?" He touched the harpy's shoulder.

The labored breathing subsided, and jade eyes slowly opened.

"Who—" he began, but Keith squeezed his hand.

"It's Keith. Remember me? Nicolas was bringing me here when the storm came. I...I saved you."

"Hardly," Corrigan grumbled.

"So you're..." a fit of coughing interrupted, "...the Healer..."

"In truth, I don't know." Keith pointed to Corrigan standing to one side. "My friend seems to think so, but I've never attempted it. I know a few things from what my mother used to show me, but as far as healing...I wouldn't even know how to begin."

Megas gazed at Keith. It was the face of a boy growing into his first years as young adult. Besides his unusual pale appearance, he seemed every bit like a normal being. Yet it was the eyes that drew his attention. He had seen eyes like that before, someplace where only those of magical abilities knew how to find. Though Megas himself had no power, he knew such a place and had seen *them*. It was that particular race that had made *No'va*, and as long as they existed, so *No'va* would itself. It was in those very eyes that Megas knew, and in that moment alone that he felt the power within. Quickly, he averted his gaze.

"You are," he hesitated, and his gaze fell upon Corrigan, who frowned and slightly shook his head, "a very gifted young man. I believe you can heal...if you believe in your strengths."

Keith glanced at Corrigan, who nodded.

Gently, the boy removed the gauze. The sight of torn flesh and feathers made him gag.

"I heard Lord Gracie suggest its removal," Megas said in a low tone. He closed his eyes while Keith slowly pulled the wing open.

The separation came at the joint. Where bone should have been, now a gap remained. Keith found he had to hold the wing up himself because the muscles had been severed. It was a pitiful sight. Even without reading minds, Keith knew Megas dreaded the loss of flight. He recalled how happy the White Wing had been on their first encounter, leading the carriage to and from Luxor Castle. Now, with bowed head, Keith placed a hand over the wound. Not sure how to begin, he called upon his magic... and waited.

He stood there for some time, the hope of healing diminishing every moment that passed. The magic was there. He could feel it, had called to

Nature and felt her stirring deep within his blood, around the room and in the various plants that adorned every corner. They stretched their leaves out to him, offering as much energy as possible. It collected in the air, like a swarm of gnats, then gathered around the boy to which only he could see and feel. His fingers tingled as the magic began to work its way into the wound.

Keith could have cried out for joy. It was working! Then he paused and watched in puzzlement while some of his magic was repelled by a different energy, one that glowed crimson when touched. Curious, Keith moved his hand where he had seen the red glow and opened his mind to the source of its containment. It was there that a trail of negative energy lead deeper into the mind, and while Keith was hesitant to enter without proper training, he knew if he did not the wing would be lost.

The room around him became a blur as he sent a mental probe into the White Wing's mind, hoping he was not detected. Deep was his connection, enough to block everything else out, even the motion of someone approaching from behind.

*****

Corrigan felt Jenario slip into his thoughts.

What is it you want now, mage?

His back is turned. He is powerless to stop you.

What are you going on about? Corrigan preened a couple of feathers while keeping a watchful eye on the boy. *I just wanted to test his abilities.*

Now is your chance! Take him now!

Corrigan ignored the comment and continued to preen.

You disappoint me, came a hiss.

Corrigan backed away from the bed when he recognized the change in voice.

You will take him. I will make you.

*****

What is this? Keith followed the trail deeper, mindful of mental barriers thrust here and there. *Is it a spell?*

Spells come in many forms, the voice of Nature flooded his thoughts. *A spell of this type leaves a trail to its source.*

I can't keep going into the mind like this! Keith thought desperately. *I may not come out!*

I will guide you.

Keith felt himself pulling out as his magic traced the glowing strand into a void of gray haze.

"It's like dream-channeling!" Keith stared at the mental projection of his hands. He brushed them across the haze to clear a view. Land opened below as his thoughts traveled quickly, defying space and time toward its source. "What is this place?" he wondered as they started descending toward a castle surrounded by a dark forest.

The haze vanished into a swirl of darkness. He recognized the beginning of another mind approaching and braced himself while his mental probe entered. Warped images drifted past. A streak of gold and silver shimmered across the tip of a blade, drawing memories from years ago when his father was struck by the same weapon.

Could this be...?

A dark figure dressed in a sable robe glided across his line of vision.

Jenario?

The silent body paused as though sensing someone. A red glow pulsed around his form. The figure warped, resembling a horse like creature rather than human.

The trail!

Keith watched it wrap around the animal. Carefully, Keith directed his probe around to where the figure's attention was drawn. A wavering image of Corrigan materialized. As the figure moved, so did Corrigan. An image of himself standing beside the White Wing appeared before the two. The shadow raised his hands. Corrigan raised his and reached for Keith.

Keith gasped when he realized what was happening. Jenario was controlling Corrigan, and he was aiming straight for *him*!

"You!" Keith's outburst shook Jenario's mind. He was almost certain he heard a scream as he withdrew through the void of gray haze. Lights and images blurred until he finally came to and twisted around to catch Corrigan's outstretched hand.

"Leave me alone..." Keith whispered in unison with Nature's power coursing through his body. A single thought threw the harpy back. There was a smack of body hitting the wall, with enough force to wake the servant. Shocked beyond belief, he scrambled from the room.

Keith took a step back as though seeing the room for the first time. His mind felt hazy and numb. He staggered back while Megas called his name in alarm.

Forgetting his pain, the White Wing darted from bed to stop the boy from falling.

In the corner Corrigan groaned and slowly pulled himself up.

"What was that about!" Megas demanded, holding Keith protectively against his feathered breast.

Corrigan rubbed his aching head. The voice was gone…for now.

"I'm fine." Keith rubbed his temple. "Just a little tired."

The Black Wing coughed and wiped blood from his lips where he had bitten the skin.

Voices shouted from the hallway before several guards burst through the open door. Lord Gracie followed behind in his nightgown and slippers, too hurried to grab a robe.

"Now what is all this fuss about?" Lord Gracie demanded, keeping his tone calm. His gaze quickly fell to Megas.

"What's happened?" Nicolas' voice carried from the hallway. Like the guards, he too rushed inside, only to stop short and stare at the harpy's newly healed plumage. "Your wing!"

Megas drew a blank. He glanced at his wing and carefully raised it. It opened smoothly, the feathers flowing properly over the place where nothing had been a moment ago.

"By *No'va*, he did it," he whispered.

Keith glanced up at the wing, but said nothing. The image of what he now knew remained fresh in his thoughts, and he intended to keep it that way.

"What magic is this?" One of the guards questioned. "Surely, not the boy."

Keith felt the White Wing release him, and he stepped forward.

"I think he'll be all right now," he said. "But if you would please excuse me, sir, I would like to return to bed," he glanced over at Corrigan before continuing, "*without* being disturbed."

Corrigan did not meet his gaze.

"You!" Nicolas gestured to the Black Wing. "You best explain yourself for this!"

Lord Gracie just shook his head, and waved a hand to end the conversation.

"I don't believe he's a threat." Just outside the door, a Foreseer poked its head around the corner, catching the headmaster's gaze. The corner of the Grand Master's lips lifted in a secretive smile. "Not now at least."

*****

A change of wind hinted the use of magic. Chronicles closed his eyes, the feel of energy moving beneath the soles of his bare feet. It was the same energy his people used for shifting. Nature always provided it. Yet it puzzled him why it pulled elsewhere, away from the clan. His questioning thoughts soon joined with his advisor not far away.

It's not from an outcast, is it? Eumaeus inquired.

No. Chronicles folded his hands together behind his back. He stood tall against the pale rays of moonlight streaming around him. *Half-breeds have no power over Nature.*

What of Windchester? He is no half-breed.

But an outcast no less. No, this amount of power can only be summoned by a person connected to Nature, someone... who is One.

CHAPTER 14

Fall quickly came and went, spreading color through the trees like wildfire. Now bare limbs carried the weight of freshly fallen snow. It was the eve of a new year, and Luxor Castle was alive with the scent of spiced cooking and festivities. To the regulars who came and went, this was nothing new. It was just another routine set aside for yearly changes.

To Keith, however, change was just the beginning.

During the course of the year he experimented more with his magic, which sometimes ended with unexpected results. Such was the time he tried to levitate a bowl of water and splashed it all over himself. At all times could he feel the presence of Nature, and he was reassured that whenever he need it he had only to ask.

He made sure he was alone when practicing his magic, sometimes in the garden when it was too cold for White Wings to fly, or in his room. No one ever bothered or questioned his doings. As one of Lord Gracie's servants he was only required to keep a section of rooms clean and help whenever needed with some of the banquets.

His expanding wisdom in many subjects he studied from Lord Gracie's history books made him a prized member at Luxor. Yet of all changes it was his appearance that stunned him, even Lord Gracie. Through the course of several months, Keith gained in height. From a frail looking boy, Keith surpassed the teenage stage and went straight for a young man's appearance, enduring Megas' light tease that he outgrew his bed in one night.

Now at sixteen years Keith gazed into the mirror, admiring and welcoming the new look. A few bangs fell over his brow while the rest was kept trimmed to the top of his shoulders. He laid aside his old clothing and pulled on his best tunic and vest. Around his neck he hung the feather, which was tucked beneath his shirt collar. To be seen with feathers meant servitude, and for once Keith wished he still had his mother's necklace to wear instead. That, at least would have been better with his evening garment. The thought of the necklace brought back memories of his mother. He thought of his friends he had made from the Thieves' Guild and Castle Mire. Yet of all his friendships, he felt alone.

If only there was someone like me, someone who also talks to voices, or even heals!

It's more than just speaking to voices, lad. A mind linked with his.

Keith looked around, using his sensitive ears to pinpoint a location of the individual. The voice in his mind chuckled.

You won't find me that way. It was not a mocking tone, as he was used to with Corrigan.

Who are you? Keith thought back.

In response, something shimmered toward the front of the room. Keith stood back as an oval-shaped substance materialized. The opening surface acted like a mirror, reflecting his startled appearance even though he could still see through. He touched it, then pulled back when his fingers broke the surface like a drop of water, sending ripples and reflections into scattered patterns.

Don't be alarmed, Keith heard. *It's a portal, not like the ones on the second floor. Those you can't see since they're disguised within the surroundings.*

The portal's transparency clouded over while a new scene materialized in its place until the young man was staring into another room. The interior was trimmed in rich mahogany, cast in golden light from a nearby fireplace. In front of the fire sat a black cat, its wings curving across its backside. Upon seeing the young man, it rose and spread its wings in a stretch. Patches of multicolored specs shimmered on the feathers when light hit them. As Keith watched, the animal trotted toward him and extended its forelegs into a leap.

A strange sensation numbed Keith's mind. While the cat's body leaned into a dive, the room began to spin and merge. A sudden light blocked everything out. When it cleared, Keith lowered his hands from his face. No longer was he in his bedroom, but the room seen through the portal. He spun around in wide-eyed amazement when he realized he now stood in the cat's spot by the fireplace.

Before him, the portal wavered in the center of the room just as the cat broke through the center. As its body cleared, it rippled like the portal's surface until it took human form.

"How did you do that?" Keith asked. "I didn't think Foreseers had other magic."

A smile spread across the man's face.

"Unless I'm not a Foreseer at all," he answered, stepping around the young man to study him. Likewise, Keith eyed the gold and green trimmed robe sweeping around his feet. Dark hair had been pulled into a ponytail, with a few loose entrails falling to his shoulders. Yet it was his ears that drew the young man's attention most. Not round like humans', these resembled an animal. Soft fuzz covered each one, darkening at the tips, and Keith was surprised when one actually moved.

The young man took a step back, mindful of the fireplace.

"Easy, lad," the man raised his hands to show they were empty. "I know this is all a bit strange right now, but I assure you. You're at no risk here."

"Who are you?" After a moment, he added. "*What* are you?"

The man chuckled and took a deep bow.

"Master Providence." He pointed to his ears. "You like?" He flicked one forward. "Perhaps I should show you yours?"

"Mine?" Keith followed his pointed finger toward the mirrored surface of the portal.

"Your mother knew she had to keep you safe," Providence waved a hand over each of the young man's ears, "so she used an illusion spell to hide them."

Keith's eyes widened at the sight of pointed ears. It was easier to feel them move without the illusion. He flicked an ear toward Providence, his voice suddenly clearer and stronger with each movement.

"Surprised?" Providence watched with amusement as Keith continued to test his ears.

"How is this possible?" He turned to the older man. "Am I not human?"

"You're more than human, Keith. You're a Healer, and Healers aren't your average magic-user." He leaned close. "You and I...we're *Lo-ans'rel*."

Keith repeated the word several times, excitement rising in his voice. *Lo-ans'rel*, as Providence explained, had only to accept a small drop of blood from an animal to acquire its form.

"You'll need proper training, of course," he warned. "Taking too many forms can corrupt your blood. But we can discuss all this at a later time. There's something more important you need to know."

At a gesture, Keith took a seat next to the fireplace, bathing in its golden glow.

"Now I know you miss your family, especially your mother." He watched the young man's expression darken. "Your thoughts dwell on her constantly. But do not despair. You still have family, and I'll be the first to announce that I'm one of them."

"A true family member, or just part of a clan?" Keith clung to the edge of the cushioned chair.

"True." He stepped over to a chair across from Keith and tucked his robe under him as he sat. "I have no doubt your mother meant to tell you, so I will do what I can to fill in her place." He cleared his throat. "There was a time before you were born when no humans existed. At that particular time, I was head of the clan, distinguished, admired. Things were good back then.

"When humans arrived, everything changed. I'm still ashamed to admit I fell in love with a human female." Providence sighed. "I never told my son, Chronicles, that he was a half-breed. Perhaps if I did, he would have understood my decision to deny him leadership after my... *sudden departure*. I gave that to Windchester, your mother's father, though in the end my son took over anyway."

Providence let his shoulders slump. Across from him, Keith listened intently.

"I left long before that, too embarrassed to face the truth." He spread his arms. "So I came here."

"So how did my mother come to live with humans?" Keith asked. "Why didn't she stay with the clan?"

Providence sighed. "From what Windchester told me, my son wanted Greverlend." He shook his head. "She was a prize for any young man at the time. So beautiful."

Even before the words could reach Providence's lips, Keith heard the thought.

Chronicles is my father!

Providence nodded once. "So now you know how I'm related, but it doesn't just end there."

"There was a conflict," Keith replied as more thoughts came. "Between us and humans? Why?"

"Because your father couldn't keep relations like Windchester could!" An animal growl erupted from his throat. "Like myself, more became...involved...with humans. As you can imagine, those born were no longer pure. It disgusted Chronicles! So he forced all half-breeds to leave the clan, including your mother when she refused to have him. I helped Windchester find his daughter a better place to live. Thus, that's how she met your stepfather. The rest of the clan moved elsewhere. Needless to say, Chronicles has burned into their minds that they are superior to everyone else."

"He thinks he's pure," Keith replied. "Am I?"

Providence nodded. "Albinos are always pure. Comes from your mother's side."

"There are more like me?"

"In the past there were." Providence rose from his seat. "But for now, that's about all the history I can give. I'll have to teach you that transportation spell sometime. It's quite easy." He motioned for Keith to stand. With a wave of his hand, he returned the illusion to cover the young man's ears. "You'll be needing that."

"Do I have to go back?" Keith's eyes pleaded. "I hate being a slave." He felt his grandfather's strong arms embrace him in a hug.

"Shafari's curse upon the slave documents would find you," Providence whispered in his ear, then pulled away. "But I have faith that you will break from it someday. Just remember what you are. Nature will always be there for you, as will I."

He guided Keith back to the awaiting portal.

"Better get going. The banquet's about to start."

"Are you coming too?" Keith asked, pausing in front of the rippling surface. The image of his bedroom opened on the other side.

"How else do you think I survive?" Providence crossed his arms. "Besides, I enjoy the company, something Foreseers don't always provide."

CHAPTER 15

Luxor Castle loomed above the mass of clouds, an image of splendor and mystery. When hit by the setting sun, its white stone briskly reflected golden rays in between the changing cloud formations. A constant breeze whisked a few puffs over the entrance, temporarily veiling its location from an approaching carriage pulled by two dark pegasi. As the carriage drew near, a growing darkness washed over the sun, drowning out its warmth until a clinging chill hung in the air.

Two guards stepped forward at the carriage's approach. The horses whinnied in eerie unison as their hoofs skidded on the icy path before coming to a stop. A heavily cloaked passenger departed, and the guards greeted their guest with spears turned down. While being led inside, the traveler removed the dark green hood, revealing short hair to match his eye color. Despite an unshaven appearance, he was otherwise well kept.

"Good afternoon," Lord Gracie greeted the new arrival. "I hope your journey was pleasant," he continued as they stepped into one of the grand ballrooms. Banners swept across the high domed ceilings in elegant arrangements, which drew his guest's eye to its fine detail.

"Having your yearly banquet, I'm assuming," was the reply. There was no need to mention food at this point. Its contents drifted in and out of the hallways, pleasantly conjuring images of what wonders awaited at mealtime.

"Ah, yes." Lord Gracie dipped his head. "Business as usual. But what of yourself? I don't forget faces so easily, but yours is unfamiliar."

The stranger chuckled.

"Mine, yes, but my partner you *do* know. I regret to say he could not make the journey with me, and instead asked me to carry a message to you."

"Oh?" The headmaster's smile never dimmed. He studied his guest, paying particularly close attention to his voice. It seemed a bit constrained, as though he had memorized his conversations beforehand, stuttering here and there on certain words, and only gained momentum when he was comfortable. "What message is that, and the name of your partner?"

"The message? Simply an interest in one of your slaves. The name is Jenario Onyx."

The headmaster's smile vanished almost before the last name was pronounced.

"Jenario..." he breathed in a husky tone. His gaze fixated onto the stranger's face, taking in his every movement, flesh tone, every pore and hair follicle, stripping him of any false barrier until there was none left to critique. "I had hoped he might change from this...*need*...to grasp power. Seems the company he keeps is no better."

"I'm flattered," the stranger mocked.

Lord Gracie noticed the fingers of his guest twitch ever so slightly, curling around emptiness at his leather belt as though trying to grasp the hilt of a sword, but with nothing to grasp they were left itching for something to hold. It was a small gesture compared to the rest of his composed form, though not small enough to go unnoticed.

"If you please, my private chamber is this way where we can further discuss your message," the headmaster said. "After you." He gestured down the corridor.

"Obliged."

"And if you don't mind, your name please?"

"Nathaniel Woodston."

"A name easily forgotten."

A faint chuckle passed the traveler's lips as he stepped alongside the headmaster.

"Oh, believe me. It's usually the *last* thing remembered."

Lord Gracie could not help but glance sidelong at his still-curling fingers, and he realized that they were not trying to grasp his belt. They were loosening something within the sleeve.

*****

Keith made final adjustments to his new set of clothing before heading out to the banquet located in the grand ballroom. Arriving guests were beginning to trickle in as he entered through a set of arched doors. An array of decorations cast many a gaze toward the grand ceiling.

"A sight to behold, isn't it?" Nicolas joined the young man. "Most of the decorations were done last night while you were asleep."

"I said I would help with those."

"Not to worry," Nicolas said. "Lord Gracie meant for you to be one of his guests today, not just a servant."

Keith eyed two long tables near the back wall filled to the point of overflowing with food. One of the tables contained the main course. The young man let his eyes take in the menu's finest: turkey, stuffed hog with an apple in its mouth, rabbit, venison, and quail. Everything had been garnished to perfection, though it was the vegetables that held his fancy. Keith's mouth watered at the sight of steamed potatoes, peeled and sliced, surrounded by steamed broccoli, carrots and onions all mixed together. There was cauliflower and several cabbages, zucchini, squash, and a mix of lettuces, turnips, and spinach. Further down the table was bread, along with several jams and crackers. Then there were the desserts, all waiting in cake-sized servings.

Nicolas leaned close. "They say that Luxor expands to accommodate the multitude of guests it receives."

Keith peered around the room in awe. "Will I see the walls move?"

The servant chuckled. "You'll probably start noticing more space before you see anything move."

A set of steps brought the two onto the main floor, shared by a grand staircase that lead to a second floor balcony. A small alcove off to the side drew his attention. Curiously, Keith walked over to inspect it. In this room, a long table contained some of the same food, a treat made just for the servants that would come with their masters that night.

"You don't have to stay in here if you don't want to," Nicolas said. "Right now, you don't look like a servant, so you'll be free to mingle among the guests." He raised a finger. "Just be on your best behavior."

"Yes, mother," Keith teased.

With those words said, the young man was left to enjoy. He eyed some of the food. After a quick glance around the room, he dipped a finger into the icing of a white frosted cake.

At least I get to eat like I'm free!

A few more guests wandered in, and Keith greeted them politely as though he were one himself. He could hear a great many approaching from the hallway and decided it best to stay on the outskirts of the room. An open balcony provided a brisk breeze that ruffled his hair when he stepped outside. The setting sun had been replaced by a pale moon through the misted clouds, so close he felt he could reach out and touch its glowing surface.

"To walk in darkness is not always the best intentions," came a low voice from behind, and the young man turned to spot Corrigan on the edge of the roof, his knees drawn up under him in a crouched position. The Black Wing gazed down at Keith and smiled faintly. "Full moons are best for hunting. Nothing escapes my sight." He ruffled his wings, prepping them for flight.

In a blink, the Black Wing pushed off from the roof, his wings easily stretching the width of the balcony. When they pulled tight, he dropped through the clouds, a silent shadow in pursuit of game.

Keith peered over the edge, trying to see through the thick mass of clouds. There had been no sound, no wind rustling the feathers in the night. There was only the gathering of guests within the castle and the startup of musical festivities. When nothing appeared after a few minutes, Keith figured he had found what he sought and had perched elsewhere, but on turning a large mass drew itself up through the swarming mist, rising high until its body was cast in silhouette from the surrounding moon.

Corrigan drew his wings up, his body arched in landing position. Sable wings beat furiously as he lowered himself to his perch. He landed on all fours, letting his wings stretch out in the breeze to cool them. In his right talon a feathered body limply dangled.

"Your banquet meal, I take it." Keith looked away as the Black Wing sank his teeth into its flesh and ripped out chunks of feathers.

"Owl," Corrigan said after swallowing. "Not bad compared to what I've been catching around here." He took another bite. Swallowing was just as loud. "What's wrong? Can't stand to see a few drops of blood?"

Keith forced a laugh.

"It's not that. I know you must. It's just that…well…I don't eat meat." He heard the snap of bones.

"Don't eat meat, huh?" he heard Corrigan mutter. "No wonder you stayed small for so long."

Keith chuckled. "I could bring you something from inside."

"I take what I hunt," came the reply. "Besides, I'm sure their meat is not *that* fresh."

Keith peered over his shoulder to see Corrigan finishing the last of his supper.

The harpy wiped the back of his hand across his chin. Any leftover bones were tossed into the clouds before he began preening.

"You might want to get something yourself." Corrigan paused to glance down at the young man. "Otherwise, you might be left with nothing *but* meat."

"Oh, I'm not worried about that," Keith replied in good humor. "There's so much, it's enough to feed several realms over a week!" He glanced to the doorway. "I am curious about those desserts."

Corrigan continued to preen while Keith made his way back inside. The room seemed much larger than before, and still guests kept pouring in, even more than at auction.

Nicolas was right. Luxor can enlarge its rooms.

The young man was greeted warmly with several nods and verbal introductions. He paid little heed to those who stared at his pale features and retrieved a plate from the servant's quarters. A seat near the room's entrance provided the perfect place to eat while watching guests come and go. For a moment he thought he saw a recent master, but was quickly forgotten as good food filled his stomach. A round of music started up, and he was lost in its resounding melodies.

*****

Nathaniel's hand stopped twitching.

Lord Gracie, though fascinated at such craftiness, was now more than convinced that he had not merely come to stake a claim to one of his servants.

"It's clear to me now which slave Jenario's looking for," the headmaster began. "And I can almost assure you that your attempt to threaten me into giving him up is nearly impossible."

Nathaniel raised an eyebrow. His hand cocked so that the dagger could fall into his grasp.

"Threaten you? *No'va's* Grand Master?" He let out a cackle. "It matters not to me whether you care about your darling little slave or not. I can pay you whatever you desire."

"What do I need with more money?" Lord Gracie asked. "I'm as rich as any filthy slave owner around these areas—and better off." His face enlightened with the change in his tone. "What do you get being around such a person, Nathaniel? He has to be paying you for your services. I couldn't see you working for him if he wasn't."

Nathaniel gave him a skeptical look, but said nothing.

"I know about you," the headmaster continued. "Liquor likes to talk. Then again, so do the people who cared most about you. Whatever made you leave your family?"

"What family?" Nathaniel spat, thrusting his fist down in between them. A silver dagger with a gold stripe down the center penetrated deep into the wood.

Lord Gracie never flinched and kept a steady gaze into the assassin's burning eyes.

"I wasn't the one who walked away. *She* left me!" He pulled the dagger roughly from the wood, chipping off several pieces, and pointed it accusingly at him. "I earned my keep, but it wasn't good enough."

"Is that what you believe?" Lord Gracie inquired. "Or did someone just tell you this?"

The assassin's face swelled red with hatred, but he held his tongue.

"What has Jenario told you?"

"That's *my* business," he whispered, lowering his gaze to the large dent in the wood. "I get the job done. That's all that counts."

"You need to get out more. I would invite you to the banquet if I knew you wouldn't do anything to my guests."

"What do I care about your guests?" Nathaniel sheathed the dagger within his sleeve. "I only came for one thing."

"So tell me," Lord Gracie probed, "how *is* my friend getting along? I understand he has discovered a new type of magic. From what source did he achieve it?"

"Source?" Nathaniel was struck dumb. "It's not like he read about it in some ancient tome, though I wouldn't be surprised since his nose is always stuck in one."

"Well, I only know one other place to get it from. Perhaps two." He tapped his nails on the table. "Tell me he didn't capture one of *No'va's* mystical creations."

"Whether it be mystical or not, he has it. And if you think I'm going to give you any answers on it, you're wasting your time! I only came here for one thing. I can't leave here without it."

"The boy is not yours for the taking, Nathaniel Woodston." Lord Gracie's tone thundered with authority. "Or should I mention, *Nathan Agecroft*?"

Nathaniel's temper was already short, but at the mention of his real name his cheeks swelled in fury. When he had last spoke, it was all he could do to keep from thrusting his dagger in the master's throat.

"That name is dead."

"As is this conversation." Lord Gracie abruptly stood. "I bid you good day." Turning his back, he began walking from his guest. A shuffle from the chair behind made him pause. There came a ting of metal as the dagger was let loose.

Even before the assassin had fully released it, Lord Gracie had already sidestepped from its path as though expecting the motion. Once the dagger had ricocheted harmlessly off the wall and clattered to the floor, the headmaster reached down to retrieve it. Gold down the blade's center held his fascination. He turned it several times to admire its reflective surface, for there was no other blade like it.

"I trust you will not do that again," Lord Gracie said quietly. "Otherwise, the guards outside this door will have no problem tearing you limb from limb and locking you in the dungeon for the rest of your life."

With a bow, Lord Gracie swept from the room, leaving the dagger on an empty plant stand for its owner to retrieve.

CHAPTER 16

Keith felt a ting of excitement in the air. Guests turned toward the main entrance. A moment later Lord Gracie entered, instantly greeted with applause. A robe of crimson and gold trailed behind him as he descended the steps. Upon reaching the bottom, he was quickly lost in the crowd.

Keith sighed heavily, his thoughts wondering to the outdoors. He thought of the Black Wing and if he had succeeded in another catch for the night.

Ah, lad, there's no need in worrying over something you can't control.

A familiar mind linked with his. The young man searched through the crowd. His grandfather's presence was close.

If I were a snake, I'd have bitten you by now, it teased.

A dark robed guest leaned against the balcony's railing just overtop the main entrance. As Keith's gaze fell upon him, the figure slightly turned and nodded. The link between minds disappeared when soft music began to play. A violin started, followed by a flute. It reminded Keith of his own musical instrument tucked away in Shafari's drawer, and he began to wonder how Lanchershire was fairing.

It's been a while since I last spoke with him. But at least he's safe for now that Shafari quit the game. Keith chuckled. *He couldn't stand losing to his own rules.*

As guests began to gather around the tables of food, Keith decided to venture out among them. Unconsciously, he fingered the ring hanging around his neck and thought of Glory. Had her family been invited?

"Oomph!" Someone backed into him, a scrawny stork-like figure.

"Watch it, y—" The voice was unmistakable.

"Master Reuphas." Keith bowed respectively to him.

Jaw agape, Reuphas stood inspecting him with a scrutinizing stare.

"Keith, wasn't it?" he managed hoarsely. "Who else would it be, what with your appearance and all, and certainly you've grown since," he shot him a placid grin, "the last time I saw you."

"It *was* a bit unexpected," Keith returned.

"Well..." Reuphas cleared his throat, his eyes trailing to the young man's bare wrists.

Keith slightly turned his hands so that the sleeve pulled back. With no dispelling bands, the servant was free to use his magic, and Reuphas knew it.

"Well..." His former master cleared his throat. "Enjoy the evening. Not like anything pleasant ever lasts." He backed away with a slight bow, then turned and hurried off.

Keith could not wipe the grin from his face as he continued through the crowd, occasionally bumping into other masters he knew. He kept his mind open to hear the many thoughts passing around. Quite a few were concerned about an albino magic-user and thought it best to head back out to the balcony where he was least visible. The last thing he wanted was a mass panic from Lord Gracie's guests.

"Excuse me, sir." Someone tapped his shoulder.

Turning, Keith was greeted by a young lady. She was nearly his height, perhaps a couple years younger. Her fair skin and wavy dark hair held his gaze, down to her revealing ball gown sleeves trailing off slender shoulders. He smiled warmly.

"I wondered if you'd come."

"It *is* you!" Glory exclaimed and clasped her hands together. Her eyes brimmed with joy. "I knew it had to be. No one else has the same looks."

Keith could feel his face flush.

"I...guess not," he stammered, feeling rather childish.

Glory laughed when she saw the rosy color fill his cheeks, then recomposed herself.

"Forgive my ignorance. But," she sucked in a breath as she took in his well-toned appearance, "weren't you smaller before?"

Keith grinned. "Being here seems to be what I needed. Everywhere else, I was kept in tight quarters."

About to answer, she noticed the gold chain around his neck. A glint from the ring hanging from the end caught her eye.

"You found it!" she said at last. "I thought it'd been lost."

Keith nodded. "Thought I'd save it for when we met again." He started to unclasp it. "It was your mother's, wasn't it?"

Glory watched while the ring was slipped between her fingers, warm against her palm where it had rested against his skin. Her fingers caressed it, rolling it around to cool its smooth surface. It was not the most valuable, a simple trinket from her mother when she had been old enough to wear it.

"Keep it." She took his hand and folded the fingers over the small token. "Consider it a gift."

Keith's wide smile deepened the dimples on either side of his cheeks. He nodded in thanks and replaced it around his neck again. It showed well against his dark shirt.

"Would you care for a drink?" the young man asked, and Glory nodded.

With her hand on his arm, Keith led her to a table and poured some punch. It did not matter whether people stared or questioned his appearance. The only thing that mattered now was Glory, and Glory was all he saw even when her father approached.

"You remember Keith? I don't think we formally introduced before. Keith," she gestured to her father, "this is my father, Master Roland from Central Valley Clan."

Keith took an awkward bow. He remembered the man's expression from before, and from the looks of it, Roland had not forgotten about the albino magic-user.

"So it is." Her father glanced him over. "You're quite the talk tonight, young man. Shouldn't you be with other servants?"

"Don't be rude!" His daughter scolded. "Keith is the nicest young man here. You should have seen the way some of the others acted."

"You are like your mother was, captivating in every way. Of course, they would try to impress you."

"Impressing is not trying to kiss someone on first contact!" Glory crossed her arms with a huff.

"Don't fuss like a child. You're old enough now to know better. Anyways, your mother sends for you."

"*Step*-mother," Glory corrected and rolled her eyes at Keith. "She probably wants to introduce me to some of her flirts."

"Now see who's being rude?" Roland took her arm and set her drink on the nearby table. "If you would please excuse us a moment."

"Certainly." Keith bowed again.

"Until next time?" Glory lifted her hand, and Keith took it in his and raised it to his lips. When he released her hand, she opened her fingers to find the black plume he had hidden beneath his shirt collar.

"As a gift," he said.

Glory's father eyed the thick plume but said nothing while his daughter tucked it away safely in the folds of her dress.

"A gift for a gift." She grinned before being led away by her father.

Keith watched the two until they were swallowed among the many guests feasting and dancing to the music.

CHAPTER 17

A shadow is produced on the darkest side of a person, but what if that shadow was on more sides than one because that darkness had expanded elsewhere? What if I were this shadow? I'm always lurking where you can't see me, and yet you know I'm there. But if I am to be your shadow, then who, pray tell, is mine?

Corrigan clung to a beam in the ceiling. The hallway had been deserted for some time, deeming it worthy for a quick nap. Wrapping his wings around his body, he comfortably settled himself. His drooping eyelids halfway closed as voices still drifted from the ballroom. With hunger more than satisfied he was ready to sleep the rest of the evening.

A shadow is something that never leaves, can never leave. It is always attached somehow, somewhere. Of course. The name of my shadow is the name of a mage, one who ever waits in the Realm of Darkness.

Footsteps softly entered the passage, interrupting the Black Wing's thoughts. They stop directly below.

And then of course there's another shadow, one that lurks unbeknown to the usual. The name of my shadow has but another, and that one stands beneath me in utter stupidity! Corrigan silently ruffled his feathers in recognition. *Ah, yes. Jenario must have sent him to do my job. Let's see how far he can get without drawing attention to himself. Little does he realize a shadow doesn't always have to follow his every move.*

*****

Nathaniel waited, his assassin instincts alert and ready. His encounter with Lord Gracie had proven unsuccessful, and with the added attempt at murder he was at high risk of failing altogether.

Fool! Rage boiled inside him. *Once he finds out I haven't left, he'll have the halls flooded with guards!*

After making sure the corridor was clear, Nathaniel crept from hiding and down the main hallway toward the ballroom. With the banquet over, guests were now retreating to sleeping chambers or returning to their own homes for the evening. That left only servants to tidy things. Nathaniel's carefully trained eye picked up all the characteristics on each one. Thus far, none were what he sought.

Laughter, and then an unusual looking youth stepped from the room.

"White hair, blue eyes," he whispered. "My how you've grown since we last met." His lip curled into a sneer of delight.

The boy's chambers are at the end of the second hall, a voice from his thoughts beckoned.

The assassin crossed over to an adjoining passage that led directly to Keith's bedroom. It pleased him that the halls grew darker the further he moved from the main locations, and because nearly all the guests had departed there was no need to keep all the corridors lit. Beams of moonlight streamed in through four large windows. As he passed them, light and shadow cast haunting rays over his body, a night stalker, skilled and ready at the slightest sound. A reflection from something moving caught the corner of his eye. He halted, ears straining.

Silence.

Something landed at the foot of his robe. He glanced down at the single black feather, far too large for the common fowl. Nathaniel let his breath out slowly. His wrist twitched within his sleeve, loosening the dagger, then stepped from the moonlit passage into Keith's bedroom.

Nathaniel's choice of dark green suited him, as it blended well within shadowed corners. In the pocket of his robe he pulled out a vial of mixed poison designed to instantly cause drowsiness. In a separate pocket he kept a piece of torn cloth. A single dose was all that was required to spare him enough time to sneak his victim from the castle to the awaiting transportation Jenario had provided. In a crouched position, the assassin had the advantage of rushing his target should he be seen before the appropriate time.

Carefully uncorking the lid, he covered the mouth of the vial with the cloth and let the contents soak through, then placed the empty vial back in his pocket.

Ingenious, he thought. *It has no odor.* A cloud passed over the moon, casting the room in complete darkness. Alone to his thoughts, he waited.

Footsteps approached from the hall, and Nathaniel calculated their weight and placement. They fell lightly, like a child, yet were distant in stride. They were unhurried, calm and expecting no company. Halfway before reaching the bedroom door they paused.

Take your time. I've got all night to do my job.

Clouds moved aside, allowing a full moon to shine. Although some of the beams threatened to reveal him as they slipped under the balcony doors, Nathaniel felt confident that he was far enough in shadow not to be seen.

The door opened. Accustomed to the dim lighting, Nathaniel could make out every detail on the young man. White hair. Slender form. Nathaniel had not been led astray.

*****

Amber eyes peered through the moonlit passage. The young man's scent came strong, and Corrigan cursed himself for just missing him. Across the way, an open doorway caught the Black Wing's attention. When a soft breeze ruffled his feathers, he smiled to himself. His wings ached to be in flight again. It was no use keeping them tight around his body, so he let them open and dashed for the door. It was a small fit. He was sure a few feathers scattered in the attempt to squeeze through.

Ah well. He's not after me anyway. He made for the open window.

It felt good to be free again, the air currents billowing under his wings. Gracefully, they arched into a climb, his body rising with each stroke. He passed the hallway where the large windows were located. Peering down he could see his shadow gliding along the wall, and he hoped Nathaniel could see it.

He landed overtop the balcony where he would be able to hear anything that went on inside. Already, he could hear Keith's footsteps. The young man strolled to the balcony wall, humming softly as he stared out into the night sky.

Corrigan strained his ears.

Enjoying what little freedom he has.

Quick footsteps interrupted his thoughts. Without hesitation, he landed behind the assassin, already smothering his target. With talons spread, Corrigan dug deep.

Nathaniel bellowed in pain and released his victim. A flash of blade in the moonlight prompted Corrigan to pull back before attacking again. Like a rag doll, the assassin was tossed with ease across the floor by the harpy's powerful wings.

Then it was over. Blood soaked through Nathaniel's clothing as he staggered to his feet in a hasty retreat. There was no messing with a

Black Wing, even a half-breed. While the assassin left the way he had come, Corrigan turned his attention to Keith. The young man lay crumpled on the floor, whimpering from the drug's effects. His eyes fluttered, and Corrigan glimpsed their sapphire brilliance before they closed a final time.

Just as well, Corrigan thought as he lifted Keith and himself into flight. *He won't know anything that's happening. Course then he'll be full of questions when he wakes. What a responsibly!*

Nighttime blended around the two. It was their sanctuary, their chance of hope and escape. Under the cover of darkness Corrigan glided with ease over the forest canopy. So low was his flight that he could have reached down and touched the leaves. In his arms, Keith snuggled close against his feathered breast. For now, at least, they were safe from the alchemist's clutches.

The Black Wing descended when he came to a small clearing. Moonlight filtered over them as Corrigan gently landed, then wedged himself into the brush. He cradled the young man in his arms like a father would a fledgling. With wings of nightshade comfortably pulled around them, Corrigan soon joined Keith in sleep.

It was a few hours before dawn when Keith awoke. At first he had no idea where he was. Everything was black, save for a slither of light between the wings. Feathers pressed in all around, warm and soft upon the breast of the sleeping harpy. The young man could feel his chest rising and falling with each steady breath. In the dim light, he could faintly make out the harpy's head and curving beak-like nose tucked against his chest feathers.

"Corrigan?" Keith whispered. He attempted to move aside one of the wings.

The Black Wing mumbled in his sleep. Keith tried again, this time rewarded with a yawn.

"You're no longer at Luxor, if you want to know," Corrigan said, pulling his wings back so the young man could see the rest of his surroundings.

Keith brushed aside some twigs as he climbed to his feet to look around. Nothing but forest surrounded for miles. He tried to recall why

Corrigan would have taken him from the castle. A flicker of faded memory stirred. He recalled struggling, but nothing more. He glanced at his friend.

"What happened last night?"

Corrigan smirked.

"You had the honor of being visited by a man named Nathaniel Woodston. Jenario sent him to bring you to Sapphire. You remember Jenario, don't you? That was the first time we met."

Keith remained silent, inclined to stare up through the trees at the light blue replacing night's dark violet.

"You were going to take me there too, weren't you? That's why there was a connection between you two."

Corrigan eyed the young man with raised eyebrows, then shrugged.

"What can I say? I slacked."

"What I don't understand is *why* he wants me." He shook his head. "Okay, so maybe I can heal, but other than that I'm nothing special." He stepped away, his eye catching some berries growing against a tree, and he stooped to pick some.

"Oh, no?" Corrigan's feathers rose on end. "How many people do you know who can heal? How many *humans* do you know who can heal? Keith, you're not—"

Keith turned abruptly, a glow of power dancing in those brilliant eyes, and Corrigan hushed.

"I *know* what I am," he said. "My grandfather, believe it or not, lives at Luxor. He showed me...."

Corrigan drew in a sharp breath.

"So you know you're not human."

The young man nodded.

"Then you know why Jenario wants you." Corrigan added.

"Because I'm not human? Neither are you! No, there has to be another reason."

There was a moment of silence as Corrigan considered the young man's words.

"So what now? Return to Luxor?" the harpy inquired.

Keith weighed his options. By staying, he would remain a servant to the only master who treated slaves with respect. Yet, a slave was all he would be, and all he would know unless he finished 'the game' and discovered more about his kind. *And Glory? What chance do I have with someone like her? I'm a nobody at the moment. I need to get out!*

He took a breath. "No. I can't go back. Lord Gracie will know my reasons." He then lowered his voice. "I'm sure Lady's already told him."

"So..." Corrigan stretched each wing, prepping them for flight. "Where to, Healer?"

Keith turned to him. "To Castle Mire. To finish the game...er...slavery."

When Corrigan gave him a puzzling look, Keith just smiled.

"You must understand. I can't just run when Shafari holds the documents of every slave he owns. Magically, he'd be able to find me no matter where I ran."

"Then I guess you have no choice after all." The Black Wing stated flatly, lifting his wings into flight with Keith gripping his chest feathers. "Careful with the plumage. Hope you realize you're on your own after this."

"Fair enough. Shafari knows me." Keith glanced over his rich clothing. "He just won't expect me to look this good."

CHAPTER 18

Shafari stepped from his morning bath and grabbed a nearby towel to wrap around his waist. He began fumbling with his clothing and had just pulled a white shirt over his head when someone spoke from behind.

"So you *do* have a softer side," came a young man's voice.

The headmaster turned abruptly, half in and out of his shirt.

"How dare you come in here! I'll have you know I'm the most powerful—" The headmaster froze, one hand raised in the start of a spell, his other hand still holding the towel.

"Keith? What are you doing here?" Shafari pulled the rest of the shirt over his shoulder, then reached for some under garments. "Do you mind?" He nervously chuckled. "It's one thing to catch someone off guard. It's another when their pants are down."

"Certainly." Keith turned elsewhere while Shafari finished dressing. He eyed a large chess game in a lone corner. Pieces were laid out over a double board in an attempted match, however, unfinished. A layer of dust had settled over top.

Could this be the same one Lancheshire played?

"So," Shafari began, and Keith turned once the headmaster was completely clothed. "You've escaped your master, I see. Funny. I thought the person who bought you would have taken better care of his servant. Certainly I know he does because no one's been returned."

"Let's just say, those five years were running a little slow."

There was no amusement on Shafari's face at the comment. Instead, he cleared his throat.

"And how did you get here? Sprout wings and fly?" He waved the comment aside. "Yes, well. He has plenty of those who can."

Keith grinned and kept his mind closed in case the headmaster could read thoughts. He did not want any information about Corrigan to leak while the harpy made his escape out the back window. It was risky, but with luck no guards paraded the lawn like they did the compound.

"And you've grown...quite a bit." Shafari stepped around the young man, looking him over. "I'm impressed."

"That's only looks, Shafari. You've yet to see what I can do magic-wise."

The headmaster frowned. "Ah, yes. *That*." Shafari plopped himself in a chair by his desk. "And nothing to contain it either. I'm sure my old friend had something to do with it. Did he have you entertain his guests? Pah!" He pulled out his pipe and lit it, puffing large rings in the air.

"Don't tell me you've forgotten so soon. I was once your every pride when it came to auction."

"You still are, young one." Shafari tapped his fingers on the edge of his desk. "But I'm still wondering how you managed to leave a floating castle."

Keith's gaze fell upon the smoke rings. He could have supplied the answer simply by transforming them, and from the look on Shafari's face, he was expected to.

The slave turned away. "You're a magic-user. *You* tell me."

Shafari narrowed his eyes. "Fine then." He dumped the remains from his pipe and thrust it back in a drawer. "You want to keep secrets from me? Then I'll keep mine from you. How's that for a game?"

"No different than the one you play with Lancheshire."

In an instant, the headmaster was on his feet, hands balled at his sides.

"You little cheat!"

"Well, I had to do something to keep you from changing him into a hound!" Keith protested.

The headmaster balked. "You didn't learn that from me. Someone else would have told you."

"Is it true?"

"Well, I have to do *something* with slaves when they don't sell."

"You could free them." Keith watched the headmaster ease back in his seat, knowing he would probably be on his feet again at the next comment. "You could destroy the documents that bind us here."

Keith never saw him move. If anything, it was himself that did the moving, or rather, the room that blurred passed. He felt his body slam against the wall and stick like a bug in a web. There was nothing under his feet as they dangled in midair, and nothing overhead. Suspended by the headmaster's will, Keith was helpless. The young man dared to look, to see whether Shafari was casting a final death spell over him.

To his surprise, Shafari calmly stood and stretched. He glanced over at the young man and scratched his beard in thought.

"You're smart, and your magic is strong. But you're still just an underling." He tapped his forehead. "Get that through your head before saying anything else." In several strides he was across the room. With a finger he raised the young man's chin to force eye contact. "Now hear this, young one. Smarts doesn't mean be rash. If you plan on surviving your remaining months, then I suggest keeping your mouth shut! Furthermore," he stepped away, "how do you expect to see your friend when you've roused my temper into killing you?"

A wave of his hand released the slave, who landed on his hands and knees.

"Killing me wouldn't bring you much money," Keith said quietly.

"Neither would I receive any after five years and you leave," Shafari returned. He gestured to the door. "Well, do you or don't you want to continue?"

Keith glanced toward the chess set sitting in the corner. Shafari proved a powerful piece, and it would take more than just magic to win. As he followed the headmaster to the compound, he compared his life to the board game.

Lancheshire played white, as am I. And Shafari? He plays black...everywhere he goes!

*****

The balcony doors were already open when Corrigan landed. The castle was dark, like a draping curtain snuffing out any warmth. Yet somehow he was relieved to be back in Sapphire, and let his wings fade as he entered the bedroom. A single candle flickered on a table next to the bed. With a sigh, he stepped to the small furnishing and lifted the candle in salutation.

"A small token of welcome," he whispered to the shadows. "You obviously knew I would return."

Dust stirred in the corner, then spiraled upward until the form of a cloaked figure stepped from its core. With a sweep of sable cape the dust was caught on a draft and dispersed.

"I only knew you wouldn't go back to your kind," Jenario replied.

Corrigan set the candle back on the table. An argument was not what he wanted now.

"I should, for the way you acted."

"It was only a boy. I didn't ask you to bring back the conquered world." He lowered his voice. "Less to be forgotten."

"You didn't just *ask* me! You tried to *control* me!" His wings ruffled into view. "Thankfully, Keith was smart enough to know the difference. He *knew*!"

"Course he does." Jenario shrugged. "That's how powerful he is." With a sigh, he smoothed back the bed drapery in thought. "Nathaniel was quite a mess, you know."

"He'll get over it." Corrigan smirked. "What did he expect me to do? Sit there and watch him stuff his handkerchief up Keith's nose?"

Jenario chuckled and folded his arms within his sleeves.

"Amusing. Well, I suppose there's no harm in watching, if nothing else."

"Watching?" Corrigan repeated. "What are you talking about? There's no need to watch Keith anymore. You already said he was powerful!"

"Yes, and I have every confidence that our young magic-user will survive no matter what condition he's in." Jenario hesitated while a voice hummed through his thoughts. *Don't give him any reason to doubt your actions. Let him believe he's doing it for the boy's sake.* "But just in case, Corrigan, I would like for you to continue watching over him."

The harpy doubled over in laughter.

"First you want him. Now you want me to play guardian!" He turned away, shaking his head. "I don't get you sometimes. He already knows you're watching him now. He knows you sent me. Don't you think he'd figure it out if I returned?" He smirked. "I'm not that hard to miss, you know."

"Then I'll adjust your fading ability," the mage replied. "Not only will your wings fade, but you yourself. You will become like your surroundings."

"No! No more of this! No more in my head!" He waved his talons in the man's face to prove his point. "Or *these* will be in *your* head!"

Jenario smiled and nodded.

"You won't need to intervene anymore, not if you're just...*watching*."

With a slight bow, Jenario slipped into shadow, as if an opening was there waiting for its master's return.

*****

"When what do me wondering eyes behold. Keith!" Lancheshire chimed with strained vigor. He had been lying on the bottom bunk daydreaming when footsteps had unwillingly forced him back into the real world. As soon as his gaze fell upon Keith he knew it could be no other, though he was shocked at how much he had grown.

Lancheshire listened intently as Keith spoke of the storm while traveling to Luxor, the Foreseer who helped win against Shafari's game, even Corrigan. When Keith mentioned the assassin, Lancheshire spat in disgust.

"I tell ye, Keith." Lancheshire sat on the edge of the bunk next to his friend. "Magic's a messy business. Word gets 'round fast. People either like ye or hate ye. I guess this Jenario fellow really likes ye."

"I don't really know what he thinks of me. I only met him once. Seems if he liked me he'd go about helping a different way." He smiled faintly, then suddenly sat up in remembrance. "I saw the game in Shafari's room! It's just like I saw in the dream-channeling."

"Ye won't find it anywhere else." Lancheshire leaned back against the side of the cell and propped up his feet behind Keith. He glanced back the way Shafari had gone. "I ain't a hundred percent sure what would've happened if he'd won. Me thinks he aimed to be rid of me."

"He is." Keith slid off the bed and kicked some of the dirt from his feet. "Lancheshire, he's got documents on all of us. We can't leave slavery until those papers are destroyed!"

Lancheshire sighed.

"I ain't liking it, Keith. Things been getting rough while ye were gone. A lot'a slaves been missing lately, but Shafari sure got himself a lot'a hounds." He chuckled. "Ye'd think with all this guarding stuff that slaves'd be hard to miss."

"They're not getting out." Keith lowered his voice and leaned closer to his companion. "Shafari's changing them into hounds when they don't sell. If he had won, you'd be a dog by now."

Lancheshire laughed and waved a hand in disbelief. "What's the point of more hounds? Ye still gott'a feed 'em!"

Keith shrugged. "Experimentation? Who knows? All I know is what I've heard from other masters. And if what they say is true, then it would explain why more hounds are appearing." He glanced down the aisle where guards were bringing in more slaves and lowered his voice. "You still have the key?"

Lancheshire nodded and patted his side pocket.

"Ain't shown a soul," he said softly.

"Good. You'll need that to get everyone out."

The slave stared. "Ain't this our cell key?"

Keith shook his head.

"Opens everyone's cell. We just need to act at the right moment." He yawned and curled up beside his friend, too tired to move to the top bunk.

"Just hope ye know what ye're up against," his companion's words faded as sleep closed Keith's eyes, and his last thoughts drowned out the familiar noise of cracking whips and dog howls.

CHAPTER 19

Shafari invited his guest to take a seat. He was the same height as the headmaster, broader in shoulder, with arms of toned muscle from years of hard work. His dark sienna skin was thoroughly tanned, adding an exotic appeal to his lissome form. He combed a few fingers through his thick black hair, his attention never wavering on the topic of slaves.

Shafari stared into those crescent eyes, unafraid even in the presence of a powerful magic-user. Now and then his guest would rub the tuft of beard just beginning to grow. The conversation was just warming to the reason he had come.

"You have a magic-user, you say, Shafari?"

Such richness. Shafari lavished in bargains that promised success.

"Master Conrad," Shafari dipped his head, "my apologies for not mentioning him earlier."

"Has he a strong spirit?" Conrad's voice purred to the headmaster's ear.

"Wild. So, too, is his magic." It was just the right touch, spurring his guest's interest.

"I would be concerned if I were you. A magic-user that does not wear dispelling bonds can be quite dangerous. Has he tried using magic against his current restraints?"

Shafari's smile widened in answer.

"I would be *very* interested in seeing this slave." Conrad's sharpness caused the headmaster to flinch. "Prove to me he has this 'wild' spirit and I'll be willing to pay whatever it takes."

"Of course. If you would permit me to retrieve him for you, I think you will find him every bit what rumors claim."

*****

They had caught another harpy. Screams of agonizing pain ripped through the compound. Keith could hear flesh shred and bones snap. Desperately, he pushed his face into the pillow to drown out the horrific sounds. It did not last long and was soon replaced by soft whimpers.

Clanking chain resonated as their newest slave was bound and placed in a nearby cell. A repulsing glimpse of two gaping wounds in the harpy's backside made the young man turn away.

"It sickens me the way they treat them." Keith slipped to the side of the bunk and leaned over so he could see his companion. "Are you awake, Lanc?"

"Who ain't?" The slave blinked up at his companion.

"I'll be really glad when it's all over with."

"Ye ain't kiddin'."

Keith cracked a small smile.

"And I hope when that time comes that you never change."

"If sanity holds." Lancheshire turned over in his cot.

Keith sighed and slid away from the edge. He could still hear the harpy's whimpering. Curious, hoping its back was not facing him, the young man cast a glance through the bars.

It was only one cell away. Flecks of dried blood mixed in between silver curls of shoulder-length hair. Its face was a mask of unusual colors, and Keith wondered if they were natural or painted. The patterns may have continued but stopped at the collarbone where guards had plucked its feathers. From this vantage point, the harpy was no bigger than a child. It huddled in one corner, keeping well away from the cell door with its eyes fixed upon the lock in wide-eyed paranoia.

Keith leaned over the side again.

"Did you see the new harpy, Lanc?"

"Hard to miss," came a muffled reply.

"This one's different from all the others, like it came from another race. How many different types of harpies are there?"

"Too many."

Keith lowered his voice. "What do you think they intend to do with him? He's too small to be a regular slave."

Lancheshire turned to meet Keith's gaze.

"Anything non-human has more strength than ye'd ever imagine."

Keith stared at him. *Non-humans...* An image of his grandfather came to mind. *Non-humans are stronger...*

A commotion of several voices alarmed the two slaves. From the top bunk Keith searched the aisles. His sharp eyes pinpointed Leventés pushing his way between guards.

"Got company?" Lancheshire snickered.

Keith nodded.

Leventés was at the cell door faster than the two realized. After fumbling with the keys, Leventés unlocked the door and motioned for Keith to follow.

"Shafari needs you," the servant said in a dry tone.

"Me?" Keith glanced at his friend as he climbed down from the top bunk.

Lancheshire slid to the edge of the cot.

"Guess I ain't the popular one no more," he teased, then crossed two fingers and held them up. "Can remember a time when Shafari and myself were like this."

"Trying old tricks to gain new favors." Leventés frowned. "He's only aiming for some new slave dealer."

"Ah, yes." Lancheshire leaned back against the bed frame. "The temptation of riches. Ain't he enough to buy ten other castles twice as large as this one by now?"

Leventés snapped his fingers.

"Enough! Come, Keith." He locked the door. "We cannot delay." He snapped a pair of shackles around the young man's wrists.

Keith could hear the two discussing him even before reaching the private lounge. He eyed both masters sitting across from one another as Leventés scooted him into the room. The urgency felt before seemed less upon Shafari's calm nod of approval while smoking his long pipe.

A dark-haired man rose from his seat to study the young man's figure, admiring the rich clothing still worn from Luxor. He lifted Keith's chin, gripping firmly but gently in attempts to seek the slave's eye color.

"A blue-eyed albino is a rarity in itself. Magic-user all the more."

With that comment, the sound of shackles clattering upon to the floor startled his new master.

Shafari continued puffing his pipe in amusement.

"So they say," Keith replied.

Conrad looked down at the young man's freed wrists.

"Shafari?" He turned to the headmaster. "Name your price. I want him."

"You're sure you won't consider any other?" Shafari asked, placing the still smoking pipe on his desk.

"No other will suffice, and you know it."

With a nod, Shafari slid a parchment of paper to one side of his desk.

"Price is at the top. Just sign and he's yours."

CHAPTER 20

The Realm of Trully was quite different from Lexington. The landscape was more open with small plots of farmland just passed the border. Further down, a quaint town provided its citizens with supplies received weekly from a nearby port. The smell of salt drifted from the shoreline, enticing Keith's curiosity, and he wondered what plans awaited him.

Soon the road began to narrow. Trees thickened on either side until it was all the young man could see. He could hear the horses huffing in the humid weather. Winter had passed as quickly as spring could arrive, bringing new life in colorful displays. A raging growth of mimosa spread on lean branches throughout the area. Threadlike petals of feathery pink blooms dangled from its limbs, its soft balls of fluff perfuming the air with a sweet aroma.

Keith almost missed the looming gates in front of the carriage, preoccupied with the sweet-smelling mimosa. Iron creaked inward to allow passage into the Northwestern Clan. Two guards stood watch as the carriage passed, moving little but to close the gate.

The young man could hear the sound of washing as they neared the castle. Women clothed in white aprons and dark wine skirts held washing boards in large wooden tubs. Soapy water sloshed continuously as they took in bundles of garments at a time. A clothesline on the other side of the yard provided a windy location for hanging. Already a great many flailed in the warm breeze as they dripped dry.

Others tidied around the yard. Several gardeners, Keith noticed, scuttled from shrub to flower, carrying pails of water to pour what was needed onto the dense vegetation. A display of yellow and violet intertwined with lilacs and white lilies. The soil was a rich black, which the gardeners pushed and pulled with forked tools. Several guards staked themselves around various points in the yard. As the carriage passed them, Keith received a nod from one.

The carriage stopped at the front entrance where a waiting servant rushed to open the door for Conrad. Another opened Keith's side. When the carriage was cleared, it pulled away to the backside of the castle.

The women paused in their washing to see the new slave. His pale appearance captivated them, especially the younger ones. Keith, however, ignored them as he followed his master inside. A short hallway lead to a lounge. A dining area off to the right was already full of busying servants rushing back and forth. Keith watched them go in and out of the narrow passage. It would not take much for someone to slip unseen between the busy bodies and noted several other passages close by.

"I'd have thought it'd taken longer to get back," a hasty voice spoke, and a rather squat man waddled from around the corner. His appearance reminded Keith of Nunnelly. His voice was flat. At times it wheezed, in need of a cough to clear his throat. A wide, leather brown belt contained several small pouches at his side and also aided in holding down a long gray shirt, its course material loosely hanging from under his stocky arms and neck. He was in no condition to even *look* like a person of wealth. Instead, he looked like a lucky peasant who had been offered the chance to live a rich life.

"As long as need be," Conrad spoke sharply as his companion approached.

"Doesn't look like much." The man squinted to examine the slave up close. He cast his gaze upward to his tall friend. "He took the money without offering a show, didn't he? Most of 'em do."

"Really, Barnaby, if your thoughts could hold what your stomach can, it'd be a different story."

The plump one chuckled.

"Aye, let me see. That'd be two meals already I've had."

"And another for supper, no doubt." Conrad shook his head. He motioned for Keith to follow as he headed for the back hall. "I presume the others are outside?"

"Where you left them, of course," Barnaby replied, waddling behind.

Conrad lead his slave out to the backyard, a mini compound in Keith's opinion. A row of slave houses took up the left side where a stonewall sectioned off the lawn. Guards stood around the wall heavily armed with crossbows that pointed at all times down into the yard.

What struck Keith was that each structure had been built inside its own cage. Around the perimeters of those cages was yet another, but without a top. There, slaves were free to mingle out in the open, with what seemed to be little confines once out in the yard. The wall around acted like a pen, in case one happened to escape the first two.

There are still the guards to contend with. Keith swallowed nervously. He noticed slaves occupied the larger section of the pen, their cell doors open to return to the huts if desired. On each of their wrists he noticed slave bands. *No doubt, I'll be wearing those too.*

As they approached the pen, slaves scattered either back to the huts or behind foliage. Keith could see their wide-eyed faces curiously examining him from a distance. He watched their movements as Conrad opened the pen for the young man to go inside. Fear was in the air.

The gate doesn't even have a lock on it! And the fence that makes up the pen is short enough to climb over. Is it the guards they fear?

"In with ya now." Barnaby grasped Keith by the collar and tugged him inside the pen. He closed the gate. "You have them, Master Conrad?"

Nodding, Conrad pulled a pair of silver bracelets from an inner pocket.

"Good! I'll take those." Barnaby grabbed hold of Keith's wrist and snapped on a bracelet. Keith waited patiently for the second. Then both masters backed away.

"Come here, lad." Conrad winked at Barnaby, who suppressed a smile.

Unsure what the two were doing, Keith did as told.

A tingling started in each wrist. Keith stopped and looked down at the bracelets. There was nothing unusual about them, no markings or designs that meant anything. He took another step. This time a sting of pain flared up his arms. Confused, Keith backed away. Instantly, the pain subsided.

"Now you understand the power of those bands." Conrad smiled mockingly at Keith. "And they won't come off as easily as you think." He held up a finger. "As for the pain you felt, that's nothing compared to what you'd feel if you touched the gate. The closer you come to the perimeter, the stronger the pain." He started to turn. "One other thing. Don't try using magic with those. Just a forewarning."

Keith watched the two masters depart, their chatter carrying on even as they retreated inside the castle.

"Slug," Keith breathed. He raised his wrists to examine the bands.

"You'll never get them off," came a quiet voice from behind. When he turned around, the girl crept forward. She looked a few years younger with long cinnamon hair that set off her pea-green eyes. "Not without a key."

"These aren't the ones that have all those locks on it," Keith said, turning his wrists to inspect for hidden openings.

"Not here!" the girl whispered harshly. She looked at the guards standing at their posts. "This way!" She led him to one of the huts. "The guards are ever watchful, though they're not really supposed to shoot without our master's consent."

"Which one?" Keith grinned. "Or both?"

"Only Conrad owns us. The other has his own. Once in a while he'll open the gates for us to go into the yard, but that's about it. Conrad does everything else." She watched him fumble with the bracelets. "So you're Keith. I'm April."

"You know my name?" he glanced at her.

"Conrad has spoken of you several times." She blushed as his brilliant eyes held her gaze. "When he heard there was an albino magic-user he could buy, he immediately began making preparations for your coming."

An oncoming chuckle was cut short, turning into a gasp of surprise as Keith's wrists flared as though on fire.

"They're very sensitive. Pulling only activates it."

"That'll be a trick." Keith grit his teeth until the pain subsided. "Now I understand what he was talking about."

"He knew you'd try to take them off?"

"He saw me take a pair off before I came here," Keith admitted. "A mistake on *my* part."

He followed April back outside. A few others crept from hiding to inspect the newcomer. "So what's with all this?" He gestured around the yard. "Are we supposed to be his special collection or something?"

April nodded.

"Special would definitely be the word. I'd probably be one of the maids if I weren't half centaur."

"Half what?"

She pointed to her feet. Soft feathering grew down to the ankles from the back of the kneecap. Tiny hoofs grew in place of toenails. A swish of movement under her skirt suggested a tail.

"Pretty unusual, huh?" April laughed. "My father was a centaur, my mother human. I'm the only one like this."

She guided Keith's attention to an older boy.

"That's Shaifer. Thinks he's part wolf. Don't do anything to frighten him. They say he has fangs, but I've never seen it myself because I'm fairly new."

As Keith watched, the boy's tongue rolled to one side of his mouth in a pant. Short black hair bristled on the top his head, and he lifted a hind foot to scratch it. For a human, the act gave an awkward appearance, and Keith suppressed a laugh.

With a shake of his head, Keith found his gaze drifting to another slave. A girl, shoulder-length blond hair and thin shoulders, was digging up bits of dirt, spitting in it, then rolling it around in her palm until creating a ball. When the dirt was completely round, she placed it in a circle with others.

"What's she doing?" Keith nodded in the girl's direction.

"That's Chase. Her specialties are throwing stones and shooting marbles." April's eyes sparkled in excitement as she told the girl's story. "Chase can throw a stone farther and more accurately than an arrow can fly. Now she has nothing. So every day she makes new marbles from the soil to play with."

Chase placed another dirt ball on the circular line, aimed, then flicked it toward the center. The ball did not go far, crumbling back to soil before it had reached halfway.

"I wouldn't think someone who threw stones would be anything special," Keith remarked. "Sounds like Conrad collects more than just oddities."

"One of a kind." April nodded. "If there's no other of the likes, he has it."

"But I'm not the *only* magic-user. Where I came from, the headmaster was one himself."

April's tail swished beneath her skirt. "Have you ever seen another albino?"

Keith grinned. "I guess I *am* the only one."

*****

"I won't leave him unattended for too long." Conrad took a sip from his goblet.

He shifted his weight in the large cushioned chair. Barnaby, who sat across from him, poured himself more wine, then pulled out a pipe. When he could not get his pipe to light, he rose to dump the remaining ashes in the nearby fireplace.

"You've got the pen guarded." Barnaby shrugged. "And I wouldn't worry too much with those bands on him." He returned to his seat.

"Shafari claimed the magic-user was clever enough to slip them off if he finds a way. He promised me the challenge of having him. Besides, I've *seen* him do it!"

"Already?"

"Not mine...yet. First, I want to see what he's capable of."

"Of course." Barnaby stared into the unlit fireplace. "But remember. You're dealing with a *magic-user*. They're quite different from the others, capable of using their minds to levitate objects, unlock things, illusions even!" His eyes flicked to his companion. "Then you'd be getting your money's worth."

Finishing his drink, Conrad set it down and rose from his seat.

"You mean *your* money."

Barnaby raised an eyebrow.

"You'd best check that slave."

"You don't miss a beat, do you?" Conrad grabbed a harness hanging by the door on his way out.

*****

Keith could hear his master coming before anyone else. When he warned the others, they scattered like flies. Most went into the huts, but a few stayed in the yard to peer from behind foliage. April tugged at his arm.

"Don't just stand there! Move!"

Keith laughed.

"What will they do, take a whip to me? Should be used to it by now."

"You don't understand! Conrad knows how to master a slave in seconds! I've seen the most fearsome slaves follow him around like dogs – like they're under a spell or something. And just because you have magic—" The thud of castle door made her stop. With a final glance, she hurried toward the structures.

The click of gate opening announced Conrad's presence inside the pen. Slowly, Keith turned to face his master.

"Waiting for me, I see." Conrad stepped toward him.

"You came to test my magical abilities, didn't you?" Keith remained still, his eye instantly drawn to his master's hands held behind his back. "Your bands may keep me from using magic, but your thoughts are as clear as running water."

"A mind-reader," Conrad breathed. "Those bonds should've controlled that."

"Sight-reader," Keith corrected. "Has nothing to do with magic. I cannot read minds...yet."

"Do not try to deceive me, young one." Conrad stepped closer. He brought his hands around.

Keith took a step back when he recognized what his master held. A brace, often used at Castle Mire, kept slaves and harpies securely bound for better handling. It joined both wrists and ankles together, with an extra length to secure wings. The thin straps were reinforced with metal, not easily breakable.

Conrad smiled pleasantly. "Most slaves think it's some type of harness for animals." He chuckled. "Little do they realize it's meant for *them*."

"And now the game starts," Keith whispered.

"Keep still, young one." Conrad readied the brace. "You'll only hurt yourself if you struggle."

Keith felt the familiar sensation welling in his wrists. He had backed away until there was nowhere else to go. Now the pen stood behind him. Any closer would release painful jolts. Panic set in, and a sound welled in Keith's throat, a sound he had never made before. It was fairly strong, like the tapping of a woodpecker. It lasted only a few seconds, but it was enough to give Keith the time he needed when his master paused to listen.

Without a thought to the guards nearby, Keith leapt at his master. The force of his jump surprised even himself, for it knocked Conrad back several feet. Anger flooded his master's face. With no time to reconsider what had occurred, Keith waited for his master's next move.

Conrad's sudden speed threw the young man off guard. Before he could blink, Keith found himself flat on his back with a knee on his chest. A quick snap confirmed a secured wrist.

Suddenly, Conrad retreated with a yelp. His own hand sought the deep gash across his cheek and left eyebrow where Keith had swiped his nails. Unlike fingernail scratches, these were made as though talons had just raked his flesh. Conrad grit his teeth, foam dripping from his lower lip. No less angry, Keith pulled his hand free.

The crack of door hitting against the wall startled Keith, and he peered over one shoulder to see Barnaby rush outside.

"What's happened?" he yelled across the yard. He waddled quickly toward the pen, but one look at Conrad's bleeding face told all. Without wasting a moment, he called upon the guards. "Shoot him!"

The guards took aim.

"No, wait!" Conrad was too late as volleys of arrows were released.

With nothing to protect himself, Keith dove sideways to avoid what he could. He could feel air whipping past his cheek. One grazed his side. Another flew overhead. A cling against metal, followed by a snap turned his attention to his wrist. An arrow had jolted the lock on the band. It now dangled unlocked. After casting it aside, Keith raised the other as another volley of arrows came.

"Stop, you fools!" Conrad yelled, waving his arms frantically. "The dispelling band!"

Keith positioned his arm just as an arrow whizzed past, snapping the lock open. He used the band to knock a few arrows from him, then tossed it aside while the guards reloaded.

He could hear them coming. The arrowheads were thick and heavy, and whistled through the air when let loose. There was no way he could dodge these, and instead raised a commanding hand and closed his eyes.

Think of Blackavar's love for you, a voice came to mind. *Think of your love for Nature. Your magic is still with us. You are One with it.*

Barnaby had frozen. He watched with mouth agape as the bolts came to a halt within inches of the young man. At Keith's command they stopped in mid-air, and with the freedom to control his magic he caused the arrows to turn until they pointed back at the guards. A single gesture returned them. Shouts penetrated the air as the arrows struck home.

April, who had been watching from the hut, suddenly applauded him. Several other slaves soon joined her. Shaifer lifted his head and howled victoriously, thumping his foot against the ground as if wagging a tail.

Keith's triumph lasted only until Conrad withdrew a thin black dart from his robe. He pulled a hallowed cylinder-shaped reed from his opposite pocket. Slipping the dart into the reed he raised it to his lips and blew.

Time slowed to a crawl. Keith saw the dart launch, knew it would come quicker than the heavily built arrows. His gaze fixed upon its rapid approach. Most of his mental energy had depleted. Desperately, he sought another use for his remaining energy.

Is it possible to catch something like that? His mind focused on fusing strength and magic together. He had to be quick.

Conrad had never seen such speed. In one swift motion, the dart was caught just before puncturing the young man's chest. Yet just as quick he let go, jerking his hand away as though he had been bitten. Gasping, Keith felt his flesh crawl where he had touched the dart. Poison seeped into his skin, slowing heart and mind. Vision blurred. Sound slurred when he tried to think, to focus. All connection with his limbs went numb, and his next step landed him on the ground, and he remembered nothing more.

CHAPTER 21

You are still with us. You are still One....

Sapphire eyes slowly opened as the poison wore off. In a daze, Keith tried to focus his attention through the haze on what lay in front of him. The darkness cleared, and as it got brighter he realized he was in a room. To his left shelves lined the far wall with strange metallic objects, things he could not find names for. On his right colorful liquids in crystal glasses cast rainbow prisms on the wall.

His head felt heavy, and when he tried to move his arms he found he could not. With closed eyes, he took in a deep breath and let it out slowly. He was not hurt, though the hard surface he lay upon was making him uncomfortable.

Why can't I move?

With heavy head, Keith attempted to sit up as best he could.

Something yanked at his throat, choking him back down. He gasped, trying to catch his breath. He tried again, slowly, and managed to glimpse down at his feet. Both wrists had been bound at his waist. A strap trailed to the ankles. What he had not felt before was a separate strap connecting from his ankles back to a collar around his throat. Trying to move his limbs only pulled the collar tighter.

Even if I could use magic, this thing would probably prevent me.

He lay back again and closed his eyes, thankful for the peace at present.

The sound of a door opening sent shivers down his back. Long strides between footfalls identified his host. When his master approached, Keith avoided eye contact.

"Any closer and I'll spit in your face," he threatened, though he knew it was a useless defense.

Conrad only chuckled.

"So encouraging," he mocked. "I take it the next thing you'll do is try to bite me."

Keith glanced at his master to find him smirking. It was then that he saw four white scars running down the left side of his face.

"Well, wouldn't *you*?" Keith countered.

In reply, Conrad moved around the table to the shelves with all the liquids.

"I don't think I'm in a position to consider the same options," he said finally, lifting a vial containing a red tinted liquid from a wooden test tube holder.

You would if I got free.

Keith watched his master pour some of the contents from the vial onto a series of plants beneath two small palladian windows. He breathed a sigh of relief. Whatever was in that vial had not been intended for him.

"So what *are* you going to do to me?" he asked when Conrad had put the half empty vial back on the shelf.

"Do?" Conrad picked up another, swirled it around, then poured it onto the plants. His eye flicked to the instruments glistening on the opposite wall. "Hopefully, I won't *do* anything to you." Then, after reconsidering, added, "Maybe trim those nails of yours."

Keith twitched. He kept moving his head, trying to keep it from resting on the hard surface. His bindings offered little movement, and at every attempt the collar would pull tighter. His distress, however, intrigued his master. With hands behind his back, Conrad came to Keith's side with unhurried steps.

"Still trying to fight it, are we?" He watched the young man's futile efforts. "Shafari said you were a spirited one, but there's never been a slave I couldn't break. And I intend to prove this through *you*."

"By doing what every other master's done?" Keith questioned. "Starving, beating, caged?"

Conrad smiled and rested a hand over the young man's forehead.

"Ah, but that's where they all failed. I, on the other hand, believe in doing the necessary to calm a slave. But I like do so…painlessly."

Whether it was the warmth of Conrad's hand against his skin that made him look, or the fact that he was being stared at, Keith was unsure. Whatever the case, the young man found his gaze hopelessly lost in his master's intense stare. All trace of thought suggesting freedom ceased. He continued to stare, even as Conrad moved away. His struggles stilled, and he relaxed. Entranced, he never felt the brace removed, nor his nails carefully clipped.

*****

Shafari paced the length of his bedchambers, his mind contemplating his next move. Rumors had reached his ears of a slave rebellion. He could hear their whisperings at night when he sometimes roamed the compound, and the night guard dozed while on patrol. Even the hounds were restless. No longer did he hear their lonesome howls. Bared teeth met the guards when they were fed. One guard he lost, becoming food himself.

Could it be...? He paused. *No, that's impossible! They're hounds, not slaves. Their minds would surely have become canine by now. All knowledge of any past existence would have been lost. Unless....*

He closed his eyes, allowing his thoughts to steady.

Unless both human and animal could co-exist without damaging past memories.

Shafari opened his eyes and sat at his desk. There had been rumors before, always when a strong individual came to the compound. Yet *these* rumors were spreading far too quickly. Nearly every slave was on edge. Nearly every guard had to work harder to control them *and* the hounds.

Unheard of! Agitated, he plucked at his beard in a nervous twitch. *To whom do I owe the honor of addressing* this *time? I've never seen so many problems as we're having now, especially when....*

Shafari glanced at the file cabinet holding all slave documents. Rising quickly, he went over and unlocked one of the drawers. He searched through all his inventory, slave names, and money income. When he reached the last file, he paused. Slowly, he lifted a piece of paper from its folder and read the name at the top.

Larson.

Shafari remembered the first day the boy had arrived – such a small child! The headmaster smiled, remembering all the money he had received from the boy's first auction. The trouble keeping him had been worth it.

But at what cost in the end? Shafari's temper rose slightly. Where he gripped the edges of the paper was now damp with sweat. His eyes skimmed the yellowed surface until they reached the signature. Underneath was a curse, *his* signature. With this, he could track a slave no matter where they went, and even kill them if necessary.

Shafari gently touched the spell with the tips of two fingers. As he let his fingers slide over the words, his lips moved, silently pronouncing each one. His eyes halfway closed, feeling his blood rush at the familiar use of magic. Gently lifting his fingers from the page, he watched as each word lit up with a faint glow, then dim and return to its normal state.

"A safe-guard to me, dear boy. Nothing more." He replaced the contract neatly where he had taken it and locked the drawer.

*****

Chase had her usual dirt marbles, trying to hit the center one without crumbling it. She crouched low so that her eye was level, then flicked her thumb upward and snapped the piece of dirt forward. The shot sent the dirt marble crumbling toward the center, less than halfway. Chase pulled herself up and stared at the game.

Keith watched her from a distance, relieved to be back in the pen. From what he could remember, he wore new dispelling bands and his nails had been cut. Anything else Conrad might have done was beyond his memory.

"You're lucky." April approached after he had fully waken. "He usually only takes a slave once, maybe twice, in order to calm them. From the looks of it, all he did was clip your nails."

"I think he hypnotized me," Keith replied as he stared at the bands. "It was strange, like being awake and asleep all at once."

"He's very good at it," April continued. "That's why we run. Don't look him in the eye. He'll control you that way."

Keith shrugged. "Some type of magic-user then."

He continued to watch Chase, her frustration mounting each time her dirt marbles fell apart. Finally, she wiped a hand across the dirt, carefully cleaning off the surface so she could shoot again.

"I wish she could have real marbles," Keith whispered. "That, at least, would be much better than dirt."

His eye fell on the sphere of dirt in front of her hand. At the flick of her thumb, it flew forward. The marble bounced once at the halfway point, creating a soft thud, but continued to roll. Chase's face lit up in surprise as a faint click of two glass marbles touched.

Keith blinked. Whereas before only brown balls of mud had been, now two turquoise marbles sat in the circle's center.

With trembling hand, Chase reached for one, but when she picked it up it crumbled back to dirt. Her eyes lifted, seeking those who had also seen. Even Shaifer stopped his wallowing and sat up to look.

April glanced between Keith and Chase. They were only a few feet away when a dry, monotone voice crackled like static as though not used in a long time.

"H...how did you do that?" Chase cleared her throat several times before speaking again. "How did you make them real?"

"Me?" Keith pointed at himself. "You must be mistaken. I can't do magic with these." He held up one wrist to show the new dispelling band.

Sudden high-pitched laughter came from Shaifer, who rolled over on his back with arms under his head. He tilted his head back so the three were in sight.

"Not magic." He chuckled. "Magic would've been real. Didn't you see the marble crumble after she touched it? It was only illusion."

"Illusion?" April asked. She pointed at Keith. "He can do that wearing the bands?"

"Course," Shaifer's grin never faded. "Illusion's not real, so there's no way the bands can prevent it. You can do most anything you want with illusion and not waste energy."

"You know this?" Keith asked with interest. "I thought I was the only magic-user."

"You are," the boy continued. "My grandpap used to be a magician. Slight-of-hand tricks are usual when dealing in trade business. Could take a whole crowd and make 'em believe they either saw or felt something that didn't exist." He grinned, and when he did Keith thought he saw two upper fangs before the boy turned the other way.

The young Healer smiled to himself. *Illusion.* The very word held the key to his escape. *But I've only just used it once. I need more time before trying something more...* The familiar sound of the outside door shutting suggested the arrival of their master. *Complicated...*

At once, the servants fled. Keith took up a hiding position under a low cut bush, its dense leaves covered him completely while still allowing him to view everything in sight. He saw Conrad approach the gate and open it. The young man's eye traveled along the narrow wooden board that his master's hand rested on to open. It slipped once, found its mark, then silently closed the gate again. Keith glanced at the guards standing around the courtyard. Not one uttered a word.

Next to him lay Shaifer. Overhead, the sound of thunder rattled.

"Maybe it'd be best returning to the shelters. Getting' late anyhow," Shaifer suggested, and without awaiting an answer he bounded off toward his own hut just as the first drops of rain began to fall.

Deciding it best to follow the boy's lead, Keith left the underbrush. He made it to the hut when a gust of wind sent a sheet of rain slanting down. Keith covered his face with his hands and searched through the heavy rain for any last stranglers. Soaked to the skin, Keith was about to enter when he saw April crossing the compound toward the gate. The young man started to call her, then stopped.

He's good! Keith realized. *Even in this weather he can control someone.*

He could not hear what Conrad told the girl, but she obeyed without hesitation and went straight to the castle. When Conrad turned, he stumbled into something. With a slightly confused expression, he backed up. Whatever he had hit did nothing the second time he attempted to shut the gate. He hurried in the direction April had gone, splashing puddles of water already collected around the back entrance.

Soon Barnaby came waddling out like an obese pig. A clap of hands signaled to all others who might still be out to return to their huts. There were no windows to peer into the other shelters, only dark solid walls. Not even a whisper would have been able to pass between them.

Barnaby came with a jingle of keys to lock each hut. He peered into each one, first making sure every slave was accounted for, then locked the doors. Keith lay on his cot when Barnaby peered in at him. He heard the metal key fidgeting with the rusty lock, heard a click, then footsteps passing on into the rainy night. His departure signaled the beginning of a plan.

Keith lay a few minutes more to be sure his master was gone. Then, throwing off the thin blanket, he got to his feet and made for the door. He inspected the lock, chuckling to himself when it easily pushed open.

If only I had known about illusion before. It would have made all the difference in the world.

Keith pushed the door open just enough so he could peer out into the yard. He could see dark shapes of armed figures pacing along the garden walls.

So maybe I can fool a couple of people, but what about a large group? There's no way I can get across the yard to the gate without them seeing me.

Keith studied the layout of the yard. Clouds obscured the moon this night, so the yard was black with shadow and thick with rain. He glanced down at his clothing. That, at least, was dark enough to get by. The problem was his hair.

Even in the dark I'd stand out like fire. His eye caught the blanket half hanging off the bed, and he scooped it up to unravel.

"May not be perfect," he murmured as he draped it over his head. "But at least it covers me completely."

Holding the blanket together beneath the chin made it seem as though he had a cape and hood. Satisfied, Keith scanned along the walls to check on the guards' positioning. There was at least one every three feet around the pen. Yet their bodies were slack, their weapons lowered. Several had even left their posts. Though their eyes sometimes glanced at the quiet huts, the wind and rain made it near impossible to make out a partially opened door, and thunder drowned out any footsteps smacking in the mud. The gate was also something they had missed, for when Conrad had last entered the courtyard, he failed to close the real one. Instead, an illusionary gate closed in its place.

The storm was Keith's greatest advantage. Illusion allowed the rain to thicken around him. Step by step, he came closer to freedom.

How will I get out if these dispelling bands start going crazy on me?

His shoulder scraped against something, and he halted. Drawing in a breath, he looked around to see if he had been noticed. Then, reaching out, he carefully slid a hand across what his shoulder had touched.

"The pen..." he murmured. *I've touched it? Why didn't anything happen?* He lifted the metallic band to study it up close. *Before, I couldn't come within several yards.* His gaze went to the opened gate. He thought back when he had first arrived and Conrad had called him to come. Keith remembered the gate being firmly shut when the bands activated.

Keith drew closer, so close he could almost reach out and touch the gate. Instead, he made for the fake one, the one that kept the guards at bay. Cautiously, he touched it, feeling the wood grains beneath his fingers.

But it's only illusion, he thought. *And nothing that's fake is going to hold me back.*

The gate's visibility wavered, dimming as Keith passed through. The trick had slipped. Hoping he could still catch it before the guards saw the real gate, he paused to recreate another in its place.

A voice to his far right caught his attention. One of them had seen the opened gate. Keith used what illusion he had left to cover his tracks and quickly made his way to the castle.

Once inside, Keith waited for his eyes to adjust to the dim candlelight. Removing the blanket, he let it fall to the floor. He shivered slightly in the dampness, letting his clothing and hair drip dry in a puddle around his feet.

This is it, he realized. *Once I find something to get these bands off, then I'll be free.* He carefully made his way down a narrow hallway into a lounging area. The pupils of his eyes expanded so he could take in more details.

Nothing. Only a metal brace hung by the doorway he had just entered.

I could make it seem as though I've no bands on, so they could be taking them off while thinking they're putting them on. But that means being found....

Keith hurried down the hallway. A single light flickered at the far end, accompanied by a set of voices. Ducking into a vacant room, Keith waited as a couple of servants finished their daily chores before heading upstairs for the night. One of them, a woman, exclaimed something about a slave accompanying their master to the second floor. Where, they never said, but it was enough to get Keith started.

Shrouded in illusion, Keith followed them through the servant's passage and up a narrow flight of stairs. It took great effort not to slip, for his feet were still slick from the rain. At the top of the steps stretched a long corridor with multiple doors on either side. Some rooms were open. Some were not, and when the two servants went their separate ways, Keith was not sure where to go next.

A door opened down the hall, and Master Barnaby slipped out in a night robe. Keith backed into the servant passage until the stout man passed and watched him rap on one of the doors.

"Come in," came the voice of Conrad.

Perfect timing! Keith thought. He listened at the door after Barnaby went in, not knowing if April was in the room with the two or not.

"...And the girl?" Keith heard Barnaby ask. "I can fetch her now."

"Good," Conrad replied. "Across the hall. You know the one. Now that it's finally raining, I can begin my experiments without being bothered."

Keith backed away when he heard footsteps approaching the door.

"You weren't bothered before." Barnaby waddled into the hallway. He fumbled with his keys while bobbing from side to side with each step. He paused to examine the multiple keys on the metal ring, then carefully placed one to the lock. There was a faint click, followed by a gasp.

Keith made sure to mask Barnaby's collapse with illusion, holding his sore hand after striking the back of his head. It seemed as thick as his body, and far too heavy to drag elsewhere. He would have to be quick.

"April?" Keith pushed the door open.

"Keith, is that you?" The girl rose from her solitary corner. Streaks of wet tears smeared her cheeks. "But…how—"

The young man held a finger to his lips. "No time. Conrad's across the hall. Let's get the others out while we can and leave this place." Locating the smallest key on the ring, Keith unlocked his dispelling bands and placed them gently on the floor. "Watch your step." He guided the girl around Barnaby's body. "Sorry. Couldn't move him."

The two quietly made their way through the servant passage and down the narrow steps. Keith grinned when they entered the main hallway. Straight ahead was the door leading to the backyard. A few more steps, and they would be free of Conrad's control.

A tall figure stepped from an adjoining hall to block their path.

"Going someplace?" Conrad asked with a small grin.

Keith swallowed a forming lump while moving in front of April. A sound from behind made them turn to find Barnaby blocking the back hall.

"I may not be the quickest," the man began, "but I'm not the easiest to discard. Your hand felt more like a light tap rather than a hit." He chuckled. "My best advice to you is be prepared for a *long* nap."

"If you're not the quickest, then how'd you get down here so fast?" Keith asked, but it was Conrad who answered.

"My dear boy, do you not think we don't know our home? I anticipated you coming when one of the guards rushed to tell me the gate had been left open. Therefore, I knew you would come, and where you would go."

Keith glanced at April. He knew a guard had seen the opened gate but had not noticed anyone trying to reach the castle.

"There were no guards inside."

"Trust me," Conrad said. "They have ways of reaching me." The master pulled a dart and reed pipe from his robe.

"And now it's only fitting that you two, as my friend put it, take a *long* nap."

"Careful! He doesn't have the bands on!" Barnaby warned. "We should call the guards."

"That won't be necessary," Conrad returned, holding the objects at his side. He stared at Keith with pensive expression. Slowly, hypnotically, Conrad moved closer to Keith. "Easy, lad," his voice seemed to purr. Rich and cool, even April was entranced by it. "That's it. Don't be afraid."

Keith tried to clear his head. *It's his voice. There's something in it that makes me want to...follow....*

"Come to me," Conrad's voice grew stronger.

Keith lost track of April as he fought against the hypnotic stare. In front of him a chess piece appeared. On the floor around him was the game board, sectioned off into a grid of squares. A knight rose before him, extending a hand to take.

Suddenly, that hand was gone, replaced by a dagger with jagged edges. It wrapped the hand with spikes that spewed black blood along the cracks in the floor. The chessboard rose up from the floor, its pieces moving toward a lone pawn trapped in the center.

No! I won't let this defeat me!

There came a scream, and in the confusion, the young man swiped his hand across the board, shattering it as though it was made of glass. In the haze of it all, Keith came to realize that the scream he heard...was himself.

"Enough!" Keith tumbled back on the floor. He glanced behind to see April in the clutches of Barnaby.

"So you've learned to cope with my little trick," Conrad said.

Vaguely, Keith was aware of his master's hand moving to his mouth. Something was placed to his lips and he puffed up his cheeks to blow. From behind, he heard a gasp as April elbowed Barnaby. She ran to help Keith up.

"Look out!" she cried, and they both dived away from the low flying dart. The dart whizzed overhead and implanted itself into Barnaby's hand.

Startled, the man stumbled back from the poison's quick effect. Not another sound was heard from him except the thud of his body hitting the floor.

In silent frustration, Conrad closed his eyes and took a quick breath. He tried to control his anger, though his face was turning redder by the minute.

"Check..." Keith breathed.

Conrad licked dry lips. "You *really* like testing my patience, don't you?"

"That makes two of us," the young man answered.

Keith met his master's sudden attack still on his rump. Fists locked together with Conrad's full-grown strength at his advantage. The young man had to scoot himself back to keep Conrad's knee from pinning him down. The master of oddities would not let go of his hands, and Keith knew the reason why. Though the slave's nails had been filed, their unbreakable surface could still inflict dark purple bruises upon the flesh, a few of which Conrad already had. Over and over they rolled, Conrad's anger getting the better of him. Releasing one of Keith's wrists, he aimed for the young man's throat. Keith could feel his long fingers slipping around his flesh, squeezing with each passing breath.

He would rather have me in death rather than escape alive!

Keith grit his teeth as they rolled over and managed to slam a foot into Conrad's stomach. A second kick flipped his master on his back and sent him skidding across the floor. His head collided with a heavy brass candleholder. After swaying back and forth several times, it finally fell across his body with a heavy thud.

Keith staggered to his feet.

"Keith!" April rushed to help him. "You all right?"

Keith smoothed his hair from his eyes and nodded.

"I'm okay," he answered. In the corner, Conrad did not move.

April approached him as Keith limped over to the body. He nudged it with his foot.

"Is he dead?" April stared down at him, keeping her distance.

"I don't think so." Keith bent down to see if he was breathing.

Conrad's hand twitched, then shot up and grabbed his wrist.

April shrieked.

"Slave!" Conrad cried breathlessly. "Little magic brat!" His other hand grasped the broken candlestick. Then, twisting Keith's wrist over so that the underside was upright, he jabbed the still burning flame onto his flesh just beneath the palm.

Hot, melting pain flashed up Keith's arm so that he jerked his hand back from his master's grasp. He stared at the place where the flame had scarred his flesh.

"You belong to me!" Conrad snarled. "And that scar proves it! *Forever!*"

Keith's eyes narrowed. He could not see his master anymore. Instead, he saw an audience. The room he was standing in vanished. The block was in front of him and he was supposed to stand on it. Behind, a guard raised his whip. In front, the young man saw food flying through the air. It was like the slave market all over again, and through the midst of it all Conrad stood laughing.

There was a roaring in Keith's ears. The mocking died. A rush of hot blood swelled at his temple, beating to the thump of his heart. How he hated this foul creature tormenting him as though he were not even human!

Keith's lip curled into a sneer. *But I'm not human....*

The laughter died. The audience began to scatter. Then Keith remembered why. He had caused the food to be thrown back. Yet somehow he missed Conrad. The young man grasped for something and threw it with all his might. It hurtled through the air, sending smoke and ash along with it.

The next thing Keith knew, he was being pulled back. The crowd vanished, along with the block and food. When he turned around, instead of the guard was April shouting and tugging at his arm. When he turned back, the body of Conrad lay engulfed in flames.

Keith did not linger. Running alongside April, they burst through the back door. The rain had worsened.

"Get yourself away from here!" he shouted, and pointed to the surrounding forest. "I'll get the others!"

There were no longer any guards, the heavy rains driving them to seek shelter. With ease, Keith crossed the yard to the huts and unlocked each one. One at a time, Keith sent them through the gate, using illusion to cover their tracks in case a guard showed. When he reached Chase, he tossed her a small pouch.

"Ready to shoot some marbles?"

At first, Chase just stared at it. Then, with trembling hand, she untied the top. Turning it to one side, she poured some of its contents into her hand.

"These aren't dirt," she managed to say, rolling the marbles between her fingers. "Where did you get them?"

"Some fat guy." Keith laughed as they went to the sound of Shaifer scratching at the door.

"Smelled ya coming!" The boy grinned.

"Ready to go?" Keith returned.

"Ready and willing. Where to?"

"The forest," Keith said. "Let's hurry! This rain is drowning everything!"

They crossed the yard together with Shaifer and Chase slightly ahead of Keith to be sure the illusion covered them. Puddles of water sloshed around their ankles, though it did little to slow their pace. Drenched and shivering from cold, Keith hurried on. The thought of freedom was enough to warm his spirit.

Almost there....

A streak of lightning blinded him. When his vision returned, something black loomed in front. Keith stared up at the thing, unable to make out what it was.

A hissing voice snaked out from charcoaled lips, and Keith gasped.

"Magic...smuck!" Conrad's voice cracked. His lips frothed in madness. One melted hand reached for the young man's throat.

Keith was frozen in place. Another streak of lightning revealed Conrad's horrid appearance. One eye had been burned shut. The other looked ready to drop like one of Chase's marbles, the lid burned away. His once silver robe was shredded and charred. The fabric itself had melted onto his skin.

As Conrad staggered toward him, some of his ragged clothing flaked off.

"Magic...."

He staggered again. His only eye rolled up in his head, and he lurched forward. Keith jumped back to avoid the attack. Instead, the master fell face-first in the mud, a marble embedded in the back of his head. When Keith looked up, Chase stood where Conrad had been.

She shrugged.

"So I didn't have a stone," she said. "But I thank ye for the marbles."

Lightning flicked from one cloud to the next. The collection of oddities was now free to the world. And now so was Keith.

CHAPTER 22

Lancheshire carefully turned the skeleton key between his fingertips. Keith had stolen it from the headmaster himself with the promise to free the compound. Yet there was no telling how long the young magic-user would remain with any one master. The minimum may be five years, but masters could sometimes keep slaves longer.

Sighing heavily, Lancheshire sat up where he had lain on the bottom bunk and slipped the key back in his pocket. The guards were restless, checking more often than they usually did down the many rows. Many rumors had escaped about a breakout. The air was thick with tension. Even the hounds were oddly silent.

"It's never been this quiet," Lancheshire mumbled. "Something's wrong."

A few voices started squabbling across the compound until a commanding voice ordered their dismissal. Lancheshire peered in that direction, catching a glimpse of crimson robes. He cocked one leg over the other and leaned against the bunks with arms crossed. When the headmaster reached his cell, he offered a crooked smile.

"So ye finally came out of hidin', eh?" the slave began.

Shafari, however, did not respond with the same enthusiasm. "Don't play games with me." His usual dangerous tone when upset was replaced with a hint of worry, which surprised the slave.

Shafari ain't one to worry. Bet me bottoms it's about Keith. He watched the headmaster approach the cell door.

"We both knew he was strong," Shafari started, "but from what I've just heard, he could bring down the whole place!"

Lancheshire chuckled. "It'd give ye a little break from the normal routine."

Swift anger drove Shafari forward, and he gripped the bars so fiercely that Lancheshire was sure he would rip them apart.

"His master was found dead – *burned* alive! A whole slew of slaves have escaped, and I'm now responsible for tracking them down!"

"And ye're blaming this on Keith?"

The headmaster bit his gums, contemplating a plan of action. "He should never have come here..." His voice trailed off as he loosened his grip on the bars. Where his fingers had touched, steam drifted upward.

"He's coming back. It's been three days already. On foot – maybe four to reach Lexington." He grasped the key ring at his belt, but failed several times to slip it into the lock. His hand shook slightly before a faint click sounded.

Lancheshire stared at the opening door. "So what now?"

The headmaster turned slightly to glance over his shoulder at the vats against the far wall.

"What say we take a little walk?" he replied, his tone a bit more controlled.

I ain't liking this! Wherever ye are, Keith, better hurry!

*****

Hiding among the rows, Keith kept his mind open to Shafari's course of action, with thoughts coming as frantic patterns of random chants and images. The disturbing report of Conrad's gruesome death had undoubtedly unnerved him. To take control of the situation, the headmaster's thoughts revealed using Lancheshire as bait to lure the young magic-user close.

Keith, however, would not be fooled. He waited until his friend stepped from the cell before releasing the illusion disguising his position.

The look on Lancheshire's face told all, and Shafari whipped around.

"Thanks for unlocking the door, but we already had a key for that." Keith grinned. He tossed a stone from one hand to the other, then held it up for Shafari to see. In the blink of an eye, the stone turned to dust and drifted to the floor. "Illusion can be quite amusing if you know how to handle it."

"Illusion..." Shafari studied the young man, then suddenly laughed. "So you think since your five years are up that you can simply walk out?" His tone darkened. "You've a lot to learn, *little* mage." In one swift motion, he yanked Lancheshire in front of him. Pulling a dagger, he thrust it under the slave's throat. "This isn't a game anymore. Now get in your cell where you belong, and I'll let your friend go."

Keith locked his gaze with the headmaster. "You're right. This isn't a game." He cracked a grin. "Or maybe it's just another attempt that went wrong. Look around you, Shafari. Aren't there a few guards missing?"

Shafari shifted his attention down each of the rows in search of support.

"Dozing off on the job again!"

"Well, now that you mention it," the young man began, snapping Shafari's attention back to Keith. "Seems in your absence, some of the guards made the mistake of unlocking some of the cells. I guess you could say they were...overwhelmed? Just a little trick I learned while wearing dispelling bands."

At this, the slaves simply opened their cell doors and stepped out, leaving the bodies of guards behind where they had stood around to hide. The mass surrounded both magic-users, some with wide grins, some with serious expressions. A few cowered as far from Shafari as possible.

"By the way, Shafari, unless you think you're holding my friend I'd put down the dagger."

A low growl announced the presence of the hounds as they stepped through the crowd in great numbers. Slowly, Shafari let the dagger drop. Wondering what he held instead, he looked to find one of his own guards in place of the slave. When he looked back up, the real Lancheshire had joined the surrounding group.

"My compliments, dear boy." Shafari let the guard's body drop. "But let's not get hasty." He gestured to the group. "These are mere trifles to deal with." He shook his head. "You, on the other hand, I knew would be a challenge. You've managed to thwart my initial attempt. But you weren't around earlier when I placed a curse on your document." He spread his arms. "You can't touch me, just as you couldn't touch the guards during the auction."

Keith's expression soured.

"You want to leave? Fine." Shafari pointed to the compound doors. "You have my permission." He then gestured to the large vats bubbling against the far wall. "As for the rest, I'll boil the lot of you before you even *attempt* to leave this place!"

"Not without contracts, you can't!" someone exclaimed, and the group looked toward the stairway as Leventés spread his wings and swooped overhead. A piece of torn parchment dropped from his hand. "Don't worry about the documents," he called from above. "That's what's left of the spell Shafari put on it. He can't complete the curse if it's not on paper."

"Ungrateful bird!" Shafari clenched his fists. "I'll have those wings from you!"

"You'll have nothing 'til you deal with me first," Keith threatened. "I'm leaving, yes. But not alone." He smiled inward, knowing the magic-user would accept his challenge. It was the moment he had been waiting for - the lone pawn had reached the king, but it would not go down without a fight.

Slowly, they circled each other, closing the gap between them with each step. *The king can only move one square at a time while I can only attack sideways. Yet he has the ability to move in any direction. I can only go forward.*

"Now we shall see who is strongest," Shafari broke the silence. "We'll start with a simple duel. I say a word and you counter by saying its opposite. Very easy...at first."

Keith lowered his eyebrows.

"What do you mean, start with a word? Why not start with a phrase, like 'I'm going to free you now along with everyone else since I can't control my guards anymore.'"

A few chuckled.

Shafari was not impressed.

He's preparing to throw spells at me. Keith shuddered. *Can I really expect to handle a full-grown magic-user who's had years of experience?* Doubt edged its way into his heart. He flexed his fingers against clammy palms.

"Why, Keith! Your face is white as snow," Shafari taunted. "Feeling doubtful now that you've boasted your greatness to your companions?" He chortled. "Come now and let us begin."

He lifted his hands outward. A breeze whipped through the room. Several candles flicked out, and an unnatural darkness settled. Lowering his arms, Shafari let the palms of his hands face downward, bringing them even with the floor.

Keith was lost in the entrancing weave as the headmaster's wrists seemed to touch when they crossed paths. In surprise, a brilliant glow of red-orange circles formed an outline around the two.

A pleasant smile broadened on the headmaster's face.

"After you," he indicated to Keith. "Think of a word that can be countered by its opposite, such as fire and ice." He clasped both hands calmly at his waist and waited for the young man to begin.

"How do you win?" Keith asked cautiously.

"By ensnaring your opponent with either a word that cannot be countered or by weakening them to the point where they cannot continue."

"So this is a test for strength."

"Oh, it's more than just that. Cunning is the *real* key." Shafari raised an eyebrow. "And now we will see whether those thieves taught you any or not."

Keith was silent. He regarded Shafari suspiciously, recalling how Lancheshire had described the chess game with the enchanted pieces.

Guess there's only one way to find out. He concentrated on what word to start with. Already, he could feel a pull in the back of his mind. His eyes glanced at the glowing rings that encircled them. The pull seemed to be coming from them. He took a deep breath, then spoke the first word.

"Frost." His own voice startled him in the still room. From the corner of his eye, Keith spied Lancheshire staring intently.

"Spring."

The counter took Keith's breath away. One moment he was standing with his eyes locked on Shafari, the next a heat stole through his body, traveling from the circles over the floor and up to his chest.

Shafari laughed at his expression.

"You're lucky I didn't say summer," he said. "Counter more quickly if you don't want any more nasty surprises."

"Silence!" Keith caught his breath. He braced himself as the pull of magic changed course.

"Good one." Shafari nodded "Uproar!"

A dull roar clamored to Keith's ears, but he grit his teeth and clung to a list of rapidly forming words.

"Teeth!" he shouted and watched with amazement as Shafari's garments ripped down one side. The headmaster staggered a moment, but only to regain his posture.

"Claws!" Shafari countered, sending pain up Keith's spine.

"Steel!" Keith retaliated.

"Armor!"

"Night!"

"Day!"

A white light suddenly blinded Keith. He had to think quickly.

"Rock!" he breathed.

"Chisel!" the headmaster answered.

"Waves!"

"Wind!"

When the light faded, Keith saw the headmaster's body rock back and forth like a ship on the ocean's torrent. Yet at his counter, Keith found himself trying to keep his own footing as a hefty gust nearly toppled him.

What if I should cross the circle? What if I become ensnared and lose the game?

Keith began to feel what the headmaster had warned. Not more than five minutes had passed, and already he could feel his strength drain every time he said a word. The more powerful or creative the word, the more strength he lost. Shafari, too, began to look weary, though Keith knew he was not about to lose to a slave. The young man glanced at the glowing circles.

"Tired yet?" he heard Shafari's mocking voice.

What word doesn't have an opposite? Think, Keith! What's one thing I know that has ultimate power? Even something as simple as...

Before Keith could finish the thought, Shafari blasted his opponent with a fiery storm, which the young man countered with ice.

"Curse..." Shafari breathed, closing his eyes as a crimson glow lit up the floor beneath him.

Keith saw it coming in wide-eyed horror. Shafari's confident expression told all as he crossed his arms and waited to see what the young man would say. Exhausted, beaten down by each spell, Keith could not think fast enough.

The floor shuddered beneath the young man's feet, and with each twist sheer agony arched its way through his body. The force of the blow threw him to his knees. He dug his nails into bloody sand. Eyesight dimmed. Waves of dizziness numbed his thoughts while faintly aware of laughing.

"Too bad illusion couldn't help you now." The headmaster chuckled wearily.

"Illusion..." Keith whispered.

He had not intended it to be a spell, but as soon as the word escaped his lips the circle of power shifted. Shafari must have sensed it, for he called instantly upon another word he thought would surely bring victory.

Keith waited.

It's not shifting, he realized. The haze in his eyes began to clear, and when he looked up he could see fear on Shafari's face.

Illusion…it doesn't just have to be something sharp or strong. I could say crickets or mice or…

Keith peered down as he pulled himself up, and his gaze fell upon his prints in the sand. It reminded him of Chase and her game of marbles, which brought a sly smile to his lips. Getting to his feet, he ignored the cheers from his comrades as he concentrated on what had to be done.

"No more countering." Keith narrowed his eyes at Shafari, who was recovering from firing random words, only to have nothing happen. Instead, he lapsed into silence. "This ends now!"

Standing straight with hands clenched tight at his sides, the young man centered all thought on his few chosen words, words that had no opposite.

And the ultimate one, he smiled, *I'll save for last.*

"Marbles!" Keith commanded the word like no other, then under his breath he murmured, "Check."

"Marbles?"

Shafari shifted his weight and regretted it, for at that moment his feet slid out from under him. Keith caught his breath as the headmaster tumbled sideways, catching himself at the last possible moment before he could break the circle.

Keith did not wait for him.

"Unicorn!" he exclaimed, pointing at the headmaster. His mother's stories of mystical beasts raged through his thoughts.

Half lying on his side, Shafari cringed at the word, and he looked up to see a white fire form from the tip of Keith's finger. The flame expanded, growing larger in the space between the two opponents. Taking shape, it pulled itself in a rear. A horn of pure ivory protruded from the forehead. Its cloven hoofs curved into two sharp points.

It came galloping down with its front hoofs ready to pound Shafari's body into the floor. Keith felt no sorrow as the creature dispersed just as it struck the headmaster in the chest. Never had anyone heard such a cry of agony. While the headmaster still wallowed in pain, Keith let loose his ultimate, most powerful creation he could aid with, tying it all together with a burst of his own will and magic.

"Nature!"

The crowd scattered when the floor began to tremble. Some of the walls crumbled. Bits of stone scattered through the air.

"Everyone out!" Lancheshire waved his arms, trying to herd people to the main exits. The hounds provided perfect protection. Their muscular bodies did not mind the batter from falling debris.

A large chunk crashed through several pillars. Candles were tossed from their stands, but their landing proved more dangerous. Filthy straw strewn along the rows instantly ignited in a rush of billowing smoke and flame. Screams echoed throughout the complex as slaves pushed to get out.

Keith continued to stand in the circle, not leaving until one of them was defeated. A large crack opened in the floor where Shafari lay. Dark green roots unfurled, drawn to the power the young man had unleashed. Their long vines snaked themselves around the headmaster's body, winding so tightly Keith thought he heard bone breaking. A half choke, half sob sputtered from the magic-user. The young man saw a hand dangle from underneath its binding. It rose, trembling in a feeble attempt, then went limp.

Weary, with dust settling on his shoulders, Keith stood alone with heaving chest. Drained of all his energy, the young man bowed his head in silent victory.

Checkmate.

The vines did not loosen, but the circle faded. For the first time, Keith looked around at the desolation. Darkness fled at the battle's end, replaced by smoke and fire.

"Keith!" Lancheshire choked from the thick smoke. "Hurry! We have to leave!" The slave stumbled over fallen rubble, avoiding flaming pits and keeping low.

Keith limped to Shafari's side. The magic-user's eyes were closed. Gently, Keith placed a hand over the headmaster's heart.

"He's still alive."

After glancing over the thick vines, Lancheshire shook his head.

"It's too late!" He coughed, holding a sleeve over his mouth and nose. "After all he's done to us, and you want to help him?"

Keith began to choke and sputter from the thick clouds of smoke slowly filling the compound.

"I know. But I won't be like him." Keith placed a hand on the roots and concentrated. The plant loosened just enough to get the body out.

"Let me take him!" Lancheshire hoisted the headmaster in his arms. "You'll need your strength!"

There was no denying the request. Keith was exhausted. Together, they picked their way around flaming rows and loose stone. At the gate, Lancheshire handed Shafari to another, then turned to help Keith. Their fingers nearly touched when suddenly Keith froze.

"Wait!" he exclaimed. "My mother's necklace and pan flute! Shafari had them in the main castle!"

"Don't be a fool! Come on, take my hand!"

An explosion shook the castle. To Keith's right the vats of boiling water had toppled; however, their liquid did little to quench the magnitude of fire and only thickened the air with poisoning fumes.

"Keith!" Lancheshire threw himself back to avoid several planks that toppled from the ceiling.

Inside, Keith had no choice but to find another exit. He felt foolish, risking both his life and Lancheshire's for two little items. He tried calling to his friend, but over the roar of fire it was near impossible to hear a reply.

Keeping low, he turned to make his way back through the maze of cells. Smoke burned his eyes and cast everything in a dark haze. Liquefied flames flared up behind him as a river of spilled contents ran between aisles and began gushing his way.

Terrified, Keith staggered around uprooted floor and squeezed between cells. He turned down an untouched row. Behind, the fire picked up speed.

Panic was the last thing he wanted. He needed to reach the stairs, for it was the only route that would take him to his treasured items. Unable to see, he had only the memory of where it was located, and when his foot finally hit the bottom step he felt relief wash over him.

His head throbbed from all the heat and breathing smoke. When nausea threatened, he lowered himself so he could crawl up to the second landing. He could not hear the fire beginning to devour the bottom steps. All he knew was to climb. He had barely reached the top before the bottom half collapsed.

Pain cramped every muscle. Dizziness plagued him, and it slowly dawned on Keith that he was dying. Intense heat and fumes whittled his strength away. Faintly, he felt the platform he was on swaying, or was it just another wave of dizziness? Spots of yellow dotted his view, followed by a growing swarm of blackness.

He lifted a hand and felt along the wall until his fingers slipped over warm metal. Hinges perhaps? Reaching up, he gripped a doorknob. It turned, and he shoved it open to escape the blackened compound.

The door shut behind him and a pair of hands gripped his body. Cool white feathers brushed against his skin, and Keith looked up to see a hazed version of a face, but a face nonetheless.

"I've got you, Keith!" Leventés hoisted the young man in his arms.

Weakly, Keith pointed down the hallway while smoke began billowing under the door. He coughed when he tried to speak.

The harpy lowered an ear to the young man's rasping lips, then gazed down the darkening hallway.

"We still have time," he said.

Leventés hurried to Shafari's study. On the floor lay torn pieces of parchments, contracts that identified each slave. Once torn, any spells upon them faded, including the transformation of hounds.

The harpy laid Keith in bed before opening the bottom desk drawer. The smell of burning wood hurried his search, and when he found the pouch containing the pan flute and necklace, he scooped it up and returned to Keith's side. Quickly, Leventés carried the young magic-user to one of the balconies where fresh air eased its way into their lungs and pushed out the stale smoke and smell of ash. The harpy made sure Keith's pouch was secured where the young man could find it before he readied himself to join the other freed slaves.

A shadow cast itself across the balcony. At first, Leventés thought it was from the rising smoke. Yet when he sought the cause of it, he was surprised to see the silhouetted form of another harpy. He waited until the creature landed, but recoiled in shock to find the silhouette nothing more than a Black Wing.

Leventés snarled, ruffling his wings in battle stance. To his surprise, the dark *'Keyarx* just stood. Not a feather shifted in response, not even to defend himself. Even his size was a bit off, being nearly the same as the White Wing.

In response, the *Ken'* spread his wings in an elegant display of greeting and bowed his head. He lifted his gaze to meet the other.

"Is he all right?"

"And why would a Black Wing care about a human?"

"I don't." He pointed a talon at Keith. "You hold a Healer, not a human."

Leventés nearly dropped the young man. He glanced at Keith, whose pale cheeks were beginning to gain color.

"Let me take him where he belongs," the Black Wing offered. "Now that he's free of this place, he no longer needs to be lingering about in the human realms. They don't even care enough for their own kind, let alone a Healer. Or us, for that matter. Think about it."

"A Healer…" Leventés repeated softly. "They are so rarely mentioned."

The Black Wing smirked.

"Perhaps that's a good thing, considering."

Slowly, Leventés stepped forward and surrendered his burden. Like a mother taking a newborn, the Black Wing was careful not to wake Keith and snuggled him close against his breast feathers. They would protect him from the harsh high winds in flight. Then, with a nod, Corrigan turned for the balcony wall.

"It would be wise if you returned to your kind as well," he added. Then he was gone, nothing more than a silhouette against the sky.

Part Three

Wisdom

CHAPTER 1

Rusha curled a wing around, extending the long snowy feathers so he could preen. His skilled fingers weaved through each one until he was satisfied. A good flap set everything in its place, then returned to their normal state of rest. Dawn began to filter through the treetops where the White Wing leader perched overlooking Crystal Valley, and only turned when he felt a presence approach from behind.

"You could at least say good morning, Chronicles." The White Wing welcomed the *Lo-ans'rel* to join him on his perch, but a single shake of the head denied it.

Chronicles stepped to the ridge that overlooked the valley. Another would have sent him toppling over, though Rusha was little concerned for the Healer's safety. As a master of magic, the Healer could do everything the White Wing could not, besides fly and fade his wings.

"You look as though you haven't slept for days," Rusha spread his wings long enough to glide down to the ridge where his companion stood. A quick glance confirmed bags of weariness under each eye. "Something wrong?"

Chronicles sighed heavily and let his shoulders droop.

"I cannot expect you to fully understand my burden, unless you wish to compare leader-wise."

"I expect your being attuned to Nature has its complications."

"It's never *just* about Nature anymore." His gaze shifted to the White Wing. "You above all should understand that reasoning."

His response was met with a frown.

Humans, Rusha thought bitterly.

Chronicles turned an ear in Rusha's direction as his thoughts were revealed, but said nothing. Their silence lingered while the sun rose lazily in the sky. Few clouds passed overhead. Now and then their shadows would travel across the valley.

Chronicles stiffened to the sudden disturbance of wings slapping the air. With ears perked forward, the two leaders turned toward the approaching sound.

"One of yours, I presume?" Chronicles inquired.

Rusha shook his head.

"Too heavy sounding."

"Black Wing?" The Healer flicked an ear forward.

"Not...heavy enough."

The Healer snorted. "Must be a half-breed."

A tremendous crack of leaves and branches toppled from above. Rusha spread his wings and jumped back from the oncoming debris while Chronicles merely stepped aside. Directly following, a dark shape flung itself between the two and over the cliff's edge with a curious bundle in its grasp. Sable feathers flew everywhere.

Corrigan? With...wait! Was that a human?

Rusha rejoined his companion to see the harpy's wings beating furiously to regain height. Yet something was wrong. The wings were uneven in their rhythms. With no air current to properly sustain the harpy's body, he began descending at a rapid pace.

At once, Rusha flung himself from the cliff to help the struggling harpy. He released a high-pitched whistle, then let out a second, this time letting the sound rap from his lips. Instantly, two harpies answered the call, flying directly to the Black Wing. They came from the sides, leveling themselves at the same speed of the fall. One took hold around his waist. The other grabbed his legs. Together, their wings beat the air as One to slow their descent.

The first few branches passed by before they finally stopped, hovering a few moments to steady their burden. One of their balconies was close by, and they carried the Black Wing over and gently laid him down.

"Corrigan!" Rusha landed on a nearby bridge and hurried to the scene. Many had gathered, but quickly stepped aside for their leader. He knelt beside his son, who lay gasping on his side. One wing covered him, which Rusha gently pulled back. The slight movement caused the wing to tremble, then fall limp.

"He's exhausted!" He pulled the other wing back. "What's this?"

What seemed to be a human was securely held in Corrigan's clutches, but a quick glance over the young man revealed cuts and burns to his clothing, more-so by the harpy's talons than anything else.

Rusha's youngest, Chanté, peered over his father's shoulder.

"Why would he bring one of *them* here?" he asked suspiciously.

His father shook his head.

"I don't know." Gesturing to one of his kin, he instructed to take the young man to one of the shelters. It mattered not which building, for all his attention was focused on Corrigan.

Chanté knelt beside the Black Wing and placed a hand over his racing heart.

"He'd have to be flying for days without rest to end up like this," the young harpy deducted. "Was he trying to evade the humans? I thought you said he intended to stay in their realm."

"That was my understanding," Rusha replied. After a moment, he scooped Corrigan into his arms and stepped to the balcony's edge. "I'll take him to the *Na'nafrétts*. He's better recovering away from the clan."

"And the human?" Chanté asked.

"I'll deal with him when I get back."

Rusha's large wings were strong enough to carry the broad-shouldered Black Wing with ease, so there was no difficulty transporting Corrigan to the other end of the valley. The edge of the forest was more thickly populated with Redwoods than where the White Wings made their home. Branches covered in thick foliage cast deep shadows, ideal for a dark *'Keyarx*. Rusha knew Corrigan would not want someone hovering over him like a protective mother. He enjoyed his privacy, which had led many to distrust him.

Rusha landed and inched his way through the thick foliage. He let his wings fade to keep them from tangling. Curiously, he looked up to see threads of moss-like webbing hanging from a branch. Below him, the same type of wavering gray-green web weaved between the branches.

So I see they've built up from the last time. He noticed new threads dangling from a tree next to him. *They must be close.*

A noise startled him down in the pit of darkness. So little was sunlight the farther down he climbed that he had to squint to see his surroundings.

"*Na'nafrétts,*" he breathed.

Several clicking sounds came from below as the White Wing stepped on a mesh of threaded nets. Not once did Rusha doubt its ability to hold him, for the creatures that built it were huge. For a White Wing to walk across was like an ant crawling on paper.

The image of the nets brought memories from years ago when the first *Na'nafrétt* cubs had been introduced to the clan. White Wing fledglings especially loved playing with them due to their speed and ability to climb trees. Yet over time, the creatures had grown too large for play, and their tremendous appetites for tree bark and sap destroyed many homes and surrounding trees. Thus the creatures were transported to the outer regions of the forest where they could grow and multiply at a safe distance.

A couple of jabbering creatures tumbled out onto the webbing, skittering around the White Wing before rushing back up the trees again. Gray fur covered their melon shaped abdomens. Six legs on either side of their plump bodies gave them a spidery appearance. The two *Na'nafrétts* scampered back and forth, communicating through various clicks, growls and screeches. Rusha shook his head as the two tumbled from the net down into darkness.

Cubs! He chuckled.

A tree branch next to him shuttered and swayed. When he looked up, a plump, round body pulled itself across the top of the net. Multiple joints allowed its long, hairy legs to bend in difficult positions to help the humongous body along. Two eyes rotated on either side of its head while two smaller ones took up the top. Its square-shaped jaws parted, resembling a turtle's mouth. The upper jaw extended slightly over the lower half with the corners of the mouth elongated into short tusks. Rusha watched the creature wrap its legs around the trunk of a Redwood. Its tusks grated against the bark, ripping off large chunks. Oozing sap ran from beneath the torn bark, a tasteful treat to the *Na'nafrétt's* double tongues. Oval nostrils flared at the point where its jaws connected to the face. The smell of harpy had drawn its attention.

Rusha knelt to lay Corrigan down. Above him, the *Na'nafrétt* moved closer, its eyes rotating to bring in a better view of the White Wing. Tapping its two tongues together, it created a series of soft clicks. Though unable to decipher its language, Rusha knew these sounds to be friendly.

Though I'm quite sure the Lo-ans'rel would know what it's saying.

With barbed hooks for feet, the *Na'nafrétt* gripped the branches and lowered itself upon the web. Its first two legs were shorter than the rest, so were used to feel along the web until it reached the Black Wing. Next, it touched Rusha. After several moments, the *Na'nafrétt* pulled back, admitting several more clicks in question.

"No harm," Rusha said. "Keep him safe." He gestured to himself. "Will return later."

The two cubs returned and skittered to where Corrigan lay. Curious to the strange creature in their play area, they felt his body with their feelers and played with his wings and hair. Then, looking up at their guardian, they jumped and squeaked for explanation.

The cubs were answered with a snort before the giant *Na'nafrétt* finally pulled itself up into the dark trees. Continuing to circle the figure, the cubs turned so their abdomens faced the Black Wing. A string of webbing ejected from the rear, encasing him with a pale green web of silk. Once completely covered, they scampered off after their parent, their jittering never ceasing.

Alone, Rusha knelt to examine the webbing. It was wet, but not sticky. Through raising the first *Na'nafrétt* cubs, White Wings had learned that a special healing chemical resided within the webbing when first extracted.

"Until you can regain your strength," Rusha whispered, "rest easy, son. I will return soon." He kissed two fingers and laid them upon Corrigan's forehead before climbing back to the canopy.

Now to deal with the human.

*****

He was falling.

Below, a pool of flaming liquid waited to devour him. His fingers were numb from holding on so long. In the distance he could hear the chanting of Shafari adding strength to the fire. It flared upward, licking his bare feet. He tried to pull himself higher, but his fingers lost their grip, and he was falling....

Keith woke with a yelp. His breath came short from the fowl taste of stomach fluids, and he closed his eyes to allow his pounding heart time to calm. An ache along his spine prevented him from sitting up all the way, but it was just enough to survey his surroundings. The room was a strange shape, a hexagon rather than the usual four-sided bedroom. Birds chirped outside his window, accompanied by several voices. From the amount of sunshine coming through the three windows in the one-roomed hut, he guessed it nearly the middle of day. Other than himself, the cot was the only furniture that adorned the space, and a strange one at that. Bits of downy feathers created a soft bedding while the rest was assembled from leaves and twigs.

Where am I?

Keith lifted his hands. Thin strips of white cloth wrapped around the palms and tied at the wrist. Another strip wrapped his head. He turned his hand over. The cloth did not completely cover his right wrist where Conrad had branded the mark on his flesh. He stared at the star-shaped scar while his other hand went to touch his mother's necklace.

He froze when his searching hand came up empty. Forgetting the scar, his hand sought the twin chains around his neck: one with the ring, the other his mother's charm. In a panic, he searched his pockets only to find no pockets at all, for his old clothing had been replaced with new.

My pan flute! Where's the pouch? Didn't I have it? Fear of losing the precious gift soon turned to weariness, and he lay back down.

He had just closed his eyes when the door creaked open, letting in the smell of fall leaves and wood. Keith turned his head to catch a view of tree branches and leaves before the door closed. His eyes readjusted to the slight dimness as he focused on the figure.

"I see you're awake."

Keith was faintly aware of rustling feathers as the figure approached. His garments were decked in the colors of coming autumn: a broad amount of yellow, flecked with red, brown, and several greens.

"You *can* understand me, can't you?"

Now Keith was sure he had seen feathers. As the harpy came closer he opened snowy wings, showing off his golden underside mixed with cream.

"You're a harpy," Keith said, receiving a nod.

"I am Rusha, leader of the White Wings. And you are?"

"Keith..." A cough froze his voice. When it passed, he tried again. "Keith Larson, from..." He paused. To say he was from Castle Mire might upset his host. Instead, he chose a friendlier location. "The Realm of Trully."

"Long way from home." Rusha's calm tone eased the young man's doubts, even more when he produced a leather pouch held from behind his back.

Keith gasped in recognition and strained his aching muscles to reach for it.

"I thought this was lost in the fire." He lovingly held it to his chest in a welcoming embrace, then peered inside. With trembling hand, he pulled out the two necklaces and pan flute. Immediately, he secured the jewelry around his neck.

Rusha rubbed his beard in thought. "A fire would explain the burn marks on your clothing. What were you doing when this happened?"

Keith pulled himself into a sitting position with great difficulty.

"I was...helping some friends when it started. Slaves, actually. We were escaping a place called..." He hesitated at Rusha's changing expression, wondering if he had already said too much. "Castle Mire...."

The leader's wings twitched to his thoughts.

"Should have known that human would betray him!" Rusha's gaze rested upon the young man. "Were you also helping Corrigan as well, the Black Wing?"

"Corrigan?" The mention of his friend caught him off guard. "He's here? I don't recall much after the fire started. But what's this about betrayal? As far as I know, he's not a slave. Then again, it's been some time since I last saw him."

"He is here, recovering after a long flight. Though it's still unclear why he'd bring another to Crystal Valley."

Keith followed the leader's gaze to the open window. As he peered in the direction of Lexington, afternoon sunlight that filtered across the bed reflected off his irises. In the next instant there came a gasp, and when Keith turned he found Rusha taking a step away from the nest.

Those eyes! The harpy's thoughts came to the young man. *Only such color belongs to one race alone.*

"You know of Healers?" Keith suddenly questioned. "Are they close?"

The White Wing nearly laughed, used to Healers catching wind of his thoughts and responding.

"Indeed they are. In fact, their main dwelling is directly beneath us."

CHAPTER 2

He was angry with the horn. He was angry with Corrigan. Why did the harpy have to get involved when he had made a promise to *just* watch? A wave of mind controlling energy was sent to stop him, but the horn had intercepted. Now as Jenario relaxed with head rested in his hands, he let his fingers caress his temple to subdue a wave of painful headaches from the amount of energy spent – for nothing. The horn had its reasons. So, then, did Jenario. A single candle burned next to him, the pale wax all but melted away in its brass holder. His tired eyes watched puffs of smoke slowly dissipate in the air.

"Now if only this pain would do the same." He sighed.

"What was that?" a crude voice boomed from behind, and Jenario cringed at the unexpected company.

At least he's sober, the alchemist thought bitterly.

Nathaniel entered the small study, his heavy boots vibrating the floor with each step, little help to Jenario's headache.

"Did I hear something about pain?" The assassin thrust himself into a chair across from the mage. Leaning back so the two front chair legs lifted off the floor, he kicked his feet onto the table with a thud. "What's wrong with you? Been working hard reading all these books lately?" He gestured to the shelves of leather-bound tomes encircling the room. "Quite a collection ya got. Added anymore?"

Not wanting to start an argument, Jenario swallowed a biting comeback.

"I have a headache. And would you mind getting your muddy boots off my table?"

Shrugging, Nathaniel removed his boots and tossed them to the floor, then slapped his soiled feet on the table and leaned back again.

"That better?" He smirked.

Jenario's gaze reflected his disgust.

"I've been having these headaches off and on," he said quietly, leaning back while still rubbing his temple. He lowered his hand, the headache subsiding finally to a mere throb. "I've never felt so tired, like the energy's being sucked from me."

"Well, you're not sleeping, for one." Nathaniel put one hand behind his head while gesturing with the other. "Think how much time you *do* sleep when you're trying to deal with a harpy using your magic to spy on someone. Then there's that newfound power you keep doting over night and day. Always locking yourself in your study, constantly talking to yourself—"

"Talking to myself!" Jenario rose in anger, sending his chair toppling and causing the throb in his head to worsen. "What do you know about magic? Nothing! So keep that drunken tongue of yours still! Better yet, why don't you go have another drink and slay a peasant? At least maybe then I'd have some peace and quiet!"

Without warning, the assassin's chair was thrown back, sending Nathaniel flying against a bookshelf. The bookcase tottered back and forth several times, causing an avalanche of books to pile on top of him.

"And you can clean that mess up while you're at it!" Jenario whisked from the study into the hallway. "I want each and every book back in its correct order – alphabetically!"

A hand pulled itself up from the rubble, throwing books off as Nathaniel attempted to rise, slipped, then picked up a book to look at the wording down the side.

"But I can't read!"

"Start learning!"

Having no patience left, Jenario hurried down the hallway and vanished into a portal of darkness. The comfort of his soft bed beckoned when he reappeared in his bedroom. He threw off his thick black robe and tossed it on a nearby chair. Dressed only in a silken sable gown, he lay down without uncovering the top layer of sheets.

"You despise not being in control, don't you?" a voice cooed.

Jenario let his body relax, comforted by the familiar inner companion.

"He forgets too easily that it was *I* who took him in when no one else would," he answered.

"He is a fool," the voice purred, soothing Jenario's rising anger. *"You don't need him to do your work, not when you have me."*

The alchemist held his breath for a moment, savoring the words like tasteful wine. A sly smile spread upon his lips. Yes, the horn was with him. He could feel the necklace that held the fragment of ebony horn upon his chest. The throb of his heart pulsed against the blood-red stone. Unconsciously, he let his fingers wrap around it. He could feel its warmth increase with each breath he took. When the stone became too hot to hold, he rested his hand on top, allowing the warmth to spread from his chest down into the depths of his soul.

"*You have only used me sparingly, Jenario. Let me be a guide. Why should you have to suffer lack of sleep as though you fear to use me?*"

Jenario opened his eyes. "I fear nothing."

"*Then let me show you the depths of endless power. Give in. Give up. Let go.*"

The stone pulsed against his flesh. A crimson glow spread from its core over the front of Jenario's chest. With every beat of his heart it crept further down his body. In silence, Jenario tensed.

"*Relax...*" the voice soothed, sending its warmth coursing up his spine into his mind. Thoughts became hazy. At his sides, his clenched fists relaxed. Without warning, the light shot from the mage's body and burst through the stained-glass doors. Glass shattered over the balcony floor.

Jenario opened ruby eyes. Long wisps of black hair draped across his brow. He rolled to one side and edged his way from bed on all fours. The mage turned to look where he had lain, an imprint of his body burned into the covers. Where before he had felt drained of energy, now his soul swelled with revived life. Each step he took clapped on the slated floor. As he passed by a mirror, Jenario glanced at his reflection. He laughed in wondrous delight, his voice exulting in the form of snorts and whinnies. The image of the black unicorn left the mirror as he trampled broken glass and jumped the balcony wall.

"*Now experience the true power of the horn!*"

*****

Keith rested against an entwining branch that created the balcony's railing. Sunlight poured through the canopy, warming several balconies where White Wings basked. It was curious, for these wooden platforms had been built smartly to receive sunlight throughout the entire day.

He turned and walked across a bridge, still getting used to its slight sway under his weight, until he reached the next platform. The treetops were peaceful. If not for the fact that he was a Healer, Keith could almost call this home. At random, he would pause to look through openings in the vast foliage and see the valley below, thankful he no longer dealt with masters or guards. Still, he missed his friends at the Thieves' Guild and wondered if Lancheshire had returned to it.

A peculiar sound drew his attention to a Redwood the platform had been built around. The young man squinted as he approached the large trunk, its bark unmarred except in one spot above his head where a chunk jutted out. Something about the pattern seemed out of place. Curious, he reached up to touch it and was surprised to find soft feathers instead of bark.

He stepped back to see a pair of golden eyes open. A head turned halfway around to peer at him. Now Keith could see the body. Clawed fingers and toes securely gripped the tree. It was a harpy, as far as he could tell, slightly human with wings folded behind its back that contained the same textured appearance of the bark. The little harpy readjusted itself and opened one wing to stretch. Keith caught a glance of its underside, a soft creamy white.

"That is one of the woodland *'Keyarx,"* a voice said from behind, and Keith turned to see a young White Wing approach. The same dark patterns on his face reminded Keith of Rusha.

For a moment they watched the creature. Then, pursing his lips together, the White Wing whistled. The melody was low, too low for humans to accomplish. The woodland harpy ruffled its wings in response, then opened its mouth. A shrill cry erupted from that small body, combining that of a pileated woodpecker and a screech owl. Some distance away, a similar cry was heard. The young White Wing chuckled and turned to Keith.

"I'm Chanté." He held out a hand, and Keith clasped it in greeting. "Rusha said you'd be this way." He beamed. "You and I look to be about the same age, though your kind would outlast me by far."

His gaze returned to the woodland harpy, which spread its wings and jumped out from the tree over their heads. Both watched it glide from tree to tree until it disappeared in the thick foliage.

"They don't fly far from the trees, do they?" Keith asked.

"Na. Should've named them Treehoppers." Chanté turned his full attention to Keith, "So... heard Castle Mire was destroyed. Can you imagine our relief? How did it happen? And..." He paused. "Why were you even there? Did they mistake you for a human? I see your ears are like them."

Keith lifted his hands to his ears. He had forgotten the illusion that still hid their true appearance.

"No wonder Rusha didn't recognize me." His cheeks flushed pink as he removed the charm. Only when he felt the soft hairs on the tips did he lower his hand. "My mother used her magic to hide them before her death."

"You didn't know what you were?" Chanté's feathered eyebrows rose in surprise. "I imagine you must have a lot of catching up to do with your kind. You know, they don't take lightly to untrained members. The biggest thing about them is shifting. Hope you've managed to learn that, at least."

The two began walking over the next bridge.

"Unfortunately, shifting's one of those things I need to learn."

The White Wing groaned.

"Good luck explaining yourself." His eye traveled to the leather pouch strapped around Keith's waist. "So what do you keep in there?" he inquired, changing the subject.

Keith glanced to the bag, then lifted the flap to pull out his pan flute.

"It was a gift from my parents, though it's been a while since I've actually played it," he admitted. "The headmaster of Castle Mire kept it locked away while I was enslaved."

"That's ridiculous!" Chanté ruffled his wings in anger. "I can't imagine being treated like that." He glanced at Keith. "I've seen humans come into our valley, though never this far. They usually hunt along the borders and take those that are too weak to resist."

"Your kind permit this?" Keith smirked.

Chanté narrowed his eyes. "My father would never let *anyone* take someone from *this* clan."

*****

Not far from the valley, a group of Dark *'Keyarx* prepared for their daily hunt. Their massive wings beat the air as they lifted their muscular bodies skyward. Talons flexed in eager anticipation for the kill to come.

A large buck would have easily sufficed, but today they thirsted for different blood. Only one creature paid any heed to their changing course. Crimson eyes stared silently after, a horn of twisted ebony pointed toward their destination.

*****

Keith brought the pan flute to his lips. He sucked in a breath, then let it out slowly over the reed openings. A single note rose, echoing around the two as it faded into silence. Where the first note left off, a second took its place. The melody was low in pitch, slowly rising in harmonious song. Nearby White Wings stopped what they were doing to listen. The song soothed them, filling their spirits with peace. As the last of the notes faded, Chanté let out a breath.

"That was incredible! I wouldn't think something so small could sound like that."

Keith slipped the instrument back into his bag. Nearby, a few harpies watched with interest.

A rush of beating wings drew their attention upward as several red-winged harpies flew overhead. There were not many, but their startling wing color across the sky drew several other stares. Keith glanced toward a tree house to find Rusha inspecting the skies.

In a heartbeat the group shifted direction, doubling back where they had come from like sparrows avoiding a hawk. Keith squinted, trying to focus on their expressions as they passed.

"What are they doing?" he asked.

"Not sure. There's a Red Wing clan not far from here, but we never really converse with them unless it's necessary."

Keith's ear caught the movement of air beneath the platform, a soft whoosh that slightly vibrated the boards. Carefully, Keith peered over the side. Without thinking, his hand went to the two chains around his neck.

Silence. The Red Wings had moved on. Not far away, Rusha watched his son.

"That's strange." Keith shook his head. Chanté joined him at the edge, following his gaze down into the depths of foliage. "I could have sworn something came underneath us."

"Na." Chanté brought a wing around to preen. "Just a low breeze, that's all."

"I don't think that was a low breeze," Keith said, noticing the platform around them darken in shadow. The two sides of the shadow moved to the beat of wings, and Keith glanced behind to see a large Black Wing hovering overhead.

A high-pitched whistle from Rusha caused his son to whip around as the Black Wing touched down upon the platform. His eyes widened in surprise at the sight of the towering *'Keyarx.* Fangs dripped with saliva when its mouth opened, and it sprang at the smaller White Wing with outstretched talons.

"Watch it!" Keith shouted, grabbing his friend and diving to the left. The Black Wing managed to swipe a piece of Keith's clothing before lunging off the platform's edge. Keith rolled over and immediately got to his feet. He started to help Chanté up when the Black Wing returned.

There was a blur of white wings between them as Rusha swooped down to stop the attack, drawing its attention away from the two young men.

"Fly!" Keith shouted.

Spreading his wings, Chanté jumped from the balcony. He flew alongside the young Healer as he raced across the nearest bridge.

"Get to the densest part of the forest!" Chanté returned, ducking under branches. "They're too big to follow!"

Keith glanced over his shoulder as he ran to see if the Black Wing was following.

"Look out!"

Keith nearly fell over himself trying to stop. A second Black Wing blocked his path, its giant wings slapping the air with each down stroke. Quickly, the young man retreated over a second bridge. His thoughts were only upon reaching a part of the forest too thick for Black Wings to follow. Directly to his left, another dark 'Keyarx joined the hunt, the same on his right.

An enraged battle cry rang out as Rusha, followed by several guardians, sprung to Keith's aid. Like smaller birds attacking a large one, the delicate White Wings swooped and dived around their dark cousins. More White Wings joined, ripping and taunting, giving Keith more time to dart over a platform and enter an area where the branches began to thicken.

"Up here, Keith!" Chanté called from above. His wings faded as he slipped through the many branches onto the narrow platform.

"I didn't see what happened to the others. Do you think Rusha's all right?" Keith asked when the young harpy jumped down.

"He's dealt with Black Wings before, so I'm not worried."

Keith opened his mouth to answer, but shut it. Behind the young harpy, the forest was dense with leaves and heavy shadows. Sure he had seen something move, the Healer cautioned his friend toward the forest opening.

Even before the harpy had a chance to move, black wings unfurled from around a russet body and struck Chanté across the back. The blow sent the harpy sailing across the platform, and only stopped when he slammed into a Redwood.

Keith saw the Black Wing spring past, its thoughts only on obtaining the flesh of a White Wing. He saw Chanté's gaze fall to the face of his predator. Still dazed from the blow, his body refused to move.

Without thinking, Keith raised a hand. In his thoughts, the scene replayed itself over and over. He had to do something, to stop it! Colors blurred, sounds mixed, and the faint sensation of ground moving from underneath caused him to close his eyes. He reopened them to find himself in Chanté's place.

The blow came faster than Keith had anticipated. Talons sunk into his arm. The next instant found him tumbling over the bridge, but he was far from done. Ignoring the pain in his arm, Keith clawed at his attacker's face. When that did nothing, he began yanking out feathers. One such pull drew blood. In the mad struggle to free himself, he never saw its blood splash onto his wounded arm. Only when a blue aura engulfed his body did the two cease fighting.

A sickly feeling of stomach churning dizziness made Keith gag. Blood rushed to his fingers, neck, and shoulder blades. Bones crunched and pinched at his fingertips and back, and when he looked at his hand his eyes grew wide in amazement. The changing light had dimmed slightly, though it stayed with him as he watched his fingers extend. Nails curled down, blackening into talons. Without thinking, he flexed his back muscles, surprised when glossy sable feathers curled around.

Wings?

The Black Wing snorted, but did not let go.

"Healer...."

"Surprised?" Keith smacked a taloned hand across its face, receiving a satisfying yelp of pain. When its grip loosened, Keith did not hesitate to use his newly formed wings just as an approaching tree slammed into the Black Wing's body with a splintering crack.

The Healer pumped his wings, trying to adjust to the newly added weight to his back. The long feathers closest to his body could be adjusted separately from the rest of the wing, and he quickly learned how to use them as he dodged trees in his mad dash. A snarl of frustration came from behind, and Keith glanced over his shoulder to see the Black Wing gaining speed. The Healer dived sideways to avoid ramming into a Redwood's wide trunk. He was flying so fast the forest around him was little more than a blur of color. Weaving and diving, Keith circled back and headed toward the main dwelling. He glanced behind.

The crashing of branches brought his attention back around just as the Black Wing shot up through the dense foliage. Keith swerved, breaking through a thin mix of limbs and leaves. The Black Wing half turned, trying to strike with its giant wings.

Keith felt something slam into his back, temporarily stunning him. Another blow came to his right wing, harder than the first. The Healer could feel himself shifting back. He tried to slow his descent, but his wings were retracting too quickly. The dark *'Keyarx* dove with him down through the trees. Its long talons grasped Keith firmly, holding him where he could not turn and fight, then felt it turn up into a landing position.

They broke through the foliage into a small clearing. Spreading its wings, the Black Wing landed with a painful halt. Keith tried in vain to pry the long talons from his bloody sides, and managed to clamp his teeth on a finger. The *'Keyarx* jerked its hand away, which caught one of the chains around Keith's neck. An instant snap sent his mother's necklace flying. Enraged, Keith turned to strike, but the harpy grabbed his hand and yanked him to the ground. Placing a clawed foot over his chest to hold him, the Black Wing laughed.

"Foolish creature," it hissed. *"Be still!"*

Keith's breath wheezed in his lungs. He was exhausted, and the Black Wing knew it.

As the Healer's blood seeped into the ground, a welcoming warmth spread along his backside as energy returned to his body. Surprised, Keith glanced at his wounds to find them closing as the grass around him began to whither, giving its life energy to its guardian.

With renewed strength, his foot lashed out at the Black Wing's groin, sending it tottering off his chest. Sapphire eyes shimmered as swift anger fused with his magic. Raising one hand, a gust of wind shot at the Black Wing's body and smacked him into a nearby tree. Still, the dark *'Keyarx* was not easily defeated. Its muscular body and thick feathering prevented small damage, and Keith realized that it would not take long before his own strength depleted once again.

Nature might keep giving me energy, but I can't keep giving it blood.

Raising both hands, Keith called forth a wave of vines to ensnare its body just as he had done in Castle Mire. They rose from the ground in an explosion of dirt and foliage to wrap around its wings. Though not very thick, they were easily broken. With little strength left, Keith tried once more. He was slightly shocked when the ground broke, and several large roots shot up in front of the harpy. Unable to halt its advance, the Black Wing crashed into one while the rest wove around its body like a snake. Keith could hear bones snapping as the first vine slammed overtop to finish what was left.

Overwhelmed by the sight before him, the young Healer turned away, and was startled to find someone else standing not far behind. The young man watched as an older male's hand moved with the actions of the vines. Keith looked back at the crushed body, its wings dangling uselessly from its broken form. Slowly, the vines retreated to the soil, taking its victim with them. Once in the ground, dirt pulled together with a touch of sprouting grass to cover the place of disturbance.

All was still as Keith gazed at the silver-eyed stranger. He noted the man's iridescent robe in the rays of sunlight filtering through the canopy. Gray white hair fell to the shoulders, and in his left hand he held a staff made from the Redwood tree. Neither said a word as the older male came close. No doubt, this was one of the *Lo-ans'rel* who lived beneath the clan of White Wings, and Keith was thankful.

The Healer stopped a few feet from the young man when a glittering object on the ground caught his eye. In one smooth motion he reached down and scooped up the charm that had broken from around Keith's neck.

"My necklace," Keith said.

Hastily, he advanced to take back the jewelry, but halted when the Healer made a series of low-pitched growls in his throat. Keith recognized the sound from when he had used the same defense against his last master. He noted the Healer's laid back ears as a sign of warning and raised a hand to his own. Before, illusion had shrouded their true appearance from humans. Now they reflected what he truly was, and he flicked an ear in puzzlement.

"I'm sorry," Keith began. "I should've introduced myself. I'm—"

"Where did you get this?" The Healer asked, ignoring the comment. His piercing gaze made Keith uneasy.

"It…was my mother's. She gave it to me before she died."

The look of surprise on the Healer's face was quickly replaced by one of fierce suspicion.

"How long ago was this?" he inquired sternly.

"Nearly seven winters, sir."

Keith tensed as he felt something flash through his mind. Quickly, he closed all thoughts, leaving only what he was thinking at present.

"Sir?" the Healer stepped toward him with disconcert on his face. "No. You shall address me as Master Chronicles."

"Chronicles..." Keith stared at him. *My father!*

"*Master* Chronicles," he corrected. "And what are you staring at? Submit!"

Taken back, Keith did not know how to react.

"Perhaps you didn't hear me the first time. I said *submit!*"

"I...don't know what you mean." Keith backed away. He pointed at the charm. "And that is my necklace you have. I would like it back, if you please."

Swift anger made the Healer's eyes glow a brief instant.

"This necklace once belonged to a member of our kind. How you got a hold of it—"

"I just told you; my mother gave it to me." Keith held his temper in check. Another pry into his mind sent a barrier slamming against the intrusion, and he watched as Chronicles pulled back in surprise.

"How dare you!" Chronicles hissed. "Do you know who I am?"

"Yes," Keith answered boldly. "Do you know who I am?"

The question received a raised eyebrow. "I do, for the most part," Chronicles turned and pocketed the charm in his robe. "You are the one we've been sensing lately. One with Nature, I see." He glanced over his shoulder at the young man. "Weak though you are."

"I'm not weak," Keith defended. "I just wish I could settle down and stop getting dumped from place to place. I want to be where I can safely say 'this is home.' But so far that hasn't happened. And from the looks of things, it's not going to."

Chronicles turned toward the young Healer. For a fleeting moment Keith's sight-reading picked up broken pieces from the Healer's thoughts: a rebellion, the clan splitting. What had happened to his kind that his mother had kept secret?

Unbeknown to Keith, another member had ventured into the clearing. Eumaeus quickly interpreted his leader's thoughts.

"Grand sake, Chronicles," he breathed. "'Tis your own flesh and blood before you."

"I am aware of that." Chronicles glanced at his advisor. "However, he knows nothing of our ways."

"He is first-born," the advisor said. "By your decreed, he receives the clan as leader after you."

"*Shy* is the one who will receive the clan. Not *him*!" Chronicles replied. "I've spent an entire lifetime preparing Shy for it, and *this* shows up!" The leader pointed at Keith. "Look at him! He wears the mark of humans. He reeks of them. His magic isn't at all what it should be at his age. And he doesn't even know how to properly submit!"

"Well, how can he?" Eumaeus stepped toward Keith. He circled the young Healer, looking him over. "All that's needed is time and patience. You felt it. He just needs practice. He's albino, like Shy. Besides, he's managed to deal with humans on his own and we weren't there to teach him." The advisor stepped to his leader's side to whisper in his ear. "He can help Shy; teach him about humans before we send anyone."

Chronicles raised an eyebrow, an intriguing thought coming to mind. Yet before he could reply, the sound of two harpies descended from the treetops.

"Thank goodness you're all right!" Chanté skidded to a stop next to Keith while his father landed more gracefully. "I thought for sure that Black Wing had killed you!"

Keith grinned and gestured to the Healers.

"Well, I did have a little help."

Rusha acknowledged the *Lo-ans'rel* leader with a nod. "You're in the right place now, lad. I was going to wait until I was certain you were feeling better."

"Good thing," Eumaeus added, giving Keith a tender pat on the shoulder. "We'll see to it he gets the care he deserves."

Then, with a nod from his leader, Eumaeus beckoned the young Healer to follow.

"Does he understand your language, having been with humans so long?" Rusha asked.

Chronicles never turned his gaze from the departing couple.

"We shall see."

CHAPTER 3

Amber eyes lazily opened as Corrigan stirred under the threads of silk encasing his body. He sniffed the air, taking in his surroundings. Muscles flexed in anticipation for flight, renewed strength flowing through his veins. A slight tug using his wings broke free of the web like a dark butterfly rising from its cocoon. The netting swayed gently under his weight as he stood and stretched, then strode to the nearest Redwood. In the distance came a couple of clicks and low grunts.

"*Na'nafrétts,*" he muttered.

He gripped the trunk with his talons and began to climb. He could not remember arriving in Crystal Valley. How he had ended up in the northern part was beyond him. Only the thought of Jenario trying to usurp his thoughts brought anger. Yet anger soon turned to hunger as his stomach quickly settled his next course of action. Wings folded neatly behind him as he made his way through the thick foliage. From above, rays of light played over the leaves, casting moving shadows from a cool breeze. Halfway to the top he paused to peer down into the darkness. Though midday, the forest below was blanketed in constant night. A slight shiver ran down the Black Wing's spine, and he hastened his climb.

A Black Wing frightened of the night? How pathetic! Corrigan lifted himself out into the sunlit sky. Perched upon a limb, he scanned the surrounding area for signs of movement. *I'm starved!*

Movement in the distance caught his sharp eye. A couple of sparrows dived in and out along the borders where the White Wings dwelled. Hungrily, he watched, arching his wings in preparation for the hunt.

"As long as the clan doesn't mind me grabbing a quick supper, I won't be in the area long."

Silently, Corrigan lifted to the sky. He held his wings in a glide, letting the air currents carry him as he dipped below the canopy, dived and came back up under a pair of nesting birds. A series of frightened chirps erupted as he grabbed one in mid-flight and stuffed it in his month.

A war cry from above startled him, and Corrigan had only moments to barrel-roll to one side. Turning, he slowed to a hover as a White Wing dashed by. A high-pitched whistle alarmed the rest of the group, and he was soon surrounded by angry clan members.

"I thought they were all gone!" someone demanded.

Corrigan turned to the voice. "Well, I see I wasn't sorely missed."

"Corrigan?"

The Black Wing looked up to see the leader land on a nearby limb. "I thought you were still resting." Rusha waved a hand to disperse his clan. "My apologies. We had a bit of trouble earlier."

"No doubt," Corrigan grumbled, taking up a place next to his father. "I come back to find you people all in a twit!"

Rusha chuckled to himself and waited until the area was clear before speaking.

"I'm glad to see you've returned safely. And I'm sorry about the confusion. We've had a few Black Wings attack." He noted his son's sour expression. "Chanté was nearly killed. If it weren't for Keith—"

"Keith?" Corrigan's facial feathers pulled tight against his skin, giving him almost a human appearance. "Keith made it here?" He grabbed Rusha's arm. "I'd forgotten all about the little runt! Where is he? Is he all right?"

"Calm down!" Rusha soothed. "He's fine. He's where he's supposed to be now." Corrigan looked below where Rusha's gaze trailed.

"Well, it's about time! What did they say to him?" He chuckled, letting his facial feathers relax. "I suppose they were pretty shocked to see him, weren't they?"

Rusha only shrugged.

"Chronicles didn't seem impressed."

"Him?" Corrigan stuck his tongue out. "He doesn't count. What of the others?"

"There was only one other – that I *saw*. Doesn't mean others weren't nearby. You know how they are."

Corrigan took in a deep breath, letting his neck and chest feathers puff out, then slowly drew them back.

"The important thing is, he's with his family." Rusha laid a hand overtop Corrigan's. "And so are you." There was a faint twinkle in his eye as Corrigan clasped his other hand overtop his father's. "Welcome home."

*****

Vegetation heavily concealed the perimeters, protecting the home of *Lo-ans'rel* from outsiders. With a gesture from the advisor, the vines parted to reveal a vast clearing. Sunlight shone brilliantly down as Keith ducked beneath the vines, which closed as soon as the two had passed. Keith's pupils constricted in the bright sunlight, and he blinked several times to adjust after traveling through the shadowed forest.

"Wow," Keith breathed, looking all around.

Gardens of flowers in every shape and color adorned the grounds along worn pathways. A variety of blooming trees spread their fragrances throughout the air. When passing a Silver Maple, Keith paused. A breeze shivered the leaves as sunlight reflected off each one, creating the illusion of silver sparkles dancing on the wind. Beneath the tree, a series of dandelions swayed in golden patches.

"You like?" The older Healer placed a hand on the young man's shoulder as he gazed up at the shimmering leaves.

"I've only seen these in one other place," Keith replied. Casting a final glance at the silver tree, he continued with the advisor.

Keith approached the center of the clearing where a wide stone foundation was located. Beside the foundation were two stonewalls. When Keith came close, a hidden door within slid aside. Two Healers stepped out, letting the wall slide back in place. At the end of the foundation were two steps that led to a platform. A throne, or what looked like one, was oddly constructed from different lengths of vines entwined over marble.

As he drew near, the young man noticed Healers gathering along the sides of the foundation. A thin red carpet of flowers trailed down the center, stopping at the bottom step. Keith lifted his gaze to see Chronicles step in front of the throne.

The young man halted at the beginning of the walkway, all eyes upon him. Nervously, he looked to the advisor, who gave the young man a gentle nudge.

"Go on, lad," Eumaeus whispered. "They're waiting for you."

Swallowing a lump, Keith stepped onto the walkway and made his way down the center. He kept his gaze straight, though now and then he would glance at those around him. Unlike harpies, *Lo-ans'rel* had no facial markings to distinguish between family members. Besides a slight variation in hair color and height, they all looked the same. Even age did little to hinder their slender appearance. In fact, Keith could not tell whether someone was old or not. There were very little wrinkles, and he began to wonder how old some of the members truly were. Decades? Centuries?

Movement turned his attention back to Chronicles. Two younger members had stepped to the side of their leader. Unlike earlier, the leader wore a pleasant expression and spread his arms in greeting as Keith stopped at the bottom step.

"I welcome you, young Keith, to Crystal Valley, and to the clan of *Lo-ans'rel*." He gestured to the Healer on his right. "May I present to you my son, Shy, whom will be your mentor."

Shy stepped forward, his emerald eyes locking with Keith's sapphire ones. Length-waist silver-white hair draped down his backside.

He looks just like me! Keith realized.

"And may I also present Jangus." Chronicles gestured to the young man on his left.

Keith caught a satisfied appeal in Chronicles' eyes as the leader watched Jangus approach. Unlike Shy, Jangus' hair was the color of charcoal. The young man beamed with pride as the leader continued his announcements, unaware of Shy's skeptical glare. While the dark-haired youth thrust his chin up like a proud stag, Keith heard Shy sigh in boredom.

"I am pleased to announce that Jangus has passed all his tests," Chronicles continued. "Should something befall myself or my son, it shall be Jangus to continue in my stead."

The word 'son' made Keith wince.

Can't blame him. I was never a part of this family. Like he said, I reek of human scent and harpy's blood, not to mention I must look a mess. Keith could feel the torn clothing down one side. *Why didn't I think to cover it with illusion?*

An ending announcement broke his concentration, and Keith was aware of the assembly applauding. Chronicles then motioned for Shy to join Keith. The young male held his silver robe up as he descended to his brother.

"May you learn well in our ways." Chronicles nodded toward Keith. With a wave of his hand, the clan dispersed.

Keith was amazed at how fast the *Lo-ans'rel* could move, and in no time the foundation was clear once again. Even the leader had vanished.

Shy smiled, sensing his confusion.

"Don't worry," his soft voice soothed any doubts. "You'll learn to do the same."

Keith looked around the still clearing.

"Where did they all go?"

Shy motioned to the trees.

"We don't always have to stay in the clearing. As Nature's Guardians, we each have our respected locations to tend."

"Except the river," a voice said from behind.

Keith turned to find Jangus watching him with folded arms.

"Crossing the river leads to the humans realms. Try to avoid doing that." The dark-haired Healer approached, then suddenly turned up his nose and took a step back in disgust. "Ugh! You smell human!" He eyed Keith's ripped clothing. "Look like one too."

"Well, *you* don't smell much better." Shy swiped a hand at Jangus, his silver hair spilling over his shoulders.

"Actually, this came from Rusha," Keith fiddled with one of the tears. "But...."

"Don't worry about it," Shy said. "It won't get in the way of your training. Besides, tonight you will be given proper clothing. Here." With a small gesture, illusion closed the rips and hid the bloodstains. "Good as new."

"Pah!" Jangus shifted into a raven and flew off into the woods.

"Don't pay him any heed." Shy rolled his eyes. "Just because he passed *his* tests doesn't make him the know-it-all around here." He leaned close and lowered his voice. "It took him *ages* to obtain various animal forms, always picking those of the shadows, easily hidden. Although, I'm not sure why he had to pick one with the worst stench!"

"Seems you have competition," Keith said.

Shy only shrugged.

"You two look like twins," a younger voice added. A dark-haired youth strode toward them with silver streaks fading from the forehead to the tips of his hair. Amethyst eyes met Keith's gaze.

Shy held out a hand toward the unexpected guest.

"Keith, may I introduce Twilight."

Keith grinned. "Like the time of day."

"It's my *favorite* time of day." Twilight grinned. "So you came from the human realms. Do tell! What was it like?"

"*Ni'ki, Twilot,*" Shy said sternly.

Keith cocked his head at the strange, yet familiar words. He recognized Twilight's name, but with the word 'light' pronounced 'lot.' When Shy switched back to Common, he retained a strong use of the accent.

"Now I know where I've heard that before," Keith said.

Shy smiled pleasantly. "The language, you mean? Of course! Only those One with Nature can hear it. Takes a bit getting used to. But if you understand Nature, you won't have any trouble understanding someone else who speaks it."

Keith blinked.

"You said, 'not now.'"

Shy nodded. "Good. Our language won't be a problem for you."

Twilight shrugged.

"That's the easy part," he said. "Everything you do must be perfect beyond what humans are capable of." He began counting off numerous items on his fingers. "Writing, speaking, moving, fighting, song—"

"Song?" Keith asked.

"Everything!" Shy intercepted. "*Qi'et?*"

After a moment's hesitation, Keith answered.

"I think so."

Shy stepped close so that he could whisper in the young man's ear.

"Remember, Keith. Chronicles will be watching your every move. Make one mistake and he won't hesitate to correct you. He's very strict about our training. We must be precise in *everything*!"

He stepped back and eyed Keith a moment before turning toward the perimeters.

"The best place to establish skills is in the forest. It's also where you'll take your first test: shifting."

"Our specialty," Twilight chimed in. "They say long ago when the first humans discovered us, they called us 'shift-wizards' for that very reason." The three began heading for the border. "I know a good spot where you can begin. Just follow me."

"I smell one animal within you," Shy said as Twilight took lead.

"You can *smell* my shifting abilities?" Keith breathed in deeply. "I can smell the flowers."

Ahead of them, Twilight laughed.

"That's because you haven't been given anything you can use to your advantage. The more animal gifts you obtain, the more you can do."

When he was given a quizzical stare, Shy explained.

"What he means is, you take the different animal abilities given to you and use them to heighten your own senses. For example, I used a wolf's sense of smell to determine what type of animal you had within. Well, maybe *half* an animal." He chuckled. "*'Keyarx* don't exactly make good shifts."

"You think?" Keith smirked.

Upon reaching the edge of the clearing, Twilight waved his hand for the vines to lift, and the three entered the thick woods.

"Don't worry, Keith," Twilight said. "Once you start acquiring different forms, you'll understand. You'll probably even start using them without realizing it."

"Despite what *some* people may think," Shy finished. "And Twilight's correct. After a few shifts, you'll start hearing and seeing things you've never known before. And you can switch from different senses."

"But what is the purpose to all this?" Keith questioned. "Is it necessary to become One with Nature in order to shift?"

"Anyone can shift, brother," Shy answered with serious expression. "For many generations, we've been expected to protect Nature. We are her loyal guardians. In exchange, she grants free use of her energy to call upon in times of need."

"It's why we're called Healers," Twilight added. "We can use this extra energy to replenish ourselves – plants and animals included."

"And other people?" Keith asked.

Shy nodded. "At one point even humans knew the word 'Healer.'" He stared off into the distance.

"And then the clan split," Keith finished.

Shy shook his head. "That was before our time. Now we must focus on the future. Healing and shifting is what we were born to do."

The giant Redwood trunks were even thicker than Keith realized, their root systems curling high over their heads before entering the rich black soil. All around, Keith was aware of eyes peering through the darkness at him, possibly those of his kind. Now and then he would hear an animal's song. Mostly, however, it was the continuous crunching of leaves and twigs snapping as they pushed aside overhanging foliage.

"What animals am I to shift into?" Keith broke the rhythm of their pace.

"All types," his brother answered. Stepping alongside, he continued. "For now, we'll start small. When you get through, you'll be able to change into creatures thrice your size."

Keith smiled. "I guess wings don't count, huh?"

"A half shift never counts!" Shy snapped. "You need to be able to fully shift, to feel the form of a new body – and control it! Twilight!"

The dark-haired youth snapped to attention.

"Take us to your spot, *je'sé*."

Reaching under his shirt collar, Twilight lifted out a silver chain containing a sapphire stone. Its inner glow reflected the young man's eyes as he held it up for the others to see.

"Ready?" he asked.

Shy nodded and took hold of Keith's hand.

"Hang on to me until we're inside."

"Inside?" Keith lowered white eyebrows in confusion. "Inside what?"

He remembered that mischievous twinkle in his brother's eye – that twinkle reflecting the light suddenly flaring out from the necklace. There was a puff of air across the back of his neck, the feeling of being pulled by an unseen force. All in an instant, Keith felt tucked into a small space, his body bending and twisting, and when he opened his eyes he was standing in a bright room with no boundaries that he could see. Glancing down, he saw that his hand was still held by Shy.

"Where are we?" Keith's voice echoed in the hallow chamber. For several moments after he could still hear his words asking the same question over and over.

Shy laughed.

"We're inside Twilight's crystal," he said.

"The necklace?" Keith looked around in amazement.

An image took shape in front of the two, like a window being opened. Beyond the crystal's surface they could see the wooded areas. When the window shifted views, Twilight's enlarged face beamed at them.

"Quit playing around!" Shy mused. "We're wasting time."

Keith saw the young man nod, all the while his appearance began to change. Fur sprouted down his neck, overpowering his clothing, which disappeared as though a thick blanket had just been placed over his body. His face elongated into a snout. The window plane shifted views, and they watched the forest floor approach as Twilight fell to all fours. The scene before them lurched forward as their friend, now a wolf, leaped into action. It amazed Keith that they were inside a stone going at full speed, and never once did he feel any movement. Only the window showed where they were going.

The wolf sped through the forest, pausing only to catch his breath atop a log. Overhead, a raven landed on a branch. It fluttered its wings and gave a rasping cry.

"Come on, fur-ball!" Jangus teased in his bird form. *"Think you can outrun something of flight? I know where you're headed."*

Ignoring the cackling bird, Twilight bounded off the log. A thick patch of moss cushioned his landing, and he hastened the journey. Behind, the flap of wings confirmed the raven was following. It was not long before he had passed the wolf and reached the clearing first. He watched Twilight shift back, returning the two brothers to the forest. Exhausted from the race, the younger boy collapsed in a pant.

"Look at him wallowing in the mud!"

Both Shy and Keith peered upward to see the raven perched above their heads.

"I'm not in the mud!" Twilight picked himself up and dusted off his clothing.

The raven fluttered down a limb or two before shifting to its true form. Letting his feet dangle, Jangus glared at the trio.

"You came all this way just to shift?" The young man shook his head. "Then here's a tip for you. Whatever you do, don't accept any gifts from a skunk. Twilight here had the pleasure of sleeping outside for a week because of it."

"That was *you* who did that!" the younger boy protested. He grabbed a stick and threw it at the Healer, who shifted and flew off.

"Serves him right," Shy murmured.

"Pompous brat!" Twilight grumbled. "Thinks he's better at everything."

"That's 'cause Chronicles favors him," Shy replied.

"But is it true?" Keith glanced from one to the other. "Can certain animal forms leave a bad odor?"

Shy shrugged. "Like Jangus said – a good week or more."

Keith glanced around the clearing. He could hear the trickle of running water nearby. Overhead, various birds sang.

"So when do we start?" he asked. A tension swelled in his belly, and rising excitement dried his throat. Already, he could feel his palms sweating, and he hurriedly wiped them on his pants.

Don't worry, Shy's thoughts came to him. *With my help, you won't lag behind long.* In response, a songbird alighted on Shy's shoulder, its cheerful chirps and whistles erasing all doubts from Keith's mind. Puckering his lips, Shy returned the song with his own whistle.

"Can you understand?" Keith asked.

"Of course." Shy raised a hand, and the small bird hopped onto his finger. "Here, you try. It's almost like sight-reading. Just hold out your hand."

Keith did as told and watched the bird flutter to his open palm.

"I'm going to be this small?" He watched the little creature preen under one wing and ruffle its feathers upon its breast. A tiny bit of red speckled its beak now, but before Keith could question, it suddenly pecked his finger.

In surprise, Keith shook the bird off and raised his hand, staring at the bead of crimson swelling from the prick. His head was swimming with an array of sounds. All around, he could hear voices. It was unlike Nature's multi-voiced sweetness echoing in the difference languages. These new voices were high-pitched, singing their words rather than speaking them.

"I understand," Keith whispered.

He raised his eyes to the canopy. Trees and sky grew larger. Or was he shrinking? Sounds became more acute. His vision began to extend to the sides of his head where normally he would have been blind. What he thought were slim trees rising above turned into blades of green grass. When he opened his mouth to comment, a chirp came out instead.

A pair of hands gently lifted him. Turning his head from side to side, Keith realized his brother held him. He peered down at himself. His round body was covered in burnt sienna feathers with a tan underbelly. A touch of white to the forehead indicated where his hair used to be.

"Test your wings, *brethusus*," Shy whispered. Then he released the bird to the air.

Keith spread his wings instinctively as he sprang from his brother's grasp toward the canopy. It was unlike shifting into the harpy form, for there were no extra limbs to worry with, besides having a tail.

He landed on a branch above the two Healers. Twilight waved to him.

Think you're better than me? A thought came from Jangus.

Keith jumped when the raven landed beside him. It gave a cackling cry as sable feathers extended into fur. Tufted ears pricked up around a whiskered face. A pink tongue licked one paw.

How 'bout a little game of...catch? Crouching low on its haunches, the bobcat prepared to pounce.

"Jangus!" Twilight shouted from below. "Leave him alone!"

Keith dived below the branch just as the bobcat pounced. He turned around in time to see Jangus shift into a hawk and swoop down upon him, claws extended. The two birds collided in mid-air, causing Keith to shift. He landed on his back with a loud thud.

"You're weak." Jangus stood over him.

"*Phv'in!*" Shy commanded, and Jangus shrugged and stepped away. "I will not tell you again." A deep sound emitted from Shy's throat. "*X'no ento'aqaen.*"

"Don't worry." Jangus tugged his shirt collar higher. "I won't."

Before Keith had gotten off the ground, the dark-haired youth was gone.

"Is it just me?" Keith asked as Twilight helped him up.

"Na. He's what we like to call...*irritating.*"

Shy's serious expression, however, did not waver.

"Ever since Chronicles took him in, he's been a problem. I'm sorry Keith. You'll just have to excuse his behavior."

"I can live with that, so long as he doesn't try to eat me."

Twilight laughed. "No worries, Keith. We don't eat meat anyway. Part of Nature's law, you know."

The comment brought back memories of Keith's mother. Slowly, he nodded in understanding.

"It all makes sense now."

"Then this should be easy," Shy said. "Before the day is over, you will have mastered shifting within your element. All our energy comes from the forest. We are earth bound." He indicated to the ground. "Nature grants only two other opportunities to change to a different element, in which case we'd have to purge all forms corresponding to it in order to take in the new."

"How many elements are there?" Keith asked.

"More importantly," Twilight added, "how many different types of *Lo-ans'rel* exist?"

"Do we have contact with them?"

Shy shook his head. "It's rare. The elements keep us separated. So in truth, we're not sure how many others exist. We just know."

CHAPTER 4

Jenario could hear Nathaniel's footsteps reverberating along the slab floor even before the assassin reached the bedchamber. Such disturbances usually upset the alchemist. Yet this time he greeted the bloodstained assassin warmly as he slung back the bedroom door.

"Out for a little morning kill, I see," the mage teased, reclining in bed with hands behind his head. "Pity it doesn't help your reading ability." He smirked. "Still, you could have invited me to breakfast."

Nathaniel halted in mid-step. He was accustomed to Jenario's normal rebuke; however, his good humor caught the assassin off guard.

"Ah." Jenario took note of his companion's hesitance. "I understand." He moved to the bed's edge and leaned closer. "In fact, I can *hear* your every thought."

"Something new you've been practicing, I suppose." Nathaniel shrugged and, pulling up a chair, plopped himself down.

"Indeed." Jenario stood with an heir of newfound dignity.

The assassin chewed on his bottom lip as Jenario strolled past his seat to the opened balcony doors. An unusual stream of pale yellow light filtered in through rising mist outside. He had not paid much attention to it until his companion stood basking in its eerie silence.

"You look more alive than you've ever been," he commented.

Slowly, Jenario turned, a grin of malign satisfaction etched into his features.

"That I am. More...*alive*."

There was a faint twinkle of color in those dark eyes, a color Nathaniel was certain he had only imagined.

Red. Blood red.

"Does my nature disturb your single-minded self?" Jenario's voice hissed.

"Single?" Nathaniel snapped to attention. "Oh, not that liquor quote again! I'm as sober as—"

"A well-fed ass," Jenario finished. "Yes, I would be able to quote you by now, wouldn't I?" The corners of his mouth cracked in scheming pleasure. "No, my friend. Your soberness concerns me not." He stepped back inside. "So long as it doesn't affect my plans."

Nathaniel bulked.

"Plans? What plans?" The assassin took out his blade and wiped it across his shirt, flaking off crusted blood. "I don't see a cursed thing of yours going the way you've said it should."

Jenario raised an eyebrow. "Don't you?"

"Well, you had the harpy – who knows where it's at now. You never got to study the boy. Then there's that power you seem to value as world-domination-at-your-fingertips!" Nathaniel rattled a hasty laugh.

"Interesting word choice," Jenario mused, rubbing the tuft of hair on his chin. "Not exactly how I'd phrase it…but close enough."

"Phrase away then!" Nathaniel rose from his seat, his thick boots grating against the floor. "Anything I can get you? Liquor preferably."

Jenario chuckled.

"Just tell me about your latest victim, and was it worth the trouble."

"Venison. And no; more hair than meat on its hide – something the harpy would've enjoyed."

Jenario sighed and turned away.

"Pity you couldn't use your talent for something more exciting, say…a unicorn perhaps?"

Nathaniel's expression reflected his doubt, but the mage continued.

"Have you ever wondered where magic comes from? How we as magic-users can conjure spells and such using formulas to control the amount of energy we take into our bodies? You haven't, have you?"

Nathaniel shook his head, lost in the mage's conversation.

Jenario held up a finger. "I know you can't read, if any at all from the amount of work you did putting my books away for me." He caught the assassin's faint scowl. "But those books hold more information of the way things work in this world than you will ever realize. Did you know, for example, that unicorns carry their souls in their horns?"

"What about it?" Nathaniel yawned. "It's where all their power is stored, or so I thought."

"But it's when they die that their souls are released, thus giving us free access to their energy."

"Uh huh." Nathaniel rolled his eyes. "So basically what you're saying is you're taking power from a corpse."

"Something to that affect. Though it's how you use it that counts."

"And *how* exactly are you using yours?"

A thin smile spread across the mage's face. Those eyes flashed a hint of crimson in the glow of eerie sunlight.

"The same that one would use a horn to gain power for himself," came a dry hiss as Jenario stepped around the assassin toward the door. Before leaving, he turned and added, "As for the boy – studying him could never be easier." When Nathaniel's brow furrowed in question, Jenario slipped into the hallway with the last phrase, "The harpy has proved more useful than you realize."

*****

Keith listened to the sounds of water trickling along the bank, marking the borders of Crystal Valley. All day he had practiced shifting until he could feel his blood racing to deliver the newly acquired forms. It amazed him what his body allowed. He could shrink as small as a butterfly, or grow as large as a bear.

As the day drew to a close, Keith finally found peace among the mossy soil and fallen leaves. The ground was moist from the nearby river and stained his clothing. He did not mind, for soon it would be replaced with the *Lo-ans'rel* garments.

He recalled the information Shy revealed throughout the day, especially pertaining to their clothing. Using his own as an example, the Header had demonstrated its durability by pulling on it. He then instructed Keith to rip one of the sleeves. When Keith had tried, he found it impossibly strong to break, even at the seams.

"Nature provides us with everything we need," Shy had explained as he showed Keith a webbing of spiders working together to create a piece of clothing for the Healers. Amazed, the young Healer watched how quickly they wove the strands. "It won't be done until morning. We can come back then."

Keith thought about his brother's warning concerning severe weather. Caught out in the cold was instant death for a Healer. The same went for extremely warm climates.

"But why doesn't Nature protect us during these times?" Keith had asked.

In reply, Shy explained, "It wouldn't be fair if Nature didn't find time to rest and replenish her energy. Winter is that one chance, but in doing so we are left without a connection."

Keith closed his eyes and brought to mind all the things his brother had told him. It had been a lot to take in his first day. His entire body ached, yet that unyielding desire to learn more about his kind propelled him to please his brother. The more he excelled, the more his brother revealed.

The distinct smell of Twilight triggered his wolf-like senses, and he called to him in greeting.

"Care to join me this evening?" he inquired as the younger boy approached.

"So I see you're getting more familiar with your abilities," Twilight replied with a wide grin. "How do you feel?"

Keith let his shoulders droop. "Exhausted."

"I wouldn't doubt it." Twilight took a seat beside the young man, then glanced up into the darkening sky. Leaning back, he placed his hands behind his head and watched the remaining yellow-orange sky gently fade into violet-blue night. "Was it hard to live around humans?"

Keith followed Twilight's gaze as he drew his knees up and wrapped his arms around them.

"It wasn't bad." He rested his chin on his knees and thought of the guild, of Luxor Castle, of Glory....

"You have fond memories." Twilight picked up Keith's thoughts using sight-reading. "According to Chronicles, humans were responsible for the loss of our first home."

"Why would humans attack us? What did we do?"

Twilight pulled himself into a sitting position and shook his head.

"Whatever it was, they were pretty upset about it." He glanced at the sky, now a rich midnight blue. "Best we head back. Shy will be waiting."

Keith stood, brushing leaves from the backside of his pants while Twilight grimaced at the grass stains.

"I don't know how you can wear that stuff! Least what we wear doesn't ruin so easily."

Keith smiled wearily. "You get used to it."

Twilight scrunched his nose in disapproval. "I hope I never have to."

Together, the two started toward the clearing. The way was shrouded in shadow, for no moonlight could slip through the high canopy to guide them. Yet Keith had no trouble seeing. The young man's pupils enlarged twice their normal size, taking in all the light available and adding in several animalistic senses to further heighten it. The sounds of trickling water faded behind, replaced by crickets and strange calls throughout the forest.

Probably 'Keyarx, he thought. *Or else my kind.*

"*Na'nafrétts* make them," Twilight read his thoughts. "Huge creatures." He spread his arms to elaborate his words. "I've never seen one, but I hear they look like furry spiders. They live just on the edge of the forest." He paused to listen. "Hear it? They make those clicking sounds."

Keith tuned his ears for the clicks and, like a wolf's, they moved to direct in more sound. Overhead, *'Keyarx* settled in for the night. Nearby, a moth crawled on a leaf. A twitch of antennae from a praying mantis turned his ear another way. Even the sound of earthworms squirming beneath his feet could be heard.

"Kind of loud tonight." Keith shook his head to clear it. "Think I preferred the quiet."

Twilight laughed. "Oh, there!" he exclaimed. "Hear it?"

It came again, a low series of clicks like the snap of a twig. Eventually, it grew louder into gurgling snaps and grunts.

"They sound close," Keith whispered. "Do they ever come here?"

"Hope not," Twilight replied. "They eat bark. The *'Keyarx* would be forced to leave if they ever did."

Ahead, they could see the vines that surrounded the clearing.

"You try opening it this time," Twilight suggested.

"Will it let me?"

"You're *Lo-ans'rel*. Why wouldn't it?"

Keith was both tired and excited. After obtaining his many shifts, he could not wait to have some time alone to practice. Upon reaching the vines, he lifted a hand like what Twilight and Eumaeus had done and watched with satisfaction as they pulled open.

"What took you so long?" Shy greeted when they entered.

"We were listening to the *Na'nafrétts.*" Twilight grinned.

"Yeah, well, at least you could have spared me one of Jangus' fits." Shy grit his teeth. "He hates that noise."

"Ha!" Twilight laughed. "I'd like to see him change into one of those things. Be a nice little addition to what he's already obtained."

"I should think by now he's learned not to shift into a skunk, so quit fussing." Shy gestured to his brother. "As for you, I've done a little preparation, which I think you will like better than what you're accustomed to."

Keith followed his brother, who led the way to the center foundation where twin walls contained a secret passage. At his presence, the wall slid to one side to allow entry. Shy went first, followed by Twilight. Keith was about to enter when a glint of white caught his eye. Though a thick layer of vines protected the clearing, he swore something had moved in the distance.

A tug on his sleeve turned his attention to the passage.

"You'll love your new home!" Twilight pulled harder. "Come on!"

Ducking low, Keith stepped inside the stone structure. The sound of wall sliding back into place shut the outside world away, and he was lost in the wonder of his new surroundings.

CHAPTER 5

The corridors of the underground home were alive with Healers. Keith could hear them even before stepping out into a vast chamber where many of his kind socialized. Redwood root systems curved in and around the stone foundation, supporting the vast number of chambers that wound further into the earth. Soil and rock formed the interior, which branched upward into hollowed Redwood trunks. Large roots overhead provided natural walkways, turning the upper portion into a fortress with the trees as watchtowers.

They probably knew I was with the White Wings all along, Keith realized as he watched several Healers come and go from within the trees.

The twisted root stems fascinated Keith. Suspended from the ceiling like giant ropes, they provided the perfect place for young Healers to test their climbing skills. A young boy scampered up the long vine, his nails digging into the wood for a firm grip. Though merely fun and games, Keith noticed the elders carefully keeping watch. Now and then they would glance at the newcomer, which Keith greeted with a nod. From behind, he heard Twilight's soft voice.

"I've heard that humans raise families in solitude. Here, we're all family. Everyone looks after each other."

"That must be nice," Keith said to himself, "to have a family...."

The three departed the large chamber and turned down a narrow passage. Eagerly, Keith followed with Twilight flanking his heels. For light, candles lit the interior, one on either side of the walls every few feet.

"How far does this go?" Keith asked his brother.

"Some go for miles," Shy replied, glancing over his shoulder. "I prepared a room for you while you were out practicing."

"Down here?" Keith wondered, but Shy's chortle of amusement eased his concerns.

"I made sure you were close to Twilight, so don't worry. You won't be far."

"Besides, it's impossible to be alone," Twilight chimed in. "The elders' responsibility is to check on the younger. So don't fret should you hear someone enter your room a couple of times during the night."

"These tunnels are vast," Shy continued. "Sometimes it's good to check until you get used to it."

Keith peered down a few side tunnels and wondered if he would come to know them like the rest of his kind.

"Here we are." Shy's voice brought his brother's attention to a doorway.

Carved from Redwood, the thick maple-brown frame arched overhead and curved down to the floor. Sap green vines delicately followed the patterns of the wood midway across. Upon the archway were calligraphic symbols, each graceful stroke perfectly etched into the wood.

"*No'aeco,*" Keith read slowly. The symbols looked nothing like a language. He had never seen anything to equal, yet he understood its meaning as though the translation had been written alongside it. "Newcomer."

"Fancy it'd say welcome," Twilight said. "But 'new' you are."

Keith watched his brother open the door.

"Hope you won't mind, as we do treasure color," Shy explained as Keith took his first step inside the enchanting room.

Colorful bottles of wine, cerulean blue, yellow-green, and lavender lined the mantle to his left. A small oil lamp close by illuminated the room with a soft golden glow, causing the bottles' colors to reflect across the wall as light shone through. Against the far wall stood a canopied bed, its bedposts carved in the shape of animals locked in intricate patterns. Keith admired the elk's entwined antlers with swan wings at the top of the canopy, with a transparent silver curtain draping down and over the foot and headrest, which were then tied at the corners to allow one side to remain open.

"Where's your room?" Keith asked, turning to the doorway where his brother stood.

"Near Chronicles," Twilight answered for him, striding into the room. "Nice." The fresh aroma of rose petals drew his attention to the bed where a single white rose lay atop the pillow. "Hey, I never got flowers in *my* room!"

"Then go pick some." Shy grinned, moving to a vine-encased wardrobe. At a gesture the vines parted, and the doors to the wardrobe opened to reveal Keith's new clothing.

"These are mine?" Keith gaped at the silken garments. Several long robes, along with an abundance of tunics and shirts, hung from the vines inside. Silver designs adorned each outfit. Carefully, as though afraid to touch the delicate fabric, Keith lifted one of the sleeves. "It hardly feels like it's there," he said, letting the silken material slip through his fingers with ease. Sifting through the rest, he came across an ankle-length, silver gown. He glanced at his brother. "This is not for going out, is it?"

Twilight chuckled.

"Nightgown," he corrected. "Honestly, Keith! What did you wear when you slept in the human realms?"

"Which you should probably be wearing now," Shy replied, glancing sidelong at Keith's ripped clothes when the illusion faded. "You might as well toss them away."

Keith carefully took the gown, watching as the empty vine curled back into the wardrobe.

"There's water for bathing in the room down the hallway," Twilight suggested.

"Thanks. How 'bout you, Shy? You coming with me?"

His brother shook his head. "There are a few things I must do." He smiled reassuringly. "But I promise to be back in the morning."

Keith gave his brother a brisk nod in understanding.

"Goodnight, brother."

Shy hesitated at the doorway, then replied in a quiet tone, "Goodnight, *brethusus*."

*****

Shy could still hear Twilight's chatter even after he had departed the passage toward his own room. He was quite pleased with how Keith was progressing, especially his shifting.

He took in more animal forms than I on my first day!

"I hear thy thoughts," a deep voice interrupted.

Knowing full well who it was, Shy froze and allowed the Healer to approach.

"So he's doing well," Chronicles said, hands behind his back in relaxation.

"He learns without question," Shy replied. "He would make you proud."

"No doubt he would, if not for his human upbringing." Chronicles walked a few steps ahead as they started down the passage together.

"He can't help it," Shy dared to say.

Chronicles came to an abrupt halt, nearly causing his son to collide into his backside. Without turning, the *Lo-ans'rel* leader spoke with fierce persistence.

"And I suppose he couldn't help throwing his magic freely about as he pleased." The leader's eyes glowed for a brief instant as he peered over his shoulder. "Our powers are for Nature alone, *not* casual play. We take our duties seriously." Chronicles looked off into the tunnel ahead of him, eyes unseeing while his mind sought the right words. "I can see the same arrogance in him that I see in humans."

"Then why are we allowing him to stay here if he is nothing more than a human's pet?" Shy bowed his head in submission when his father turned to grip the young man's shoulder.

"He will learn his place…as will you."

Shy watched Chronicles silently slip down the corridor.

You will speak with him, won't you? Shy tuned his sight-reading to his leader's thoughts.

Yes.

Have you read his thoughts?

His past separates him from the rest of us. He will always be part human, no matter how pure his blood.

*****

Keith returned to his room shortly after bathing, relishing the feel of fresh linens against his skin. While adjusting the gown, the scar on his wrist caught his attention. Why had that not healed? The talon marks had been long and deep while the flame of a candle had hardly broken the skin. He recalled the fire from Castle Mire. How terrified he had been!

Could fire be a weakness even if it's one of Nature's elements? Maybe it's something we can't control.

The gown grazed the floor as he walked to his bed and pulled back the covers. He picked up the rose that still lay on his pillow, stirring its fragrances, and placed it on a nearby table.

There was a faint tap on the door.

Keith turned, one knee resting on the edge of the bed when it opened. He could tell by the fingers that wrapped around the frame that it was neither Twilight nor his brother. Instead, Chronicles swept into the room and shut the door quietly behind him. The young man could feel his chest tighten with unease as his father approached, pulled up a chair and made himself comfortable.

"You don't have to keep still for my sake," Chronicles spoke softly, eyebrows lowered in vacant expression.

Realizing he still had his knee in bed, Keith slid the rest of the way under the covers and snuggled beneath them. To him, the downy mattress was like resting on air. After all the years he had spent in filthy cells, hard cots and ripped blankets, the change was welcome.

"I'm sorry I'm not what you expect," Keith whispered. That tense feeling of being judged lingered in the pit of his stomach, and he turned away from his father's gaze.

"Expect?" Keith flicked an ear toward his father's voice. "What would I *expect* from someone who's lived a human life? I can only assume you'll achieve close to or as much as Shy."

A rustle beside the bed told Keith his father had moved closer. He looked up when he felt fingers lightly touch the scar on his wrist.

"Flames," Chronicles began, "cannot be healed, no matter if we are One or not. It is as deadly as the nectar from the *Eúgliactmaent* plant."

"A plant that can harm us? But I thought—"

"Not all things in Nature can be controlled," Chronicles interrupted. "Now, had you chosen Fire as your element instead of Earth, that mark on your skin would have never shown. But because it is not our element, Fire is nothing more than heated energy spurred by what's around it. It's about as controllable to us as the air we breathe. There's nothing connected to it, to hold it back. But should it scorch the forest floor, what then? Does Nature die? No. She simply transforms and continues growth. And we are here to make sure she does just that.

"We are her guardians, her loyal servants and trusted advisors. We care for her young, the plants and animals that prosper in her wake. In return, we receive her gift of energy, to shift, to control the magic that's around us. It is the same way with other elemental Healers." He lifted his hands to the ceiling. "We are supreme! There is no equal to our knowledge of the way things must be."

Gradually, he lowered his arms and turned a weary silver gaze to his son, who after a moment asked, "What about the things that happen when I use magic? I can't explain why it acts the way it does, especially when I'm angry."

"Emotion," Chronicles replied, "can affect our energy. Be it love, anger, or sadness. The more powerful the emotion, the more energy involved." He raised a gray eyebrow. "Seems we've been sensing yours even before you arrived. Must have been quite an experience to shift the balance of magic that much."

"Magic has a balance?"

Chronicles sighed to himself as he moved the chair back to its original location.

"Such ignorance."

"But is it normal to do that? I mean, could magic become powerful enough to upset even Nature?"

"*Normal* is a human term, and usually does not pertain to us. There is nothing greater than Nature."

"But if there were?"

The door shut, leaving Keith alone. From the hallway, he could still hear his father's thoughts.

You have much to learn.

CHAPTER 6

"Tell us more!" Twilight urged.

From early morning to late afternoon Keith was surrounded by a group of young *Lo-ans'rel*, eager to hear his adventures from the human realms. Now as the sun shone brightly overhead, Keith regaled days of slavery and how he had called upon Nature to bring an end to Castle Mire. He spoke of the Thieves' Guild and even demonstrated how to steal without getting caught. All the while questions poured from every member.

"How did you survive; what did you eat; were you frightened?"

"Yes," he answered. "Yes, I was afraid, afraid I'd never be free to do the things I was meant to. But you know something? Even though I'm glad to be here, even though I left such a miserable place, I still made a lot of friends. There were many people who helped along the way. Without them, I probably wouldn't have made it this far."

"Does this mean you'll go back one day?" Twilight's question hushed the group in eerie unison. "What?" He shrugged. "Just asking."

"Go back?" Jangus frowned, standing off to the side of the group. "He should be grateful our leader even took him in, especially since outsiders *aren't* allowed." Opal eyes narrowed at Twilight, who dropped his gaze. "Revealing our location could bring in humans." He scrunched up his nose. "Having to smell like one is bad enough."

"I know why you say that," Keith defended quietly. "But not all humans are interested in stealing your homeland. As I said before, I left a lot of friends."

Jangus smirked. "Rats and thimbles?"

"Oh, be quiet!" A young female pushed him from behind.

"What was that for?" Jangus demanded from the auburn-haired female. Angry eyes flashed in warning, only to meet one of equal authority.

"Because he knows more than you or I will ever understand," she replied coolly, sweeping a hand through her long curls. Her cheeks flushed when she turned back to Keith. "Sorry about that." She glanced over her shoulder as Jangus stormed off. "He still has a bit of growing up to do." Her brilliant eyes met Keith's. "By the way, I'm Katherine."

"Uh, thanks." Keith grinned sheepishly.

"And I apologize for that rude interruption. Please continue. Your story is fantastic!"

"Yeah, especially when you threw the guards!" Twilight pretended to battle with a Healer sitting next to him, who fell back like he had just been thrown. Their lips formed fake sounds of battle, and as the fight came to an end, they were congratulated with claps and cheers. Even Keith was amused.

"You laugh now, but you must realize it wasn't funny at the time," Keith said. "Besides, I didn't mean to. It just sort of...happened."

"Everything happens for a reason," Katherine said. "You only learn with each ability you use, and from that you can only perfect what you learn."

"No!" Twilight blurted. "From there you can only get more powerful, and from the looks of things, he already is."

"I'm sure Jangus would argue the latter." Katherine smirked.

Keith sat back and listened to the chatter. He looked down at his new clothing, an earth-toned tunic and short pants with gold lining down the front. The sleeves stopped at the elbows with enlarged cuffs pulled back, exposing a rich maple-brown interior. Wisps of white hair curled over his brow, complementing his appearance to the young females surrounding him.

Both he and his brother had similar features, though at seventeen summers Keith held the advantage of courting sooner than Shy. Already, many young females had taken an interest in him, to Chronicles' discretion.

"Aren't you going to finish the story?" Twilight's unexpected question returned Keith's thoughts to his surroundings.

"What?"

"The story." Twilight rolled over on his stomach and propped his hands under his chin. "Remember? We left off after that one guy bought you – the fat one who called you 'feather.'"

A few chuckles followed.

"He can get to that part later," Katherine interjected. "What I'd like to hear is about humans in general. What's their homeland like? Do they live in clans like us? How are their social behaviors?"

"So very curious, are we?" Keith raised an eyebrow, then nodded. "Yes, they do live in clans. The land is divided into realms with a series of clans in each one." He spread his arms. "They're so vast! I've only just seen a portion of what human realms look like. That's why I'd want to go back – to explore, to expand on what I already know." He sighed. "I want to see things, to learn, to discover."

"I think you've already managed quite a discovery," Katherine replied. "And your descriptions are so vivid." She closed her eyes and opened her mind to sight-reading.

Keith smiled and allowed his thoughts to fill hers with visions of human encounters.

"I feel like I know them already." When her eyes opened, they glowed for a brief moment before returning to their normal color.

"I'd be scared to," Twilight admitted with a shudder, "after hearing so many things about them."

"You shouldn't judge someone until you've gotten to know them first," Keith said. "Fear only thickens the rumor."

"Well, listen to you." Jangus' familiar mockery turned everyone's attention to the side of a Redwood where the young man leaned against the trunk. He smiled in sarcastic sweetness. "How nice," he cooed. "Little words of wisdom. I'll put that to use the next time I enter the human realms." His smile quickly soured.

Keith got to his feet as Jangus stepped toward him, circling like a hungry wolf.

"And what would Chronicles say? He'd laugh. Probably say it's mere foolishness."

"Maybe." Keith met the Healer's intense gaze without blinking, his sapphire eyes aglow with a rising temper. "But mere foolishness would come from one who's never known what they speak. Chronicles knows this. I've read his thoughts."

Jangus balked.

"Pah! No one can read his mind."

"He's not above the rest of us, and he's not perfect," Keith continued. "Leaders *can* make mistakes."

Jangus snarled. "We don't make mistakes. When we train, it's to perfection. No human can equal us."

Keith took in a deep breath. He thought back to the Thieves' Guild, to Blackavar and Medallion. He thought of Castle Mire. He remembered the corky phrases Lancheshire used to say, and suddenly he knew – the answer to any question that treaded the edge of ridiculousness.

"Pish posh," he said.

Jangus' brow crinkled in confusion.

"What?"

"Pish posh," Keith repeated. "Ain't no point to a word unless ye make one," he imitated Lancheshire's voice. "The same in which ye make ye point, and if there ain't a word to make yer point with then there ain't no point in making a remark involving it!"

The other Healers watched in concentrated silence. The only movement was the turn of heads keeping up with the conversation. The last phrase had caught Jangus off guard; they could see it in his eyes. He had no answer, tried to stutter a response, then clamped his mouth shut.

This is only the beginning, Jangus' thoughts reached Keith before backing away from the group in embarrassment.

"That was brilliant!" Twilight hopped to his feet and scuttled to Keith's side. "Confusing, almost to the point where it didn't make any sense. Yet…it did."

"You actually out-worded him." Katherine watched the dark-haired youth slink into the underbrush. "That's a talent I'm not accustomed to."

"But I thought we were supposed to be perfect in *everything*?" Keith cracked a smile.

"Aw, he had it coming." Twilight dismissed the remark with a wave of his hand. "'Bout time someone put him in his place, the pompous bird."

"Speaking of which." Keith tapped a finger to his chin. "He reminds me of an old bird with the same attitude. I wasn't at all surprised by it." He chuckled. "In fact, I almost prefer it. Makes conversation much more lively."

"Careful," one of the Healers approached. "Jangus is no fool, nor will he deal with one who is. He takes everything seriously."

"Does he, or just pretends to?" Keith asked. "Usually, the one who speaks loudest wants the attention." He shrugged. "Well…at least that's what a friend used to tell me."

"You're just full of advice today, aren't you?" Katherine raised an eyebrow. She glanced over his shoulder at the small group beginning to disassemble. "Eumaeus usually says things like that. Guess we'll just have to stop calling you Keith and start calling you Wisdom."

Keith's cheeks swelled with pride.

"Wisdom? Me?" He waved a hand. "Na! I was just making a point. Like my friend used to say, 'Ain't no use in making a point 'less there's a point to be made." He thought about the nickname. "Although," he paused. "*Vistom.* Has a nice ring to it, actually."

Twilight nudged Keith's elbow.

"See? Not a bad name to grow into. By the way, do humans have nicknames too?"

*****

Vistom....

Shy tried to discern any expression from Chronicles, though he knew the effort was futile. The two stood together, like two trees on a hillside, watching the small group around Keith.

What he lacks in our ways, he makes up in knowledge, Shy thought to his father. *Surely something will come out of it.*

Shy heard his father sigh. *Perhaps. He still has a lot to learn. Tomorrow, begin his mental training. Magic is no good without the ability to withstand Nature's forces around him.*

CHAPTER 7

A line of young *Lo-ans'rel* assembled into the clearing, walking in perfect unison. Led by Shy, they were taken to a secluded training ground where they could safely learn how to develop their skills. Among the group was Keith, who was third in line behind Jangus. Twilight and Katherine were also present, which Keith was glad. He had been watching them all morning while they took turns showing off their individual skills. He mimicked their movements, taking in all he saw.

The Healers wasted no time and made a single row in the middle of the clearing where Chronicles patiently waited. Keith marveled at the staff their leader held. Made from Redwood, it spiraled down in smooth arcs with relief carvings of wings flowing along the curves. On the tip of the staff perched a sapphire stone. Calmly, Chronicles walked down the line, giving a nod of satisfaction. Upon reaching Keith, he paused to study the young man before continuing.

"Today," the leader's voice penetrated the silence, "we come to celebrate our Gifts." All eyes were upon their leader as he spoke, his rich voice drowning out sounds of Nature around them. "As *Lo-ans'rel*, we are *One* with Nature. No other can equal her grace. No other creation is made to perfection. *No one...*" He weaved his fingers through the air, dancing them upon the breeze so quickly that it was hard to follow the gesture. "*We* must be perfect in our ways, for that is how we were made."

He dipped the tip of his staff toward one of the Healers.

"*Twilot.*" The name rolled from his tongue in their language.

Twilight stepped forward.

Chronicles made a simple gesture, which Twilight responded to by leaning back, arching his body so his hands touched the ground behind his head. Though much younger than Keith, his body was built of solid muscle. As smooth as flowing water, he completed the flip and righted himself to a standing position.

"Perfect," Chronicles purred. The boy beamed proudly and returned to his place in line.

The leader turned to another. Like Twilight had, a Healer stepped forward. Extending hands out, palms down, the Healer closed his eyes in concentration. Beneath bare feet, the soil quivered. A twist of the wrist turned palms down, fingers spread, and Keith felt the flow of energy pull from ground up. Nature stirred. Flowers that were not present before suddenly rose from the dirt to open yellow-petal faces toward the sky. Vines reached for the open palms, but at a gesture from Chronicles the young Healer ended the flow of energy by closing his fingers over the palms. The growth spurt halted abruptly, and as the Healer lowered his arms, that which had risen returned smoothly to the earth as though nothing had occurred. A nod of satisfaction from the leader was all that was required, and the youth returned to his place in line.

When the leader's eyes fell upon Keith, the young man nervously swallowed. Thoughts like icicles formed in his mind, ready to tear him apart at the slightest mistake. He would have to be perfect. As Keith stepped from line to approach the *Lo-ans'rel* leader, all eyes were upon him as he awaited instructions.

Chronicles remained devoid of any emotion. Silver eyes penetrated through all the young man's confidence, leaving nothing but fear and doubt. A quick gesture told all Keith needed to do: a simple show of skill on what forms he had obtained.

Ah, something easy! Keith closed his eyes and tried to picture the animal he wanted to change into. *But what's more impressive? An eagle or a wolf? Or did I even gain them?* He could sense Chronicles' impatience and thought of his brother. How shamed he would feel having taught this *human's pet*, as Jangus usually mocked. *Just pick something!*

Magic flooded through his veins. The familiar sensation of shifting brought relief. At least he was changing, but into what? The two images he had thought locked together, and a new wave of panic took over. Half his body was shifting one way while the other half shifted into something else. The crunching of shoulder blades made him twist in agony. They extended from his back, long quills of feathers pushing outward. His fingers elongated into talons, almost like when he had changed into the dark *'Keyarx*. Instead of growing, his toes shrunk into furry paws. His face felt contorted, and he looked down to see his shadow elongating. The nose and mouth drew up into a wolf's snout. Fur bristled down his neck and onto his back. No longer able to stand, he dropped to all fours. Even before he had finished shifting, he could sense the group's confusion and shock.

Keith stared at his shadow. *What have I done?* Lifting a forearm, he examined the clawed hand. *So my head and body are part wolf while the rest is...some type of bird?*

Chronicles backed away when Keith flexed his wings. He tested their power by giving them a good stroke, nearly sending him airborne. He quickly folded them.

"How is this possible?" Chronicles' voice, usually deep and commanding, sounded frail and uncertain. Even his face was a shade paler.

Keith cocked his head, smelling fear rise from the leader's body. He pricked his ears forward in innocence, which did nothing to calm the situation. Shy and Jangus exchanged looks between Twilight and Katherine.

"*Lo d'hess!*"

Keith flattened himself to the ground at the sound of his father's voice. *Hold still*, he had said, and so Keith did.

Chronicles approached his son, who lay with head upon his forearms. Kneeling, he ran a hand over the soft fur from the nape of the neck to the ears. Keith felt his father probing his thoughts, searching for the secret behind his son's double shifting. Disappointment soon crossed his features when he realized it had been nothing but a mere accident.

"Return to your place." He sighed and stood, keeping an eye on his son while he began the transformation, then nodded to Shy. "You'll need to be conditioned to expand your talents."

Bowing, Keith returned to his place in line, though he was given a wide girth from those around him. *So this is possible for all of us?* He heard Shy think to his father.

It is rare, Chronicles returned. *But it takes more than just a careless shift to accomplish it successfully.*

Keith felt the biting sarcasm, but had it been more than just a 'careless shift?' *Has no one else been able to shift like that?* The thought remained with him throughout the rest of their training. When the session was over, many did not linger. Too eager to practice their newly developed talents, they quickly dispersed. Shy, however, stayed with his brother along with Twilight and Katherine. All three itched with the desire to learn his secret.

"It's all the talk now!" Twilight exclaimed.

"I could *hear* them," Keith said, walking alongside his brother. He ducked under a low limb as the group made their way toward their home clearing.

"Some couldn't even concentrate on their training," Katherine said. She brushed a hand through her bangs, smoothing back a few loose strands. "I'm sure Chronicles was thinking your talents were more of a nuisance rather than anything special."

Twilight laughed. "Jangus sure got his fair share of scolding. Did you see the way he looked at you? I thought his jaw would drop to the ground when you finished shifting!"

"How did you do that?" Shy broke the question. "And don't tell me you can't remember what you did." His eyes narrowed. "A gift like that is rare to have, and too valuable to lose."

Keith tried not to laugh. "Actually, it wasn't that hard. When Chronicles asked me to shift, I wanted something that would impress him, but I couldn't decide. So I just thought of two animals and started shifting." He shrugged. "Guess I'd shift into something worth looking at."

"What'd it feel like?" Twilight asked. "Was it still the same?"

Keith scrunched his nose in remembrance. "It was a little painful, not like regular shifting. Your body goes in two different directions rather than one." He caught his brother's raised eyebrow.

"That's it?" Shy blinked in disbelief. "You thought of two animals and just shifted?"

"Wonder what would happen if you tried three?" Twilight snickered, receiving a cynical look from Shy.

Katherine closed her eyes, but shook her head in dismay. "I can't do it."

"Let me try." Twilight was quick to frown when he realized he too was not capable. "It's impossible!" he exclaimed. "I can't think of more than one form at a time."

"I can," Shy announced without batting an eye. "Is that all, *brethusus*?" He turned to his brother. "And then you started to shift?"

Keith nodded.

Twilight glanced from one to the other, his fingers in a constant twitch of excitement.

"Well, go on!" he urged. "Try it."

Shy shook his head. "Don't have to."

"Why not?" Twilight's voice squeaked, receiving a pat on the shoulder from Katherine.

"Because he already knows he can," she stated. "None of us can do it. Maybe it's because you both are albinos. Like you said. It *is* rare. Then again, so are albinos."

The vines were about a yard ahead of them. Twilight yawned, arching his back in a stretch and eager to turn in for the evening. As

Keith waited for the others to enter, something caught his attention through the trees, something that lurked with the perfect wing coloring to hide among shadows. Smiling to himself, Keith lingered behind.

"Aren't you coming?" Shy waited in the opening for his brother, who waved a hand in refusal.

"I think I'd like to stay out a little longer, if you don't mind. I'm not tired yet."

Shy regarded him a moment before nodding.

The vines closed, leaving Keith alone. Behind him the shadows shifted. Slowly, Keith turned and brushed past some low branches. A cackling bird overhead drew his attention to its silhouetted flight. The tall Redwood was dizzying to look upon past its great trunk. His eyes darted back to the shadows only to find someone blocking his path.

"Think you're special, don't you?" Jangus stood with arms crossed. He reeked of negative attitude. "Anyone could have shifted like that. We just don't do it very often."

"Sure, Jangus." Keith shrugged, stepping around the dark-haired boy.

"You think you're better than us. You couldn't even shift properly when you came, and now this? Think you're good enough to become next leader?"

Keith ignored the comment.

"Hey! Where do you think you're going, *human's pet*?"

A pair of hands gripped Keith from behind while something snagged underneath his feet. He went down hard, scraping both knees. From behind, he could hear laughter.

"If I didn't know any better, Jangus, I'd say you were jealous." Keith spat, tasting blood on his lips. Only when his bottom lip began throbbing did he realize he had bitten it, but knew it would not last long when the familiar sensation of Nature's energy quickly healed his cuts.

"Oh, that could be anyone, not just me." Jangus strode around Keith until he was facing him. "Aw," he cooed. "Pathetic little human's pet."

"Quit calling me that!" Keith started to brush the dirt from his pants when he was shoved once again.

"Come on, human's pet!" Jangus taunted, circling. "What's the matter with you? Let's see what you can do." He pushed him back down. "Oh, I'm so very frightened!" He held a hand to his forehead in mock fear. "Little human's pet is going to shift into a half flying freak!"

A sound bubbled in Keith's throat, something he had only heard a couple of times. Both ears laid back, serving as a warning along with his threatening growl. Jangus laughed, failing to notice a shadow stealthily moving along the upper branches. It was only when the Black Wing dropped to the ground and raised himself with outstretched wings did Jangus turn to glimpse the *'Keyarx* at its full majesty.

Corrigan made sure to display his long talons in front of the boy's face, which sent Jangus stumbling over Keith in terror. Keith watched him flee in his raven form before bursting with laughter.

"Doesn't he ever change into anything else?" Keith mimicked the boy's expression.

Corrigan smirked and held his nails up proudly to examine them.

"Priceless," he said softly. Holding out a hand, he helped Keith to his feet. "Rotten little mouse, wasn't he? Like to have shown him a thing or two with these rather than wave 'em in his face. But..." He shrugged, letting his wings relax. "Oh, well."

Keith brushed himself off, then examined his knees. Already, the scrape had healed.

"I appreciate your help." He twitched his ears for any signs of his kind. "But you'd better go. I'd hate to think what Chronicles would do if he found you here."

"Him?" Corrigan rolled his eyes. "Word spreads quick." He let his wings ruffle up as a cool breeze swept through his feathers. "Is that pompous peacock truly your father?"

Keith grinned. "You've been spying on me, haven't you?"

Corrigan shrugged. Raising his wings, he lifted into the sky, climbing with each stroke.

"You should join me for a fly one day – show off your new forms!"

Keith grinned and watched his friend gracefully weave between the branches until he was swallowed by the canopy.

*****

"Ah, the joys of young magic, and the beginnings of great power."

Jenario leaned against the balcony wall with eyes closed and listened to the voice in his head. Such malign sweetness, he realized, but such a vast opportunity to gain more knowledge.

Too easy. Jenario opened his eyes. *I'm consumed with this endless watching. Why not turn my attention elsewhere?*

"*If you had, you wouldn't have me.*" A sweet voice edged its way into his thoughts. "*By watching him, you learn. If you stop watching, you lose track of how the race develops and what powers they gain. Don't you want to learn the same power? Don't you want to obtain it someday?*" The voice was drenched like sweet nectar, caressing his desires and luring his thoughts to where it wanted. "*The ultimate source of magic is the ability to shift. There is no equal.*"

"But I already can," Jenario remarked. "A unicorn—"

"*Is not enough!*" the voice intervened. "*Think what shifting gains you. Not just the ability to transform, but to manipulate, to control, to create. It is the key to controlling Nature herself! It is all there in one individual. That's why you watch. That's why you wait. The key to shifting is an albino Lo-ans'rel.*"

Jenario sighed. He was tired, but the voice in his head was relentless.

"*He'll come back,*" it continued. "*Humans fascinate him. He'll seek the place of his birth. He'll be drawn by mere curiosity.*"

Jenario stopped listening. He was so very tired. His mind was split into separate individuals. One side wanted sleep, the other – power. At last, the voice calmed, allowing Jenario his rest. The horn could afford to wait. It had all the time in the world.

CHAPTER 8

Seasons came and went, each bringing new discoveries as Keith continued to grow and learn from his kind. It was now his twentieth winter. Frost sprinkled fine crystals over the still earth, a sign that Nature was preparing to deny her energy to the world while she slept.

The forest was quiet except for the crunch of footfalls over frosted grass as Keith stepped out into the fresh air. A light blue robe grazed the tops of his ankles as he made his way to the center of the clearing. The day was gray with no promise of sunshine, and a brisk wind sent shivers through him. Memories of when he had first arrived flooded his thoughts – Chronicles on the raised platform, his brother and Jangus flanking his sides. He remembered Twilight, a playful boy no longer, but still curious about human ways; and Katherine, her long auburn hair like flowing wine. Even Jangus had grown, though Keith still detected that hint of jealousy now and then.

And myself?

Keith continued his stroll, pausing to stare into a frozen puddle. Yes, there was change, from the graceful gestures when performing magic to the way he walked and spoke. Kneeling, he swept a hand over the frost, testing the strength of remaining magic before its winter sleep. He nodded with satisfaction when it melted, allowing him to see his reflection more clearly. He smiled at the well-groomed image. His hair fell in waves around his face and shoulders. Silky eyebrows had been neatly trimmed and smoothed back. *Mother would be proud.*

"One day you will find out..." He squeezed his eyes shut, his mother's words echoing through his thoughts. He touched the charm hidden beneath his collar, Glory's ring; he had never forgotten her. He studied his reflection, watching the water slowly freeze over until his image was lost beneath a thin layer of ice.

He left the clearing in the form of a white wolf, relishing the wild freedom as Redwoods flew by in a blur. When the trees became more expansive he knew he was not far, and soon the ground began to tilt upward. Steeper still it became until the path took a sharp turn, curving around the side of a hill until smoothing out at the top.

He stopped, heart pounding, and stood overlooking his homeland. After a few moments to catch his breath, he shifted back and stepped to the cliff's edge. A breeze caught his hair and robe on a small draft. The smell of coming snow tinted the wind. It would not be long before Nature shut her powers completely off from the *Lo-ans'rel*, and they would be left to fend for themselves.

Keith chuckled. *I'm so early the 'Keyarx haven't risen, save but one.*

A fallen log provided the ideal spot to sit and wait. From this vantage point he could just make out where the edge of the valley met the realm known as Unicorn's Glade.

"Where all flowing water comes – the land of unicorns," Keith spoke to the wind. His pupils enlarged as he strained to see more, but a faint mist clouded most of the valley. Disappointed, he turned his attention elsewhere. Stories he had heard from other Healers concerning unicorns came to mind. To his knowledge, none had ever seen one, though rumors claimed it was the most beautiful creature to grace *No'va*.

"They say our last leader, Windchester, met one." Twilight had said. "According to him, there are no males, only white females."

"Why's that?" Keith had asked.

"Something to do with the balance, I suppose," was the reply.

Keith scanned the treetops, hoping to see Corrigan.

He should be here any moment. He grinned. *Unless he forgot to wake.*

A shimmer of white drew his attention below where the leaves were not as thick, then again in the distance. Ears pricked forward to the tune of repeating thumps against earth, something that ran on all fours. Another streak of white, this time appearing in a distant clearing. In the moment it appeared his gaze followed its every move, from the swish of mane and pallid fur, to the tip of its....

Keith jumped to his feet. "That couldn't have been..." His stomach lurched, glad he had come to the top of the valley. Fear mingled with awe, still uncertain if what he had seen was real.

His heart skipped a beat at the crack of a twig from behind, and he turned toward the shadows of overhanging vines and vegetation leading back into the dense forest. His ears flicked forward, ready to pinpoint any signs of movement. Slowly, he inched closer.

"Corrigan?"

"Took you long enough." The harpy's wings pulled back from around his body as he descended from the branches. He gave them a good shake when he reached the ground, then folded them neatly behind in a fade. "What were you doing? I've been here all morning. If I hadn't made a sound, you'd never have taken your eyes off the valley."

Keith fidgeted in embarrassment.

"Looks like your wings aren't the only things that can disappear," he said, feeling his cheeks grow warm. "I know it's out of place for me *not* to sense you." He gestured to the valley. "But didn't you hear it?"

Corrigan cocked his head curiously to one side.

"Hear what?"

"Don't tell me you just sat there and didn't hear anything."

The Dark *'Keyarx* shook his head, raising his wings in preparation for flight as he strolled to the cliff's edge.

"My eyes may be sharp, but my hearing is not nearly as good as yours." His wings stroked the air. "Besides, it was probably further than you thought. You were just concentrating too much."

Keith was about to reply when Corrigan dived off the ledge, his massive wings beating the air to lift him skyward. He circled above.

"Forget about it, Keith, or should I say – *Vistom!*" Corrigan spoke in the *Lo-ans'rel* tongue. "Come join me."

With a mischievous grin, Keith followed, curling his body in a graceful somersault before letting his shifting abilities take control. From above, the Black Wing watched in amusement while his friend's body took on a similar appearance – a dark *'Keyarx*.

"You should keep that form more often," Corrigan said when the Healer had climbed to his height. "It suits you."

"I don't know." Keith looked down at himself. "Chronicles already despises harpies. I don't think he'd appreciate it if I went around looking this way." A vision of Chronicles shoeing off a fledgling came to mind. Curious to see behind what appeared to be an unguarded door, the young *'Keyarx* soon met his match against a furious *Lo-ans'rel* leader. From then on, Chronicles viewed them with distaste, especially during molt season.

"It's how you know they're living in a particular area." The words of Chronicles brought a smile to the young man. "Constant shedding! I'm surprised they don't choke on their own plumage!"

"Harpies..." Corrigan lazily glided on the wind currents over the valley with Keith trailing beside him. "You still haven't lost that human touch."

Keith flapped his wings a couple of times to catch the high winds, his current thoughts forgotten.

"I know. Chronicles believes it's my downfall." Keith peered at the passing *Lo-ans'rel* clearing.

Corrigan snorted, barrel rolling underneath his friend and allowing his wings to slap at his belly.

"Hey!" Keith laughed. He swung over to one side and dived to Corrigan's level.

"Why do you let that old man bother you?" The Black Wing turned so that his backside faced down. "I've lived in the human realms for years, and look what became of me. You remember how it was, don't you?"

Keith raised an eyebrow.

"How could I forget…" He stared into the distance, letting the wind currents hold him. *I wonder if Jenario is still interested in my kind?* He glanced at Corrigan, who was enjoying the free ride on a current below. *Or has he chosen to study through the means of another?*

Folding his wings, Keith dived past Corrigan, swooping around and back toward his friend.

Corrigan grinned merrily and followed suit, folding his wings close to pick up speed.

Keith skimmed the tops of the trees. By chance, an opening gave him an idea, and he dived down, narrowly missing several limbs. Behind, he could hear Corrigan calling his name.

"Bet you can't do that!" Keith laughed as he weaved between branches. Pockets of space allowed his wings to open a brief moment in order to control his flight, but not speed. Another opening provided a quick direction change, only to realize a thick wall of foliage blocked his path with nowhere to turn.

If I crash into this, there's no way Nature will be able to heal me! His mind raced to find a solution, for he had only seconds to spare. *Shift! Shift now!*

Keith's mind burned with the power to transform as pure energy ripped through his body. He could feel branches tearing through him as he hit, or was *he* the one passing through? All feeling vanished. It had become a mere thought, a source of power that emerged on the other side in the form of a glowing blue orb. He had *become* his own power; however, it was draining rapidly, and soon the light began to dim.

Keith navigated his spherical being by thinking in which direction he wished to go. A curious web-like substance stretched in front of him and connected between several tree trunks.

I can't believe how far I've come! Keith realized, his light source beginning to flicker. *I'm in the northern section where the Na'nafrétts live.*

Keith had just floated overtop the webbing when he suddenly shifted to his true form and tumbled down, bouncing a couple of times before the net adjusted to his weight. He lay sprawled on his back, the feeling of nausea churning his stomach.

"Wow!" Keith breathed, unable to say more. *Just that nearly consumed all my energy.* He stared up at the canopy. *Guess I'll have to get Corrigan to carry me back.* He tried to sit up, then lay back down to wait for his strength to return. *Corrigan...He doesn't know I'm here.*

Keith placed a hand over his heart, its rapid pulse beginning to slow. Carefully, he sat up to take in his surroundings while his pupils enlarged to better see in the darkness. The webbing gently swayed between the trees, then pulled to one side as though a great weight were upon it. Turning, Keith heard a series of clicks. Leaves blended with tree trunks, creating masses of shapes that could not be distinguished from one another. If one of the *Na'nafrétts* was there, its body was just another shape.

Until it moved....

Keith closed his eyes, detecting his surroundings using other senses. A faint, musty odor lingered in the air. Here, there was no passing breeze, and the young man crinkled his nose in disgust. Sounds of munching alerted his sharp hearing.

He nearly jumped when a *Na'nafrétt* feeler touched his shoulder. An enormous furry body stepped to the side of the net, its bulging eyes rotating in their sockets as it peered down at its smaller guest. A commotion of quick chattering from the trees attracted Keith's attention toward two cubs scampering out across the net.

"Faun'dusc-té," Keith spoke his native tongue. He bowed his head to the *Na'nafrétt* adult. *"You must be the proud parent."*

A rhythmic grumble answered.

"Oh, I see. You're only a guardian." He watched the cubs tumble over one another in order to get close. The larger cub was far bolder than its younger sibling, venturing close enough for Keith to reach down and touch the soft fuzz on its back. At the feel of the stranger's hand, the cub shrieked and dashed up a tree, eventually creeping back for another look.

The guardian purred loudly, followed by a sneezing grunt. Keith looked up as a feeler patted his back.

"No, I'm not hurt," Keith said gratefully. "But I can't shift right now."

A snort.

"Show me a way down? That'd be grand, but how so?"

The *Na'nafrétt* used a feeler to point at a spot behind its head. Hesitantly, Keith stumbled over the net, holding onto the *Na'nafrétt's* forearms to keep his balance until he reached its side.

"*You'll take me?*" Keith noted where the *Na'nafrétt's* neck curved in a crescent shape, suitable to sit in like a saddle. The young man chuckled sarcastically. *Certainly, I'll just ride this thing like some fat horse. So dignified! I'll probably get thrown off halfway down.*

Gripping its fur, Keith climbed up the neck and swung a leg over.

"*Ready when you are,*" he said, feeling the creature lifting itself on its long legs.

The *Na'nafrétt* moved faster than what Keith considered possible. Its spindly legs hooked onto the limbs and lowered its great body down the tree trunk. The Healer quickly learned how to sway with the feel of its strides when walking across flat surfaces, mostly using the woven nets from place to place. Then they came to a place where nets had not been built, and the branches were too far apart to climb.

"*What now?*" Keith asked.

A rumble in the distance greeted them, and something hit the tree beside them. Keith stared at the dripping goop. It did not take long to solidify to a rubbery appearance.

"*It's web!*" He realized. "*So...you're great shooters as – what are you doing?*"

Keith suddenly leaned forward and pressed his legs tighter to the *Na'nafrétt's* body when it started tilting to one side.

"*This is crazy! A single thread is going to hold us up?*" He gasped when the giant swung its legs around the line and started walking across the treacherous gap upside down. Once or twice he felt himself slipping, but the *Na'nafrétt* pressed a feeler over him to hold him in place. The Healer was much relieved when they finally righted themselves at their destination. He rubbed his protesting stomach.

"Hey, I can see in these parts!" he exclaimed in Common, then translated for the *Na'nafrétt*. He noted a slight green tint coming from somewhere below, which seemed to be moving. "*We must be near the ground.*"

They had no trouble getting down. Plenty of webbing allowed quick access, and Keith was grateful when the journey ended.

"*My appreciations.*" He slid from its neck to the ground, then waited until the *Na'nafrétt* had returned to the treetops, its great body blending into the shadows.

His ears perked at the sound of trickling water, and he licked dry lips.

Keith soon found a narrow stream coursing through the forest. Clear water created a mirrored surface. As his hands disturbed the stillness, he watched the white of his hair blend with his features, a little lower than it should have been. The forest around him was still illuminated in a green glow. Although he could not fathom its cause, the taste of liquid soon bade forgetfulness.

His thirst satisfied, Keith rested with his chin on one knee. He closed his eyes, envisioning the angry expression on his father's face when discovered missing.

No doubt, he'll suspect I've left for the human realms. Keith's brow creased in thought. *I've been from one end of the valley to the next.* He sighed. *What else is there for me to learn from my kind?*

A shimmer of white gathered his attention to the water. He noted the hair in the reflection falling over a pale neck, the face slightly elongated. At first he thought the ripples were manipulating his features, but a closer look revealed something a little more animal-like. Blue eyes stared. A horn of pure ivory perched upon the forehead. Nostrils flared in a snort.

Keith raised his head, for the sound did not come from the water, and stared in awe at the most beautiful animal he had ever seen. Its fur was snow-white with a silken mane and tail. While solid muscle rippled through its chest and hindquarters. Delicate legs took a proud stance with soft feathering flowing down to its cloven hoofs. The face gently curved like a marvel sculpture, so perfect and defined it could not have been real. Yet the horn was the source of green tinting the forest. Keith could not tear his gaze away, for its majestic beauty captivated him.

Is this real?

"*Do you not trust your own heart?*" A soft-spoken female's voice entered his thoughts.

"That voice," he said, unable to move as the unicorn gracefully approached the water's edge.

"You have heard the many voices of Nature," it replied. *"Mine is but a single thread connected to a larger spool."*

"I beg your pardon?" Keith held a hand to his face to block the rays of light coming from the horn. There came a chortle, and the light dimmed just enough so the Healer could lower his hand.

"Some say we are the physical forms of Nature. Others believe we are the source of No'va's magic."

"Is it true?" Keith asked.

The unicorn stepped through the water, hardly disturbing the surface.

"Words will only confuse, and time is precious to us both." It halted just a few inches from the young man. *"The only way for you to learn is for me to show you."*

Keith's gaze froze upon those eyes filled with love and forgiveness. Entranced, he did not move even when the pearly horn lowered over his heart. His eyes shut tightly at a sudden pain that gripped his insides. Two powerful minds opened to each other, and Keith grit his teeth as visions flooded his thoughts.

Just as quick, the pain was gone. The Healer opened his eyes and turned, searching for the unicorn. No longer was he in a shadowed forest, but standing on a ledge overlooking a familiar landscape.

I'm in Unicorn's Glade. No sooner had the thought come than the scenery changed, opening up into the center of the valley with a full moon overhead. In awe of the sudden events, he blinked several times. *This can't be real.*

"These are my memories," a sweet voice sang all around. *"Keep watch to the phases of the moon. Only then will you understand."*

Keith did as told and lifted his eyes skyward. Drifting clouds cast deep blue shadows over a full moon. Or was the moon itself blue? The Healer continued to watch, consumed with the need to know its importance. Shadows lengthened until threatening to engulf it. Then, like the fluid that runs from a pricked finger, a crimson stain began festering over the moon's surface. Even when the clouds had cleared away, the moon still retained its color. It was too red. *Blood red.*

A whinny echoed in the distance, and Keith turned to glimpse a unicorn galloping toward him. Just past the forest's edge, it ascended a low rock formation in the clearing. Aligning its horn with the moon, it poised as if a majestic stag, its proud posture hinting a mighty task to complete.

What does it watch? Keith followed its gaze past the moon. Stars gathered in that never-ending blackness, too many to count. One such cluster gave the impression of something more solid, spherical in appearance. It was not until he saw more lined behind it that he realized what was happening.

The moon had aligned with others of its make across the galaxy until it created a perfect line, a line that pointed directly back to the unicorn. Keith could feel a gravitational pull toward that horn, and he braced himself as the balance of magic was drawn to it. In that moment, a beam of red light spiraled down from the moon. Through time and space, the beam collected energy from other sources and directed it back into the horn.

The intake of Nature was suddenly released, and a surge of power swept over the land. It was not an explosion of physical energy as Keith thought, but mental, one that blanketed the land in cleansing.

It's not damaging, he realized, feeling the light flow over his form. Eventually, the light cooled in color, and the moon slipped from its formation. The chain broken, all normal activities resumed.

"*This is the way it has always been,*" the unicorn explained. "*Each new millennium brings purity and balance, but that balance isn't without consequences.*"

A new image flashed before him, returning Keith to the forest where two unicorn foals lay.

"Twins?" he asked.

"*It is not uncommon to have two souls created at the same time.*"

Keith twitched an ear at the distinct sound of footfalls. A huntsman burst through the thicket and drew back an arrow. The young unicorns scrambled to escape. Without thinking, Keith jumped in front of the bow to block it. Still, the arrow sped through him as though he had been made of air.

It's just a vision. He closed his eyes. *I can't change the past.*

Keith awoke on his back. Dizzily, he pulled himself to a sitting position and gazed up, half expecting to see the unicorn. Instead, a regular white mare stood in front of him. The eyes had darkened to hazelnut brown. Even its once glossy coat had dulled.

"I'm not dreaming, am I?" Keith rubbed his head and slowly sat up. "What just happened? I feel like my skin's on fire!" He held a hand over his heart. "You...that was *you* I saw." He swallowed in nervous excitement. "I heard a name – Osha? You called to the other, the one that was being hunted…Merla. That was your sister."

"Yes – was." The mare lowered her head and heaved a heavy sigh. *"Her story is not without its own twist of fate."*

Keith took a guess. "She didn't die, did she?"

Osha's thoughts were faint, forcing the Healer to strain his mental energy to understand.

"Her fate was decided long ago by one whose greed consumes him, one who still watches and waits your return to the human realms."

Keith was silent while his thoughts drifted elsewhere.

"Jenario…" he said at last. *I thought he had forgotten.*

"The human mage that spared my sister could not spare his own soul. Long forgotten you would have been, but for another – he will wait until the time is right." The mare sighed. When she spoke again, her voice was barely audible. *"You are probably wondering why I have taken this form."*

Keith cracked a smile. "That, and more."

"I give you a gift, something to both protect…and be protected."

Keith got to his feet. Laying a hand on her shoulder, he tried to grasp what little connection remained between them.

"Remember these words, my Wisdom. Trust in your heart, for there lies the key to greatness. Let your love guide you. Only then will the doors be opened and reveal your true destiny."

As the last of her words echoed through his thoughts, the two minds closed, leaving only silence to answer the young man's many questions.

"Wait! I still don't understand!" He held a hand out to her mane, letting the threads run through his fingers. "Has something happened to this balance with the moon? And why me? What can I do that's any different from the rest of my kind?"

His questions were in vain, for the mare made no attempt to reply.

A noise from above startled the animal. Without warning, she turned swiftly and bolted back across the stream to the other side, spraying Keith with water droplets.

"Osha!"

Branches broke over Keith's head. Without the horn's radiance, the forest returned to darkness, and the young man was not about to let himself be caught unprepared by any opponent.

One encounter is enough for me today, he thought while readying himself.

"Keith?" came a familiar voice, and the Healer let out a breath in relief to see his friend climb down a Redwood. "So this is where you've been hiding."

Keith chuckled. *Good ol' Corrigan.*

"You know, it'll be a miracle for you to get back undetected." Corrigan ruffed his wings in frustration. "What were you thinking? Going through the trees like that! I had to bribe the *Na'nafrétts* to show me where you'd gone!" The Black Wing pretended to backhand the Healer across the face. "And I hope you can shift, 'cause I sure ain't carrying ya!"

The Healer almost faltered, remembering how he had drained his energy earlier. Yet now with each beat of his heart, he felt it increase in strength. The flow of energy running through his veins had nearly doubled to more than what he was accustomed to.

What did you give me? He repeated to himself. *What am I protecting?* He glanced at Corrigan, then nodded.

"I can."

It took less time getting out of the forest. With Keith as a dark *'Keyarx*, the two companions quickly made their way back to the ledge from which they had departed.

"You're very quiet," Corrigan noted as he landed beside the young man. "Didn't hurt yourself flying like that, did you?"

The Healer's lips curled into a sly grin. "On the contrary. You learn more that way."

"Stop playing and get home, or do you like the sound of yelling?" Corrigan flapped his wings so that the draft they created tossed Keith off the ledge.

"Good point!" Keith waved farewell and let himself glide down. As the young man headed home, he glanced over his shoulder to see Corrigan departing for his own territory. As he landed in the *Lo-ans'rel* clearing, his thoughts trailed back to the image of Osha.

"I give you a gift, something to both protect...and be protected," her words came again. *"Trust in your heart, for there lies the key to greatness."*

Hesitantly, Keith held a hand over his heart. Its beats were slow and steady.

"Trust in my heart," he said softly, "for there lies the key of greatness." He began slowly walking to the secret walls, still mystified by the day's events. "I give you a gift...."

He stopped suddenly, remembering how Osha had looked after showing her memories. He glanced down at his hand, and when he pulled it away from his chest a faint shimmer of green faded away.

"Oh, Osha..." He breathed the words in a long sigh of regret.

"Trust in your heart...."

The secret wall slid aside for him to enter, and as he stepped inside, he realized what the unicorn had meant.

"You gave me your horn," he whispered to the wind before the wall closed. "Your horn lies in my heart, to protect it...and myself."

CHAPTER 9

Several weeks passed since that fateful day. Yet life for the *Lo-ans'rel* continued, and Keith soon learned how to push the memories to the back of his mind for later use. The day was young, and many Healers wanted to go out for some fresh air.

Keith waited impatiently for the wall to slide open. Beyond the warm interiors of the *Lo-ans'rel* home lay a fresh batch of fallen snow. The trees were patched in ice crystals, and the ground was slick to walk upon. Still, the young man bounded out like a child. A few others followed, relishing the fresh air and change of setting.

One of the Healers bent to pick up a handful of snow. He raised it high, and a brisk wind sent it airborne. Dark brown hair blew around his face as he watched it whisk away. It was not long before it started snowing again. Triumphantly, he turned to Keith, his older cousin.

"Did you see that?" he asked, his eyes an icy blue. "I've been practicing how to make snow. Do you think I could create an ice storm?"

"You did pretty good last time," Twilight intervened, approaching the two from behind. "Wish I were gifted in weather-making."

Keith laughed merrily. "What are you talking about? Jeremiah, tell him!" He gestured to his cousin. "Twilight *does* have that ability, *giu' rik*?"

Twilight shook his head.

"Not like *he* does. Look how it comes to him, and Nature's not even awake."

"A talent less to be forgotten," came the voice of Shy as he stepped from the underground passage. "Are you feeling better, *brethusus*?"

Keith's smile waned, but only slightly. His daily flights with Corrigan had been discovered, receiving strict punishment. He could still feel the sting of his father's hand across his cheek.

"I'm fine," he replied. "Just glad to be out."

Shy studied his brother's face, not bothering to read his thoughts. Presently, a large snowflake landed on the tip of his nose, and his eyes momentarily crossed to examine this distraction. Its icy touch caused a twitch of discomfort, which was met with several chuckles.

Keith glanced around. The group had nearly assembled, and at a thought from another the game was set into motion.

Hide-and-seek? the thought came.

In the snow? We'd all stand out! Twilight complained.

Not unless you're albino, Keith teased.

"We're the ones who'll have the advantage here, brother," Shy said. "What do you say?"

Brother...It had become easier to say over time, and it would seem Chronicles had accepted that fact as well, welcoming his eldest son into certain festivities that others normally were not permitted. Though there were still times Keith felt drawn to the human realms, he was nonetheless content with his home. It was paradise, with no masters and unlimited freedom within the boundaries of Crystal Valley. Why then should he ever need to leave?

"*Vistom!*"

Keith snapped to attention.

"*Qot'ax!*"

Another call signaled a wave of shifts, and Keith was momentary caught up in a swirl of sparrows.

Come, brethusus! Shy beckoned, fluttering upward into a thin twister of brown and white birds.

Keith stared through the spiral's center, deciphering their chirps and songs to identify each member. A flash of white became his brother, the darkest being Jangus. Closing his eyes he let his shifting take control, rising among them in the form of a dove.

Show off! Jangus swooped in front of him, but Keith dived the other way, enjoying the feel of magic coursing through his veins.

Jangus, gui'et! All at once the birds scattered through the trees, leaving a lone and bewildered Jangus seeker of the game.

Not fair! I'll find you! he thought wildly. His form changed to a falcon, and he hastily departed after the others. *And when I catch you....*

*****

Keith shifted into a sparrow to better dart through the thick branches. In the back of his mind he could feel Jangus trying to probe his location, and quickly closed all connections. Now he would have to rely on sight and sound.

He took a different path from the rest, heading for the border of Unicorn's Glade. Most others, he was certain, had gone to the northern woods. The thick trees would make it difficult to find anyone in that section, even in snow.

Keith rose to the canopy, not completely breaking the treetops for fear of being seen. Nesting places from *'Ken* flew by, not a single White Wing in sight. For now, the weather kept them indoors. Swooping down he came to rest at the border's edge. Snow sprinkled his shoulders as he shifted to his true appearance. Keith's footfalls faintly crunched over the icy ground. He observed the glade beyond the valley's borders, quietly recalling the day he had met Osha.

I wonder where she went...

"Going someplace?"

Keith turned at the sudden voice.

"Or are we just out for a winter stroll?" That sarcastic tone, one that could only belong to one being.

"I hear you," the Healer scanned the trees, "but I don't see you."

A chortle came from above.

"I do enjoy the solitary lifestyle." The sudden appearance of the Black Wing's body took Keith by surprise. Corrigan saw the young man stall before approaching, and his lip curled into a sneer. "Mostly I enjoy what I do – disappearing. Fits my nature, wouldn't you agree?"

Keith eyed his friend.

"And does that charm keep you warm as well?"

Corrigan snickered. "How kind of you to notice."

The two stood quietly in the snow. Eventually, sounds of laughter faded in the distance, and Keith twitched an ear to pinpoint its location.

"Wouldn't you rather be with your family?"

Corrigan stretched his wings in response.

"Do you even have one?" Keith tried again. "Is it too much to ask? At least a 'yes' or 'no' would suffice."

With drooping wings, Corrigan plopped himself on a log and heaved a heavy sigh.

"Look, um..." Corrigan began. "I know it must've been..." his voice came and went, "hard for you never to have known a family...until now." His head bowed as though shamed to speak it. "My family's been here all along. All I have to do is fly up and they'll be there." He shut his eyes, trying to hold back stinging tears.

Suddenly, he grabbed a fistful of feathers and yanked them out in frustration. Pain blinded him, and he let the tears fall freely. Around his feet, ruby droplets spotted the snow. Beside him, Keith remained quiet.

"Damn my father's stubbornness!" Corrigan wept, smearing blood over his brow as he tried to hide his face with his talons. "Taking a Black Wing for a mate – what was he thinking? He cursed me! I'll never be more than a half-breed, a misfit between races! Small...helpless. I'd never be able to stand up to a true Black Wing. Might have been different, maybe, if my mother hadn't been taken..."

A hand gently touched his wing, but Corrigan yanked it away. Too late, he realized what the Healer had done as he raised the newly developed feathers in place of shredded stubs.

"I don't like to see you hurt," came a soft voice.

Corrigan met Keith's eyes, the glow of energy fading.

"Healer..." The harpy bowed his head. "Don't waste your energy on my behalf." He slowly rose to his feet. "I should be going."

"He loves you, Corrigan." A pause. "I have faith you'll find her one day."

"That day is not now." Corrigan shook his head, and he raised his wings in preparation. "You're free to be with your family. I am not." His gaze trailed over the forest toward the direction he headed. "For me, there's still some unfinished business to take care of first before I'm free."

Keith stood back as the giant wings flapped once to knock the snow from his feathers. Just before leaving he glanced over his shoulder at the young man.

"Maybe you were right all along," he said. "Maybe I *am* a slave, for how could I be free if someone constantly has me under their charms, even if only illusion?" As he took to the skies, a small voice came to mind, and he looked down a final time at the Healer he had come to admire over the years.

Illusion isn't real. Magic is... Keith watched the shifting clouds draw back together where the Black Wing had gone. *He's gone back to Jenario, to finish his own game.*

With a heavy sigh the young man began following the border to where the frozen river stretched between the valley and human realms. A break in the trees provided a faint glimpse of human development in the distance. Smoke rose from chimneys in puffs of gray haze, the houses stacked together in rows.

Lexington... I hope the guild is still holding.

When he reached the bottom of the slope, he paused. A breath of cold wind brought smells of cooking.

It's too strong to be from town. It has to be in this area. Keith scanned the trees, straining his ears to locate his kind's whereabouts. The river was not very wide. He could easily make it across and come straight back.

"Don't cross the river," Jangus had warned. Was it worth getting caught, if only to check?

I won't be but a moment. In the form of a wolf he quickly crossed, his nails tapping lightly over the ice. Once on the other side he paused to look back. *Only a moment....*

Keith let his nose guide him through unfamiliar territory. Each step carried him closer until he faintly saw a small trail of smoke rising on the other side of a snow bank. He slowed his pace to minimize sound, then climbed a small hill. His fur bristled around the neck when he heard sounds of clanging, and he peered down into a small clearing once he reached the top.

A solitary figure huddled close to a dying fire. A black frying pan barely sizzled with leftover scraps of meat. The clanking Keith had heard came from a utensil scraping the pan's bottom as the stranger stirred its contents. Beside the fire lay a torn traveling pack, its worn material barely able to hold the few items he carried. A walking stick lay at his side, a hand's reach away to ward off animals.

His curiosity satisfied, Keith was about to depart when a tiny thought came to mind. Using sight-reading, the young man opened his mind to allow it in. It was a simple thought, but in it lay the traveler's present complications.

I'm a failure.

Keith watched the human poke the fire in a last desperate attempt to keep it going. The flames flickered once, then went out. The sound of crying took its place.

I can't leave him like this. Keith's ears lay flat against his head. He did not like staying any longer than needed, especially since his kind thought he was still in the valley. He watched the figure pull his cloak tighter, faintly shivering from a brisk wind. *Let's just hope I don't go back smelling like a human.*

The sobbing continued until movement caught his attention, and he jerked around to stare at the young man approaching. Instinctively, he grabbed the walking stick.

"You look cold." Keith tried to sound friendly. "Would you like an extra cloak? You're welcome to have mine." He held out the cloak he had removed before entering the clearing. Illusion disguised his pointed ears to resemble human's; however, no amount of magic could mask his eyes. Their liveliness shone clearly through the haze of snow still lightly falling.

"H-how...where dddid you come fr-f-from?" The man's teeth chattered when he spoke. It did not take long for him to accept the cloak, which Keith pulled snug around his shoulders. The stranger's quivering soon ceased. "I didn't even hear you."

"Oh, I was in the area." Keith knelt beside the damp wood and tried to rebuild the fire. A few prods revealed still warm coals, and with a little energy left to spare he soon had it blazing bright. The traveler quickly warmed his frozen hands.

"You're a magic-user." The stranger stared into the fire. Keith remained quiet and stood off to the side. "You couldn't have gotten it so quickly unless you were...which I am," he added softly.

"Are you?" The young man studied the traveler. Sandy-brown hair matched his eye color. His clothing was mud soaked in places and stained in others. Now and then a rose-orange color could be seen under the double cloaks.

"At least I'd like to *think* someday I'd be a great magic-user," the traveler sighed, "or I'd have done what you did." After a moment's thought, he added, "And if I was, I wouldn't be here." His gaze shifted to the young man, and he extended a hand to shake. "Name's Abraham."

"Keith." The Healer shook firmly, then took a seat beside his companion. "So what brings you out this way?" The question brought hurt to the traveler's eyes. He adjusted his cloak before extending a hand and watched while flakes lightly touched his palm. Feeling too warm, he removed the extra cloak and handed it back.

"Thank you again." He folded his hands in his lap. "I apologize if I seem a little distant. You see, my father is one of *No'va's* greatest magic-users. My mother always feared one day I'd too take up magic, and forbade me to ever practice it. Perhaps I should've listened." He gazed at his hands. "Little it's done for me."

"But if your mother was afraid of magic-users, why then would she marry one?" Keith asked, and Abraham's cheeks reddened.

"A fit of passion, nothing more," was his reply. "My mother never married."

"Oh." Keith paused. "And your father? Does he know?"

Abraham was swift to answer. "Oh, I plan to meet him one day! I only wish to meet his standards before doing so."

"Well, then. What can you do magic-wise?" Keith implored. "If you've been practicing, then I'm sure by now you've mastered a part of it."

Abraham balked. "Yeah. Illusion."

"What's wrong with that? I know illusion. It's always worked wonders for me in the past."

Abraham gestured to the fire still burning strong.

"It takes more than illusion to do that," he said. "Illusion is fake. My father didn't become well-known for fake magic."

"Listen to me." Keith sought his companion's gaze. "Illusion is just the first step to using magic. Do you not think your father became great right away? It takes great practice, and above all *great* patience. What you're looking at now is not how I started. I was once like you. I lost both my parents at an early age, so I didn't have anyone to teach me. Like yourself, I too am self-taught."

"But...no one respects illusion." Abraham hung his head.

"And why would you care whether they know what you can do or not? Not knowing what I could do saved my life on several occasions. I remember times when my magic was barred from me, so I relied on illusion to trick people into believing I still had it." He gazed intently at Abraham. "Respect comes from knowing how to use what's limited to you, not about how much power you have. There's always a limit, always a weakness, because when magic *does* fail then you've always got illusion. Besides, illusion doesn't take energy to use; therefore, you're in constant supply." Keith chuckled. "You also have to realize that some people are not meant to be great magic-users. I know plenty of people who are great at the simplest things, and they aren't magic-users at all."

He let the words sink in before adding with a smile, "It's not about what you have; it's who you are that matters. And if your father can't respect that, then perhaps your mother was right not to have married him."

Keith waited to see what his companion would say.

Eventually, Abraham sighed. "I've been running like a fool trying to discover the reason for my lack of talent, never thinking that maybe I wasn't the type destined to use magic." A smile cracked the corner of his lips. He lounged back against the frozen log they sat on and laughed. "I haven't felt this good since...I can't even remember!"

Keith grinned.

"So where exactly do you live?" he asked, and Abraham pointed toward Lexington.

"Just past town. Come visit sometime. I've few friends who understand why I won't live in luxury."

Keith nodded. The smell of his kind told him it was time to return.

"Well, I should probably be going."

"You from Lexington too?" Abraham stood, along with Keith.

"Originally, yes," Keith replied. "I plan to return some day. When I do, I'll stop by for a visit."

"So where are you staying out here?" Abraham rubbed his chin in thought. "Nothing but woodlands and harpies toward the north."

Keith backed away.

"Like I said, I was in the area." The smell of his kind was stronger now. He quickly turned and headed for the snow bank. "Take care. Keep warm!"

The Healer gave little time for a response as he quickly departed. In his wolf form, he made haste for the river. Once across, he shifted to his true form. A twitch of ears confirmed that he was alone.

Hope I wasn't gone too long. The young man started toward the clearing. *Poor Abraham. I probably left so fast there'd be nothing left to see if he had tried to follow.*

He paused again to check the area just past the vines.

"They may still be in the game," he said to himself as he stepped toward the hidden passage.

"They may," a soft voice startled him from behind. "Then again, they may not."

Slowly, Keith turned to find Chronicles coolly regarding him from the borders. A sharp pain in his head made him wince. Keith's heart fluttered in panic. Did he suspect? Immediately, he closed his mind to keep all thoughts unread. Usually, such methods were not successful against the accomplished mind-reader.

Keith braced himself for the worst when the probe suddenly withdrew. He watched his father nonchalantly turn and walk along the edge of the clearing, a slight smile upon his lips. He was teasing. Keith was almost positive he had known all along. Turning on his heels, Chronicles slowly returned.

"Wisdom, Wisdom..." he sang in good humor, hands clasped behind his back. "You've been with us three years. Surely by now you'd know not to hide things from me." He raised an eyebrow. "If you'd truly been with the group, there'd be nothing to be ashamed of, now would there?" He frowned, an expression Keith was used to seeing.

A flutter of wings drew his attention away from his father, and he ducked as a raven flew overhead. It landed on Chronicles' shoulders and cawed wildly.

You're in for it now! Keith heard Jangus' cackling thoughts. *You crossed the river!* The bird regarded him with its large opal eyes, making Keith shutter. A Healer could never disguise his or her eyes. It was their only flaw in shifting.

Keith wanted to smack it, but Jangus only cackled and flew off, probably to alert the others.

"I didn't mean to," the young man began. "I thought I'd see—"

"A human?" Chronicles glared at his son, who clamped his mouth shut. "And did you once consider that this human could have followed you back? That we could've been discovered, and have to move yet again?" Keith backed away as Chronicles' face flustered dark red in anger. "Do you realize how difficult is it to find a suitable place to live, someplace where humans have not festered? They're like insects! They spread and devour as if this world spawned their kind from the very beginning! This is not their world! They do not belong here!"

By now Chronicles was screaming, drawing a circle of Healers around the two. From the corner of his eye, Keith glimpsed his brother.

"What could possibly provoke a human to attack us unless they've been attacked in the past?" Keith returned. "Is that what happened? You wanted to know about them because other leaders before you had done so, but when you finally came face to face you didn't know what to do." He could see the loathing in his father's eyes. "That's what's missing here – a link with humans. That's why you banished the other leader. *He* was successful. *You* were not."

Keith never saw the leader move, only felt it as the wind was knocked out of his body. The next instant he was on his back with Chronicles' staff pointed at his chest. With the flick of his thumb a hidden blade slid from the bottom, stopping just above his heart. Shy started to stay something, but was abruptly silenced. Keith just stared up at his father.

"So that's been your secret all along," he breathed.

"I hold no secrets!" Chronicles hissed.

"Is that why you hate me?"

"I see the same arrogance in you as I saw in Windchester. He too wanted us to be a part of human life. It was because of them you lost your mother."

Swift anger rose in Keith, and he was quick to reply.

"That wasn't some random person who happened to find out what she was. That was someone who'd known, who'd been planning for some time." His expression softened. "But Chronicles, not all humans are like that. If I told you there was someone who understood us, would you be willing to meet that person?"

Chronicles lifted the staff, taking a deep breath as he replaced the dagger within the wood.

"The only good humans are the ones that don't exist." And he walked away.

Keith got to his feet. "Then neither do I."

Barely a whisper, it was enough to halt their leader.

"What did you say?"

"I'd been so long without a place to call home," Keith said. "Clearly, this is not it."

"*Brethusus*?" Shy sought his brother's thoughts. "What are you saying?"

"I'm leaving."

His kind fidgeted uneasily, waiting for Chronicles' reaction. Keith could hear their thoughts, detesting this young rebel. Twilight's thoughts were full of questions, as was Katherine's. He could not read his brother's, and assumed Shy had closed his mind to ponder alone. Now he understood why Corrigan felt the way he did.

At the sound of his father's throat clearing, the clan silenced.

"Humans nearly destroyed you," he said gently. "Now you wish to return to them." He approached his son. "Is that truly what you want?"

"It is." Keith's gaze never faltered under his father's stare, though his voice quivered when spoken. "We're One with Nature, but not with those who live within it. Just...give me a chance to prove that our connection means more than this."

He knew he had stepped over the line, had gone beyond what any Healer dared against their leader. Yet he had reason. Osha had given him that the moment the horn transferred to his body. He could feel his father testing this reason. Again, the mental probe tingled on the outskirts of his thoughts, but the young man refused to lift the barrier.

Chronicles tapped his nails impatiently on his staff as his son continued to speak.

"Just because I'm leaving doesn't mean I want to sever all my connections here. I may not want to stay forever, but I don't want to lose the only family I have left – if 'family' means anything to you."

Keith let his gaze drop. Grief had closed his throat, and he could say no more. He longed to hear his father say, "Yes. Come and go as you like," and embrace him like a father should. Instead, there was a long silence with only the icy wind breathing down his neck. It was getting colder. He thought back to the human he had left across the river, hoping his fire still held.

"I will give you until the spring," Chronicles began, snapping Keith to attention.

"I'm sorry?" he said.

"When the first flowers bloom, I will ask your decision."

Without another word, he shifted into an owl and was off through the trees. The familiar raven's caw soon followed. Most of the Healers had already left upon Chronicles's departure, which Keith was glad. He needed time to consider.

A hand to his shoulder made him turn to find his brother beside him. Not far away, Katherine and Twilight waited, only leaving when Shy signaled to them.

"I disappoint you," Keith said once they were alone. "I know I did the others."

Shy shook his head. "You stand your ground. I've always admired that part of you." He sighed. "If only I had it in me to do the same."

Keith grinned. "I'm going to go back to the human realms and make the necessary connections so people will accept us. Then you and the rest can come see for yourself."

Another brisk wind sent shivers down their spines.

"You should go in," Shy suggested. "We can discuss this at a later time."

"Aren't you coming?" Keith asked, not wanting to leave his brother in the cold.

"I have to wait for Jangus."

"Since when do you wait for the likes of him?" Keith chortled, but stopped when his brother did not find it amusing. "Alright. See you in a bit."

*****

Shy watched his brother enter the hidden passage, waiting a few moments to be sure he did not come back out. A single gesture was all he needed to alert the owl in the nearly tree. It swooped down and landed at his side, shifting back into the slender form of a dominating leader.

Shy did not even look at him to know he was there. Instead, he bowed his head and repeated what his brother had told him.

"You did well, my son." Together, the two began walking toward the passage. "Everything is ready. All we do now is wait."

CHAPTER 10

Why can't I remember? A flicker of light illuminated the room, a faint memory of where he was. *How long ago did I leave?*

Corrigan lay still. Beneath him, the softness from the cot's sheets made him itch. Stubbornly, he ignored it and kept trying to retrace his thoughts.

There was not much that frightened a Black Wing, except somewhere between Crystal Valley and Sapphire he had lost his memory. How long he had lain, he could not remember.

Is winter over?

Corrigan focused on a light beginning to move closer, bobbing up and down to the rhythm of someone walking. Only when it was a few feet away could he see the person carrying it, and suddenly the memories all came rushing back.

"You make me sick!" Corrigan snarled.

Jenario set the candle on a table next to the cot. It was then that Corrigan recognized the place. He was in the alchemist's dungeon. A steady drip of water in the corner confirmed any doubts.

"I hope you enjoyed your rest," the mage replied with a slight hiss.

"I'm *not* your servant!" Corrigan made the motion to rise, but his body refused to co-operate. His wings felt weighted down, so instead he wrapped them around himself to hide his trembling. He was furious. "I know why you blocked my memory. And you can forget about me spying on Keith. *Ever!*"

Jenario bent to his eye-level.

"Oh, but I'm not concerned with spying on him. He'll eventually come back to the human realms."

Corrigan shivered at the change of voice. Jenario's smooth words now cracked in a dry whisper, as though another had taken control of his tongue. The mage cleared his throat, and when he spoke again it sounded his usual self.

"I only blocked your memories to read your thoughts." He straightened and waved a hand over the harpy's wings. The weight upon them lifted, and Corrigan sat up to gingerly test them. "I knew you'd protest, so I simply cast a sleeping spell over you."

"Because you knew I wouldn't tell you anything about Keith."

"I knew you wouldn't reveal the Healers." That voice again. *"Even with you as my eyes I learned very little. You made sure to stay well away from their home, didn't you?"*

"Quit doing that!" Corrigan demanded, backing away from Jenario. "What's wrong with you?"

"Never mind *that*," the alchemist muttered. "My power has taken me to new levels. I can control so much more."

"More like *it's* trying to control *you*! Do you even realize what you sound like?"

Jenario straightened, then shrugged.

"I hear it, yes."

"What exactly do you want with Keith?" Corrigan asked, never taking his eyes off the mage. "Is it *your* idea to study him, or the horn's?"

Jenario narrowed his eyes, a crimson glow engulfing them. With a single gesture Corrigan found himself airborne, though his wings never had time to move. Like a puppet, he was suspended upside down in front of the alchemist, who laughed bitterly at his inability to move.

"Foolish creature! What do you know of magic when you have none yourself?"

Corrigan looked directly into Jenario's eyes.

"I've been around long enough to know the difference."

"And what difference would that be?"

"Those with magic, and those who are going insane! You're not the same person you once were when I left. I can feel it now. There's something here that's growing. You can see it all around. Everything's black, black like the clothing you always wear, black like that thing you've got hanging around your neck." Corrigan's gaze did not waver under the intense glare. "It's the horn!" He pointed to the ruby necklace. "Jenario! It's not trying to join with anything. It's trying to overtake you!"

As if coming out of a trance, Jenario snapped to attention.

"Put me down!"

Not realizing he still held the Black Wing, he let his hand drop, and Corrigan fell to the floor on all fours, mad as a hornet.

"Jenario, you oaf!" Corrigan raised himself to his full height. "Take that damn thing off! Get rid of it!"

"I created it," Jenario whispered, holding the stone tightly in one hand. "I'm more powerful than ever. There's only one thing I lack: the ability to shift."

"You *can* shift; I've seen you," Corrigan corrected, but Jenario shook his head.

"With the ability to shift into different creatures gives the user control over other possibilities: an understanding of animals, healing, and the ultimate power source – *Nature herself!*"

It was then that Corrigan understood Jenario's intentions. He was not interested in studying the *Lo-ans'rel*. He intended to take their power for his own purposes!

"But why Keith?" Corrigan dared to breathe. "Why not another?"

Jenario's lip curled into a sneer, a mimic of Corrigan's own sarcastic smile. *Now* he was afraid. A Black Wing playing cat and mouse with a powerful mage overtaken by a black unicorn was not something he enjoyed.

"You underestimate the power of albinos," the horn hissed. *"They are the most powerful of their kind, and your little Keith is no exception. I was created from the greed that rules humans' hearts. My own body was destroyed, and now I seek one that will not yield to my full power. Once I was pure and roamed the forests with my sister. Now I am forced to live off another until such time when I can regain a new one. A Lo-ans'rel's body is ideal for my purpose. One drop of blood by the light of the Blue Moon will complete the transformation, and I will be returned to my formal self."*

Behind the mage, Corrigan glimpsed the stairwell shrouded in darkness. If he was quick, he could make it out. Jenario must have read his thoughts, for he raised a hand to stop him.

A wing smacked him across the chest, knocking Jenario flat on his back. Then the Black Wing was flying up the stairwell. Beneath him, he could hear Jenario screeching something incoherent. Or was that the horn's commands?

Corrigan grabbed the handle and flung open the dungeon door. Too late, he saw a shadow move from the corner of his eye. Corrigan sprang at the dark figure, talons outstretched. A glimmer of crimson was the only indication of someone there in the web of darkness. There was a murmur of soft words as he struck solid wall. Corrigan hardly felt the impact, just cold floor as his body collapsed.

"Sleep, my Black Wing puppet. Your services will be rewarded in the end."

WISDOM

The last thing Corrigan remembered before his world became a void of numbness was a crimson light pulsating to the beating of his heart, then winked out.

*****

The morning was still. A circle of Healers gathered around a nest made from soft moss and leaves. Eumaeus, elder and counselor to Chronicles, lay dying. His last few moments were spent carrying him to a secluded location in the forest and preparing a nest where he could lie in comfort.

For Keith, it was an honor to take part in the ancient ritual. He stood with the others, watching his father kneel by the Healer's side. His time of passing was near.

Weakly, Eumaeus lifted a hand toward Chronicles, who tenderly held it. The elder's lips formed silent words only their leader could understand. His hazel eyes fluttered a brief moment, at last losing all focus and closing a final time.

Keith could not see his father's face, for he had placed a hand over his eyes and bowed his head. His shoulders gently shook.

Would he weep for Twilight or Jangus? Would he weep for Shy? For me?

Slowly, Chronicles stood, murmuring soft words and sweeping a hand over the nest. He stepped back into the circle, head still bowed. Where tears smeared along his cheeks, the skin flushed pink.

All eyes fixed upon the nest. Keith had heard but never seen a *Loans'rel* burial. Now as he watched, vines began to sprout around the sides holding the deceased Healer. The soil sank from underneath, pulling nest and body with it. As it disappeared, vines covered the opening to prevent the surrounding Healers from peering below.

"An honorable soul is treasured by Nature," Chronicles spoke. "A dishonorable soul is stripped of their bodies and dispersed bitterly among the decay of unused magic."

A touch to Keith's shoulder made him turn to find Shy standing behind him. When he looked back to the nest, it had completely gone under. The ground had recovered itself with blooming flora.

They were very close, Keith heard his brother's thoughts. *He led a good life. I'm sure Nature will release his spirit. His memories will be kept as guidance for others who're in need.*

When there was no more to see, Chronicles concluded the meeting with a few remarks, then sent the clan on its way. Keith watched the Healers disperse into the surrounding forest. Shy, however, remained with his brother.

"It's spring," he began.

Keith took note of the flowers wavering in the breeze.

"I suppose you want my decision," he replied.

"I already know." When he spoke again it was merely a whisper, and his mind closed so none other could penetrate his thoughts. "I only wish I could go with you." Then, like the others, Shy departed, leaving his brother alone.

Keith did not leave right away. Instead, he went where Nature had taken Eumaeus and stood staring at the spot. Questions played over in his mind, questions that made him doubt his final decision. Was *his* spirit worth keeping? What kind of honorable life had *he* lead when all he had done was discover what he was and where he had come from?

"At least I found the answers I needed." Memories of his mother came to mind. "You did all you could for me. What more could I ask?"

An ear twitched at the approach of footsteps. From the way each step fell, he knew it was Chronicles. The leader stopped beside the gravesite. He did not make eye contact but gazed at the ground as though half expecting Eumaeus to come back up. At last the two turned toward home and began walking side by side. Keith could not remember when his father had stayed by him for more than an instant. Yet, like his brother, Keith knew the reason behind it.

"I know your question," Chronicles began, keeping his gaze ahead. "You may return during certain times. I daresay, three years of discovering your kind is not nearly enough."

Keith froze, all attention on his father with his ears pricked forward.

"I...I can?" he stuttered.

"However—"

Keith's heart sank. *And now the compromise,* he thought bitterly.

Chronicles paused at the clearing's edge.

"When you leave, you shall be given a mark, which you will bare upon your left shoulder." He gestured to the area. "It will be a permanent reminder of what you are, and where your loyalties lie."

"Is that what the mark means?" Keith laid his ears back.

"*Jae'to.*"

Keith's face flushed red.

"I'm no traitor!" he protested. "You know that's not true!" Yet there was no use arguing, and Keith knew it; the leader's decision was final.

"Secondly, unless you are summoned, do not expect to walk past those borders without being noticed. I *will* know."

Keith clamped his mouth shut and walked a few steps ahead.

Guess it's better than nothing. He could've decided something else.

At the border's edge, Keith stopped at the stern touch of his father's hand.

I mean what I say, mesemon, came the thought. *Just because you've lived with humans doesn't mean you know everything.* When Keith gave him a questioning stare, Chronicles only replied, "Don't come crying to me if you get yourself in trouble. You leave here, you're on your own...*completely.*"

CHAPTER 11

The blindfold kept him from observing their work, though it did nothing to dull the pain inflicted to his sensitive flesh. Chronicles supervised the two *Lo-ans'rel* in charge of creating it. Using heated needles, they built the mark from tiny dots burned into the skin.

"As you may well know from experience in the human realms," Keith listened to his father, "fire is the one thing that can harm us. The only way to keep a mark like this from being healed by Nature is to use a different element than the one we have to create it."

Keith remained still, never flinching even when they applied a burning solution to keep the area clear. He was relieved when they finished the last dot and dabbed his shoulder with a cool cloth. The blindfold was removed, and Keith was allowed to see the mark branded upon his left shoulder.

If its meaning had meant something else, Keith would have dubbed it the most beautiful design he had ever seen. The tattoo arched gracefully from the top of his shoulder and curled to the back. It was large enough to be seen from several yards away, but small enough to hide under clothing.

Satisfied with the work, Chronicles sent his son straight to his bedroom to dress. Keith wasted no time in gathering the few items his brother and friends had prepared for his journey. From Shy, a special mixture labeled *mu-kaj'*. Keith smiled and quietly repeated the name in Common.

"Pure water." He lifted the top to inhale its honeysuckle fragrance before slipping it into a pouch on his belt. He thought of Blackavar as he did, grateful to have it now that he was returning. He patted its leather top. "Serve me well and fail me not."

From Twilight, the sapphire necklace used for storing items, which Keith immediately secured around his neck. The last was from Katherine – food packed into several smaller pouches. He added those with the larger one on the belt. With room left to spare, he placed the pan flute along with the Pure Water.

I must look quite the traveler, he thought while pulling a cloak around his shoulders. He made sure Glory's ring was well hidden under his shirt collar. Being the last day with his kind, he allowed Twilight's necklace to show.

WISDOM

A portion of white scar caught his attention, and Keith glanced down to the wrist where Conrad had burnt the star-shaped mark into his flesh. It was the mark of slavery, one he almost wished he could proudly wear to symbolize his defeat of Castle Mire. Yet now it served as a mere reminder that Nature had her way of cruelty, that his kind were not the grand power source his father boasted when chance permitted.

Should I reveal myself to humans, I would not want such a mark revealing the harm that can be done to us.

Swiftly did he approach the wardrobe containing the precious *Loans'rel* garments. Such material was not easy to destroy, so Keith found use to command Nature's energy to slit one of the gowns into a thin ribbon. With it, he wrapped firmly around the area so that part of the hand was covered without drawing much attention.

Satisfied that everything he needed was packed, Keith stood in the underground bedroom that was once his. He admired the colored glass along the far wall, the canopied bed with the animal carvings, and even the white rose that still bloomed every season. He stepped outside and looked up at the doorway to see 'newcomer' still written at the top.

I'm sure they'll find a better use for it after I'm gone. My kind are not ones to waste space.

He started down the tunnel, peering into rooms that had left their doors open. When he came to the main chamber where young ones learned to climb and play, he paused to take in its surroundings. The chamber was empty today, for the warmth of spring had drawn everyone outdoors. Now and then he could hear squeals of delight from those playing close by in the clearing.

With a heavy sigh, Keith continued through the sliding doors. The afternoon sun shone brightly down through wisps of clouds lazily pulled along by an upper breeze. Upon seeing him ready to depart, some of the Healers stopped their play and watched him with growing curiosity. Such fascinating tales he had told from the human realms! What more could he conjure up upon his next return?

"*Vistom!*"

Keith barely had time to look before Twilight was in his arms, hugging his friend one last time. He noted the sapphire charm.

"Thought you might need it, just in case. Come back one of these days and tell us more about humans." His eyes pleaded for the answer to be *yes,* and Keith was not about to disappoint.

"Of course I will," and got squeezed tighter. "Thank you for the supplies," he choked, holding back tears. "I'll miss you all so much."

Their goodbyes were short-lived, for at the approach of Chronicles the two parted. Behind their leader walked Shy and Jangus. From the smirk on Jangus' face, Keith could tell he was glad to be rid of him. Shy did not meet his gaze until he came forward to embrace his brother.

"Are you sure you won't come with me?" Keith teased, but Shy's expression remained serious.

"You shouldn't say what you don't understand," Shy whispered, then backed away when Chronicles cleared his throat.

"Ready?" he asked stiffly.

Keith nodded.

"Then come with me. I will see you to the border."

The young man took one final look around the clearing, acknowledging those who bid farewell. As he passed Jangus, the dark-haired youth turned up his nose and ignored him, though his opal eyes followed his every move. Shy stepped beside Katherine and Twilight and watched the vines close behind the two as they left for Crystal Valley's borders.

The sound of rushing water from the river perked up Keith's spirits. Although he was leaving, the thought of a fresh start in a world with no boundaries livened his steps. Even Chronicles took note of his eagerness.

Keith stopped at the river's edge and stared across to the other side. It was the end of Crystal Valley, and the beginning of a new way of life.

I crossed the borders once before, knowing I had to return shortly. Now I can cross freely and go where I wish, but cannot return without permission. If only I could come and go when I wanted. Still, the thought of humans finding our location – Chronicles would never risk it.

There is already too much at risk, came his father's thoughts. *Your risk, for one. The other, human settlements are getting dangerously close, and there aren't many places left to relocate to—at least not in this area. We would have to travel north in order to find something else.*

Keith turned to his father.

"But surely you wouldn't have to," he replied. "Not if I can reestablish a link between us."

Chronicles snorted in disagreement.

"You've yet to even know your true strengths, and here you speak of compromising with humans."

For a moment, the two stood quietly observing the forest beyond the river. Then, after adjusting his pouches, Keith moved forward to step across the rocks.

"Wait," Chronicles' command stopped him. When his father suddenly embraced him, Keith did not know how to react.

Does he truly care? Even love?

When his father pulled back, Keith did the one thing he could think of in return for his father's affection. He bowed low, nearly squatting on the ground in order to show his loyalty. Chronicles laid his ears back in content, then nodded once, pleased at his son's performance.

"Here. Take this with you." He held out a hand. At once his staff appeared.

Keith held his breath. The sapphire stone on the tip matched the stone on the necklace.

"It will protect you."

Keith accepted the gift in awe. He held it in both hands, testing its weight. Then, with a gesture, it vanished within Twilight's charm for safekeeping. He slipped the necklace under his collar.

"Thank you," he managed.

"And...this."

Keith stared at his mother's charm Chronicles had taken from him three years ago. He had not seen it since, though it still glimmered with polished radiance as though his mother had given it to him that very day.

"You were right to have it. Your mother would have wanted it so."

Keith could say nothing as he took the necklace and slipped it around his neck. He nodded once in thanks, then turned toward the river. It felt good to have the charm back. He could feel it against the other two as he carefully picked his way across the rocks to the other side. Each stone brought back different memories. He remembered his first shifting lesson and how his father had tested his abilities, only to find he could combine animals into one shift. He remembered the silent nights spent with Twilight at his favorite location. He remembered Katherine and his brother, how she secretly admired Shy. He thought of his cousin, Jeremiah, trying to control the winter weather. He thought of Jangus.

I'm sure he's glad I'm gone. Keith smiled. *But not for good.*

He stepped from the last rock onto the bank. It was so different with everything in bloom. He looked back. No one stood on the bank to watch him leave. Yet he knew they were there. He could sense the shifting energy in the air and knew his father was not far.

Gathering his courage, Keith turned away from his homeland. When he came out of the woods, he was on a hill overlooking the Realm of Lexington.

Blackavar... If I hurry, I can make it before dark.

No longer in slavery, he was free to go where he pleased, to learn and be where he was originally raised. As he started downhill, he began to whistle a tune his brother had taught him. The call of humans drew him forward, and for once in his life he felt like he was coming home.

EPILOGUE

Golden eyes flashed in the dim lighting of the forest, eyeing the tall figure invading its space. Even the *Lo-ans'rel* knew better than barge into this territory. A low growl warned the approaching figure that he had come far enough.

"*Delexi.*" The wolf recognized Chronicles' voice and crept from shadow. Sable fur bristled around the neck. Its nostrils flared, taking in the leader's smell of pine and dried leaves.

"*Healer,*" it snorted. "*Why do you summon me?*" The wolf began circling the leader. Chronicles, however, did not flinch from the animal's behavior. He knew the wolf's limits. So, then, did the wolf know his.

"*E'nox-avi.*"

"*And what favor would that be?*"

Chronicles met the wolf's hungry eyes.

"*As you may have heard, my eldest son has returned to the human realms. I need someone to see where he goes, what he does, and report back to me. In return, I will offer you human transformation. That would easily let you follow where a wolf may not be permitted.*"

Delexi snorted in silent amusement.

"*I? Disguised as a human?*"

"*It would be a temporary form. You know the boundaries where humans dwell. You're used to hunting around them without being seen. Sending one of my own may cause more trouble than it's worth. That's why I need you.*"

"*And degrade yourself in the process!*" The wolf flattened its ears and bared its teeth. "*You must be joking.*"

In response, Chronicles knelt and extended his arm.

"*I do what is necessary to keep this clan safe. And if it means degrading myself in the process, fine. I must know about human development. How far have they come? Where are they building next? This, I plan to use when the time is right to fight back, and reclaim our home!*"

Delexi considered the advantages. He could remain a wolf as long as Keith stayed near or in the forest, then transform when he went into town.

"It's probably wise you didn't send one of your own. He might sense their magic."

"Then you accept?"

Delexi eyed the Healer's hand a few feet from his nose.

"I want your blood before mine."

"Remember that this is a temporary shift. It may only last a few hours, a day at most." Then Chronicles bowed his head and turned his wrist face up.

Pain came quickly, and the Healer had to bite his tongue to suppress the urge to jerk his hand back. He knew what was happening. A piece of his own shifting ability was going to the wolf, and to make it work in a non-magical body, the wolf needed energy. It took all Chronicles' mental strength not to cry out as a jolt of energy left his own body. He could hear the animal trying not to whimper, though by now they sounded more human as the transfer neared completion. When Chronicles finally came to, he was lying at the feet of a human similar in appearance. Golden eyes stared down at the leader, and a sly smile arched across his face.

"Need a hand?" Delexi noted his human accent as he clasped the Healer's arm and helped him up. "I will be a shadow, nothing more." He looked down at his dark clothing, then pulled the black cloak around himself.

Though unsteady after the transfer, Chronicles nonetheless retained the dignity of a leader who had experienced magic transfers many times over, and Delexi doubted he would be last of these.

"Don't stay in the human realms for long," the Healer said, letting Nature's energy run through him to close the wound. He flexed his fingers, relishing the feel of blood flowing through his veins.

"I shall report back what I find." Delexi bowed his head.

He turned and dropped to all fours, thick black fur sprouting from his clothing as he returned to his true form. His sable coat blended well with the deep shadows of the forest, and Chronicles listened to him go until he could hear no more. Without a second thought to his plan, the Healer headed back toward the clearing.

He failed to notice a white feather drifting down where he had stood as Chanté watched from hiding. Throughout the conversation, the White Wing had scarcely breathed. A scolding from his father he could handle, but a scolding from the *Lo-ans'rel* leader himself? A shutter ran down Chanté's spine. Only when he was sure the Healer was out of earshot did he rise from hiding and stretch his stiff joints in each wing before taking to the skies.

ABOUT THE AUTHOR

Bonnie Watson was born in Richmond, VA with an interest in art and writing. She graduated from Virginia Commonwealth University in 2005, having completed several shorter works of fiction. In 2010, she published her first novel, and has been diligently working on the series ever since. Her love for medieval fantasy is apparent in much of her artwork, and can be viewed, along with various other writing projects, on her main website: www.WisdomNovels.com

AUTHOR'S BLOG
www.WisdomNovels.wordpress.com

STEP INTO THE NEXT ADVENTURE...

PRINCE
BOOK TWO OF BLUE MOON RISING TRILOGY

After uncovering the truth behind his secretive upbringing, Keith returns to the human realms to restore harmony between his kind and those they once protected. To do so, he must first find a location to work from in order to gain the trust of humans, and what better way than becoming a prince of an abandoned clan centrally located in the Realm of Trully.

Yet running a clan is no easy task, especially if the last person who owned it still lives in town, and the surrounding clans won't work together because of that fact. To make matters worse, a runaway childhood friend suddenly shows up, along with his half-brother. Both have their own reasons for coming, though none of it helps with the steadily expanding storm forming the Dark Unicorn's territory to the north.

Meet a half-breed Black Wing caught in the clutches of an alchemist, who wields a power he hopes will make him the magic-user he has always wished to be; a runaway girl searching for a way out from an arranged marriage; a Healer seeking to destroy the very foundation which lead to the division of his people; and two sister unicorns: one Pure and one Dark.

Bonnie Watson

Wisdom Novels®

Prince

BOOK TWO OF BLUE MOON RISING TRILOGY

Bonnie Watson

Prince

Book Two of Blue Moon Rising Trilogy

PROLOGUE

Lightning flicked from one cloud to the next, followed by sporadic claps of thunder. The deafening sound drowned out pounding hoofs galloping through the forest. Another streak lit the sky, reflecting upon the twisted tip of onyx horn. Nostrils flared as it took in the scent of electrified air. A charcoal coat blended well in the night. It was nearly home.

Trees thinned out the more the ground curved uphill. At the top, no trees remained. The black unicorn stood overlooking a sumptuous tower-enforced castle in the Realm of Sapphire. It reared in tribute to its nightly run while a thin line of white lightning lit its backside. When the light faded, the unicorn had vanished, replaced by a sable-robed figure.

"Your strength is growing, Jenario." The crimson stone glowed where it hung from a chain around his neck, casting his velvety garments in a soft red hue. *"You no longer hold back your desire to be powerful. Continue to do so, and I will see to it that you become the most powerful mage in all the land."*

The familiar voice drew a smile across the man's face. As both illusionist and alchemist, he remembered the day he had severed the horn of a unicorn, hoping to obtain its power. That horn now resided within the red-stoned necklace. Although the voice came directly from the stone, it used its host's lips to speak, with a change of accent every time it did. When the alchemist replied to the horn, his voice lost the harshness of the other's tone and returned to normal. Mere illusionist he was...no longer.

"There are very few magic-users living in *No'va* now," he said with a chortle. "Of those, most are either unknown or lack the skill to become known. Compared to them, I'm already the most powerful."

He bent to scoop up a few grains of dirt, letting them deplete between his fingertips as he lifted his hand. With a few added words of power, the drizzling dirt multiplied in a whirlwind of spinning dust. Only when he felt the cloud had expanded to his liking did he simply step through and appear in the interior hallway of his home.

After stepping through the portal, he shook off the dust and crinkled his nose at the smell of alcohol. His one companion, Nathaniel, had been drinking again. He could almost taste it in the air. With a heavy sigh, Jenario headed down the hallway.

He paused. The way to his study stretched before him. To his left, another passage led to a stairwell. After a moment's hesitation, he took the stairs. At the top, he paused to peer out a window. From this vantage, he could just see the forest briefly outlined against the sky when lightning flashed in the distance. The sound of thunder was faint, suggesting the storm had moved on.

Turning his attention to a door, he pulled a key from a side pocket and slipped it into a lock. A quick turn and the door opened on silent hinges. He stepped into the round room, a canopied bed in its center. On the far side of the room double balcony doors had been left slightly open. A scant breeze sifted through curtains surrounding a still form lying on the top covers of the bed. Slowly, Jenario approached and drew back the fabric.

Soft plumage stirred. Jenario gently moved aside one of the wings to reveal Corrigan sleeping soundly. Russet flesh, specked in light gray markings, much resembled the color of Redwood bark from Crystal Valley. It was home to a vast majority of his kind. For a half Black Wing, that home was far off, and Jenario remembered why.

Corrigan had been invited to Sapphire so Jenario could study his nightly behaviors. What Jenario got instead was a tool at the dark horn's disposal, a puppet for spying and gathering information. It had been one such request to *gather* another person of interest. When Corrigan had refused, it set off a chain of events that spiraled downhill, ending with the harpy locked away in Jenario's tower.

Jenario placed a hand over the harpy's forehead and closed his eyes, allowing his mind to link with the Black Wing's thoughts. Although asleep, Corrigan's mind was well aware of the presence and thrust a barrier up to block the intrusion. The mage, however, was not about to be put aside. With power from the horn as his guide, he bypassed the mental barrier and slipped into a world where nightmares easily roused.

"Don't be frightened," he soothed.

Images faded in and out of Corrigan's mind. At last, a mist resembling the harpy took shape and approached Jenario's mental probe. So, too, did the mage project an image of himself for the Black Wing to identify.

"You!" Corrigan screeched, so that Jenario held a hand to his temple. *"Let me out, or I swear my talons will find your throat!"*

Jenario laughed. *"Unless you sleepwalk, which I highly don't recommend, you're best to stay here."*

"You're afffraid," the harpy hissed. *"You're afffraid of Keith'sss growing power."*

Jenario frowned. Keith had been his point of interest lately, and was the sole reason behind Corrigan's entrapment.

"He'sss already fffigured you out," the harpy continued. *"You'll never sssucceed in hisss capture!"*

"Be silent!" a new voice interrupted the flow of thoughts, and Jenario's mind clouded with the horn switching over. *"Still yourself, half-breed! A human has flaws, and Lo-ans'rel know that. Jenario himself cannot hope to catch a full-blooded one, but I can. And when a unicorn wishes something, there's nothing that can be done to stop it."*

Corrigan's wings ruffled in attempts to wake, but the spell upon him was too strong, keeping him locked in an endless cycle of emotion and nightmares.

His let his hissing accent drop. *"He will find a way..."*

The horn cackled. *"Even Lo-ans'rel cannot fight against the power of a unicorn. But since you so believe he can resist me, I will grant you the ability to see everything that occurs, but only where Jenario goes. And when he finds your friend, then you will see just how weak Lo-ans'rel are compared to me..."*

Made in the USA
Middletown, DE
19 January 2024